GW00371166

ANNA
JACOBS

The Nurses of Eastby End
Eastby End Saga Book One

**HODDER &
STOUGHTON**

First published in Great Britain in 2024 by Hodder & Stoughton Limited
An Hachette UK company

This paperback edition published in 2024

1

A CIP catalogue record for this title is available from the British Library

Paperback ISBN 978 1 399 729932
ebook ISBN 978 1 399 72994 9

Typeset in Plantin Light by Manipal Technologies Limited

Printed and bound in Great Britain by Clays Ltd, Elcograf S.p.A.

Hodder & Stoughton policy is to use papers that are natural, renewable
and recyclable products and made from wood grown in sustainable forests.
The logging and manufacturing processes are expected to conform to the
environmental regulations of the country of origin.

Hodder & Stoughton Limited
Carmelite House
50 Victoria Embankment
London EC4Y 0DZ

www.hodder.co.uk

The Nurses of Eastby End

I

Early 1886

When he saw the girl sitting on the reservoir wall, Dr George Nolan stopped abruptly. He'd just sat by the bedside of a dying woman and had stayed at the house a little longer afterwards to try to comfort her family.

Feeling the need for some fresh air and peace, he'd decided to walk home the long way round by the reservoir, and enjoy the last of the daylight glinting on the water.

Something was wrong here, though. He could tell by the way the girl was sitting hunched up and radiating misery, because he'd seen that look before. He couldn't simply walk past and leave her to it, so he changed direction, left the footpath and began moving across the grass towards her.

When she saw him coming she looked panic-stricken and tried to jump off the wall, clearly intending to run away, but she stumbled and fell.

She didn't even try to get up but lay there, facing away from him. He could tell she was weeping by the way her shoulders were heaving and he ran the last few yards.

He stopped where she could look up and see him and held out one hand, not grabbing or even rushing her. 'Let me help you up.'

She made no attempt to take his hand but after one quick glance at him she turned away, sobbing loudly now, sounding so desperate his heart ached for her. He'd definitely been right to stop and check what was wrong.

He waited but when she didn't move, he bent and pulled her gently to her feet, taking hold of her arm. 'It's getting cold. Let's go back to my house and talk. My wife is waiting for me there, so you'll be quite safe. She'll make us a hot drink, then you can tell us what's wrong.'

The lass didn't answer, just stared at him as if she didn't understand the words. He was a tall man and she was quite tall too, coming up to his shoulders. Then she looked sideways again towards the water, before turning back towards him.

He saw the moment she realised who he was and tried once again to pull away but he kept a firm hold of her arm. He wasn't going to let go of her, didn't want another unhappy soul to leave this life needlessly by jumping into the town's reservoir, not if he could prevent it.

'Yes, I can see you know who I am: Dr Nolan,' he said in a calm voice. 'And whatever it is that's upsetting you, I'm sure my wife and I will be able to help you.'

'No one can help me now.' She smeared away tears with her free hand but more followed.

'You can let us try, at least.'

She looked up at him so doubtfully he still kept a firm hold of that slender childlike arm.

'Come along. I'm hungry and I need a cup of tea. You look cold so I'm sure you'll welcome a warm drink too.'

He set off walking and to his relief she moved with him. Then she stopped abruptly, dragging back with her whole body, trying to surprise him and get away. But he'd been expecting this and didn't let go of her. She was young, alone and clearly in desperate need of help. He couldn't risk letting her run away.

'I don't think you're one of my patients, are you?' he asked.

'No. So you should let me go.'

'I can't. You need help and I'm a doctor, so it doesn't matter whether you're one of my regular patients or not. My wife and I will do our best to help you, I promise.' He tugged her forward again and this time, after another doubtful glance sideways, she started to stumble along beside him and kept moving.

'You'll like my wife. She's called Jenny,' he said quietly. After that he didn't try to chat or ask her any more questions, merely continued moving briskly along, still holding her arm tightly.

When his wife opened the door, he said, 'I found this lass near the reservoir. She's extremely upset.' He let go and gave the girl a slight push towards Jenny.

'Aw, you poor thing. Come in and I'll make us all a nice cup of cocoa.'

'I don't . . . I can't . . . '

Jenny had a firm hold of the lass now. 'What's your name, love?'

She stopped struggling, hesitated then gave in. 'Cathy.'

He'd seen his wife do this before when he brought home someone who was troubled: put an arm round their shoulders, wrap them up in a soothing stream of words and get them to sit down with her. She would have made a wonderful mother had fate been kinder to them, he was sure.

'Take your coat off, George, and hang up our visitor's coat too while you're at it.' She edged Cathy's coat off quickly before the girl seemed to realise what she was doing, then led her into the morning room, which had a fire blazing cheerfully in the grate.

'Make yourself comfortable, dear. I'll bring you some cocoa in two ticks of a wag's tail.' Jenny bustled out.

The girl stared at the fire and George saw her give in, sighing and holding her hands out to its warmth. He stayed as much in the background as he could.

Jenny wasn't long coming back with a tray containing three mugs of cocoa and a plate of biscuits. She handed out the mugs and gestured to a chair next to the fire. 'Why don't you sit there, love?'

The girl sat down, clutching her mug in a way that said she needed the warmth as much as a drink.

'Have a taste,' Jenny urged after a while. 'Tell me if you'd like more sugar.'

Cathy took a sip, then another. She finished the cocoa so quickly George felt sure she'd been both hungry and thirsty. He tipped his own untouched cocoa into her mug and Jenny gave him an approving nod as she pushed the plate of biscuits closer.

Jenny gestured again to the plate, their guest seemed to relax a little further and took a biscuit.

His wife pulled her chair closer and waited till their young visitor had finished a second biscuit, then said, 'Tell us what's wrong, Cathy.'

'You won't want to speak to me if I do.'

They both stared at her then exchanged knowing glances. Easy to guess what this was about. They'd seen girls in this condition before.

'Go on. Try us,' George said.

'I'm expecting a baby.' She looked from one to the other.

'On purpose? Or did you love someone who's let you down?' Jenny asked.

'*No!*' She shuddered. 'I could never love a man like him.'

'Tell us what happened.'

Her story came out in a series of short jerks. 'A friend of my father. Mr Pershore. He grabbed me. Forced me. It hurt. Afterwards he pushed me away, said I'd been asking for it. Said I'd been flaunting my beauty at him. He threatened to kill me if I told anyone what he'd done.'

'And did you?'

'No. I didn't dare. He's Dad's best friend.'

'Then later you found out you were expecting,' Jenny guessed.

She nodded and two more of those fat tears rolled down her cheeks. 'My mother realised what was wrong a few weeks later when I didn't get my monthly and was sick in the morning. I told her how it had happened but she didn't believe me. Nor did my father. They believed *him.*'

'That's not fair.'

'They said they were sending me to St Monica's, that home for wayward girls. Everyone knows it's like a prison there and they cane the girls regularly, so I ran away.'

'How old are you?'

'Thirteen, fourteen next month.'

'Where were you going when I found you?' George asked.

'I've nowhere to go so I was going to throw myself in the reservoir.' She began sobbing again, hiding her face in her hands, her whole body shaking with anguish.

They couldn't hide their anger. 'We believe you. And we're not angry at you but at him,' Jenny assured her.

'How does he get away with it?' George asked his wife. When he turned back to the girl, he had to speak loudly to get her attention. 'Cathy! *Cathy!*'

She cowered away, clearly expecting to be hit.

He spoke firmly and loudly, 'We do believe you, Cathy. And no one here is going to hurt you.'

She stared first at him then at Jenny and her words were barely a whisper of sound. 'You believe me? Really?'

'Yes. It's not the first time that man has behaved like this, you see. As a doctor I hear about such things. And we can definitely help you,' he added.

'How? You can't take the baby away.' She stared down at her stomach with loathing. 'I don't want it.'

'Others will want it, though. There are people who can't have babies themselves and are longing for children.' He didn't say that he and his wife had that problem too. They'd helped place other unwanted children for adoption but hadn't done it for themselves because it wouldn't look good to take a child from the same community, especially one whose real mother was still living nearby.

Jenny joined in. 'We'll look after you till you've had the baby, then you can either keep it yourself or let a childless couple adopt it and love it.'

'You will?' Then she sagged. 'My parents will stop you. They *want* me to suffer. They keep saying it's all my fault and I should be punished.'

'We won't let them lock you away at St Monica's,' Dr Nolan promised. 'That so-called home is a disgrace.'

There was a brief silence then Jenny gestured with one hand. 'Look round you. What do you see?'

'Boxes. And no ornaments anywhere. Are you packing to move house?'

'Yes. We're leaving this village. And if you want to come with us, we can hide you till we leave then take you with us.'

'Would that be all right with you, Cathy?' the doctor asked. 'We'll treat you kindly, I promise.'

'Where are you going?'

'We're moving to Rochdale and would be happy to take you to live with us till the baby is born.'

He and his wife would help Cathy work out the best solution when she was calmer and had learned to trust them. For the moment they were doing what they should have done with Pershore's previous victim, a girl who'd killed herself. He didn't need to ask his wife to know that she too would want to get this poor child safely away from the man.

The following morning Jenny woke Cathy early and asked her to give the doctor her jacket and shoes so that he could leave them at the side of the reservoir.

He harnessed the pony himself and drove off in his trap. No one would think twice about where he might be going. People would simply assume he was off to visit a sick person. It felt strange to be doing this but he was saving lives, which was what mattered most to him.

When he came back, Cathy was looking so anxious he patted her shoulder. 'You'll be safe now. People will assume you've committed suicide, whether they discover a body or not.'

'What's going to happen to me, though? Later, I mean.'

'We'll think about your future after we've moved. Once we're away from here, you can stay with us and help Jenny in the house for a few months. After you've had the baby we'll help you build a new future.'

She gave him one of her wide-eyed stares and considered this for a few moments then nodded. 'Thank you. I just – I can't thank you enough. I'll work very hard, I promise you.'

He was beginning to realise that Cathy was an intelligent young woman and he was looking forward to getting to know her better. Surely he and his wife would be able to set her life back on a good path once she'd had the baby?

After that Jenny took the girl upstairs to the spare bedroom with instructions to stay there while the Nolans finished their packing, because outsiders would be coming and going all day, picking up the things they'd sold or were giving away.

They gave her books to read and fed her nourishing meals. Gradually she calmed down and got some colour back in her cheeks.

'I wish I could stay with you for ever,' she said two evenings later. 'You never shout at one another or scold me.'

'We prefer to live peacefully and besides, we enjoy each other's company,' the doctor said.

His wife patted her hand. 'We'll help you after the baby is born, Cathy, I promise you. But I won't pretend it's possible for you to stay with us afterwards.' She sighed and added, 'There will be others needing help, you see. The way girls are treated in these circumstances, as if they're the only person involved, disgusts us both, so George and I do our best to help them when we can.'

'But if I can't stay with you, how shall I be able to live . . . afterwards?'

'We'll help you find a job and somewhere to live. We'd never simply turn you out on the street, I promise you.'

The girl let out a huge sigh of relief and dabbed at her eyes. 'I'm so grateful.'

A few minutes later she said suddenly, 'I want to be exactly like you two when I grow up.'

Jenny smiled. 'No. Be like yourself, but try to do good in the world.'

'I shall. I give you my word that I shall try my hardest to live a good, worthwhile life and help others.'

'That's all anyone can do. I've never met anyone yet who's perfect, though. Just do the best you can.'

When the pantechnicon drew up outside the doctor's house on her third morning waking up there, Cathy went and hid in the roof space as they'd planned, sitting or sometimes lying down on a wooden platform that had been placed across the rafters to store the empty trunks and suitcases.

The removalists were from Rochdale and they arrived at the doctor's house by seven o'clock and started stacking the furniture and other goods in their van. Once the house had been cleared they set off for Rochdale with the Nolans' possessions, travelling slowly to give the horses plenty of rests.

As Dr Nolan and his wife had explained to Cathy, he was going to take over a medical practice in that town from an elderly friend who wanted to retire to the seaside at St Anne's.

'Rochdale is close enough to drive ourselves there in our pony trap once we've tidied up the empty house, and we shall no doubt overtake our furniture on the way,' the doctor said. 'You can hide under a blanket in the back of our trap among the final bits and pieces till we're well clear of this village then you can join us on the front seat.'

'You'll have to hide again when we pass our removalists,' Mrs Nolan said. 'We'll leave a space for that on the cart.'

Once they'd set off and Cathy had come out of hiding, Jenny said, 'There's something else we need to do before we get to Rochdale and that's change your name. How about turning Cathy into Rachel and Wallace into Norris? How does Rachel Norris sound to you?'

'I like it. Can I really do that? Change my name?'

'Why not? Who's going to call the new doctor a liar when he introduces you?'

'But won't my parents come after you to get me back?'

'I doubt it. How will they know that you've left with us? Even the two removal men won't see you.'

2

When 'Rachel Norris' had been with the Nolans for about a month, they sat down with her one afternoon to 'discuss something important'.

'We've noticed that you don't even like to talk about your child,' the doctor began.

She scowled down at her stomach. 'No. I'm sorry, but I don't.'

'And I don't think you're going to change your mind about keeping it.'

She shuddered visibly, then looked from him to his wife, guessing she'd be disappointing them, but couldn't lie to them. 'I'm sure I shan't.'

'So perhaps we should discuss your future and make some plans, then. You see, Jenny and I would like to adopt your baby and it won't matter to us whether it's a girl or a boy.'

That was the last thing Rachel had expected to hear.

'Would you allow us to do that?'

She didn't have to think about it. 'Oh, yes, definitely. You're so kind you'd make ideal parents and give the child a happy life, I'm sure.' She hesitated then added, 'What's more, I'd not feel guilty if I knew it was in your care.'

'If you change your mind once it's born we wouldn't insist on keeping the child.'

'I shan't do that.'

He studied her face. 'No, that's what we both thought or we'd not have spoken yet. So may we offer you a suggestion for how we do this? It'd make everything easier . . . afterwards . . . if the child were thought to be ours.'

They kept surprising her. 'Tell me how we do that,' she said.

'If you wear clothes and padding that make you look fatter but not as if you're expecting and my wife gradually pads out her clothes into the right shape to look as if she's the one expecting, then you could have the baby at home here and it would seem to everyone else to be ours.'

'Would you like to think about it for a while?' Jenny asked.

'No. I don't need to. I definitely don't want to keep that man's child.'

'Then we'll find a scrubbing woman but apart from that you and I can manage the housework on our own for the next few months. Is that all right with you, Rachel?'

'Yes. Fine.'

'Thank you. It's an incredible gift you're giving us and we can't put into words how grateful we are. When it's all over we'll help you to find a way to earn a living, and you can always turn to us if you need other help in the future.'

It proved easier than they'd expected to keep up the deception because it simply never occurred to anyone to question that Mrs Nolan was expecting and she claimed tiredness and fear of losing another child as a reason for not going out much.

Rachel continued in good health, helping out with the housework and also sometimes now his wife wasn't available in the doctor's surgery which adjoined the side of the house. As the doctor had expected, her young body showed few signs that she was even expecting a child, though from the end of the seventh month she did look a little fatter and he had to find another helper.

She had found the work with his patients so interesting she missed it and asked his permission to read some of his medical books.

It was Mrs Nolan who knitted baby clothes and sewed little garments, looking as luminously happy as if she were really expecting a child.

One day when she was nearing her time, the doctor asked Rachel into his surgery and his wife joined them. 'Am I imagining it or have you enjoyed assisting me to treat the patients and learning about how human bodies function?'

'Yes, I do enjoy it. It's not only interesting but truly worthwhile work. And it's different every day. I shouldn't think you ever get bored.'

'I'm too busy to be bored.' He smiled. She had proved to be extremely intelligent. 'So how would you like to train as a nurse? Train properly, I mean, in a hospital. You could do that in Bristol. They've been leading the country there in providing proper training for nurses. Once you'd qualified you'd never lack for employment, believe me. Think about it.'

Rachel stared at him in surprise then, as his suggestion sank in, she leaned forward eagerly. 'I don't need to consider it. I'd absolutely love to train as a nurse.'

George exchanged smiles with his wife, then turned back to her. 'Once you've recovered from the birth, we can help you find a place on a course in Bristol to do your training. Your timing for the baby will fit in well with the next new course starting.'

Jenny said, 'You'll need to pretend to be older than your actual age to do this, though, or else you'll have to wait another three years to start. Fortunately your recent experiences have given you an air of maturity and a better understanding of life than most girls have at fourteen. If you say you've just turned eighteen, I doubt there will be a single person who doesn't believe you.'

Rachel nodded. She had been so lucky to have been helped by the Nolans. And they'd make excellent parents for the baby, which had taken away her worries about giving it away.

Three weeks later she bore the child. The birth had been easy, they told her. It didn't feel easy to her but there you were. It was necessary to expel the infant from your body and you did what you had to, putting up with the pain.

'It's a girl,' Jenny exclaimed.

'Is it? Do you mind?'

'Of course we don't. We're very happy with any child, whether it's a boy or a girl.'

A few weeks later Dr Nolan took Rachel to an interview at the hospital in Bristol. Nobody queried her claim to be eighteen and the doctor gave her a good recommendation.

The following week she heard that she'd been accepted for the next course and could live in the nurses' hostel while she did her training. She couldn't wait to pack her bags and leave but tried to hide that. She'd miss the Nolans but she wouldn't miss seeing the child. Little Julia's presence was a constant reminder of that wicked man and she still had nightmares about him .

When Rachel finished her training as a nurse two years later, she had no difficulty finding a job in another hospital, this time in London. She learned a lot there but grew increasingly annoyed by the arrogance of some doctors towards both nurses and female patients.

After a year she moved to assist a kind elderly GP working with poorer families from his own surgery. But even here she found herself hemmed in by people's low expectations of what women were capable of. Male patients in particular could be highly suspicious of her ability to help treat them.

At least there was more general acceptance these days of the need for nurses to be properly trained, but women were making slow progress towards true acceptance of their skills when they actually went out to work.

If she'd had a rich family, she'd have wanted to train as a doctor, something women were starting to do. But she was always aware of the need to support herself and to have some money put by 'for a rainy day', so she didn't mention that to anyone.

It amused her that during the eighteen months she spent working for the GP, she'd turned down three proposals of marriage from young men who would be regarded as highly eligible by most people. One of them was even a doctor himself. They were pleasant enough but there wasn't one of them she'd want to spend the rest of her life with, let alone give up nursing to become what she thought of as a resident house-keeper and brood mare.

She still kept in touch with the Nolans, mostly by writing to them. She had visited them a couple of times, but the sight of her daughter, now a small child, running round the house and garden, still brought back unhappy memories and even nightmares.

Then one day when she was visiting the Nolans, she went into town to do some shopping and saw Pershore coming towards her. Worse still, he saw her. He stopped dead, gave one of his horrible, gloating smiles and pointed his forefinger at her.

She hid in a shop doorway, trying to stay out of sight and yet be able to peep along the street. It was definitely him! What on earth was that horrible man doing here?

Even now, after all this time, her heart began pounding with fear at the mere sight of him. She had never forgotten what he'd done, still had the occasional nightmare.

He was moving towards her now, so she darted back inside. She knew the shopkeeper slightly and asked her if she could go out at the back, explaining that a man she didn't like was following her and she was afraid of him.

The woman, a comfortable motherly person, peeped out and then put the lock on the shop door. 'I've seen that man round here before. He's started visiting a newcomer to town, and I don't like either of them, the way they look at women.'

'I'm terrified of him.'

'Well, you go out the back way. I'll make sure he doesn't follow you. This way.'

'Thank you.'

Rachel used the back lanes behind shops to get back to the Nolans' house, running most of the way.

'What's wrong?' Mrs Nolan said at once.

When Rachel told her, she frowned. 'He surely can't have come here because he found out about you knowing us?'

'The shopkeeper said he has a friend who's moved here.'

'Oh dear! You'd better stay in the house till it's time to leave.'

And, Rachel thought, she'd not come here for a good while. If his presence here was by sheer chance, then she'd been very unlucky.

It was Mrs Nolan who suggested she become a district nurse, a new area of employment for women. She'd need to do a short training course on top of her original training, but she loved learning so didn't mind that.

The independence of that work and the contact with people who might desperately need her help appealed to her greatly. Her own life had been saved by Dr Nolan and his wife and apart from finding people's physical and health needs fascinating, she wanted to help others in her turn, not just by working at the behest of a male doctor who didn't always understand what his female patients were going through in their lives.

'What would I have to study? I'm a reasonably experienced nurse now, after all. I don't want to go back to being treated as a rather stupid child as I was sometimes in Bristol.'

Jenny Nolan took out a leaflet and handed it to her. 'Read this and think about it.'

Rachel read it quickly. Training for district nurses apparently covered a wide range of subjects, some of them likely to be unfamiliar to those with experience mainly in hospital nursing. These included sanitary reform, health education for patients, ventilation, water supply, diet, the feeding and care of newborn infants and young children, infectious diseases, and sexual health.

She looked up. 'My goodness! What a lot of new things there will be to learn about.'

'Does that put you off?'

'No, of course not. I'd enjoy it.'

'We noticed when you lived with us that you have a hungry mind. I've been talking to a friend and they're setting up district nursing services in various towns and cities across the country. The ignorance of some poorer people even about their own health is often apparently dreadful and regularly leads to unnecessarily early deaths. With better knowledge people can make simple changes in their way of living to improve their own and their families' health at little extra cost. My friend said if she'd been younger she might have tried doing that sort of nursing herself.'

'I'd love to try it. I can always go back to hospital nursing if I don't enjoy the work, after all.'

Mrs Nolan hesitated then asked, 'You don't think you'd ever want to marry?'

'No. Definitely not. I've been asked a couple of times, but I didn't want to give up nursing. I'd go mad with boredom doing housework all day.'

'Then I'll pay any extra expenses you encounter and give you a living wage while you're doing this course.'

'I can't ask you to do that, Jenny.'

'You didn't ask. I'd be happy to do it. You've given me the thing I wanted most in life, as well as your ongoing friendship, which I value greatly. Besides, my husband and I can easily afford to give you that sort of help. This practice isn't in a poor area.'

So Rachel found herself moving on yet again, and looking forward greatly to learning about a district nurse's work. It sounded to be just up her street.

3

Joss Townley had a happy childhood but clashed regularly with his father as he grew towards manhood because he didn't want to go into the family business. He loathed the large, noisy factory and the rows of women working at the sewing machines. The poor things always looked weary but when he suggested giving them an occasional rest, his father hit the roof.

The trouble was, he was an only child and his father was determined that Joshua, as he insisted on calling him, should take Townley's over when the time came. And since he'd been forty when his son was born and wasn't in good health, he took the lad into the factory at fourteen to prepare him for it .

He'd have taken him away earlier to train him but that was the soonest his son was legally allowed to leave school. Joss begged to be allowed to continue his studies with the other lads because he was one of the top students in his class at an expensive private school, but nothing he said would change his father's mind.

'I can't bear the thought of spending my whole life persuading shops to stock the clothes our factory produces, or trying to produce them more cheaply. I don't like even being inside the factory, Father.'

'If it was good enough for my father then for me, it'll good enough for you in your turn, so you'll do as you're damned well told. Everyone has to earn a living in this world and you're no different. You are *not* going to let the Townley family down.'

His father repeated this with an increasing degree of anger over the next few weeks, not budging an inch.

Unlike his father, Joss enjoyed being out of doors and loved to breathe fresh air and tend plants. He spent hours walking in the countryside on Sundays or any time he could slip away on his trips to sell their products into shops. And he had green fingers, as people called it. The section of kitchen garden he'd taken over as a hobby produced more fruit and vegetables for the cook than the much larger section tended by their full-time gardener.

During his last week of school, he was forced to go into the factory every day after school ended, and hated it so much he begged again. 'Please, Father. Let me at least go into some sort of work that involves fresh air and nature, farming perhaps.'

'Never! You're our only son and you don't come from lowly farming stock. Besides, who else is there to inherit the factory if you don't?' His father crashed one meaty fist down on his desk. 'You'll do as you're told or I'll throw you out of my house and family this very day, and not one penny will you get from me when I die.'

'I don't care about money.'

Silence, then, 'Well, you should do, Joshua. And what's more, I'll bring in your cousin Mark and make him my heir if you refuse to work here with me. He'll jump at the chance to run our factory.'

He smiled in grim triumph as his son fell silent. Mark Townley was in his early twenties and had already gained a reputation as a bully who ill-treated the workers in the shops owned by that branch of the family.

Joss stared at him in horror. 'You wouldn't.'

'I'd have no choice. My nephew is the only other person who carries our family name.'

When his father was out at his club that evening, his mother sat down with Joss, took his hand and said quietly, 'Please do as your father asks, darling. He means what he says about your cousin Mark and he won't change his mind. He's the most stubborn person I ever met.'

As he scowled and opened his mouth to protest, she added, 'You can sell the factory after he dies and do what you like with the rest of your life. Your father is quite old now and although he tries to hide it, he's not in good health.'

He stared at her in shock. 'You speak as though you don't care if he dies.'

She shrugged. 'I shall deny saying this, but I had to marry the man my parents chose for me instead of the man I loved. Your father has been kind to me in his own way, and once I had you to love, my life became a lot happier. But if your father brought Mark into the business, I'd have to live with him, and I'd find that extremely unpleasant.'

In the end it was this frank talk that persuaded her son to give in.

All his father said was, 'I knew you'd see sense in the end, Joshua.'

Joss tried very hard to settle into the business, but he continued to loathe the work, the sour smell of the factory and the way his father did things generally. The only thing he was good at was handling the money their business earned, which his father said proved he was in the right occupation.

He still didn't agree.

Then fate stepped in and his father died of a seizure just after Joss turned twenty-one.

When the funeral was over his mother had another of her quiet talks with him. 'Darling, I hope you don't mind, but I'm going to live with Georgina from now on.'

He wasn't surprised at how happy she looked as she said that. 'You and your sister always did enjoy each other's company. When are you thinking of moving?'

She took a deep breath, looked at him apprehensively and said, 'I'd like to go as soon as I can, if you don't mind. Georgina is going to stay on here to help me sort out my things and pack, then we could leave in about a week's time.'

'So quickly?'

She gave him a shrewd look. 'How soon are you going to put the factory up for sale?'

He smiled wryly. 'I've done that already, but these things take time.'

'Don't you think it'll sell quickly?'

'Who knows? I've already spoken to an agent who thinks it'll go fairly quickly. Give Father his due, he was a good businessman and has navigated some difficult times really well, so it's a valuable asset. And I'm quite good with money, so I won't waste what it brings, believe me.'

'There you are, then. Um, you know your father has left me nothing?'

'Yes. I think that's outrageous.'

'I do have the money my godmother left me, but it's not a lot and I'll be dependent on my sister for part of my keep if that's all I have.' She looked at him hopefully.

He didn't hesitate. 'Father had ridiculous ideas about women and money. I'll give you a decent allowance, naturally.'

When he named the sum he had in mind and asked if that'd be enough, she let out a shuddering sigh of relief. 'I can't thank you enough, darling.'

'You'll get that for the rest of your life, more if it proves insufficient.' But he didn't give her any money outright. He was his father's son in that. He wasn't risking her leaving it to someone else.

'You're a kind son.'

'*He* should have left you a proper allowance.'

'He always said women couldn't handle money, but I've been dealing with the housekeeping money all my married life and have never overspent or got into debt.'

He could guess that she wouldn't have dared point that out to his father, who always had to be right. 'Where are you and your sister going to live? Her house is a bit small.'

'Harrogate. If she and I pool our money, we can buy a house there and actually, your father's cousin lives there.'

'I didn't know he had any relatives left.'

'Your father didn't like Albert so we didn't bother to keep up with him socially, but I did like him so I sent him cards and catch-up letters at Christmas and for his birthday and he sent similar ones to me.'

'What's his name?'

'Albert Townley. He's a little older than your father and never got married. He lives quietly and he always says he's happily married to his books.'

After she'd gone Joss missed his mother's company and fretted around the house in the evenings. He couldn't wait to get away from this place after the last few unhappy years under his father's control.

Within two months Joss had sold the factory and a month later he also sold the big house which had been the family home for the whole of his life. He invested the money they brought extremely carefully because it represented freedom from now on.

He put some of the most beautiful furniture and possessions into storage, together with his own collection of books. He let his mother take any of the pieces she wished to keep and sold the rest. That included the shelves of gold-tooled ornamental books that had been bought by the yard. His father had never read a page of them or of any other book that his son had seen, but he'd considered them necessary for the house to look 'right' for people of their class.

After some thought, Joss decided to go travelling round England. He'd always had a desire to see his own country and find out whether it really was a 'green and pleasant land' but most of all, he was longing for fresh air to get what he thought of as the stink of the factory out of his nostrils.

When he did eventually set up a permanent home, he wouldn't live as lavishly as his parents had done. He was quite sure his father had eaten himself into an early grave by the years of huge evening meals that his mother had only picked at, and he'd not eaten lavishly, either. She'd been tied to his father's 'rule' even more than he had. He didn't know how she'd kept her sanity for all those years and was delighted at how happy she and her sister sounded to be in Harrogate.

When Joss left the village he started his new life with a few weeks in London, visiting art galleries and museums, then began to travel by slow stages round the coast of Kent. He spent the worst of the winter in the south of France, amazed at first to find out how bad the French he'd learned at school was.

In the spring he went back to Kent and began moving slowly along the south coast, with an eventual aim of exploring the west country. But there was no hurry and he spent longer on his journey than he'd expected.

He'd stored some of his possessions and clothing in London in numbered boxes and went back to dip into them as needed or added new boxes to the stores.

He took care to write to his mother every month and to catch a train north to visit her at intervals so that she wouldn't worry about him. He met Cousin Albert a couple of times and found they shared an interest in similar types of books.

It was all very pleasant and he enjoyed visiting some of the most famous places in England, such as Stonehenge and the great cathedrals and castles, as well as the more picturesque country areas.

He also studied the wildlife and plants he came across and had bought books about them. What a joy that was. There was so much to learn. And he joined in harvests and other physical activities, trying not to show that he was actually quite a wealthy man and enjoying ordinary people's company.

He not only found striding out across the countryside far more interesting than sitting watching it at a distance from a train but it led to a big surprise. After living like this for well over a year he'd become markedly stronger physically and had to buy a whole new wardrobe for the new, muscular body he'd developed. He hadn't realised he'd been so weak physically, but now he felt to be bursting with strength and energy.

Joss spent nearly five years travelling, with rests during the worst of winter in university cities or stops in other places of interest as well as occasional stays with his mother and aunt. He stayed for longer in some regions and he worked in all sorts of menial jobs, enjoying most of them greatly: gardener, harvest labourer, fruit picker, anything that kept him out of doors and learning about country ways.

He found he had an ability to get on with people at all levels in society and enjoyed chatting to anyone and everyone.

When he got to the north, he went to see his mother in Harrogate first then began exploring the countryside, which was not nearly as lush as the south. Then he came to the moors and fell in love with them on sight. He couldn't explain why they touched his heart strings, but they did.

He was, by now, ready to settle down but still wasn't sure how he'd occupy himself when he did. After some more exploration of the north he decided on Lancashire rather than Yorkshire, but definitely wanted to settle near the moors.

He'd buy a house when he found some part of the north that suited him and then he'd live on the interest from his savings and investments, which had proved very successful. During these past few years he'd used far less money than he'd expected and didn't feel a desire to spend lavishly on anything.

He rather fancied getting married, though, and starting a family, but he wasn't rushing into anything. He wasn't spending his life with a woman unless he enjoyed her company.

When he was in an industrial town called Oldham, he wrote to his mother to say he'd be staying in a hotel there for a week if she wanted to contact him. There were a few places he planned to see nearby so he was going to do it in a leisurely manner and not make frequent moves from hotel to hotel.

The morning after he'd sent his letter he received a telegram from his mother, saying she needed to see him urgently and would he please come to Harrogate as soon as he received this.

She wasn't the sort to panic and had never asked anything like this of him before, so it must be important. He sent her a telegram to say he was on his way and would be arriving in the late afternoon.

When he got there she rushed out of the house and asked the taxi driver to wait as they needed to go out again immediately. Only then did she turn to her son, fling her arms round him and say, 'Oh, thank goodness you came quickly!'

'Has something happened to my aunt?'

'No, of course not. Georgina's never ill, nor am I. It's Cousin Albert. He died suddenly last week, but I didn't know where you were then, so couldn't contact you.'

'I'm sorry to hear that but why are you so upset? I didn't think you were deeply fond of him and I hardly knew him.'

'I was quite fond of him, even though he was your father's cousin, but it's not that. It's his lawyer, Mr Weaver, who says it's urgent and wants to see you as soon as possible. Albert has apparently left everything to you but there's a problem that needs dealing with if you're to inherit.'

'Good heavens! Why me anyway? He hardly knows me.'

'You're the closest male relative who is a Townley. And didn't you hear what I said? A problem has cropped up in connection with his bequest.'

'I'll go and see his lawyer tomorrow morning then. I'm tired, mother.'

'We need to go now. When I told Mr Weaver you were on your way he said he'd stay late and you should go to his rooms straight away.'

'But—'

'Lawyers don't normally use the word "urgent" in every other sentence, as he did, so who knows what will need doing?'

'But mother—'

'You should go straight away. And what's more, I'm coming with you. You've done so much for me since your father died and maybe I can do something for you now.'

She was so agitated, he left his suitcase in her hall and got back into the taxi with her.

He was exhausted and it'd be something and nothing, he was sure, but she was so upset he'd better humour her.

4

Mr Weaver's rooms were in an elegant building. 'These offices must cost a fortune,' Joss said as the cab drew up.

'Never mind that. Come on inside.'

A young clerk greeted them with, 'Ah! Mrs Townley.'

'And this is my son.'

'Good afternoon, sir. Mr Weaver will be very happy indeed to see you.' He disappeared through a door and came back almost immediately. 'This way, please.'

Joss followed his mother into a comfortable office where a tall, thin man was waiting for them.

'This is Mr Weaver,' his mother said. 'And this, of course, is my son, Joshua Townley, usually known as Joss.'

'I'm delighted to meet you, Mr Townley. I hope you don't mind my saying that you bear a distinct resemblance to your cousin, even though you're much younger. Do please sit down. I'll summarise the situation and then we'll discuss how to deal with things.'

The man wasn't wasting much time on civilities, Joss thought. Maybe whatever needed doing really was urgent.

'As your mother will have told you, I'm sure, Mr Townley has left everything to you.'

'Hasn't he left anything to my mother?'

'No. When he asked her if she needed anything, she told him not to bother, said she was all right financially, and he agreed because he preferred not to split up the inheritance. There is some money in the bank, but the main thing that concerns us today is the purchase of some land in a town called Ollerthwaite, in a small valley in the northern part of the Pennines.'

'What has that to do with me?'

'Let me explain the situation and then you'll understand. Mr Townley's grandfather's family on the maternal side used to live there permanently, but when he died and his parents inherited, they sold some of their land in order to afford a move to Harrogate. Sadly, his father had become an invalid and the air there seemed to suit him better.'

Joss nodded, wondering where all this was leading.

'They kept the family home and nearby grounds, but rarely visited the house in Ollerthwaite.'

He sighed. 'Your cousin, however, regretted the sale because it broke up his estate, and when he found out that it had been bought through a proxy purchaser by the Entwistles, a family he particularly disliked, he was furious. Sadly, there was nothing he could do about it.'

'How does that concern me?'

'I'm coming to that if you'll bear with me. Just before your cousin died so unexpectedly, the owner of that land became ill and as he had fallen out with his own family, he offered to sell the land to your cousin. I'm quite sure it was to spite them.'

Joss nodded, still bewildered by all this information.

'I told Mr Townley the land wasn't worth the asking price, because it's not in a good part of the valley.

I also advised him against stepping into the middle of the Entwistles' family quarrel. But he ignored my advice because he had always wanted to get back that piece of land, said it belonged to him morally.' He sighed and paused, shaking his head and staring blindly at the fireplace for a few moments.

Joss waited impatiently, wishing the fellow would get on with the tale.

'I told Mr Townley he should at least think about it for a few days but he ignored my advice and went ahead anyway. Worst of all, he placed a deposit to secure his purchase of the land without consulting me about the terms. His offer was accepted with certain conditions. However, he died suddenly before he'd sorted out the rest of the payment.'

'Then surely the deposit can be returned?'

'I'm afraid not. The conditions were not of my making, believe me. The rest of the purchase money has to be paid by the end of this week or the deposit will be forfeited and it is a significant sum, which ought to be part of your inheritance.'

When Mr Weaver told Joss how much that was, he stared in shock because the deposit was nearly half the purchase price.

'Jim Entwistle, the one who's selling that land, is now gravely ill, with only weeks to live, and is refusing to change the terms of the sale at all. Presumably he is expecting it to fall through and is intending to keep the deposit to pass on to his children.'

'Good heavens! That is unconscionable.'

'I think so too.'

'Did my cousin have money in the bank to cover the rest of the sale?'

'Unfortunately not. He was in the middle of arranging to borrow the money temporarily from his bank, then he intended sell some of his investments and pay off the debt. The bank won't go on with that now he's dead so the sale can't be finalised in the time agreed and the deposit will be forfeited unless you have enough money to complete the payments.'

Joss's heart sank and it was a while before he spoke. 'I do have enough money, actually, but I'm not sure I want to complete the purchase. Will they at least extend the time so that I can go and look at this piece of land?'

'I'm afraid not.'

'Oh dear.'

'If you want my advice, even if you don't wish to keep the land, you should buy it. You can always sell it again later, after all.'

'But I don't even know what it looks like.'

'I'm afraid I can't help you there. All I know is that it lies in the middle of one side of the current grounds of the house that you've been left.' He hesitated then said quietly, 'What it amounts to is, are you prepared to lose the deposit?'

Joss shook his head. Of course he didn't intend to give away so much money. 'I suppose not. Are you absolutely certain there's no way we can insist on it being returned?'

'I'm afraid there isn't. Mr Townley was so eager to acquire that particular piece of land he behaved very rashly and we now have only three days left to pay the rest of the money.'

After a few moments' thought, Joss said, 'Well, I think you and I are in agreement, Mr Weaver: that deposit is too large a sum to lose.' He looked sideways at his mother, wondering what she was thinking and she smiled at him.

The lawyer nodded. 'Yes. It's far too large to give away. I've never known Mr Townley act so rashly, but I was aware that he'd always deeply regretted his parents selling that land.' He paused then said quietly, 'You're buying it, then?'

'Needs must. I'm not giving away that much money. These Entwistles must be very lacking in common decency.'

'The man selling the land wasn't liked in the valley, that's for sure. They're a farming family and seem to have made a lot of money in the past few years. The other brother seems to be better thought of, though. I don't know the details but I heard that this Jim Entwistle was selling it to your cousin merely to spite his brother Lionel. Just imagine going to those lengths!'

Joss couldn't even begin to imagine that.

'Anyway, how shall you manage the payment? Is there anything I can do to help?'

'There's a branch of my bank in Harrogate which I've been using to deal with my mother's affairs. They're well aware of my financial status, so I shall contact them tomorrow morning first thing and then perhaps you can arrange for the final payment to be made.'

Joss stared down at the floor for a moment or two. This would be one of the rashest things he'd ever done in his life. But if his cousin Albert had been so eager to buy that land back, there must be something special about it, surely?

There had better be!

And if not, he would definitely sell it again, might do so anyway.

'Where is this land exactly?' he asked.

'Just outside Eastby End, which is a rather run-down part of the town of Ollerthwaite. Your cousin's family home is near it.'

'Whatever was my cousin thinking of?'

His mother said quietly, 'Albert wasn't a stupid man.'

'Well, I'll find out more when I go there, won't I?'

Mr Weaver nodded and handed him a folder. 'Here are the details the bank will need to arrange the transfer of the money.'

As they walked outside, Joss looked at his mother. 'I hope I'm doing the right thing.'

'I think you are. It was Cousin Albert's dearest wish, and he has left you rather a nice amount of land and investments.'

'I'm not short of money.'

'Shall you go and live in the valley? Albert has left you a house there too, after all.'

'I haven't the faintest idea what I'm going to do or where I'm going to settle permanently. Once I've got the finances sorted out, I'll go and have a look at the house, though, of course I will.'

'I'm sure it'll all work out well in the end, darling.'

He wished he had her optimism.

5

Councillor Walter Crossley smiled at his wife across the table as they were finishing their evening meal. 'Out with it, Flora love. What's on your mind? It's not like you to sit silent over a meal.'

'I had occasion to go into Eastby End this afternoon and it really upset me to see the place. It's like a world of its own, not part of our town or even our valley.'

'In what way?'

'I hadn't realised how bad it was. It's so run down it's turning into a really bad slum. I don't know who owns the properties there but they should be ashamed of themselves for neglecting them. Do we own any of them?'

'I'm afraid we do and I haven't kept my eye on them as I should have done, have just left it to a rental agent. Those are the properties I acquired a couple of years ago by default when Headley Keaton couldn't pay his debts to me.'

'Then we ought to do something and encourage the other owners to take steps to improve their possessions as well. My heart aches when I see the children. Many of them not only live in hovels but go round barefoot, wearing clothes that are little more than rags. Worst of all, they have that famine look on their faces, you know the one I mean, hungry eyes. It's as if some of them have never been properly fed.'

His smile had faded completely now. 'That sort of thing upsets me too. If only we humans didn't need so much sleep. The trouble is, the Ollerthwaite town council can't tackle every problem in the valley and nor can I. And that part of the town has been a near slum for as long as I can remember.'

'Well, it's an actual slum now, Walter. Most of the houses are very poorly maintained and it's a wonder some of them haven't fallen down.'

'It's as if all the lazy, useless folk end up living there.'

Her voice grew sharper. 'And also the people who're in trouble with the authorities, sometimes through no fault of their own like not being able to pay their rents when they're ill. Even in my short time living here I've heard of that.'

He nodded, looking unhappy.

'There must be something the council can do to make a start, Walter.' She looked at him challengingly.

'It's the cost that prevents it, especially at the moment with elections coming next year. No councillor who wants to get re-elected will do something that puts up the council rates that householders have to pay. They just won't.'

'Well, I think we should make a start.'

He stared at her, eyes narrowed. 'What are you plotting now, woman?'

She grinned. 'You know me too well.'

'I'm glad to say I'm starting to know you very well since we married. Come on. Out with it, my lovely lass.'

'You still haven't spent most of the money Abigail gave you after her marriage, the proceeds of her father's crimes and thefts, which they only found out about after he died. You keep saying you're saving it for a worthwhile project. How about we use it to start something in Eastby End to help the poorest people there? That'd be an extremely worthwhile use of it, don't you think?'

'Hmm. How do we work out who the poorest people are, though? And even so, there isn't enough money to do more than ruffle the surface.'

'Better to ruffle the surface and help some than to do nothing. Anyway, it's easy to work out who are the most deprived people. You only have to look round that part of town to see that it's the women and children who're suffering most. Well, they always suffer most when their menfolk are lacking work. The breadwinner has to be looked after first when the food is put on the table, doesn't he?'

'It's usually necessary to bring at least some money into the home, even if the breadwinner can't find full-time work.'

'Well, I think we should use that money to help the women and children.'

'We've already set up a clinic for poorer women in Ollerthwaite itself.'

'Yes, and it's doing some excellent work, but it's not doing all that I'd like it to. Ida, who runs is, is a good nurse, but she's not prepared to go out among people, insists on them coming to her.'

'Well, if it's free medical care they'll get from her it'll be worth the effort to visit the clinic surely?'

'Eastby End isn't near that clinic. There are some people out there who can't walk to the end of the street, let alone the mile or more to the clinic in town. And anyway, Ida is always busy so we need more help, another nurse and perhaps one located in Eastby End. One of the new district nurses maybe, who go out to see people in their own homes.'

He was looking thoughtful now so she knew she'd caught his interest.

'Why don't you offer a large percentage of that money to fund another clinic and hire a district nurse in Eastby End, Walter? Most such nurses are hired by an institute, but we're too small a place to have one. However, we could affiliate ours to a nearby institute, or even the one in Liverpool and get them to help us appoint women suitably qualified enough to be recognised as Queen's nurses. What do you think?'

'It's a good idea, well worth considering.'

'The money you're managing should be offered to the council on condition that they match the amount you're giving. Then, if they have to increase council rates to raise their share of the money, they can explain to the voters that if they do that a very large sum will be donated to spend on the poor during the next year or two.'

He blinked in shock. 'You have been thinking hard, my dear.'

She gave him one of her determined looks and gestured with one hand as if to say, over to you, before sitting back and waiting patiently for his reply.

Walter frowned, not saying anything for a while then murmuring, 'I wonder if the council would get involved?'

'I think they would if word was spread about the offer and people who are well respected expressed their support. The newspaper could run a front-page article about district nursing, too, and I know some councillors' wives who will be happy to nag their husbands into helping their poorer sisters.'

He gave her another slow nod or two, and a wry grin.

'We could use Mrs Dacre Craven's *Guide to District Nurses and Home Nursing* as our official reference book. It's very well written and has been accepted just about everywhere. We'd not need to set up a new system; the basics of that have already been worked out all over the country. And our nurse could wear a uniform like the one they advise at the Queen's Institute in London to show she's a respected official. It's actually very practical, has to be, because the clothes need washing regularly after contact with dirty people and their homes.'

She paused for breath and he reached out to give her a big hug. 'My love, you are wonderful. Mind you, you'll need to push your lady friends to nag their husbands good and hard. A lot of the men on the council wouldn't do anything without that incentive, I'm afraid.'

'When they hear that the Queen herself has given a large sum of money from her Jubilee fund and even helped choose the uniform for district nurses, they won't take much pushing.'

He smiled. 'I think this will be a very worthwhile cause and if the councillors have any sense they'll snap up an offer like that.'

'I'm not sure sometimes that certain council members have any sense at all,' she said with a roll of her eyes, 'but I do think women of all classes will approve the idea, because it'll save children's lives.'

'Let me think about how to do it, Flora love. There's quite a lot of money left in the fund, I admit. But I promised the police inspector it would be spent wisely and under my own direction, not simply tossed at small targets here and there. And don't forget that I have to report back to him about exactly what it gets spent on.'

She knew better than to press the point further at this stage so changed the subject. She and Walter might have married late in life but she understood her man. He was very careful indeed about how he used other people's money, whether as a councillor or private citizen, which was only right and proper.

She'd give him time to think, but she was utterly determined to do something to improve Eastby End, whatever the council, or even her Walter, said or did. She couldn't bear to stand by and see children and their mothers suffering as badly as some of them were only a couple of miles away from her comfortable home.

Walter sounded out the council members he knew best and none of them seemed to be particularly worried about Eastby End, simply accepting that it was where the poorest people lived.

'You can't help people who won't help themselves,' one man said.

'It wasn't always that bad round there,' Walter protested.

'Well it is now because times are hard and there simply aren't enough jobs to go round.'

That didn't stop Walter explaining at the next council meeting that he could arrange for the donation of a substantial sum of money to the town if the council could find the funds to match it. 'You'd have to show that you'd put the donation to good use, though.'

'How did you get hold of that much money?' one of his regular opponents on the council asked indignantly. 'I often worry about how you've made your own fortune, Walter Crossley, I do that.'

'I made my fortune by hard work. I was given this money by a senior police officer. It's the proceeds of various local crimes, which is why we'd have to show we'd put it to good use and account for every penny spent.'

He paused then added quietly, 'It'd be a big lift for our valley, getting that sort of money into circulation here, and it'd be good to help the poorest people, don't you think? Especially the children. I hate to see how hungry some of them look. Have you seen how long the queues are at the soup kitchen run by the church in the centre of Ollerthwaite?'

'The council gives money to charity, don't worry,' another man snapped. 'But we have a duty to our rate-payers as well.'

'I shouldn't be surprised if doing something that brings in money won the sitting members a lot of votes at the next elections.' Walter waited a moment to let that sink in then added, 'And if we don't use it some other council will get the chance. I can't sit on that money. I've been told to put it to good use by a senior police officer.'

'Why can't it go to a more worthwhile cause then?'

'What's more worthwhile than feeding hungry mothers and children, and setting up a clinic for them?'

The discussions went to and fro for over a week, but in the end there was a special meeting and even the most miserly of council members agreed to match the donation.

'We'd be mad to miss the chance of being granted such a large amount of money,' several of them said in the end. 'But we'll be watching how you spend it, Walter Crossley, and watching very carefully too.'

While that was going on, Flora sounded out the wives of the better-off men in the valley, women who might not have the vote but who certainly had influence over what their husbands did with their votes. Many of them had supported her idea of opening a clinic for the poorer people in Ollerthwaite itself and using some of the money Walter was handling to do that.

Now, she suggested they discuss the possibility of creating another health clinic, this time in Eastby with their husbands and tried to nudge them into taking this step.

It was two months before a plan was devised and approved for raising money locally to match the donation. After that there were ongoing disagreements about how exactly to spend it, not to mention who exactly the 'deserving poor' were. And some questioned why it couldn't be spent on men as well as on women, though hardly anyone complained about spending it on the children.

In the end Flora challenged some of the council members and the wives of influential citizens to go with her to Eastby End and tell her whether they wanted to continue living next to such a slum and risking infections and epidemics being spread from there to the rest of the valley.

It was the first time some of them had really looked round Eastby End for a good many years and it came as a shock, because both buildings and people seemed to have gone a lot further downhill. This didn't at all accord with their views of their valley and its place in the world.

'I agree that something has to be done,' one of the women told her afterwards. 'Are you quite sure that we'll get that donation?'

'Absolutely certain. It's a lot of money, isn't it?'

'It is. We'd have to work for several years to raise that much for charity. I shall definitely speak to my husband about how we should use it.'

6

Once the purchase of the piece of land he'd inherited had gone through, Joss arranged to visit his new property, not just the land but the house. His mother offered to go with him but he wanted to decide how he felt about it on his own so he turned down her offer as tactfully as he could.

When he got off the train in Ollerthwaite he stood for a few moments staring round, in no hurry to move on. He was glad his height allowed him to see over the heads of most of the travellers bustling towards the exit because there was a good view of what seemed to be the main street from the platform.

Thanks to his travels, he was used to assessing a new place quickly. He took his time now because this place was more important to him than most of the others had been. He might even end up living here since there was a house waiting for him. Or he might not.

It was a small station, at the end of a short single line that led only here from the main railway. It had passed through a few villages en route, stopping at each one, and he had to admit to himself that he'd enjoyed the scenery on the way here. Good thing he hadn't been in a hurry, though.

The main street ran slightly uphill and had a peaceful settled air. Once the other passengers had dispersed, there were only a few pedestrians to be seen on the street, none of them seeming to be in a hurry. He rather liked the look of the town, actually.

Someone cleared their throat next to him and he realised that an elderly porter was waiting patiently to hand over the rest of his luggage, which had now been unloaded from the van at the rear of the train.

'Sorry. I was just looking round. Thank you.' He slipped a coin into the man's hand. 'Is there a cab and can you recommend a hotel, please?'

'We don't have an actual cab here but I can send a lad to fetch the chap with a pony trap who often takes people around. There should be a room free at the Jubilee Hotel, which is the only place where people like you would want to stay, if you don't mind my saying so. It's quite small but those who've stayed there seem to have been very happy with its services.'

'Then that's where I'll go. Can you give me the name of the proprietor?'

'Yes, of course. It's run by Mr and Mrs Shorrocks. They only turned it into a hotel recently and are still fitting out some parts of it but the food is apparently excellent and I hear the beds are clean and comfortable.'

What more can you ask of a hotel? Joss thought. 'That sounds perfect. I'd be grateful if you could get transport to take me there.'

Ten minutes later a young chap drove up in a pony trap which had a covered rear part and when the porter gestured towards Joss, the young chap came across to him, smiling cheerfully.

'I gather you and your luggage need to be taken to the Jubilee Hotel, sir?'

'Yes, please. The porter seems to think they'll have a room free.'

'I'm sure they will, sir. Is that trunk heavy?'

'I'm afraid so.'

'Could you help me heave it up, then.' He lowered his voice, 'Our porter is a bit old to lift heavy loads.'

'Of course I can.'

When it came time to get into the trap the driver said, 'Why don't you sit next to me, sir? You can see more from there and the weather is fine. First visit to Ollerthwaite, is it?'

'Yes. And the moors round here looked beautiful from the train.'

'And there are some good walks across them. The lake's pretty too, nearby.' He slowed down and pointed. 'You can just catch a glimpse of it from here. The town is just starting to put up signposts to help visitors find their way round.'

'Good idea.'

'It's a nice little town, ours is, if I do say so myself. I've visited a couple of big cities and I didn't like the crowds of strangers and all the traffic, no, I didn't like them at all.'

He drew up not long afterwards at the hotel, which had a neat little sign over the door and stood in a corner position on the main street. It wasn't far away from the station but too far to lug a heavy trunk to.

'I'll just go inside and check that they have a room,' Joss said.

'I'm sure they will have, sir. But I'm happy to wait as long as you like, then I'll help you carry that trunk in.'

The door to the small hotel was half open so Joss knocked and waited. When no one answered, he pushed it further open and called, 'Is anyone there?'

A woman hurried out from the rear of the hall. 'Oh, sorry. I was just brewing a pot of tea. Can I help you, sir?'

'I'm looking for a room, probably for a few nights.' It didn't sound as though the house he'd inherited had been occupied for a while so he'd have to set it to rights before he moved in. *If* he moved in.

'Certainly. Would you like to see one of our rooms?'

'If you don't mind. One of your bigger rooms, perhaps? My name's Townley.'

'I'm Mrs Shorrocks. My husband and I own this hotel. If you come upstairs I'll show you one of our finished rooms. They're all more or less the same size, I'm afraid, but I think they're quite roomy.'

At the top of the stairs there was a long corridor with doors on either side, two of them marked 'Bathroom'. She opened a bedroom door part way along. 'Here you are, sir. This one looks out on to the main street, which is nicer than looking out over the yard at the rear.'

The room was immaculately clean and it looked as if the furniture and fittings were brand new.

She smiled and gestured. 'Why don't you try the bed?'

'Do you mind if I do that?'

'Not at all. Beds are made for lying down on, aren't they?'

It was very comfortable so when he got up off it, he asked, 'There's just one other thing: do you provide meals?'

'We're happy to do that as long as you let us know in advance.'

'Then I'd like to take this room with breakfast and evening meals tomorrow and probably for a day or two after that. I don't know how long I'll be staying in the district, but at least four or five days I should think, perhaps longer. I'll tell you as soon as I know.'

'I'm afraid I don't have anyone to bring your luggage in or to help you with the trunk because my husband is out.'

'I can bring the suitcases in myself and I'm sure the man who drove me here from the station will help with the trunk. He seems very obliging.'

'We have a trolley you can use to help with it, on the flat bits at least.'

When they came down, she took him to see the guests' sitting room, which was another comfortable space.

'That looks good,' he said.

She called to the young chap who'd driven him here and brought out a trolley from under the stairs, then left them to bring all the luggage in.

When he came downstairs again, Joss paid his driver and added a generous tip, which brought a beaming smile to the young man's face.

As he went back towards the stairs, Mrs Shorrocks popped out of the rear of the hall to ask, 'Would you like a cup of tea? I've just brewed a pot and there's plenty.'

'I'd love one, if you don't mind.'

'Not at all. If you'd like to go into the guests' sitting room I can bring it to you there. Or else up to your room. I don't mind which.'

'I'll have it in the sitting room, if that's all right.'

'Yes, of course it is. The armchairs in there are very comfortable. There isn't a local newspaper, I'm afraid, but we take the *Manchester Guardian*, though it doesn't get here till mid-morning. I can lend you our copy.'

'No, thank you. When I've had my cup of tea I'll go out and explore the town.'

She brought a mug of tea a few minutes later. There were two biscuits with it which looked home-made.

He took a sudden decision. She had such an honest face, he trusted her instinctively. 'I'd like to ask your advice about something in connection with my visit here. Perhaps I could speak to you and your husband about it tonight, in confidence?'

'If we can help you, we will. We have someone else who's booked a room for tonight, so it might be best to wait till after the evening meal, then join us in our own quarters. That way, no one else staying here will hear what you're saying.'

'Thank you. I'd be much obliged.'

He went out and strolled round the town centre, stopping a couple of times to chat to someone. As he'd found on his travels, there were often old men hanging about, watching the world go by who were happy to chat. And if you bought something so were shopkeepers. He'd been delighted to hear that there was a small lake nearby and decided to walk round it at some stage.

By the time he went back to the hotel he was feeling pleasantly tired. It would be nice to settle down somewhere for a while, whether he made a permanent home here or not. He wondered whether the house he'd inherited was furnished, so that he could stay there if he stocked the pantry and hired some help. That way, he could try out what it would be like to live there.

When he went down for the evening meal he found that there were now two other guests, a youngish couple there to enjoy a couple of days of moorland walks. He enjoyed their company over the evening meal, which was served by Mr Shorrocks' younger sister, who'd been out at school during the day.

It was good, hearty food, and as he chatted to the couple he found out that there were several walks he could enjoy, all easy to find.

Already he was enjoying being here.

After the meal was over, Joss joined the Shorrocks in their comfortable sitting room and explained about his inheritance in broad terms, then waited for their reaction.

Abigail Shorrocks looked at him in surprise. 'So you're a cousin of old Mr Townley.'

'Yes. Distant cousin, though, and I didn't know him very well. It was my mother and aunt who saw him regularly because they live in Harrogate. And now I'm left in the position of needing to find out what I've inherited. I thought I'd go there tomorrow and look at it. Is there someone in this town I can hire to drive me there and show me round the area this first time?'

'I think it'd be best if I did that,' Mr Shorrocks said.

He was surprised. 'I can't ask you to do that when you have a business to run.'

'Unless you've taken a dislike to me on sight, it'd probably be worth your while to let me show you round.' He hesitated for a moment then said, 'Especially if the Entwistles realise you're the one who's bought that piece of land. They might pester you to sell it to them.'

Joss gave him a sharp glance at that. 'Are you warning me about them even before I've met them?'

'Yes. They don't have a good reputation for getting on with neighbours and I'm certain they'd have snapped up that piece of land for themselves if they hadn't quarrelled with their cousin a few years ago.'

'Well, I have no idea what I've inherited yet or what I'll be doing about it.'

'You'll understand why they want it when you see how their land is situated. The Entwistles were small farmers originally, but the family have gradually built up their holdings and the oldest son seems set on buying more if he can. He's the biggest landowner in Eastby End, apart from your cousin, and as Mr Townley wasn't here very often he didn't try to influence local affairs. When Jim Entwistle sold the land to you, I gather Lionel hit the roof about it.'

'I thought Jim was still alive.'

'He is, but he's gone off to Blackpool to spend his last few months in comfort, thanks to your money.'

Joss whistled softly. 'That sounds to be a bad situation for me to walk into.'

'It is. Which is why you'd be advised to take someone with you at first. They're not subtle folk. I think they'll let you know quite quickly if they want to buy that land from you.'

'How come the brothers are so at odds with one another?'

'No one is quite sure, just that there was some sort of quarrel a few years ago.' Rufus paused, waiting. 'So . . . shall I come with you?'

'Yes, please. But you'll be leaving your wife without help, so I insist on us agreeing terms for a payment for each day or half day you spend with me, plus any expenses we incur will be my responsibility.'

'Thank you. That's very fair. We shall need to hire a pony and trap and I'll get Abigail to put us up a few sandwiches. Pity there isn't a decent pub in Eastby End or we could have had a half of shandy at lunchtime. I should think we'll be there all day, especially this first visit, don't you? What time do you want to set off?'

'About eight o'clock, do you think? I'm an early riser usually.'

'Me too, so whatever suits you will be all right. Breakfast at seven-thirty be OK?'

'Fine by me.'

'Is that all for now?'

Joss took the hint and stood up. 'Yes. I'm really grateful for your offer of help.'

When he went up to bed, he took out the book he was currently reading, *Plain Tales From the Hills* by Rudyard Kipling. He was finding the short stories very interesting and learning a lot about India. He liked to vary the type of book he read.

What would he have done without these paper companions during the past few years? He'd kept some of them and sent them to join his possessions in storage, given others away that he'd never want to read again to libraries in towns and villages he visited. He could never have thrown away a book, even a tattered one.

Tonight, however, he didn't turn many pages because he kept thinking about his inheritance and the trouble he might be walking into with these Entwistles. If they'd quarrelled so fiercely with one another, they might be hard for him to deal with too, especially as they sounded to have really wanted to get hold of that land.

Well, they wouldn't find him weak at standing up for himself and he was, if he said so himself, good at managing money too. But he'd try to defuse the situation. That would make life much easier if he came to live round here.

He couldn't help wondering what the family house would be like. It'd be ironic if he liked it enough to make his home here. No, surely he'd need to live somewhere with more amenities, somewhere near a big town or perhaps a city?

Oh, what did he know? He hadn't even seen his inheritance yet, or the land he'd bought, let alone the place where it was situated.

7

Flora said she'd deal with hiring a suitable district nurse for Eastby End and Walter left her to it. She was determined this time to find someone who'd go out and about to see the sick women and children in their homes, especially those who'd have had difficulty getting to a clinic. They'd hoped to get that sort of care from the nurse hired for the Ollerthwaite clinic, but they'd had difficulty finding someone. In the end, they'd had to hire one who had excellent experience in hospitals and assisting doctors, but had made it plain that she wouldn't go out to visit people in their homes.

Ida had proved very capable when it came to tending patients at the clinic, but it was disappointing to have to accept her limiting what she would do because Flora had hoped for more.

She didn't feel like making long journeys these days for any reason but dire necessity so wrote to Pearl Grayson, a friend of many years, who was the head nurse at the School of Nursing in Liverpool, one of the main places where district nurses were trained. She spent a long time working on the letter and explaining to Pearl what they were prepared to offer in wages and other amenities. Then she outlined their needs in a separate document that could be copied and given to applicants, keeping a carbon copy of it herself.

To her delight, a letter arrived by return of post saying there was an extremely capable young woman who might be suitable, but Rachel Norris had said she wanted to find a home of her own, however small, with her next job. She didn't feel it was likely she'd get married, because she enjoyed her work too much, but she was tired of sharing accommodation with miscellaneous other women, mostly much younger than her.

Flora took this dilemma to her husband.

'I did hear that a small flat is being made in a house in Grange Street,' he said. 'It shares a bathroom with the owner, but there are two rooms, one a living room with a sink and kitchen area, so the tenant would be fairly private there.'

'You always seem to hear such things before anyone else does, Walter.'

He swept her a mocking bow. 'People tell me things. But I'm always at your service first of all, my dear wife.'

'Never mind fooling around, tell me who owns this flat.'

'Dora Prior. Now that her husband is dead, she needs the money, but I think she wants the company as well. She'll be living on the ground floor, says she finds going up and down stairs more difficult these days.'

'What is the flat like inside?'

'Nice enough, I've been told. It's newly painted but furniture isn't provided. I can find some second-hand pieces among my stock so that won't be a problem. And it's quite close to Eastby End, so not too far for our nurse to walk to work.'

'Hmm. It sounds as if that might be just the thing. If you're going out this morning, can you find a lad to take a message from me asking Mrs Prior if I can go and look at it this afternoon?'

'I'll do better than that. I'll call in myself and arrange it, then escort you there.'

It took Flora only a few moments to decide that the flat would be suitable and Mrs Prior was delighted at the thought of renting to a nurse.

'What about furniture?' she asked anxiously. 'The tenant must bring in their own things. I feel this will ensure I get someone who can afford to pay the rent regularly, not someone scratching for every penny.'

And also, Flora thought, it'd save Mrs Prior from buying any furniture.

'That's all right,' she said. 'We'll sort some furniture out. We happen to have some spare items. Can you give us a key so that we can have it delivered?'

Walter stepped forward and gave her some money. 'Rent in advance to show we're in earnest.'

Mrs Prior clutched it tightly, looking greatly relieved.

They went on to Walter's store of second-hand furniture which he used to help poorer people and youngsters trying to set up homes, though he also sold items occasionally.

Flora sorted out some pieces which were old-fashioned but in reasonable condition, promising to purchase a modern innerspring mattress for the iron bed frame, which was also sprung.

Walter said he'd arrange to get everything from the shop the following morning, together with one of the boxes of miscellaneous crockery and other kitchen items. He collected the latter when better off people would have thrown them away to give a start to young couples struggling to set up house.

'My goodness, you're a demon for getting things done quickly, Flora lass,' he said as they drove home.

'We both are. And we need that nurse if we're to improve the conditions in Eastby End. This time we'll make sure we get someone who'll go out to people's homes, not someone who insists on them coming to see her in a clinic like Ida does.'

'She's a good, steady nurse, knows the job.'

'I agree. But we wanted a district nurse, didn't we? And whatever it takes, I'm determined to find one this time because the need is even more urgent.'

Rachel was almost at the end of her studies to become a district nurse when she saw Pershore lingering outside the college one afternoon, watching the students stroll out. How could he possibly have found out where she was? The only vague idea was that he'd raided the doctor's dustbins and found one of the envelopes from her weekly letters. Or else, he'd paid someone else to look for such information.

People in the town where she'd grown up had always said the Pershores were the most stubborn people on the planet, but she was astonished that anyone would go to such lengths. She jerked back out of sight instinctively and went round to the back exit instead, checking that he hadn't come round here, then she ran to the nurses' home and stayed inside it for that and several following evenings.

What did he intend to do? Attack her again?

She slept very badly that night. She was so near the end of the course, she couldn't leave now.

What was she going to do about him, though?

Well, she'd take great care where she went after dark and as soon as she finished the course she'd try to find a job a long distance away.

It seemed that fate was on her side though. Later that day she got a message from Miss Grayson, the head of the School of Nursing, asking her to come and see her at nine o'clock the following morning.

She wondered if this was to do with the job in the north and Miss Grayson's first words confirmed that it was. Most of the trainee district nurses were set on working in a larger town, but she didn't mind going to a small place if the rest of the conditions were right, especially one a long distance away.

'I mentioned to the people in Ollindale that you might be happy to work there as a district nurse but wanted your own flat and they've found you one. It's small but they will offer it to you rent free if you take the job.'

'They must be very eager to find someone. Is there something I should know about the area I'd be working in?'

'All I know is that they have difficulty finding trained nurses because it isn't easy to attract people to a small valley in the Pennines, especially when it's to work in a poorer area, as this one is.'

'Our training prepares us for working in such places.'

'Yes, but district nursing is still something fairly new and it's hard to find enough trained and experienced women to fill all the vacancies.'

'Will they mind that I've no experience of being a district nurse, except what I've done during my six months' training?'

'No. This is a new area of work anyway and all the people who've taught you have spoken very highly of your skills and ability to get on with people. Hence the inducements they're offering to get you there.'

Rachel could feel herself blushing. 'Oh. That's very nice to hear.'

'And you do have experience in hospital work and in a doctor's surgery as well. Mrs Crossley is very determined to improve this part of town, you see, and has obtained a generous donation to be used to make employment there attractive to you.'

She smiled and added, 'I have to say Flora is the most energetic woman I've ever worked with. She says they want a nurse not only prepared to visit poor people in their own homes, but also to run classes or sessions in what they're calling a district clinic for lack of a better term. It's a place that used to be a shop, so isn't as big as they'd like but they're going to re-fit it to serve as a clinic according to your suggestions.'

'I'd enjoy helping with that.'

'She doesn't want someone too set in their ways to take on the job and admits that it'll be rather a challenge to work out the best way to do things in a rather neglected area of town. You'll have a fairly free rein about the way you do the work, but will answer to her about the nursing details particularly.'

'Now that does sound promising. What's the local doctor like? Won't he object to a nurse working independently? A lot of them do.'

'The doctor in Ollerthwaite is a woman, in her fifties apparently, and is doing well at breaking down prejudice against herself. But there's too much work for one person, so they're intending to appoint a male doctor soon as well.'

'I see. It does sound interesting. But I think it's only fair to tell you that I shan't stay if the new male doctor prevents me from working efficiently. I've met a lot of men who don't believe women can think for themselves, even when those women are experienced nurses or doctors.'

'I doubt Flora would allow the appointment of a doctor with such old-fashioned ideas.'

Rachel then took a deep breath and said, 'Something has cropped up and I'm being followed by a nasty chap. I'd be even happier to go and work in this valley if where I've gone could be kept secret.'

Miss Grayson stared at her in shock. 'You should have told us.'

'It's only just started happening again. He . . . was a nuisance before when I was younger and I don't know how he's found me again.'

'Should we call in the police?'

'And charge him with what? Staring at me?'

'Well, it's only a day or two before you leave, and I'd not only be happy to keep where you've gone secret, but to help you to leave in any way necessary to keep your destination secret.' She fell silent and watched her companion, then prompted, 'So, will you take the job, Rachel, if we keep your destination a secret?'

She didn't hesitate. 'Yes, I will. And thank you for being so understanding.'

'You don't spend years working with young women without encountering occasional problems with men.'

'I'd love to work with poorer people, women and children particularly. And the flat does make a big difference to me as well. I want a home of my own so much.' She hadn't had that since she was fourteen.

'I'm to tell you that there will even be money available to buy food for those in the most need who come to you for help.'

'Ah, that's good to hear! I've felt so – well, Shakespeare said it best, "cribbed, cabined and confined" at times as a nurse, not able to try new things, having to do what a scornful male doctor says.'

'That sort of thing used to annoy me too when I first started nursing and it's sad that it's still around twenty years later. There weren't many properly trained nurses in those days and some doctors tried to treat us like glorified housemaids, there to wipe up after them.'

They both fell silent for a few moments. It could be so hard for women trying to work in what was still regarded by many as a man's world. In the end, Rachel asked, 'What's the valley like? I've never been so far north before.'

'Neither have I. But Flora says it's a small valley with a lake at the lower end. It's surrounded by moors which are quite pretty, with one town, a couple of villages and a few scattered farms.'

'What about a uniform?'

'I didn't think to ask about that.'

'It helps to wear one, as you know. People seem to respect those wearing them more.'

'Hmm. You could use the one you've worn while doing this course if they haven't thought to provide one. As long as you change the badge, of course.'

'I can just put a patch with a red cross on the shoulder.'

'Good idea. Now, when can you leave? The course ends in just over a week and the flat will be ready and furnished by about Thursday of this week.'

'I can start on the Monday after the course ends if that's all right with them.'

'Excellent. I'll write to Flora. Oh, and she says they'll reimburse you for your travelling expenses.'

As she walked home, Rachel felt in a bit of a daze. What had she done? Hadn't she vowed to be careful what sort of job she accepted after this course ended and especially to look at the area where she'd be working before she accepted it as a part of her future life. She was, after all, better qualified and experienced than most nurses and would have no difficulty finding a job.

But it was too late to back out now. And at least she wouldn't have to dip into her savings while she looked for work if she started there as soon as this course ended.

It was going to be both interesting and satisfying to use the new skills and knowledge she'd acquired during her studies, especially if Mrs Crossley was open-minded about how they set about helping people.

8

Rufus had arranged to hire a neat little pony trap from the local livery stable, and went out to collect it while Joss ate a quick breakfast.

Abigail had prepared a picnic meal for lunchtime and Rufus put a few basic tools into the cart 'in case we need to fix anything in your house'.

'I'm glad you're coming with me. I think you're much more practical than I am. I'd never have thought of taking tools with us today.'

'Who knows what we'll find there? The house hasn't been occupied for years from what you say. I like working with my hands. I'm thoroughly enjoying fixing up our house and turning it into a hotel.'

'I'm sorry to take you away from that task.'

'Not at all. I'm also very nosy and no one in town knows much about that house of yours because it's been deserted and locked up for two or three decades. I gather someone has been hired to keep an eye on the external maintenance, though.'

'Yes, the lawyer mentioned that.'

They drove along a dirt road which ran along the edge of the lake and away from the town, then turned off on to a side road whose faded signpost said it led to Eastby End.

'It's a bit bumpy this way, but it's much prettier,' Rufus said. 'The council fill any bad potholes every now and then to keep it in reasonable condition because people use it as a shortcut to various farms and smallholdings as well as to Eastby End itself.'

The road wasn't long and they soon found themselves in among houses again.

'People weren't exaggerating when they said this was a poor area,' Joss commented. 'Is this the main route there?'

'No, just the most pleasant. There are two or three ways that lead from the parts of the town into Eastby. People joke that it sticks out from Ollerthwaite like a sore thumb. The roads all lead eventually towards what is considered to be the centre of the village, as some still call it. It used to be the main street when the place really was a separate village. They've crammed houses on some parts now, though.'

A couple of minutes later he slowed down and waved one hand. 'There you are. The centre of Eastby End.'

It proved to be a very sad-looking place, the edges filled with ramshackle buildings most of which looked to be in great need of repair. One had been partly burned down but not rebuilt, only half-heartedly fenced off. There was a small, shabby-looking church and grave-yard at one end, and what looked like the wall of a school at the other.

There were quite a few people in the streets and many of them looked like a human equivalent of 'ramshackle', Joss thought. You could tell that they weren't eating well and everyone's clothing was shabby, some even ragged. Two groups of men were lingering on opposite street corners watching the world go by, as people out of work often did. They were also watching each other, as if suspicious and hostile.

It particularly upset him to see young children looking hungry and he muttered, 'If there weren't so many children with that famished look on their faces, I'd have bought the younger ones a buttie from the baker's.'

'Don't even think of doing that, Joss, or you'll be mobbed, not only by the older kids but by those young men, some of whom would even take food off their own brothers and sisters.'

'Good heavens! What sort of people would do that?'

'Ones who've been hungry for a long time. This can be quite a violent place after dark, so I wouldn't recommend that you walk about on your own here once the sun goes down.'

'That sounds bad.'

'We've actually had a slight improvement lately, because a gentleman is having a small manor house built and that's providing some jobs.'

And if he settled here he too might create a job or two, Joss thought.

As they reached what Rufus said was the central part of Eastby they saw an open space, some run-down shops and a small and very plain church, after which they turned on to a slightly wider street that led towards what looked like the outskirts of the suburb. The houses away from the town centre gradually began to look better cared for and some of the outer ones had neatly tended gardens.

When he saw fields ahead of them, Joss was surprised at how attractive the countryside looked, the land sloping gently upwards towards hillier ground in the distance, with clumps of trees here and there at the lower edge and then the moors higher up.

'What a contrast!'

'Yes.' Rufus slowed down and pointed. 'See that low wall? It marks the edge of your land.'

Joss stared at it, then asked, 'How far behind it does my land stretch?'

'You own several acres. I'm not sure of the exact layout, but I think those trees may be near the border. The wall only seems to run along the side of the road. Isn't that a barbed wire fence down the side?'

'Yes. But this wall is so low anyone could climb over it, so it's only a token gesture of separation, isn't it?' Joss stared across meadows rather than land ploughed for crops. The grass in one part was long and looked ready for mowing to him. Why hadn't the farmer dealt with it?

'Isn't that ready to be turned into hay?'

'Yes. I don't know this area very well but I think that's the piece of land you just bought back from Jim Entwistle.'

The wall next to the road suddenly stopped at a pair of wrought-iron gates. Rufus gestured towards them. 'This is your main entrance to the house and garden.'

He signalled to the pony to stop in the wider space at a gateway where sagging double gates barred the way.

'Hold the reins and I'll get down and open the gates,'

'No, I'll do it.' Joss got down quickly but he had to shove the gates hard to get them to move gradually back. 'I don't think these can have been opened for a while. They need some work doing on them and most of the stone walls need attention too.'

'Yes. The estate must have been neglected for many years, except presumably the roof.'

When Joss gestured to him to drive through Rufus called out, 'It's not worth closing them till we're leaving.'

He nodded and swung himself back up on the trap. 'Could you stay here for a minute or two longer and let me get a good look at the whole house?'

At the other end of the drive, about fifty yards away, stood a large house which looked unoccupied. It must have been well over a hundred years old and built in a neatly symmetrical style he had seen in other parts of the country and liked. There were two floors, with two windows on either side of the front door, plus a neat row of dormer windows in the roof. He really liked that style of house, not too fussy like some modern houses he'd seen in towns.

Rufus clicked to the pony but let it move along at a slow pace. 'I'll have to take care how I go. The drive needs attention and it's so overgrown the grass can hide big potholes.'

As they moved along he noticed that some of the unkempt grass beside the drive was flattened as if someone had been treading on it recently.

'Who's been walking round here?' he wondered aloud.

'Lads from the town dare one another to come inside the grounds and occasionally they even break windows to get into the house itself. They haven't done that as much since we got a new and more capable police sergeant in Ollerthwaite, though. He and his young constable have made a good start in re-establishing law and order. The old constable they replaced was past it and did as little as possible, so the unruly lads ran wild.'

'The gardens look as if they've been running wild too, and for a long time. It could be quite a pretty house, though,' Joss said quietly. 'The roof doesn't look as if it leaks and surely those are a couple of new tiles near that end dormer window?'

'Yes. There's an old chap and his son who're paid to see that the exterior is maintained as needed to keep the place waterproof. Didn't the lawyer tell you about that?'

'He didn't give me many details at all. I took over in a hurry and we had to complete the purchase of that piece of land or we'd have lost the big deposit my cousin had paid.'

'Some folk I know were watching that situation with interest. Those two Entwistle half-brothers have always hated one another and they'd fought over the boundaries on their own land for years. The father had left the main farm to the younger son, you see, because he was by far the better farmer and there wasn't enough land for two decent farms.'

'Well, I want to look at that particular piece of land before we leave today. Such a fuss over a couple of acres.'

'Every acre is important to a small farmer, especially a good one like Lionel, who's hungry for more land.'

'Is he? It must have been a bad quarrel for the older brother to sell the land outside the family.'

'It was, though no one knows exactly what it was all about, whether just the inheritance or something else as well.'

'Let's go inside the house now, eh?'

Rufus got down, tying the mare's reins loosely to a post. Joss frowned as he went across to the front door because it was standing slightly ajar. 'How did this get left open?'

'I've no idea. It's usually locked.'

Joss pushed the door a little wider and called out, 'Is anyone there?' After waiting in vain for an answer, he said in a low voice, 'We'll go inside, but keep your eyes open for intruders.'

'I will. But you should go first, taking possession so to speak.'

But did he want it? Joss wondered.

He went right into the big, square hall and stopped to stare round, liking the feel of the interior. It wasn't in as bad a condition as he'd expected, though the whole place was dusty. Had someone broken in today or had the front door been left open like this for a while? Surely not?

Oh dear, he should have waited and checked for marks of feet in the dust of the floor.

He was standing roughly in the middle of the hall so turned slowly round on the spot, studying the place. There was a big window on the wall near the stairs, with a pretty coloured glass border round the edges.

To one side there was a pile of what looked to be pieces of furniture, covered by dust sheets. He lifted up the nearest edge and saw a small table of good quality. He brushed dust off the surface and changed that mentally to *very* good quality. It had a beautiful patina and it must have taken many decades of polishing to bring out that deep glossy gleam.

He covered the table up again and stared across through two internal doorways that led to large rooms, which had even bigger piles of furniture standing in the middle, also covered by dust sheets.

To his surprise he felt a strong sense of welcome, so strong it was almost as if someone had given him a hug. He stopped dead, shaking his head to clear it. He was imagining things, must be! This was just an empty house.

But he couldn't shake off the warm feeling and he had to admit to himself that he liked the looks of what he could see from here – a spacious room at either side of the front door with the two tall bay windows in each at the front of the house letting in plenty of light. He realised he'd left Rufus waiting outside and beckoned to him.

His companion looked round as carefully as he had done. 'Nice house. I didn't expect that, somehow. Why would you leave it empty?'

'I don't know. The previous owner was a distant cousin of mine and I'd only met him a few times. He was more a friend of my aunt. Let's look at the kitchen area.'

Joss led the way slowly across the hall towards the rear, where a half-open door showed a passage. They followed it, stopping at the end in the doorway of the spacious kitchen.

There was a faint clicking sound, as if someone had closed a door quietly, and they looked at one another, frowning. Joss jabbed his forefinger towards a wall with three doors in it and Rufus nodded. The sound had definitely come from that direction. Was an intruder hiding there?

He went across and opened each door in turn. The first two revealed only dusty storerooms lined with shelves containing kitchen utensils. The rooms had such small windows, set high up in an outer wall that they weren't as brightly lit as the kitchen. But it was clear that no one was hiding in them.

When he opened the third door, however, he found himself facing a child standing with her back pressed against the far wall and her arms spread out at either side of her torso. She was pale and looked utterly terrified.

'There's a child here!' he called out.

As he opened his mouth to tell her he wasn't going to hurt her, she gasped, put up one arm as if to guard her face from a blow then crumpled to the floor.

'She's just fainted.'

Rufus came across to join him. 'Eh, the poor little thing. She can't be more than ten years old.'

'I've never seen anyone look as afraid as she did when I opened the door. I wonder what she's doing in the house.'

'Hiding, probably.'

'Must be. But what from?'

'Who from, don't you mean? Bullying perhaps. There's a bruise on her cheek. Some kids can be cruel to others.'

'Well, we can't leave her lying on the floor. I hope this doesn't frighten her even more.' Joss bent down and scooped her up, carrying her out into the kitchen easily, she was so slightly built.

'Let's go into that room on the right. It has furniture in it. If we can find a sofa, we can let her lie down on it.'

Rufus led the way this time, hurrying ahead as they passed through the kitchen again. He turned into the next doorway and began pulling the dust covers off the furniture till he found a small sofa.

As Joss was setting her down on it the girl began to regain consciousness, staring up into his eyes, then suddenly struggling desperately to escape. He stepped quickly back, holding his hands apart and outstretched at the sides to show he wasn't trying to grab her. He said gently, 'Lie still. You fainted and we're only trying to help you, not hurt you.'

She looked from one man to the other. 'I wasn't doing any harm. I haven't taken anything. I just . . . needed shelter.'

'From the rain, or was someone chasing you?'

'From some big boys in the village. They were throwing stones at me. It hurt.' She rubbed one arm.

'My name is Joss. What's yours?'

'Minnie.'

'Did no grown-up try to stop them hurting you?'

'There weren't any grown-ups around so I ran away.'

'What village would that be exactly?'

She looked at him in puzzlement. 'Don't you know this is Eastby?'

'I thought this was just part of the town, not a separate village.'

'Everyone round here calls it a village. I come here to school.'

'Don't you live here?'

She threw a worried glance at him. 'Not in the village.'

'Where, then?'

'At the farm.'

She wasn't volunteering much information. 'Which one?'

'Moors Edge.'

'Isn't that where the Entwistles live?'

That brought a worried glance and a reluctant nod.

'Are you an Entwistle?'

'Sort of. My mum was an Entwistle then she married my dad, so I'm a Gremshaw.'

'Your mother *was* an Entwistle? Has she married again?'

'No, she's dead.'

'Oh. Sorry to hear that. And your dad?'

'I live with my grandma at the farm now.' She glanced towards the door. 'Please, mister . . . Can I stay here till all the big lads have gone away?'

'Don't you go to school?'

'Sometimes. When I can set off early enough.'

'So that these bullies don't catch you on the way?'

She nodded. 'And if they're there in the afternoons I wait to go home.'

He took a sudden decision. Helping her might be a good way of starting to break down the hostility he'd been told about between the Entwistles and the Townleys. 'Of course you can stay. You need to rest a bit or you'll be fainting again. Didn't you get any breakfast?'

'I was late waking up, and she never lets me have anything to eat if I'm not on time.'

'Your grandmother?'

'No. The aunt who married my Uncle Lionel. It's one of her rules. I daren't even ask for food if I'm late.'

Rufus felt in his pocket and offered her an apple.

She looked at him doubtfully, then took it and whispered a thank you before polishing it carefully on her skirt.

'We'll walk you back home when we've finished looking round here, to make sure no one attacks you on the way.'

That didn't seem to please her either, but after a moment she stopped polishing the apple on her skirt and nodded. 'Just to our gates will be far enough. I'll be all right from there onwards.' She took a big bite, seeming to think he'd agree to do that.

He didn't argue, but he intended to see her all the way home and speak to someone about the situation. He hated to see bullies getting away with their nasty tricks. 'I'm going to look round this house now. Don't risk going back on your own yet. They may still be there.'

She shivered at the idea. 'I won't. Thank you.' Then she took another bite.

Why had her aunt punished her that way? he wondered. They couldn't be short of food if they owned a farm, surely.

9

The two men left Minnie sitting on the sofa and carried on exploring the rooms at the rear. They stopped at the window in a smaller one at the back looking out across the fields behind the house.

Joss pointed. 'Is that the piece of land I bought, do you think?'

'Looks like it to me from that rough diagram you showed me.'

Joss smiled. 'I'm not good at making sketches.'

He could see that the field was carrying a crop of long grass that looked more than ready for mowing and wondered if that was up to him now. The fence between it and the farm seemed rough, as if hurriedly erected.

He smiled at the happy memories of joining in haymaking when he was on his travels. But the smile turned into a frown as he realised how angry and upset the Entwistles at the farm must be at losing all that hay because of their family quarrel, not just losing it but having to watch it go to waste. Galling, that would be.

Travelling around had taught him a lot about himself. One of the things which had stopped him pushing his way as roughly through the world as his father had done was his ability to see the other person's point of view.

The sad thing here was that he might own this crop but it would do him no good because he didn't have any animals to feed and wasn't planning to buy any, either. He might fancy living in a house surrounded by its own meadows and trees, but he didn't hanker to become a farmer.

On his travels he'd seen people offer the hay to the neighbours rather than let it go to waste and ... He paused on that thought and slowly began to smile. He could try doing that, offering it to the Entwistles. It'd help him to have it mown down, after all, as well as helping them if they acquired some more hay at no cost.

He peeped in at the child, but she seemed to have fallen asleep again, so he led the way to have a quick look round upstairs. There seemed nothing special about most of the bedrooms so it didn't take long. There were curtains at the windows drawn like the ones downstairs, and all looked faded and dusty.

He did stop for longer in the sixth and largest bedroom because it still had some clothing neatly folded in the drawers and hanging in the wardrobes.

'That will need clearing out,' Rufus said.

Joss shuddered at the thought of fiddling around with the underwear in the top drawers, women's on one side of the bed, men's on the other. 'Well, I don't intend to be the person doing it.'

'If you offer some woman from the village the contents of the wardrobe and drawers, she'll jump at the chance to clear it out for you. You won't even have to see the contents, if you don't want.'

'Unfortunately it'd be wise for me to check what's in the drawers and cupboards in case there's anything other than clothes. But ugh, would you like to fumble about among the women's bloomers in the top drawer?' A shudder was his response and he chuckled. 'You're right about hiring someone else to do it but I'd need to keep an eye on what they found.'

He looked round the landing. Spiders' webs seemed to decorate the upper corners everywhere in the house and dust lay thick on the surfaces. They might have maintained the outside of the building but they hadn't cared for the interior, except to cover up the good furniture.

When they went downstairs they checked the girl again. 'I'd half expected her to have run away,' Joss said. 'Look at the poor thing, still fast asleep. She has that look children get if they're not happy about something. She'd be pretty if she were happy, I should think. Why is she looking like that if she's an Entwistle?'

Joss watched Rufus go across to the window, fumble around under the outside edge of one curtain at waist height, then turn round grinning and brandishing a key at him.

'This was hanging on a hook underneath the curtain. People often put keys to French windows in that place. I bet it opens these. Let's go out and get some fresh air after all that dust.'

Joss nodded and watched him open both windows. The fresh air blowing in felt good after the stale dustiness of the house's interior but even that didn't wake the child. They went outside to stand on a paved area with weeds growing in the cracks and saw what were probably stables set back at the right with a couple of small cottages beyond them.

He turned back towards the house, which was bigger than he'd expected. Nicer, too, even at the rear. In fact, he was surprised at how much he liked the feel of the place.

'Let's take the child home before we do anything else. I want to ask her father something.' Joss didn't wait for an answer but went back inside and said loudly, 'Wake up, Minnie.'

She woke with a start, giving him a worried glance.

'We're going to walk home with you now so that no one can hit you. Is there a gate in that fence beyond the hayfield or do we need to go through the village to get to your farm?'

'I can go back on my own. I'll be safe now.'

He gave her a stern look. 'No. We're not risking anything. I'm going with you. What's the best way back?'

She stared at him, looking unhappy about that, then pointed across the grounds. 'There's a gate at that end but Uncle Lionel has put a padlock on it now. I can climb over it easily though.'

So could he, if necessary. 'Come on, then. We'll go that way.'

'You can watch me from here to make sure I get there safely.'

She started edging towards the open window, so he took a quick step sideways to bar her way. 'I'm taking you back and if you try to run away, I bet I'll catch you quickly because I'm a really fast runner. I'm *not* risking you getting attacked again and your family needs to know what's been going on. How were you going to explain the bruise and not going to school?'

She looked at Joss in dismay. 'I can say I fell over. And you don't have to worry. I can easily sneak into the house.'

'No. We'll walk across there together.'

She gave in but walked slightly apart from them. She clambered over the gate easily and they followed suit. When they were halfway towards the farmhouse, however, a man came running out of it and ran across to them, looking furious.

'What are *you* doing on my land? And what have you done to our Minnie?' He grabbed her arm and pulled her to his side. 'How did you get that bruise, love? Did this man hit you?'

'No. It wasn't him. He saved me.'

He looked down at her in surprise.

'We came with her to make sure she got home safely,' Joss said. 'And to check that you know that it was some big lads from the village who were throwing rocks at her earlier. I don't think she was going to tell you herself. She hid in my house, you see, thinking it was empty.'

A tall older woman had walked across to join them while they were talking and now joined in. 'I told you there was something upsetting her, Lionel.'

She stayed slightly behind him but held her arms out and the child ran into them, hugging her convulsively.

The man stared at them and muttered, 'Thank you.' He looked back at the child. 'Why didn't you tell us about this, Minnie? Who's doing it? We'll have a word with them.'

'That will only stop them for a week or two, then they'll find other ways to get at me. It's the Saxby gang. They don't like the Entwistle family because my uncle upset old Mr Saxby.'

'Damn Jim. He caused a lot of trouble before he left.'

'Well, he won't be back if he's so ill,' the woman said. 'You should start looking after his bit of land or it'll go to pot.'

'How can I? Jim still owns that cottage and the land on the other side of it, damn him. That's the only thing my father left to him.' He turned back to the child. 'I'll thump them myself if they don't leave you alone.'

'If you do that the other kids who're mean to me have got younger brothers and sisters in the school. I'll never have any friends.' She burst into tears.

Lionel sighed and turned back to Joss, saying stiffly, 'Thank you for helping her.'

'I was happy to. I like children. And by the way, I'm Joss Townley.'

'Lionel Entwistle.'

'Pleased to meet you.' Joss hesitated, then said, 'Um, I wonder if I can interest you in a business matter while I'm here?'

The reply was sharp. 'You must be joking. Me do business with a Townley? That'd be a first!'

'I'm serious. It'd be to our mutual benefit.'

He stood with his arms folded across his chest. 'Go on, then. Surprise me. What business could we two possibly have?'

'There's a hayfield ready to harvest.' He gestured behind him.

'I've been warned by a lawyer to stay off that piece of land now that you've bought it and I don't intend to get into trouble with the law.'

'What if I said you could harvest the hay and keep it as long as you tidied up the area for me at the same time?'

'Why the hell would you say that?'

'Because it'll save me a job and stop it looking messy. I have no stock and I'm not intending to buy any so I don't need the hay. I'll get the land cleared at no cost or trouble to myself and you'll get the hay at no cost. We could both be happy with that sort of a bargain, surely?'

Entwistle was still frowning at his visitor as if he was having trouble believing this.

Joss spoke quietly. 'I know there's been trouble in the past between our families, but I wasn't part of it. This is the first time I've even come here to the valley. And for your information, I prefer to live on good terms with my neighbours, and I usually manage to do so.'

Entwistle didn't try to hide his surprise. 'Are you coming to live here then? They were betting you'd be another absentee landlord like the other Townleys. It's a wonder that house is still standing.'

'I like the valley enough to settle here permanently but the house will need modernising. And I'm not a farmer. So . . . what about the hay? Do you want it?'

'I'd have to have it in writing. I don't want you setting a trap to sue me for theft.'

'If you must. I don't play dirty tricks on anyone, let alone close neighbours, I assure you. Is there someone you'd trust to witness a document putting that in writing? It'd be a waste to pay a lawyer's fees for it, surely?'

Entwistle looked sideways at Rufus who had been standing quietly near them. 'I've heard one or two say you seem an honest man, Shorrocks.'

'I always keep my word. And folk say the same about you, Entwistle.'

He looked surprised at that, then studied Joss again. 'We can draw up a written agreement ourselves. My mother will write it and witness it with Shorrocks. That shouldn't take her more than a few minutes. She's a clever woman.' He turned round. 'That all right with you, Ma?'

She nodded and gave Joss an approving nod that suggested she liked what he was doing. It'd be good to have her on his side as he tried to defuse the hostility.

Entwistle hesitated then said, 'If we do it now, I could make a start on cutting that hay straight away and take advantage of the fine weather that those who understand weather say will last another day or two. I'll work till late tonight and get a good start. It gives a good yield of hay, that land does, as I saw when my damned half-brother owned it.'

'All right. I can come to your house now to sign the paper, if you like? That'll speed things up even more, won't it?'

Another stare was followed by another nod, then Lionel unlocked the padlock on the gate and put it in his pocket, leaving the gate wide open, after which he turned to lead the way into the farmhouse.

When the visitors followed him inside a younger woman stared across the room at them as if they'd grown horns. She was thin and didn't look well. Entwistle introduced her as his wife Thelma.

'This Townley chap is offering us a deal.' Her husband explained it to her.

'You're trusting one of *them*?' She looked across suspiciously at Joss.

'I'm giving him a try. Nothing to lose, is there? I'm getting it in writing first, though.'

She continued to scowl at the visitor and stand at the far side of the room, not asking him to sit down. It was the older woman who gestured to a chair and said he might as well make himself comfortable. She then got out a bottle of ink and a pen, followed by a cheap writing pad.

Before she started, she said quietly, 'No one's bothered to introduce me by name, so I'll tell you myself that I'm Sybil Entwistle, widow of the former owner and mother of Lionel here.'

That made the younger woman absolutely glare at her and open her mouth as if about to yell, but Lionel spoke first. 'Sorry, Ma. I wasn't thinking.'

The younger woman muttered something then seemed to realise that Minnie was there and asked, 'What are you doing here? You should be at school, you naughty girl.' She raised one hand as if about to slap the child, who darted to the other side of her grandmother.

'Leave her alone, Thelma,' her husband said.

'You always take her side.' She left the room but the look she threw at the girl made Sybil stop writing to intervene.

'Minnie would be better staying with the Chapleys, Lionel. How many times do I have to point that out?'

She saw the child stare at her with hope in her eyes and felt sad because it was so obvious what Minnie wanted.

'They're her mother's relatives and they've offered to have her a couple of times now. Why didn't Thelma let her go to them? Why does she always have to be awkward?'

Lionel looked at Minnie. 'Would you rather live with Gran and Pops Chapley?'

'Yes, please. I'd love it.'

He sighed and nodded. 'Well, you're right about that, Ma. And what happened today settles it. Will you get her things together after we've finished all our business here. I'd better drive her over later today.'

'Yes, of course. But I can take her there. I need to do some shopping in the village.'

'Thanks.'

As they finished signing the agreement, his wife came back inside and started banging pots around, but she looked as if she was doing more listening than housework. The occasional look she threw at Minnie only emphasised how she felt about the child.

The agreement was completed quickly then Joss had another thought and looked at the Entwistles. 'I need to find help in the house and garden, especially a housekeeper to manage things for me. If you hear of anyone from round here wanting a job, could you please tell them I'm staying at the Jubilee Hotel and I'm looking to hire servants straight away so that I can open the house again?'

'I'll be the one most likely to hear who's looking for a job, if anyone from this family does, because I sell our eggs at the market,' the older woman said with a sharp look at her daughter-in-law. 'What wages are you paying?'

'Whatever is usual round here plus half a crown extra a week.' He'd found before that small increases in the usual payments generally made it easier to find and keep servants.

Thelma hadn't said anything else, just stood there scowling alternately at the older woman and the child.

Sybil ignored her. 'You'll have no trouble finding people then, Mr Townley.'

'I want to find good workers who'll be loyal. They'll only be hired on trial till they've proved themselves, mind.'

'I'd do the same. If you pay me five shillings a head, I'll *find* you some good workers and you'll have nothing to complain about in their work, I promise.'

Her daughter-in-law did join in this time, yelling, 'Stay out of this, you. It's none of your business. You're just a servant yourself.'

Her son turned to his wife. 'I've told you before to be careful how you speak to my mother, Thelma. She isn't a servant, she's one of the family.'

'Well, *she* should be careful how she behaves towards me whoever she is. *I* am mistress here, not her.'

The older woman gave her a scornful look. 'I keep my eyes open for opportunities to earn a bit extra, as you well know, Lionel, because *you* don't pay me a decent wage even though *she* leaves most of the work to me.'

Sybil had spoken so bitterly Joss could tell the two women didn't get on. Well, he'd not like to work for such a sour woman, either.

'You get the egg money,' her daughter-in-law snapped. 'Family members shouldn't need paying at all. You eat well and have a comfortable bedroom. What more does an old hag your age need?'

Joss was feeling increasingly uncomfortable with this exchange and he could see that Entwistle was too. It seemed to him to be a poor way to treat your husband's mother. He didn't like the looks of Thelma Entwistle, not at all.

Sybil took a deep breath then turned back to Joss. 'It'd help if I knew what the house was like before I work out how many staff you'll need. I've never even been inside it.'

'Why don't you come back with us now and take a quick look round? I'd really welcome some advice from a sensible woman like you.'

'Everyone in the village wonders what the place is like inside,' she said. 'I know about housekeeping because I used to run this farmhouse before my husband died. Perhaps I should explain the various relationships to you because you're a newcomer to the district. I was Dan's second wife. His first wife died young, poor thing. My son had a half-sister as well as a half-brother, Minnie's mother. Her father died when she was a baby and then her mother died too last year.'

She paused for a moment and he nodded and said, 'Go on. It's helpful.'

'Minnie came to live with us because her other grandma had broken her arm. She's made a good recovery and has asked us twice to let her have the girl. I think Thelma refused out of sheer spite.'

'How dare you say that?' her daughter-in-law screeched and Lionel shushed his wife, though it was obviously touch and go whether she obeyed him.

Joss and Sybil smiled at one another. He liked the straightforward way she'd explained the situation. But the other woman continued to scowl. What a miserable, bad-tempered person she was.

'I'll walk out with you, Townley,' Entwistle said.

The older woman pushed the girl towards the door. 'You come out with us, Minnie, then sit on the gate till I get back from his house. I'll pack your things and take you across to your grandma Chapley's then.'

At the gate Entwistle stopped and helped the child up then asked, 'All right if I leave this gate open while I'm haymaking, Townley?'

'Of course it is. Be hard to do the job if you didn't. I shan't be moving into the house till I've got help to run it and the main rooms are clean.'

'It won't take long and if Ma finds people to work for you, they'll be hard workers. She knows everyone in the village. See you later, Ma. Minnie can wait for you out here. I'll keep an eye on her.' He waved goodbye then hurried back towards his barn. There was no sign of his wife.

They started walking across and when Joss glanced sideways at his companion she was frowning as if thinking hard about something. When they got to the house, she glanced uncertainly towards Rufus, who guessed she wanted to speak privately so moved away. 'I'll wait for you in the house, Joss lad.'

'All right.'

Sybil waited till he'd gone then asked, 'Are you wanting a full-time housekeeper, Mr Townley?'

'Yes.'

'Live in?'

'Of course.'

'Then I'd like to apply for the job.'

'Aren't you needed to work at the farm?' he asked in surprise.

'I've never been happy there, only there haven't been any other jobs for a while and I'd rather stay near my son. There's nothing at the farm that can't be done by someone else and as you could no doubt tell, my daughter-in-law isn't the most cheerful person on earth to live with. She isn't even a hard worker as well as being a right old misery who counts every pea you put on your plate.'

He hadn't heard that saying but it made him smile.

'I'm a hard worker and I think it'd be more interesting and certainly more pleasant to be your housekeeper than to carry on here at Thelma's beck and call. My husband pushed him into marrying her and she wasn't as bad when he was alive. But she changed after he died and insisted she must be in charge as the owner's wife. I didn't want to leave the valley and thought she'd calm down but she didn't. So . . . will you give me a try?'

'Yes. Happy to. I'll say you're on a month's trial, same as any others I hire, but it's my guess you'll be perfect for the job.'

She glanced at him in surprise. 'You've decided it that quickly, without asking me any more questions?'

'Yes. I'm pretty good at understanding other people after spending a few years travelling round the country for sheer pleasure and mixing with people of all sorts. Frankly, I don't want to be having to tell my housekeeper how to look after things properly.'

'Then I'm happy to accept the job. We'll shake hands on it, shall we?' She offered her hand like a man, which surprised him but he didn't hesitate to shake it to seal their bargain.

'If you give me a house key, I'll come back after you and Mr Shorrocks have left and have a really good look round so that I can see what will be needed to set the house in order. I'd prefer to move here as soon as I can – well, once there are other servants, of course. You'll no doubt understand why. My daughter-in-law won't be pleased and she's hard to live with at the best of times.'

'No. I'm sure she won't from how she behaved towards you.'

Sybil rolled her eyes at the mere thought of how Thelma treated people. 'I know how to manage things for a peaceful life, I promise you.'

'I'm sure you do.'

She hesitated then said, 'Can I ask about your family, Mr Townley? Will any of them be coming here to live with you? You don't seem like a married man.'

Something about her made him trust her enough to share a few more personal details. 'I'm not. My father died five years ago and I sold the family factory I'd inherited because I loathed working there. My mother went to live with her sister in Harrogate and I spent a few years wandering round England. I did a bit of seasonal work, even though I didn't need the money, because I enjoyed the company.'

He smiled, obviously remembering something pleasant, so she waited for him to continue telling her things at his own pace.

'My father wasn't a pleasant man to work for and he ill-treated his workers. It left me feeling bad because he'd forced me to do that too. I vowed I'd never make people I employed feel so unhappy in their work.'

'I can understand that. You look cheerful enough now, though.'

'Yes, I got the misery out of my system and I've found my true course in life, which means helping people when I see a need. I'm not short of money so I have no need to push to earn every farthing.' He smiled at her. 'You're a good listener, Sybil. I don't usually tell people about my father. And please keep quiet about my money.'

'I won't tell anyone. But I enjoy chatting to people and getting to know them, and it's been too quiet out at our farm since Thelma moved in because people avoid visiting her.'

'Well, I hope you'll have time to enjoy life as well as your job when you're working for me. There was a poet who once said:

What is this world if, full of care,
We have no time to stop and stare.
No time to stand beneath the boughs
And stare as long as sheep or cows.

'I forget how it goes on. Who on earth was it?'

'I think it was a Mr Davies.'

He beamed at her. 'You're right. Do you enjoy poetry?'

'I enjoy reading anything, but I know that poem because Minnie had to learn it by heart for school and I helped her, which made me learn it too. I agreed with what Mr Davies said.'

They smiled at one another, already feeling comfortable together.

'Let's go and find the spare house keys now and you might as well have a rapid initial look round before you leave, in case you don't like the thought of working here.'

'The keys will probably be kept in the kitchen.'

Rufus rejoined them and she followed the two men to the kitchen. Sure enough, they were there and she was the one who found them. They were where she'd have put them herself – hanging inside a cupboard near the back door, all sorts of keys in neat little bundles. It seemed like a good omen.

She checked the one in the lock of the nearby door and soon found a similar one for herself. When she tried that in the door, it worked smoothly so she held it up to show him and at his nod, she tucked it into her pocket.

'I can have people here to see you for the jobs tomorrow morning or whenever you next come back.'

'That quickly?'

'Yes. They live locally.'

'Tomorrow morning would suit me best. Make it mid-morning because I'm meeting someone at the market earlier on.' Well, he was if this Walter Crossley chap everyone spoke so well of was there and Rufus introduced them. 'I'd like to move in as soon as possible, even if the clean-up isn't finished.'

'I'll make sure your bedroom is ready by tomorrow evening.'

'I'd be grateful, whether the bed is perfect or not. Now, why don't you have a quick walk round before you leave? Doesn't matter where you go because I've got nothing personal here yet.'

'All right. I'll come back later to check it all more carefully and make a few notes about details. Then I'll come in early tomorrow and start work.'

'You'd better sort out a bedroom for yourself in the attics while you're at it. There's a nice big one up there that might suit you.'

He turned to leave then stopped and fumbled in his pocket, pulling out a five-pound note. 'If you need to buy anything for the house, just go ahead and do it. We'll need the makings for cups of tea early on, don't you think? I'll set up accounts in whichever shops you think best as soon as we can discuss that.'

She stared down at the money bemused. It felt wonderful to be trusted like this.

She gave the two men a nod and they heard her moving round the front part of downstairs, then going upstairs before she strode off back across the field.

When she'd gone, Rufus chuckled suddenly. 'She's a clever woman, that one, but I bet she'll boss you around.'

'I like her directness and I shan't mind being bossed a little when it comes to running a house. What do I know about the details of that? I liked the way the child ran to her. That said something about how she deals with people, doesn't it?'

'Yes, it does. I didn't take to the son's wife, though,' Rufus said quietly. 'She's a surly looking woman and she'd obviously slapped that child hard, judging by the mark on Minnie's face. Entwistle still doesn't trust you yet, though.'

'No, but at least he's giving me a chance. I was hard put not to laugh at his surprise when I offered him the hay.'

'You handled him well. You're good with people.'

'I like to get on with my fellow human beings. But make no mistake, I'm not a soft touch. I don't let anyone cheat me and I can defend myself physically if need be.' He shook his head sadly and added thoughtfully, 'I don't like the atmosphere in the centre of Eastby, though. That'll have to change.'

Rufus looked at him in surprise. 'You think you can make enough difference to affect that?'

'I know for certain that I'm going to try once I figure out what's going on behind all this.'

'You're proving to be a bundle of surprises today, Townley. What else have you got in store for the people of this valley, I wonder?'

'I'm not sure what exactly I'll need to do yet. But one thing I am sure of is that things need changing and the valley will be in for some surprises from me, especially this part of it.'

He stared into space, then added slowly, 'I think Eastby has been badly neglected, don't you?'

'Yes. And good luck with your efforts to improve things.'

10

Another idea had been simmering in Joss's mind ever since he realised how hard it was to get around the valley with no public transport systems. The trouble was, there weren't enough people living here to see any business setting up to develop any systems in the near future. So he had to do something different.

Before they went back he decided to share his idea with his new friend and see what Rufus thought of it.

'I've been considering buying a motor car. I don't want the trouble of looking after horses or hiring a groom for just one pony and anyway, I've been itching to buy a car for a while now.' What was the point in having money if you couldn't indulge yourself occasionally? He smiled ruefully. 'When I was travelling round the country I met a chap who had a Lanchester Phaeton and he took me for a ride in it. It's a sound vehicle, doesn't break down nearly as often as most cars, he assured me, but it had cost over five hundred pounds, and wasn't cheap to run, so I had to give up the idea for now. They're still mainly rich men's toys. Pity.' He paused for a moment then asked, 'Is there anyone who knows about cars in the valley?'

'Actually, there is.'

'Oh, good. Tell me about him.'

'Riley Callan, who's the main plumber in Ollerthwaite, is itching to start dealing in motor cars and repairs, but he can't afford to set up a business yet because he's a married man and has a wife to support. He's a very capable chap and does excellent work putting in bathrooms, which I should think you're going to need quite soon. Amazing, isn't it, how many families want plumbed-in bathrooms these days? Modern ones, not the old-fashioned sort.'

'I shall definitely want a couple of them installed in my family home. The one there is very old-fashioned, and I don't want to share the family bathroom with the servants. The kitchen could do with modernising as well.'

'Well, perhaps one day Riley will get his dream of dealing in cars and you can buy one from him. I should warn you, though, that Walter Crossley doesn't approve of motor cars.'

'Oh? I wouldn't have expected a man with his reputation for being a natural leader in the community to feel that way.'

'It's not that he minds change generally, but unfortunately his son and grandson were killed in an accident involving a motor car a few years ago.'

'Ah. That would indeed be hard to get over. I'll try to tread sensitively and not mention cars in his company. I'll have to buy a bicycle though.'

'No problems with that. Peter Dodds sells new and second-hand ones, or he can get hold of a tricycle if you place an order for one. You'd be able to carry more stuff on that. A lot of people use bicycles to get round more quickly. I have one myself.'

'Living out at the edge of the town, I'll probably need a tricycle and a bicycle so that my servants can get into and out of town more easily.' He sighed. 'I think it's going to take a lot longer for motor cars to become common in

England. They seem to be ahead of us in nearby countries in Europe and America is leading the way in producing cheaper motor vehicles, not just ones for rich people. It's all very exciting.'

'I love your enthusiasm, Joss. I shall look forward to you moving to the valley. You decided to do that more quickly than I'd expected today, I must say, soon after we went inside the house in fact.'

'Yes. It was strange how right it felt inside.' And somehow he'd quickly known that the house had welcomed him, stupid as that might have sounded. He didn't say that, though. Instead he changed the topic of discussion. 'The other thing that decided me was having seen the main part of Eastby End. I think I can find quite a few things to do that will help turn that part of town from a slum into a decent place to live.' Unlike his father, he wanted to use his money to help people, not to live extravagantly. He didn't intend to reveal that he was actually quite rich, though, or some people would try to take advantage of him.

'Did you notice that people round here still call it "the village"?' Rufus asked. 'The Entwistles called it that as well. The people in the main part of the town don't seem to do that.'

'Yes, I did notice,' Joss said. 'It's surprising the term has lingered for so long and sad that the place is so backward and run-down at the moment. It's not just Eastby that I like, you know. I think the moors round here are beautiful, too. There must be some excellent walks nearby and glorious vistas from the upper stretches.'

'Yes, as long as you feel safe being alone out there.'

'I can usually take care of myself. But if things looked nicer in Eastby and there was somewhere to provide drinks and snacks, we could probably attract hikers and other visitors to tramp across the moors and spend some of their money here.'

'You're not the first person to think of that. It hasn't happened so far, not to any great extent.'

'Well, anything would help. They need more jobs round here, I can see that already as one thing that would make a difference.'

A short time later Joss said quietly, 'People will no doubt gossip and wonder about me, so I'll tell you a little about myself and ask you to set them right if you hear them making wild guesses. I'm comfortably circumstanced because my father owned a furniture factory. I had to work there and I hated it, so I put the factory up for sale as soon as I inherited.'

'And you're not courting or engaged?' Rufus grinned. 'The women will want to know that.'

'No, I'm not.' He'd enjoyed a couple of relationships during his travels, renting a furnished flat for a time during the winter months and thinking he might settle down with someone. But he hadn't rushed into anything and these attractions had faded within a month or two, so he'd moved on.

The women had been charming but they'd proved to have limited topics of conversation and he'd been bored after a while. He needed, no, *craved* the company of an intelligent woman as his wife. If you didn't have a lot of relatives, a wife was even more important to your happiness. And he wanted to have intelligent children, not slow-thinking fools. That was far more important to him than having a pretty wife and good-looking children.

Perhaps there was something wrong with him? He'd often wondered why he felt so differently from most other men about marriage. Perhaps he was asking too much of a woman and would never find someone he truly wanted to spend the rest of his life with.

That would be sad.

He was surprising himself by confiding in a man he'd only just met but then, he'd immediately taken to Rufus and his wife as well. In fact he really liked the feel of this valley and its kindly, slow-speaking Lancashire folk – well, he liked most of them. There always seemed to be a few bad people scattered around, wherever you went.

He suddenly realised something else about his current situation and grinned. It'd be even harder for the Entwistles to keep up a feud with his family if Sybil Entwistle were working for him as housekeeper, wouldn't it?

He realised that Rufus had said something. 'Sorry. Could you say that again? My mind is leaping around like a grasshopper in a field today, I'm afraid. There are so many things to take into consideration.'

'I asked what you want to do next?'

'Move into my new home as quickly as I can. And I'm looking forward to meeting the Crossleys. They sound to be the main movers and shakers in this valley.'

'They are – or they have been until now.'

Joss paused, frowning, his mind making another few leaps around. 'I can't remember the name of the poet who used that phrase, "movers and shakers", but he also talked about "the dreamers of dreams". Now, who was it? Oh yes, Arthur O'Shaughnessy. I must get my books of poetry out again once I've moved in and check, but I think he said that in the 1870s, give or take. Those books are like old friends and I've missed them. In the meantime I hope I can start making my own dreams come true.'

'You're constantly surprising me. I didn't think you'd be quoting poetry at me so often. My wife does that sometimes.'

'Well, books of all sorts were my constant companions when I was travelling, so it's no wonder I mention them. To get back to our original topic, perhaps the Crossleys will be able to give me some suggestions about how to make a difference to Eastby End. The more I think about it the more I like the idea of trying to do that.'

He had seen for himself what a difference having a job and enough food to eat could make to people, and he was going to do something about that. But he wasn't going to tell anyone how much money he had. He'd continue to use his wealth carefully and hope to make a difference to his world.

The breeze blew gently, lifting his hair, caressing his cheeks, feeding his lungs with fresh oxygen. That bracing air was one of the big attractions of his new home and he loved the way it sat just outside the town, nestling into the edge of the moors. No wonder they'd called the farm next door Moors Edge.

'It's market day tomorrow,' Rufus said. 'The Crossleys will probably both be there. They come early usually so don't be too late if you still want me to introduce you to them.'

'I do. And thank you for helping me today.'

'You're welcome. I've enjoyed your company.'

'And I yours.'

They smiled at one another then Joss offered his hand and they shook in that wordless way men do sometimes to seal an unspoken promise.

After that Joss went into the hotel and left Rufus to deal with the pony and trap. He was feeling rather tired so after he'd enjoyed a pleasant evening meal, he went up to his room early.

He usually read a chapter or two in bed and had expected that tonight he'd finish the novel he'd been reading during the past few evenings. But somehow he couldn't settle to it. Real life was proving more fascinating than fiction, even the most exciting stories, since he'd arrived here. He put the book down, extinguished the gas light and lay thinking about his new home.

When he yawned for the second time, he gave up trying to stay awake and turned over, letting sleep overtake him in a gentle tide.

He made a wish as he drifted away, wished he could move in within a day or two. He needed a home, needed it so much.

The following morning as Joss was finishing a leisurely breakfast, Rufus came into the dining room to ask if he could be ready to leave soon.

He looked round with interest as they strolled across town to the market, which must have started quite early because it already looked to be well under way. There were more people around than Joss had seen gathered anywhere in the valley before and many of them seemed to be chatting and exchanging banter rather than merely buying and selling, standing smiling at one another, like long-time friends.

Rufus looked round for Walter Crossley and suddenly exclaimed, 'Ah! There he is!' He wove his way through the crowd to where a silver-haired man was standing at one side, watching people with a benign expression on a face that was still good-looking, carrying its years lightly.

Rufus introduced the two of them, then said, 'Walter, Mr Townley is coming to settle here in his old family home and would welcome your advice about the best ways to settle into life out there in Eastby.'

'I hope you will stay here, my dear chap, and let me welcome you to the valley. I'd heard that you'd come to visit your inheritance. How do you like our valley?'

'I love it here, especially the bracing air of the moors.'

Mr Crossley beamed at that.

Rufus stepped back. 'I'll leave you two to chat. There's a fellow I want to see over there. I'll join you again later, Joss.'

Walter took over the conversation. 'Did you enjoy looking round your house? It must need a lot of work doing on it by now.'

Joss didn't ask how his companion knew that because he was only too aware that in small towns a newcomer couldn't keep much secret. 'The structure is sound but the house needs to be brought up to date. And—'

'Excuse me a minute.'

A man interrupted them just then to ask Walter something, and when they tried to start chatting again, two women came up to ask him about another matter.

Walter answered them patiently but when they walked on, he immediately suggested to Joss that they move away. 'In fact, how about we go to the café that's opened recently just down the road from here. They need customers if they're to survive and I'm always ready for another cup of tea by this time of the morning. You and I need some peace if we're going to discuss something as important to you as making a fresh life in a new town.'

When they went into the café, Walter asked for a quiet table for a private chat and from then onwards, Joss noticed the owner of the café keeping people away from them in a gentle but firm way.

'What exactly is worrying you?' Walter asked once they'd made a start on their pot of tea and plate of scones.

'Well, I'm not exactly worried, but I would welcome some advice. I hope I don't sound arrogant but I not only need to settle in myself, I have a little spare money from an inheritance and I'd like to do something worthwhile with it. I noticed how run-down Eastby End is and as that's right next to my family home, I wondered whether I could do something to help improve the place. I gather it's quite rough in the central area there after dark.'

'Unfortunately it is. That's very generous of you.'

'It's also rather selfish in one sense. If I'm going to be living there, I want it to be a happier place. Many of the people hanging around in the centre of Eastby looked extremely unhappy. And quite a few of the people actually looked hungry. It shows, doesn't it, when children in particular aren't eating regularly?'

'Yes, it does. I do what I can but my time and resources are already spread thinly so with the best will in the world, I can't do much about that part of the valley.' He shook his head sadly. 'If you're going to do something to help people, Mr Townley, I'd be delighted to hear that, but I should advise you to bear in mind from the start that you can't do everything at once. You're only one person.'

'I think that's very good advice and I will bear it in mind. It's jobs people need most of all, I do understand that and it takes time to create them.'

Walter nodded. 'Don't forget that you'll be employing some people in your home and garden. That'll be a good start for two or three families.'

'Yes. But there are a lot of others in need and it upsets me to see children looking hungry, or shivering because they don't have enough clothes to keep warm.' Joss frowned. 'Ought I to open a soup kitchen where people who're given vouchers can get a simple meal, do you think? That would only be a temporary help, though, wouldn't it?'

'Temporary measures are needed as well to tide the less capable people over till better times are with us, not to mention the better weather at certain times of year, which always helps. And believe it or not, life in the valley has gradually improved over the past few years, even if not so much out at Eastby. I've had the pleasure of nudging things along a little here and there. It can be very satisfying.'

'Yes.' Joss looked at the other man ruefully. 'I'm impatient to make a start, not only to help families but single people too, both old and young.'

'I must say I like your attitude, Townley. Hmm.' Walter put some sugar in his cup of tea and stirred it absent-mindedly for a few moments before speaking again. 'I'll probably need time to consider the whole situation before I can give you a proper answer and perhaps make some worthwhile suggestions. But if you want to run any ideas past me, don't hesitate to seek me out.' He nodded slowly and added, 'One thing I can do straight away is introduce you to my wife. She in turn will be able to introduce you to a lady called Rachel Norris, who will be arriving in our valley tomorrow afternoon. She's a district nurse and she'll be working mainly in Eastby End, so when you do start trying to find some way to help people in need, you ought to fit some of your effort at least in with what she'll be doing. And you can also get her to keep her eyes open for any desperate cases.'

He paused to look at Joss and ask, 'Do you know how district nurses do their work these days? Most people round here haven't even heard of them.'

'I do know a little about them. They started in Liverpool, I gather, and now they're popping up in other parts of the country. Going out to people's homes sounds to be an excellent way of getting help to the neediest people.'

'Yes, it is. My Flora is very excited indeed at the thought of having one working in Eastby End. She's the one who set it all up and hired Miss Norris. It isn't easy to attract properly trained nurses to a quiet little valley like ours, I'm afraid.'

'Well, that will be one thing to put on my list for certain, to assist the new district nurse. Ask your wife to tell her not to hesitate to call on me for help.'

He didn't say it but he guessed this nurse would be a fierce older woman, like a couple of the ones he'd met on his travels. She'd have to be fierce from what he'd heard from those women about the difficulties of their work.

They talked for a little longer, then Walter pulled his watch out of his waistcoat pocket and flipped open the top. 'Eh, is that the time already? I need to go and find my wife. She'll have finished her shopping by now and she'll want to go straight home and get everything ready for Miss Norris's arrival tomorrow. Come back with me and meet my Flora. It'll have to be quick, though. You can have a good old chinwag with her about the practicalities of helping folk in Eastby another time.'

As they walked along, Rufus rejoined them, though he had to walk behind because of the narrowness of the pavements. That let the other two continue chatting for a little longer.

'Did you leave all your family behind?' Walter asked Joss.

'There are only my mother and aunt left now. I have no other close relatives. They're living in Harrogate. I visit them regularly and shall continue to do that, of course.'

'Not even a stray second cousin or two?'

'Not that I know of.'

Walter gave Joss a warm smile. 'Then you'll fit in here in another way as well. This valley seems to collect people without homes and friends and finds them new ones. You've made a good choice deciding to settle here permanently, believe me. It's good that you're thinking seriously of how best to do it, though. A little forethought never goes amiss when something is important.'

'Well, I'm more than ready to settle down. I've had my fill of travelling around.'

'Ideas will come to you gradually, I'm sure.'

He liked Walter Crossley and his wife too, but her mind was clearly on her coming guest at the moment, so he said goodbye and was left looking forward to getting to know them all better at a later date.

II

Rachel arrived in Ollerthwaite the following afternoon. As she got off the train the other passengers walked away briskly, showing their tickets to the porter at the barrier. She saw two people waiting at the edge of the station move in the other direction and come towards her, stopping for a moment to stare at her, looking faintly surprised. Then they started moving again.

She didn't have any difficulty guessing that they must be the Crossleys or understanding that it had surprised them how young she looked and that she was rather pretty. She wasn't being vain about that. She knew what she looked like and often wished she were a 'plain Jane', then that horrible man might not have pursued her.

Stop thinking about that, she told herself, and summoned up a smile. She always dreaded first meetings with people who seemed to expect all nurses to be older, unattractive to men and therefore seeking fulfilment in nursing.

Mrs Crossley took the initiative by offering her hand and clasping the younger woman's firmly. 'You must be Miss Norris. I'm Flora Crossley. I'm so pleased to meet you. Welcome to Ollindale.'

'It's lovely to meet you too. Thank you for coming to collect me from the station.'

'That's the least we could do. And this is my husband, Walter, as you must have guessed.'

He shook hands too, something men didn't always do with women. Rachel considered that a point in his favour.

'Shall I go and unload your luggage, Miss Norris?'

'Yes, please. I have a big trunk and a rather large suitcase in the luggage van. They're both clearly labelled. But you'll need two people to deal with them because they're so heavy.'

'I'll find someone to help me put them on our cart.'

Walter strode off towards the luggage van and Flora stayed with Rachel. 'We'll take you and your luggage to the flat we've rented for you and then perhaps you'd like to come to our house for tea? We can show you round that part of the valley on the way and Walter will drive you home afterwards.'

'That'd be lovely. Thank you.'

'Let's get up on the cart. We can all three fit easily on the driving bench, I should think.'

When they were sitting there waiting, Flora said. 'Just to let you know, we've put some food in your flat already. Fortunately there's a corner store nearby so you'll be able to pick things up there on your way home. The best greengroceries are sold at the markets, of course, and as it was market day yesterday, my husband and I picked up a few things to get you started.'

'You must tell me how much I owe you.'

'Nothing, my dear. Just a small welcoming gift.'

'Thank you so much.'

By that time Mr Crossley and his helper were behind them, grunting with exertion as they loaded the heavy trunk on the back of the cart, then the big suitcase.

Rachel saw him slip a coin into the porter's hand then he joined them and clicked to the pony to start moving.

'This is Railway Road, the main street of our town,' he said as the neat little pony clopped up the gentle slope.

It all looked very peaceful. They turned to the right and went along a few quiet streets in what looked like a nice area.

'Is my flat part of a nurses' home? Miss Grayson didn't say.'

'I'm afraid it isn't. We don't have enough nurses in the valley to need a special home for them. The nurse dealing with the clinic in the town centre is staying with a cousin. I'll introduce you another time. She's called Ida Kelson, but she isn't a district nurse. We've had trouble getting one of the newer types of nurse to come here. Ida's very capable but she made it plain from the start that she wouldn't visit people in their homes. She runs a clinic for the poor and patients go to see her there. She manages it very efficiently.'

'Oh. I see.'

'We felt that it was more important to find a district nurse to deal with Eastby End. It's too far for most people who live there to come into the town clinic when they're sick, sadly.'

Rachel didn't know what to say to that. It certainly wasn't what she'd expected. There were usually other district nurses nearby, even if they weren't working together.

Miss Grayson, who had supervised her recent training and arranged this position for her, had spoken very highly indeed of Mrs Crossley but she hadn't known exactly how the rest of the valley's nursing services were organised. Rachel's appointment had happened in a rush, partly because of her problem with Pershore and partly because she wanted her own flat, wanted somewhere she could make into a real home where she could be private some of the time.

She was also well aware that there were more towns seeking such help than there were district nurses available to provide it so the people in Ollindale had been eager to gain her services. It had been clear that her supervisor wanted to help a friend.

They stopped outside a terrace of rather narrow houses and though all of them had a small garden at the front, the gardens were tiny strips of green with a low wall in front of them.

Mrs Crossley gestured to the end one. 'This is Mrs Prior's house. The first floor has been set up as a flat and you'll be very comfortable there, I'm sure.'

The landlady opened the front door to them, stared at Rachel as if slightly surprised and then beckoned them inside. She too had been expecting an older nurse at a guess.

After being introduced Mrs Prior indicated a door at the side of the hall. 'That leads to my flat, which takes up most of the ground floor, except for the entrance hall and the shared bathroom at the rear. I had a little catch put on the inside of the bathroom door to lock it when it's being used, by the way.'

'Very practical,' was all Rachel could think of to say.

'Your flat occupies the whole of the first floor.' She pointed to the rear of the entrance hall where there were some steps leading down. 'There's a sort of cellar down there because the house was built on a slope, but it wasn't big enough to turn into a proper flat. You can store your luggage there, though. And it's got an old slopstone and cold water tap there, though I hardly ever use them. The old outside lavatory across the back garden still works, so it's also available for your use, if necessary.'

She stepped back towards her own flat. 'I won't delay you now, Miss Norris, but you must come and have a cup of tea with me one day, and we'll discuss arrangements for taking our baths.'

'Thank you. I'd love to.' She hoped the arrangements for baths weren't too restrictive because you could get rather dirty dealing with some patients.

Between them, she and Walter managed to haul her trunk upstairs then he carried up the suitcase, though she could see that it was rather an effort for a man of his age. She hadn't been able to manage with less luggage because these contained all her worldly goods and she had no family to leave her things with.

The Crossleys moved back to stand near the entrance door of the flat and Mrs Crossley said, 'We'll wait for you outside, Miss Norris, and give you time to look round properly. No need to hurry. My husband and I always have plenty to chat about.'

As soon as they were outside Flora said in a low voice, 'I didn't expect her to be so pretty or so young. You could see that Mrs Prior was surprised at that too.'

'She's extremely pretty, isn't she? Do you think that'll be a problem?'

'It might be. It'd be better if she wasn't for working in Eastby End and also if she wasn't so young. It never even occurred to me to ask about her appearance and age.'

'Let's hope people get used to it quickly then.' He waited and when Flora said nothing, he asked, 'Is something else worrying you?'

'Her safety. She's already asked Pearl not to tell anyone where she's gone because of some chap following her. And she's so pretty I'm afraid we shall have to do something to protect her from certain types here too. She'd be all right going about in Ollerthwaite but I don't like the thought of her moving around Eastby End streets on her own, especially after dark.'

'We can hardly turn her away now.'

'No, and I don't want to. Let me think about it. I'm sure I'll come up with some solution.'

Left on her own, Rachel walked round the two rooms again, delighted with them at least. It was a pity she'd have to share the bathroom but she'd have her own space for everything else. There was even a sink in the corner set up as a kitchen. She hadn't had rooms of her own since . . . She didn't let her thoughts linger on that time and the baby she'd had to give away.

She pulled some of the drawers in and out then opened cupboard doors, smiling again now. Everything was nice and clean.

She'd better not keep the Crossleys waiting, so went down to rejoin them. There'd be plenty of time to settle in and unpack in the next day or two.

'Is there enough furniture?' Walter asked. 'We can get you some more if you haven't enough drawers and cupboards.'

'The flat will do very nicely as it is, thank you. I've been looking forward so much to having a home of my own.' She hesitated then said, 'Well, there is one other thing that would be useful: a bookcase. I love reading and have quite a lot of books. I'm hoping to keep more of what I read now that I have more room.'

'I have a bookcase in my shop. I'll bring it round for you. I think it'll fit nicely to the left of the window. It's second hand but not damaged, just a bit scratched.'

'Thank you.'

Flora smiled as they settled themselves on the driving bench again. 'Now, we'll drive you up to our farm for tea.'

'Will we be going anywhere near Eastby End?'

'I'm afraid not. It isn't far from your flat but it's at the other side of town from our farm. We'll take you to see it tomorrow.' She hesitated then added, 'Um, don't try to walk round it tonight after you get back. The central part can be a bit rough after dark.'

'Rough?'

She looked so shocked, Flora asked, 'Didn't anyone inform you that it's the poorest part of the whole valley? I did tell them.'

'I knew it was a poor area but no one told me it was that bad,' Rachel said bluntly. 'What do I do if I get called out at night?'

'Walter and I will have to sort something out to cover that,' Flora said at once. 'It'll be helpful once you're seen wearing your uniform and people get used to who you are. We've put word out that a district nurse will be coming to Eastby End and people have already been asking when you'll be starting work.'

Walter added, 'And the area is improving all the time with the town's new police sergeant keeping the peace.'

Rachel wished Miss Grayson had been more specific about what it was like here. She might not have taken the job if she'd known that it could actually be dangerous to go out in Eastby End after dark. She'd be trying to escape from Pershore and didn't want to walk into other trouble.

She hated the way her looks drew unwanted attention from a certain sort of man and often wished she were ugly, she really did. She dressed plainly, dragged her hair back into what she hoped was an unflattering bun and did absolutely nothing to attract attention but still some men pestered her.

Walter exchanged worried glances with his wife. 'If you're, er, having difficulties, Miss Norris, please tell us at once.'

'We hadn't considered that side of things as much as we should have done,' Flora said. 'But we will find some way to protect you, I promise.'

Rachel took a deep breath. 'Well, let's not look for trouble before I've even seen the place – or it's seen me. As you say, wearing a nurse's uniform does help.'

But the conversation was rather stilted during the meal at the farm and their visitor was clearly worried. What had happened to this young woman to make her dislike her own looks so much? Flora wondered.

'My wife and I will collect you in the pony trap tomorrow morning instead of the cart, and take you round Eastby so that you can judge the area for yourself,' Walter said.

'One piece of good news is that we've found a former shop just round the corner from the main street that's large enough to turn into a clinic, so we've rented it already,' Flora said. 'It needs doing up because it's been standing empty for a few years but we thought it best to wait for you to get here before we did any work on the interior, except for having it cleaned of course. You can decide how you want it setting out inside.'

Rachel brightened up visibly. 'That'll be wonderful. Small changes in layout can make such a big difference.

Flora took over again. 'We've bought some basic medical supplies, like bandages, carbolic soap and iodine, and a table and chairs. They're there already and if you'll give us a list we'll get whatever else you need. And we'll arrange the interior however you specify.'

'Thank you. It'll be interesting to think about how to set things out. I've never been able to do that before.' She ate a few more mouthfuls then asked, 'Is there a Lady Superintendent to keep a check on the situation? They usually appoint someone to keep an eye on district nurses and to help them organise their work and contacts in the community. And – well, I presume the other nurses in other areas of Ollindale will help out if things get busy, as I would do for them?'

'I'll be keeping an eye on things, but I shan't be calling myself by any fancy titles,' Flora said. 'But as for other nurses, Eastby is a small suburb on the very edge of a small town, and there is only one nurse at the town clinic and one helping Dr Coxton, so mostly you'll be working completely on your own, I'm afraid.' She frowned, feeling guilty about this. 'I'm assuming there will be another nurse coming to work with the new doctor. We've advertised for a male doctor because some men won't let a woman like Dr Coxton treat them, however well qualified and experienced she is. So stupid! But there's work for more than one doctor here anyway.'

'It's rather unusual to have only a female doctor for a whole town,' Rachel said.

'Our previous doctor was quite elderly and when he died suddenly, we had to find another one quickly. He'd objected to the mere idea of any other doctor coming to work here, male or female, and he had some of the older town councillors on his side about that. Fortunately when he died I happened to know Dr Coxton was looking to move to a country practice and I knew how capable she was because I'd worked with her before.'

'It'll be good to have a woman doctor,' Rachel said. 'She'll understand some of the problems I'll be dealing with better than a man could.'

'She's made a good start and has even won over some of what I call our local "dinosaurs" about a woman doctor's capabilities.'

It was already starting to get dark when they took Rachel back and as they returned, the Crossleys admitted to one another that they were worried that she might find things a bit difficult here and wouldn't want to stay.

'I should have planned better for that side of things,' Flora muttered.

'We weren't quite sure what would be needed. And we didn't expect someone quite so young and pretty, did we? We'll see what we can do now.'

They would have been even more worried if they'd known that Rachel only unpacked her suitcase when she got back. All she took out of her trunk were her sheets and a towel.

As she struggled to push it into a corner she decided to leave her books and personal possessions till she was more settled. *If* she settled here. That depended not only on what Eastby itself was like but how the people living there reacted to her and how safe she felt. Not to mention if Pershore found out where she was.

If only she weren't going to be the only district nurse for that part of town. She already felt the lack of someone to talk the situation over with. All the district nurses she'd met who'd been working in Bristol or London had spoken of working with others and some of them went about in pairs.

As she got ready for bed, she went across to the window a couple of times, staring out in what she thought was the direction of Eastby End. But there was nothing disturbing the peace and hardly anyone walking about, and at least there were gas lights in the streets.

Luckily she was so tired by now that she fell asleep quite quickly. It was so lovely to be on her own in a quiet room, instead of sharing a bedroom.

12

The next morning, Joss got up early and as soon as he'd finished breakfast, he asked Rufus where to find the man who sold bicycles.

'His workshop isn't far away. I'll take you there on my way out if you like.'

After he'd introduced Joss to Peter he said, 'Will you be all right finding your way to your house in Eastby afterwards?'

'Yes, thank you. I'm good at finding my way around even after I've only been to a place once. Just one other thing before you go, though. Will the shops in town deliver to the other side of Eastby?'

'They might be reluctant to send their delivery lad so far with only small purchases, I'm afraid, but they should be all right for the big weekly orders. That's not just because your house is quite a long way from the town centre but because there are some rather unsavoury young louts in Eastby who can be a bit rough on a single delivery lad, and have been known to pinch items from the basket on his bicycle.'

'I'd guessed that might be the case from how it looks and feels in Eastby.' And he wasn't going to put up with that for long, whatever it took to change things.

When Rufus had left, Joss turned to Peter. 'I think I'd better purchase a tricycle so that the people I employ can use it as needed to fetch things from the shops in town. Can you get me one?'

'Yes, of course. It'll take two or three days for me to do that, though. How much do you want to spend?'

Joss shrugged, 'Whatever you think reasonable.'

The man beamed at that.

'It doesn't have to be brand new, but I want something that's safe and good mechanically, of course.'

Once they'd agreed a price, he frowned and took a quick decision. 'I wonder if you have a cheap second-hand bicycle I can also buy for my own occasional use? I don't need anything fancy, just something to get around the valley on, and I need it straight away if possible.'

'Well, actually, I have a bicycle available now that might suit you. I've only just bought it in. It belonged to a lad who's moved away from the valley to work in Manchester. His parents are elderly and have no use for it. I was going to give it a lick of paint and smarten it up before I tried to sell it, but if you need it straight away and don't mind a few scratches, I can let you have it quite cheaply.'

They agreed on a price but Peter still insisted on going over the bicycle mechanically before he'd let Joss use it. 'I always make sure the brakes work well. How about you take a nice stroll round the town centre for an hour or so, eh, Mr Townley?'

How could you complain about someone wanting to make sure you stayed safe? 'Good idea. Perhaps you could suggest where to go?'

He set off, going up the main road as suggested but walking briskly rather than strolling. He came to a crossroads Peter had mentioned as a good destination. It was just outside the town and the prosperous looking farmhouse to the right, which was set slightly higher than the road looking down into the valley, must be the Crossleys' home.

Peter had suggested he turn back when he got here but Joss felt he had time to go further if he continued to walk briskly. A left turn here would take him along a well-defined track which seemed to lead straight towards a small building, whose roof and part of a wall he could just make out above some trees. About fifty yards along, another track to the right appeared to lead to a large building currently under construction. Like the Crossleys' farm it was up a slight slope from the crossroads.

He chose to turn right towards that because it looked interesting. He'd been told a large house was being built for a Mr Edward Ollerton, whose family had been squires in the valley until they lost their money. Edward had rebuilt the family fortunes and come back here to live. Walter had promised to introduce Joss to him, but with a bit of luck he might manage to introduce himself.

He prided himself on having learned to strike up conversations with all sorts of people and really enjoyed meeting folk from different backgrounds to his own. He could see a group of workmen putting slates on the new roof and a gentleman who looked to be in charge was standing below next to someone who appeared to be the foreman. They were both smiling and nodding so presumably things were going well.

Was this Edward or the person in charge of building the house?

The man saw him, said something to his companion and came across to ask in an educated voice, 'Can I help you, sir? Have you lost your way?'

'Thanks for the offer but I'm not lost. I'm a newcomer to the valley, about to settle out beyond Eastby End, and I'm enjoying looking round while I wait for Peter to finish checking a bicycle I've bought. Joss Townley, at your service.' He held out his hand.

'Lewis Brody, architect and builder.'

They shook hands and Joss went on, 'I heard about a house being built for the major landholder in the valley and I presume this is it?'

'Yes. It's for Edward Ollerton. His previous family home was just uphill from this site but it burned down a couple of decades ago.'

'The house looks very attractive and I should think it'll have a lovely view across the valley. If you designed it to fit so nicely on that site, you're to be congratulated. I hope you don't mind me coming to look at it more closely.' He grinned. 'I'm incurably nosy about the place where I'm now going to live.'

'That's only natural. And thank you for the compliment. The house is turning out rather well, I think. No one will mind you coming to have a look now and then. You won't be the first or the last from round here to do that. I think half the town has been out to see how things are going at one time or another.'

'Was the valley named after the owner's family or were they named after it?'

'I have no idea. All I know is that the Ollertons have been living round here for a couple of hundred years, give or take. Ah, here comes the owner now. Let me introduce you.'

Edward Ollerton looked to be about ten years older than Joss and was as friendly as his architect. The three of them chatted for a while about the valley, then Joss invited them to come and visit him once he had sorted out his new home and settled in. He smiled again as he added, 'If the valley is like other small places, rumour will let you know how I'm getting on till then.'

He took his leave and went back down the hill, stopping to peer at the glint of water that must be Jubilee Lake to the left but he'd have to save that to visit another day. To his delight his bicycle was ready, so he was able to get back to his new home far more quickly than he'd come into town.

He took another quick look round the house then cycled slowly back to the hotel, feeling tired but pleased with how things were going, and so happy at the thought of settling down and making a proper home for himself.

For that he'd need servants and was relying on his new housekeeper's help to find them. If he'd ever met a capable woman it was her.

13

Sybil Entwistle planned to set off for her new home at about seven o'clock the following morning so that she would avoid an unpleasant confrontation with her daughter-in-law over breakfast. She was looking forward to a more peaceful life there, away from Thelma's sharp tongue.

She was sure her son's wife would throw a fit once she found out Sybil was leaving, because she was lazy about housework. Well, Lionel was welcome to live with his wife's shrill complaining and nagging. Sybil had had enough. Whatever happened now, she wasn't going back.

In preparation for the coming changes, she went out after tea to see her friend Megan, ignoring a peremptory demand from her daughter-in-law to know where she was going and allowing herself the rare treat of slamming the door behind her.

When she asked her friend whether she'd be interested in working for Mr Townley as a maid, Megan stared at her in surprise.

'Really?'

'Really, truly. I'm going there as the housekeeper. There's a job for you if you're interested.'

Megan wept for joy at the thought of earning her own money. Like Sybil she was widowed and living with her son and daughter-in-law in what had once been her own home. That was hard when she'd formerly been in charge there.

There were so few jobs available for younger widows like her and Sybil in Eastby or even in the town of Ollerthwaite generally. Any that came up were usually snapped up by people as soon as they heard about them, so people in Eastby rarely heard in time to apply.

But at least her friend's daughter-in-law was a pleasant young woman and they didn't try to hide what they were talking about from Gillian, who didn't hesitate to wish her mother-in-law luck in getting the job.

Megan's son was equally pleased for her and at once offered to take her possessions across to the big house if she was successful. He was also happy to include the box Megan had been looking after. Sybil had brought her own most treasured personal possessions to her friend's home two years ago just before her son got married. These were items she'd inherited from her own family and she felt they belonged to her still.

She'd seen the gloating way Thelma looked round the farm and fingered the ornaments on her first visit. After another visit from the young woman she'd even found scratch marks on the lock of her box of small treasures in her bedroom. She'd kept quiet about that for her son's sake, but had felt furious.

Soon after the wedding Thelma had had the effrontery to ask where certain items were as she wanted to rearrange the ornaments to look more attractive.

'Those items belong to me and I've put them away safely for when I get my own home again. So they're none of your business,' Sybil told her sharply.

The next day Lionel had also asked his mother where some of the ornaments had gone and she'd told him the same thing.

He'd given her a reproachful look. 'I thought families handed down their possessions.'

'Most of those belonged to my grandma so they don't belong to the Entwistles. I may get married again, in which case I'll want my own things, won't I?'

'Get married? At your age? Surely that's not likely, Ma! Who is there for you to marry round here?'

'You never know who'll come a-visiting one of the local families.'

She'd never taken her box of possessions back to the farm, because she had been seriously considering moving away from Eastby. The trouble was, she loved her only son and worried about him.

She now occupied the smallest bedroom, had been informed by Thelma that she must leave the best spare bedroom for guests. Yet there had been no guests staying overnight, not once, because Thelma didn't seem to have any close friends and most of her relatives had moved away from the valley.

'You and I will enjoy living together, I'm sure.' Sybil said to her friend as they said goodbye.

'You sound certain I'll get the job.'

'You definitely will. I didn't like to tell people yet, but Mr Townley has already said he'd leave the hiring of other domestic help to me.'

Megan let out a squeak of joy and gave her an extra hug. 'Oh, I'm so glad. Thank you. Tom and Gillian will enjoy having the place to themselves, not in a nasty way, but every young couple needs time together to make their own married life, don't you think? I'm just in the way here and any dairy maid could do my work.'

She sighed and Sybil knew from her suddenly sad expression that her friend was thinking of her late husband. Those two had been very happy together, happier than Sybil had been with Dan, though she hadn't been *unhappy* exactly. But she'd always known that her husband still missed his first wife and had married her for the convenience of having someone to bring up his children by her.

Megan whispered, 'I didn't like to ask in front of my son and his wife, but what did Thelma say about you getting the job as housekeeper?'

'I haven't told her yet. That can wait till tomorrow morning. I have no doubt she'll get very nasty about it. She's been getting lazier and lazier about doing her share of the housework.'

'She'll miss your help in a lot of ways. Everyone knows you were the best farmer's wife in the district till your Dan died.'

Sybil shrugged. 'Fat lot of good that did me after I lost him. He'd left everything to his son and had suggested Lionel marry Thelma for the money she'd bring. When he realised he was dying he made Lionel promise to do that.' She took another step backwards. 'I'm going to see Jack Berring now, to find out whether he wants a full-time job there.'

'He will. That family's been living a hand-to-mouth existence for years, times have been so bad round here.'

Megan was right. Jack, who owned a tiny smallholding, was delighted to try for the full-time job as Mr Townley's gardener and general handyman. If he got it, his eldest son would be able to take over the smallholding and the couple of part-time jobs Jack had been doing on a regular basis, so there'd be benefits for the whole family.

He promised to come to Townley Hall later in the morning the next day and when she asked him if he'd mind picking up her trunk from her current home on the way, he said he'd be delighted to help her, whether he got the job or not.

By the time she got back, her daughter-in-law had gone to bed and since Thelma always fell asleep quickly, Sybil was able to tell her son that she was going to work for Mr Townley as housekeeper.

'Why didn't you tell us earlier?'

'I wanted to tell *you* first, Lionel.'

He stared at her but didn't make the obvious comment. 'When was that arranged?'

'This morning.'

'You didn't ask me if you could go and work there.'

'I'm a grown woman, son, not a child who needs to ask permission to do things. I've been looking for a job for a while, actually.'

'Well, I don't like the idea of you going to work for that family. The Entwistles have never got on with the Townleys. This one doesn't seem as bad as the rest of them, I admit, but you should look for another job.'

'I've been looking for a while but there haven't been any other jobs going. I really like the idea of earning my own money and doing something more interesting. As housekeeper I shall have to live in, so I'll be moving out of here tomorrow morning.'

'You're moving out tomorrow! What will Thelma say?'

When he opened his mouth to continue protesting, she cut him short. 'Aw, admit it for once: I don't get on with your Thelma and I never will. No one else does either, but you're too loyal to say so.'

He sighed. 'She'll settle down once we have children, I'm sure she will. She's really anxious about not having started a family yet. Give her time and a baby or two and she'll calm right down, I'm sure. Some women are just . . . slow starters at having families.'

He was trying to persuade himself about that, Sybil thought sadly. Thelma would never be easy to live with, but he'd made his bed and would have to lie in it.

'Why do you have to live in anyway, Ma? Can't you just go there daily?'

'Housekeepers usually live in, love.'

'But—'

'Look, son, I stayed on after your father died because I was upset and you needed me. Then I had to show *her* how we did things here and anyway, there were no jobs nearby. Now I've been offered a really good job and if I don't snap it up quickly, someone else will.'

She waited a few moments but all he did was sigh. 'Can't you be happy for me, Lionel?'

'I'm being selfish, I suppose, but I shall miss you. They're lucky to get you.'

'Thanks, love. Now, I know it's late but will you help me carry that old trunk down from the attics so that I can finish packing my things before I go to bed?'

He looked surprised. 'Can't you do that tomorrow? You surely don't need to leave at the crack of dawn.'

'I want to leave early. Before Thelma gets up, I hope.'

He nodded, clearly understanding the implications. 'Right. Come on then. Let's get that trunk down to your bedroom.'

'Thanks, love. We'll use the back stairs, shall we?' Not only did she not want to disturb Thelma but she noticed how hard he tried to move quietly, so he must have felt the same. But she didn't comment on that.

'You know you can always come back here if things don't go well, don't you, Ma?' he said in a low voice after they'd put the trunk in her bedroom.

'Yes, of course I do.' But she'd have to be desperate to come back, utterly desperate. 'And will you make sure she lets Jack take my trunk in the morning? I brought this one with me when I married your father so it truly belongs to me.'

'Ah. Hmm. Yes, of course. I'd not have grudged you any of the trunks, though. I'll, um, work near the house just to be sure of seeing him when he comes and if he doesn't turn up, I'll bring it across to you myself. Er, it will be locked, won't it?'

'Yes, of course.' She gave him another hug. She could imagine the storm of abuse he'd get when he carried her trunk down.

He didn't say anything else but he looked unhappy as he left her to her packing and she guessed he was already worrying about what his wife was going to say and do tomorrow. Thelma might not get on with her mother-in-law but she would hit the roof about losing her help around the farm. She made a poor farmer's wife on top of everything else, wasn't even an efficient worker, for all she acted as if she were superior to everyone else.

Sybil had already packed another suitcase with the essentials in case anything went wrong with the trunk. She'd carry that across to the big house with her. She now proceeded to pack the rest of her possessions in the big trunk then locked it carefully. She knew she had the only keys because she'd taken the spare from its hook on the storeroom wall as a precaution soon after Thelma moved in and Sybil realised what sort of life she would be facing.

By the time she'd finished packing it was after midnight and she'd not get much sleep but she didn't care. She sighed happily as she set her alarm clock for five o'clock and fell asleep almost immediately.

Excitement helped Sybil come fully awake immediately her little alarm clock sounded from under the edge of her pillow. It wasn't even light outside yet but she was hoping to slip out of the house before Thelma got up.

She'd always enjoyed starting the day by pottering about quietly on her own and today it seemed a fitting farewell to the farmhouse she'd once loved and cared for.

After getting the fire burning up in the kitchen range she put the kettle on to boil with only a little water in it so that it'd get hot quickly. She did like a cup of tea to start her day and there'd be no food stores at the big house yet. She ate a couple of jam butties as she worked and made some ham sandwiches to take with her for later.

Unfortunately, her daughter-in-law came downstairs to the kitchen just as she was carrying her suitcase to the door, ready to leave. Pity.

'I thought I heard a noise. Pour me a cup of that tea. What are you doing up so early—' Thelma broke off to stare. 'Why on earth have you got that old suitcase out?'

'To hold my clothes because I'm moving out today.' Sybil took a deep breath and said, 'I've got a job as Mr Townley's housekeeper. I thought I'd make an early start on my first day there.'

There was dead silence for a couple of minutes as Thelma gaped at her. Then she said, 'That's our suitcase. You can't take it.'

'It's my own suitcase, actually, came to me from my family when my mother died.'

'Everything you brought here belongs to this family now.'

'I'm not arguing. It's mine and I need it for my clothes and that's that.'

There was a brief silence, then 'Who said you could leave anyway?'

'Me.'

'Your son's the master here. He's the one who says what people can and can't do. I'm sure he won't *allow* you to leave.'

She couldn't help smiling. Lionel might be nominally in charge, but he still tried to avoid trouble. He hadn't come down to the kitchen with his wife and his bedroom was next to hers, so he must have heard her get up. He was probably avoiding the inevitable quarrel for as long as he could.

'And even if you do leave, you can't go today, or even this week because I'll need to find someone to replace you here.' Thelma looked round. 'You haven't even started your chores this morning. Get on with them at once.'

She darted quickly across to stand in front of the outer door, arms folded, barring her mother-in-law's way.

Sybil had had enough of being bossed around by this nasty young fool. 'How are you going to stop me leaving? I'm bigger and stronger than you.' To prove it, she jerked the other woman aside and opened the back door.

Thelma's mouth fell open in surprise, then she lunged forward and tried to bang the door shut again, yelling at the top of her voice for her husband. 'Lionel! Get down here this minute!'

There was no response from upstairs.

'Come down here this minute, Lionel Entwistle!'

There were footsteps coming down the stairs and Thelma tried to kick the suitcase out of the way. 'Get on with your chores, Sybil. We'll discuss this later after I've spoken to Lionel.'

But she was no match for the older woman, who shoved her aside again and sat down on her suitcase in front of the back door, arms folded, waiting for her son. She didn't like upsetting him because he was a gentle soul but there was no avoiding it now.

Thelma was just about quivering with fury and Sybil had wondered if she was going to attack her physically a minute or two ago. If she did, she'd got a shock coming because Sybil would hit her back. She'd had enough of being bullied and wasn't going to put up with any more of it. She had something worth fighting for now and would do whatever was necessary to get away.

When her son came into the kitchen, he looked surprised at the sight of his mother sitting on the suitcase in front of the door, arms folded.

'What on earth's going on?'

Sybil got in first. 'Your wife is trying to stop me leaving by pushing me around, son.'

'She deserves a good beating, she's so stupid!' Thelma yelled.

He looked at his wife in shock. 'Don't you dare talk about my mother like that.'

'I'm not *letting* her leave, whatever it takes. She works on the farm and she hasn't even given us any notice. And how am I going to manage without her help?'

To Sybil's delight, he scowled and said slowly and loudly, 'My mother has a right to manage her own life. We're lucky to have had her help for so long. You'll have to hire someone else.'

'We shouldn't have to pay that much for help when we've got family who can do the job.'

'If we'd been paying my mother a fair wage for her hard work, and treating her politely, maybe she wouldn't have wanted to leave.' He fumbled in his pocket, pulled out a five-pound note and went across to thrust it into his mother's hand. 'You'll need some money to fall back on in case things don't work out, Ma.'

Thelma shrieked like a soul in anguish and tried to snatch the money back, but Sybil shoved her hand away and stuffed it deep in her pocket. 'Thank you, son.'

'What are you thinking of, Lionel Entwistle, giving her all that money?'

'I'm thinking of my mother. Do you need help carrying that suitcase across to Townley House, Ma?'

'No. I'll be fine, love.' But she wasn't leaving it at that. 'As for you, Thelma, I've bitten my tongue a hundred times at the way you speak to me for the sake of family harmony, but I won't do it again. Never, ever. Nothing will make me come back here.' She gave herself the pleasure of adding, 'And I'm going to leave you with a piece of very good advice. If you want to get the best out of the person who takes over from me, you'll treat her politely – especially if she's older than you and will undoubtedly know far more about the job.'

'How *dare* you speak to me like that? I'm mistress here and in charge. Lionel promised me I would be before we married, so I have the right to do things my own way.'

'My advice about being polite still holds good. Your present way of behaving towards others doesn't get the best out of them.' Sybil picked up the suitcase and walked out quickly, wishing Lionel could escape too.

There was another shriek from inside the kitchen as her son followed her out. He took the suitcase from her and carried it over the rough ground at the side of the house. Then he opened the outer gate and set the case down on the grass beyond. 'The ground is smooth from here on so you should be all right carrying it. Good luck, Ma.'

She couldn't resist giving him a hug. 'Thanks, son.' She hesitated but it had to be said, 'Don't forget to make sure she doesn't stop Jack from picking my trunk up. He'll be coming here for it later this morning.'

A sigh escaped him. 'I won't forget. And I want to thank you for all your help since Dad died. You've been the best of mothers to me and I should have looked after you more carefully.'

That brought tears to her eyes, especially as he pulled her close and gave her a quick kiss on each cheek before he turned and went back to the house.

14

Sybil picked up the suitcase and strolled across the meadow towards Townley House, smiling at the sight of the pretty house, which was about twice as large as the farm she'd just left. She felt her anxiety fade as she breathed in the crisp morning air and listened to the chorus of bird calls that was just starting up.

When she got to the house she set the suitcase down and unlocked the back door. Before she went inside, she crossed to the wood store and picked up some shrivelled pieces of kindling that were still lying around at the back of the open-ended shed. There were a few smaller pieces of wood there too, so she slipped some of them into the old shopping bag she'd brought with her.

She took the wood inside and set it down near the kitchen range. Silly, but there you were. She was eager to take the first step into her new job even before she brought in her own suitcase: lighting a fire in the range to heat the water, and of course making it possible to boil a kettle and make a pot of tea.

Bending down, she piled some kindling into a small pyramid shape inside the square open fire grate at the heart of the old-fashioned kitchen range then pulled out the box of matches she'd brought from the farm. She wished she could see Thelma's face when she found no box of matches in the usual place today.

The kindling caught light quickly, which was good because it showed that the range drew well. She set the smallest pieces of wood in place over the tiny fire. They too were long dried out and would catch light quickly.

Only then did she bring in her suitcase and dump it in the hall at the foot of the stairs. After that she carried the faded wood basket outside and filled it with bigger pieces of firewood, disturbing a few black beetles in the process. Horrid things. If there were any still patrolling the inside of the house, they'd get short shrift from her. She made a mental note that they'd need to order some more firewood as soon as possible.

By this time the fire was burning up nicely, so she placed a couple of the bigger pieces of wood on it. Only then did she allow herself the pleasure of walking slowly round the large kitchen, opening and shutting all the drawers and cupboards as she waited for the big iron plate on the top of the range to warm up. She was annoyed with herself for only bringing a few tea leaves to brew herself a pot of tea. They'd need to brew more at intervals as the day passed.

The various pieces of crockery and cutlery in the drawers and cupboards had simply been left as they were, and she'd never seen so much dust in her life. But it could be a nice room when cleaned, with a huge pantry and two walk-in store cupboards in a row that filled one side.

It would be nice again once she'd sorted everything and restocked the pantry. Someone must have emptied all the food out and cleaned its shelves, thank goodness.

In the scullery next door to the kitchen there was another large cupboard, this one filled with dusty larger pieces of crockery, like serving dishes and big bowls, pans of all shapes and sizes, and bakeware. She would soon get them washed clean again in the huge square sink.

She was going to enjoy running this house.

Lugging her suitcase upstairs, she dumped it on the landing and went round checking the bedrooms. Hmm. These were nicely furnished under the dust sheets and clearly meant for the family or visitors. Mr Townley had suggested she sleep in the attic, had said there was a nice big room up there, so she carried her suitcase up.

There were several bedrooms and to her delight she found that the biggest one was at the front of the house. It was better furnished than the others and would probably have been the housekeeper's room. If it hadn't, it was going to be from now on. It looked out along the drive and the entrance gates, which she also liked about it.

She bounced on the bed, nodding approvingly at the way the springs of the metal base were still lively. She'd make up her own bed later, but she and Megan would need to take the dusty mattresses outside and beat them first.

They would still have to use the old mattresses, unfortunately, and goodness only knew how long these had been lying here and what little creatures had made homes over the years in the flock they were stuffed with. They felt lumpy. She hadn't seen such old-fashioned mattresses since she was much younger. No, they'd definitely need new ones, modern inner spring mattresses, and she was sure Mr Townley would agree to buying some. She'd check of course, but she bet his was just a flock mattress too.

She thought she heard a sound so glanced out of the window and saw someone on a bicycle turn into the drive from the main road. It took her a moment to realise it was her new employer.

She ran lightly down the stairs and was in the kitchen by the time he got off his bicycle and leaned it against the rear wall. He came towards the house carrying a sacking bundle, so she opened the door for him. 'Good morning, sir.'

He jumped in shock. 'Good morning, Sybil. I didn't expect you to be here yet.'

'I thought I'd move in early so that I could work out what was needed to start setting the house to rights.'

Heaven help her if he objected to her moving in today. She wasn't going back to the farm, not for anything. She'd rather sleep under a hedge than ask Thelma to take her in again, she decided as she waited anxiously to hear what he said.

'I'm glad you did, Sybil. You can help me make a shopping list because if possible I want to move in today as well. I've bought a bicycle, as you must have noticed. It's second-hand but works well. I've ordered a tricycle too, because you can carry more things on one of those. Do you know how to ride a bicycle?'

'Yes. I used to share one with my husband. After he died I continued to use it.'

'Oh, good. It'll be very useful to have one because we're a bit far out of town for walking in from here when we're in a hurry.'

He dumped his sack near the back door. 'I've brought another pair of my shoes with me in case these get dirty walking around outside. When I go back into town I'll have to sign out of the hotel and arrange to have the rest of my clothes and other possessions brought here.'

He indicated the bicycle, positively beaming at it. 'It's
great to have this to get around on, reminds me of when
I was a lad.'

She loved to see his boyish glee. 'Don't ride off on it for
a while, sir. If you remember, Megan Grainger is coming
to see you this morning. She'll make an excellent general
maid if you approve her.'

He grinned at her, more like a cheeky boy's grin than
that of a mature man. 'I shall enjoy meeting your friend
but as I've already told you, it'll be you who chooses our
help for inside the house. Go ahead and offer her the job
if you're sure she's a hard worker.'

'Oh. Right. But Jack Berring is coming about the gar-
dening and handyman job a little later as well, and you'll
need to check that he's suitable and tell him what you
want him to do and what you're offering to pay. It's not
a housekeeper's job to choose the male servants who'll
be working outside. I'll tell you, however, that he's well
thought of round here.'

'Oh, very well. I'll speak to this chap if you insist. I trem-
ble in my shoes at the thought of going against your wishes.'

She didn't know what to say to that, then realised he
was joking and relaxed, speaking without thinking, 'Eh,
you're teasing me, aren't you? I've grown out of the habit
of having a bit of fun, living with a sour-faced daughter-
in-law like mine.'

'Well, please get into the habit again. I enjoy looking on
the lighter side of life sometimes and I'm not one to stand
on my dignity with people who help me, either.'

She clapped her hands together and beamed at him.
'I'll be happy to do that, sir. My husband was a nice chap
who used to like chatting with people.'

'You must miss him.'

She felt her smile fade. 'I do. A lot. He was good company.'

He waited a couple of minutes for her to pull herself together and smile at him again to tell him she was ready to continue.

'Is that a pot of tea?'

'It is indeed.'

'And . . . is there any left?'

'I haven't really started on it yet. Do you want a cup – no, a mug would be better.'

'Yes, please. You don't waste time sorting things out, do you? I like that.'

'I don't waste anything if I can help it, time or food or whatever.' Unless someone rearranged the tasks and insisted you do them in a stupid inefficient way as Thelma had done.

She remembered something else she needed to check with him. 'We're going to need a scrubbing woman, too, but I have someone in mind for that, say two days a week after our big clean-up at the start. I'll send word to her later to start tomorrow and come in full-time this first week to help go through the house and remove all this dust. Is that all right?'

'That's fine. Is there any sugar or milk for the tea?'

'Sorry. I don't take sugar and I couldn't carry milk as well as my suitcase.'

'Never mind then. I'll take it black. It'll still be nice and hot, and I'm thirsty.' He took a few sips and sighed happily. 'That's better.' Then he frowned as he looked round. 'I know the whole house is in a mess and very dusty, but can you get a bedroom ready for me to move into today as well as for yourself? I don't want to miss the fun and games of being involved in setting up my new home right from the start.'

'It will be ready enough if you'll set up accounts for me to buy food and other household items and let me walk into town later to get them. I can order a lot of groceries to be delivered but I'll need to bring back the basics we'll need straight away for our midday meal.'

'You said you knew how to ride a bicycle, so you can use mine to ride into town. I've already set up an account at the big grocer's shop on the corner of Railway Road. Mrs Shorrocks at the hotel suggested that one and they were very nice to deal with.'

'Painter's, yes, they are well thought of.'

'They said that if we put in a big order, they'll deliver groceries and cleaning materials straight away.'

'Oh, good. That'll make things easier.'

'Order whatever you need to start off with and tell them to put it on my account. Ask them to deliver it all immediately. Don't stint on anything. You can walk across to your son's farm later and pick up your husband's old bicycle, then you'll find it a lot easier to get around any time you need to.'

She hesitated because she'd rather have kept her quarrels with her daughter-in-law to herself, but she doubted it would be possible. 'I think my son would be happy to let me keep using that old bicycle because his wife won't even try to ride one and he has his own. But she's in a huff with me for getting this job so I don't think she'd let me take it.'

He smiled. 'Like that, is she?'

'Unfortunately, yes. I'm really glad to be away from her.'

'Then speak to your son another time about sneaking that one of yours out to you. And remember, don't stint on anything at the shops.'

'You trust me that much?'

'Yes, I do. You have an honest face. I think you're more likely to speak too bluntly to someone than cheat them.'

She had to chuckle at that. 'You're right.'

'I'll get on with checking the contents of the various rooms I'll be using, then. I'll leave the kitchen to you.' He walked out, looking happy.

Shortly afterwards footsteps sounded outside the back of the house and she went to see who it was, pleased to see that Megan had arrived early too. 'Come in, love. You're hired.'

Her friend stopped dead for a moment, looking astonished.

'Mr Townley insists that he trusts me to find good workers and he's not going to waste his time doing it. So you're hired.'

'That's wonderful.' She gave Sybil a quick hug. 'Thanks, love.'

'You can go back and fetch your things later, after I get back from town. I'm cycling into Ollerthwaite later to buy some food and supplies, so we need to check what cleaning equipment is needed as well as thinking of groceries we can't do without.'

'Is there nothing left here at all?'

'Nothing except a few cleaning tools. There aren't even rags to act as cleaning cloths. But I've looked into all the drawers and seen things that are already ragged, so we'll be all right.'

'It's been years since Townley House was occupied, hasn't it? I vaguely remember someone living here when I was a child, but no one permanent since then.'

'That all I remember too. Anyway, at least someone cleared all the food out of the pantry, so the shelves aren't mould-covered underneath the dust. In fact, you can make washing down all the pantry shelves your second job. First, we need to beat the old flock mattresses we'll have to use tonight and leave them outside to air.'

She waved one hand. 'Go and have a quick walk round all the rooms. I can see you're dying to see what it's like.'

Megan went across to peer into the storerooms and pantry, then turned to smile at her. 'There's a nice lot of storage space, isn't there?'

'Yes. It's a lovely big house. You'll have a bedroom in the attic. Choose which one you want while you're up there. It'll be small but all yours. I'm up there too in the biggest one, which is the official housekeeper's room. Eh, what's up? Don't cry, love.'

Megan mopped her eyes. 'There's nothing wrong. They're happy tears, that's all.'

'I just thought of something. You'd better let me introduce you to Mr Townley before you do anything, so he knows you're not an intruder. Come on.'

He was in one of the other downstairs rooms pulling the dustcloths off the furniture. 'I think I'll use this as my sitting room, Sybil, and – Oh, sorry. Didn't realise you'd got someone with you.'

'This is your new maid, sir. Megan Grainger. She came early so I hired her, as you said I should.'

'Pleased to meet you, Megan. I hope you'll be happy working here. It'll probably be a bit chaotic at first, I'm afraid.'

'I shan't mind that, sir.'

'Good. We'll all have fun, then.'

When they got back to the kitchen Megan smiled and nodded to her. 'He's nice, isn't he?'

'Yes, he is. And not at all uppity. We'll be all right working here.'

They clasped hands for a minute then got on with things.

15

Adam Dean had just started working on a customer's car that had broken down for no obvious reason and been towed into town by a highly amused farmer and his large carthorse.

He was surprised when his boss and friend came into the workshop and said, 'Leave that for the moment, Adam lad. There's a gentleman here to see you.'

'Who is it?'

'A Mr Genner. I've left him in the waiting room. He says he's a lawyer and it's about something important, so take as much time as you need.' He chuckled and added, 'Maybe someone's left you a fortune.'

'That'd be very nice. I wouldn't mind at all. Not likely, though.' He frowned. 'I don't know anyone called Genner, Tom. And I've not had anything to do with any lawyers either, come to that. He must have made a mistake.'

'Well, go and find out, one way or the other. He refused to tell me any details.'

'I won't be long.' Adam wiped his dirty hands on a rag and went into the waiting area where a balding and rather plump middle-aged gentleman was pacing to and fro. 'Mr Genner?'

The man looked across at him and gasped. 'I don't need to ask who you are. My goodness, you look so like your father, Mr . . . um, Dean. Is that what you call yourself?'

He was so shocked by that it took him a few moments to answer. 'I do, because that was my mother's name so I've always been a Dean.'

'It's as good as any other for the moment, I suppose.'

'What on earth do you mean?'

'Shall we sit down to talk?'

'Oh, sorry. Do take a chair.' He waited till the other man was seated then followed his example, covering the chair seat with a page from the newspaper, because he was wearing overalls daubed here and there with oil.

'Do you know my father, then?'

'I definitely did. I was his lawyer.'

'How can you be so sure your client was my father?' Adam had never met his father or even seen a photo of him. His mother had always told people she was a widow but had refused to give her son any details about his paternal family, so he had only her word for it.

'Now that I've seen you, I'm utterly certain our investigator was right and that you are James Entwistle's son.'

He waited as Adam gaped at him and repeated the name. 'He was called James Entwistle?'

'Didn't you even know his name?'

'No.'

'Goodness me. Well, I was his lawyer for many years. Sadly, he died a few weeks ago after a short illness. He'd already instructed me to take certain actions but he wasn't expecting to die so quickly. Unfortunately, he came down with severe influenza at the beginning of last winter.'

'A lot of people died in that epidemic.'

'Yes. It was very sad. Anyway, when I opened the envelope he'd left with his will, I found that it contained a letter to you as well as the one giving me certain further instructions.'

'I can guess why his name was different from mine. Bastards don't usually take their father's name, do they?'

'Um, no.'

'My mother told people she was a widow, but she refused to give me any details about my father and she had no photographs of him. When I grew older, I guessed that she'd never been married. She died two years ago from a seizure. I had no one left to ask about my father's family or I might have tried to inform him of her death. If he'd been interested, that is. He certainly never visited her – or me.'

'He kept watch on her and knew when she died, but we had trouble finding you after he died because you'd moved from the address he'd given us and not left a forwarding address.'

'There were no debts to pay, just a house to clear of furniture, and that sold quickly. I thought there was no one left who'd want to keep in touch with me as most of my school friends had moved away.'

'Well, your father owned the house you grew up in and he bought the furniture. He didn't expect you to move out so quickly after she died, though.'

'I moved because I'd already finished my apprenticeship and had been working on motor cars. I was offered a job by the proprietor here, not only repairing cars but building them. I was eager to begin doing that.'

'I see. Well, now that I have found you, it's my pleasant duty to tell you that your father has left the house you used to live in to you.'

Adam could only gape. This lawyer was giving him one shock after the other. Not only a father but a house.

Owning your own home was rare for someone from his background, but was a wonderful thought.

'Why did you move so quickly, Mr – um Entwistle?'

'I knew I couldn't afford the rent on such a house and anyway, the job I'd been offered was here in Blackpool. I didn't keep in touch with the neighbours, who were pleasant enough but much older than me.'

When the lawyer shook his head sadly and made a tutting noise, he asked, 'What happened to the house after I left then, if I own it now?'

'A neighbour has been looking after it because your father hoped you'd contact someone, perhaps at Christmas to wish them well. But you didn't. When he died suddenly we had to hire a private investigator to find you.'

'Where did this James Entwistle come from?'

'He only ever answered to the name Jim. He was a farmer in a small Pennine valley called Ollindale. Your mother came from there originally too. I'm surprised she refused to tell you about him after you grew up.'

'I think she was afraid I might go looking for him. When I turned twenty-one and completed my apprenticeship, I begged her to tell me but all she would say was that he'd never told her he was married, so hadn't earned the right to get to know me. She said I was not to think badly of him, that he'd done his best to look after us, given his own circumstances. She could be very stubborn about that, so in the end I stopped asking.'

'From what he told me, Mr Entwistle loved your mother greatly and had been very happy to have a son by her to carry on his bloodline. He paid her through me to bring you up decently and see that you got a good education and then an apprenticeship to some trade. He didn't want you to grow up to be an idle gentleman.'

Adam took a deep breath and felt anguish spike through him as it did every time he thought or spoke about his mother. She'd been a good mother in every other way than providing him with a father. 'What did the letter he wrote to you say?'

'He told me that he wanted to leave everything he owned to you, as he'd specified in his will, and trusted me to see to it that this was done. He expressed sadness that he'd not been able to share your life. Here's his letter to you. I have no idea what he wrote in that.'

He opened his briefcase and took out a sealed envelope, which he gave to Adam. 'I think you'll understand the situation better if you read that before I go on. He told me he'd explained things to you.'

'Very well.' Adam took a deep breath and faced it, sadness washing through him, because this was as close as he was ever going to get to meeting his father now.

My dear son,

I'm not good with words but I want to tell you that if things had been different, I'd have married your mother like a shot and brought you up myself.

As it is, I've been legally tied to a bitter, childless woman and all I've been able to do for you is pay your mother an allowance, provide her with a home and put away money so that when I die, there will be something left for you that's worth inheriting.

I shan't tell you what to do with it, Adam. That's entirely up to you. I've been told what to do all too often in my life, and with poor outcomes.

Mr Genner will give you the details of your inheritance and hand everything over to you. Use it to have a good life and please don't think badly of me.

Your loving father,
Jim Entwistle

PS *I'd be very happy if you changed your surname to Entwistle but that too is up to you.*

Adam read it through again, then looked up at the lawyer. 'I find it hard to believe that he's left everything to me! Had he no other close relatives?'

'None that he cared about, or even liked. I could do nothing about that. I suggested Jim contact you first when his wife and then again when your mother died, but he said it was too late and he was too old and infirm to change his way of life. And anyway, he didn't get on with his family so he felt there was nothing to be gained by introducing them to you.'

He paused to let that sink in then continued, 'I wonder, could you finish work now and come to my hotel room to go through the details of what you've inherited in private? It amounts to a comfortable independence and unless you wish to live lavishly, you'll never need to work again. But you will need to deal with a few things and plan your next few steps, whatever your ultimate decision. If I can be of assistance in any way, I am at your service.'

By this time Adam felt as if the world had stood him on end and was shaking him about mercilessly, like a child's rag doll. He didn't know what to think or say about all this. 'Yes. I suppose I'd better come and discuss it.'

Mr Genner gave him a gentle smile. 'A bit of a shock, eh?'

'A lot of a shock, sir. Um, I'll have to explain this to my employer and change out of my dirty working overalls before I leave here. Tell me which hotel it is and I'll join you there.'

'There are a lot of hotels in Blackpool. I don't know it at all well and we don't want to miss one another, so I'll wait for you here, if that's all right with you? I've told the cab driver to wait for us, and I have some other legal papers I need to go through, so I shan't be impatient if I have to wait. Take as long as you need to wash and change.'

'Thank you.'

There was something kind and trustworthy about Mr Genner and that more than anything else reassured Adam that this was all genuine. He really had inherited a fortune, as Tom had joked. Well, it would seem like a fortune to him if there was more to come.

When Adam went back into the workshop and explained the situation, Tom was just as amazed by it all as he was.

'And you had no idea, Adam lad?'

'No idea whatsoever. Not about any of what he's just told me.'

'I don't know what to say.'

'I don't know what to say, think or do, except find out more from Mr Genner. Um, is it all right if I take the rest of the day off? I—'

'Of course it is. You can tell me all about it tomorrow. I'm very glad for you, lad. Go and get changed out of your overalls and make yourself look as smart as you can. You want to make a good impression on this lawyer.'

He turned as their apprentice came in. 'You can clear up Adam's tools for the day, Jack. He's had a bit of a shock and needs to go and speak to his lawyer.'

Jack stared from one to the other. 'I hope it's not bad news.'

It was Tom who answered. 'No, it's good news.'

The lad nodded and began to clear up the day's mess, whistling cheerfully.

Adam walked across to what they called the 'wash-up room' and changed his clothes quickly, making sure he scrubbed his fingernails till they were pink and clean. He even combed his dark, unruly hair till it was lying neatly for once.

When he came out to join the others again, Tom nodded and said quietly, 'That looks much better. Good luck, lad.'

'I think I'm going to need it to cope with all this.'

'Nay, you'll manage just fine. No one's ever accused you of being stupid. And this is good news, think on, not bad.'

'I hope so.' He went to collect Mr Genner from the waiting room and followed him outside to where the cab had been waiting all this time. The extravagance of doing something like this shocked him.

Indeed, everything that had happened during the past hour had shocked and astonished him and he was finding it hard to think straight let alone speak sensibly. To his relief, the lawyer didn't try to chat as they jolted across town in the hackney cab, just stared at what they were passing, only speaking to express amazement at the sight of how tall Blackpool Tower was. It had only been open a few years and visitors often gaped at the height of it. Some went up to the top, and Adam had done that too. But he'd found it a bit boring after he'd stared round a bit at the view and hadn't bothered to go up it again.

'I didn't expect it to be so big!' the lawyer exclaimed. 'Or so high. I'd not like to go up to the top.'

He nodded and Mr Genner craned his neck to get a last sight of it, then leaned back in his seat and kept silent.

Adam was glad of that. The whole world seemed so strange today. The sea to the left of them that was sullen and heaving wearily up and down beneath a grey sky. Like him, it seemed to be simply putting up with what was happening around it, helpless to change things.

Entwistle, he thought. His name ought to have been Entwistle.

The lawyer's hotel room turned out to be a suite in a large hotel Adam had never even gone inside before. It was very luxurious indeed, which only increased Adam's feeling of disorientation. Surely this was a nightmare and he'd wake up any minute, struggling to get down to breakfast with the other lodgers, then to work on time.

But the strangeness continued unabated. Mr Genner rang a bell and asked the maid who answered it to fetch them a pot of tea and some biscuits, then gestured to Adam to sit in a comfortable armchair near the fire.

'I'll go through the details of the bequest now, if that's all right with you.'

'Yes, please.' Perhaps that would make it seem real.

'You are now the owner of several small houses and a large sum of money lodged in a savings account with a big national bank which has a branch in Ollerthwaite.'

Adam couldn't speak, he was so shocked.

The lawyer allowed him a few moments for that to sink in then gave him a few more details, smiling at Adam as he'd finished with, 'My client said you'd have no knowledge of him or what he owned, and I can see from your astonishment that he was right on all counts.'

'How could I? I didn't even know his name until today.'

'He said he'd trusted your mother implicitly to keep his identity secret as she'd promised.' Mr Genner waited a minute then said, 'So you can't possibly have any idea what you will want to do next.' He wasn't asking a question, merely stating the obvious.

'No. I'm still trying to take it all in. Still trying to believe this is real, actually.'

'Well, it is real but there is no hurry for you to do anything now that we've found you, and are sure you're the right man.'

'If you have any advice or suggestions, I'd welcome them.'

'I suggest you go back to your lodgings and think hard about what you want to do, what sort of life you want to lead from now on. Might I ask, are you courting anyone?'

'No. I've never met any woman I want to spend the rest of my life with.'

'Then that's one problem you don't have. How about you come to see me again tomorrow morning and we'll have another chat.'

'Yes. I think that would be best. At the moment, I haven't the faintest idea of what I want to do with my life.' Except finish the car he'd been building for himself. He could buy any part he wanted or needed for it now.

'Finish your tea, then, and I'll ask them to call you a cab.'

Adam drained the cup, welcoming the liquid's warmth, but turned down a refill. 'I don't need a cab, thank you, Mr Genner. I'd rather walk back to my lodgings and let the fresh air clear my head.'

The lawyer pushed a large envelope across to him. 'As you please. You'd better take this with you, though. It's a complete list of what you've inherited. You can re-read it tonight.'

Adam didn't even want to touch it, which was foolish. But he felt as if once he opened it, he'd be trapped in a world he didn't understand. 'I must seem stupid,' he muttered as he stood up.

'No. Not stupid at all. But definitely in a state of shock. My best advice is to do nothing till you've grown used to the thought of what's happened. Then you'll be able to think things through logically and make sensible decisions.'

'That sounds to be sound advice to me.'

'I do my best to advise my clients sensibly. I've lived long enough to learn a few things about life.'

Adam walked home along the seafront, arrived at the end of the street where his lodgings were and hesitated. After a moment or two he continued past it, not going back again till he'd walked for miles and the sun was beginning to set.

He looked at his watch as he went inside. Nicely in time for tea, and nicely tired too.

As he washed his hands before joining the other men, he glanced out of the window. The days were getting longer and spring was under way, but the rain that had been threatening for the last hour or so of his walk suddenly rattled against the windows.

Plenty of time to sit and think tonight. Why could he not deal with the situation more sensibly? Because it was such a big shock, that's why.

He looked at the big envelope, which was crumpled where he'd clutched it during his walk. He didn't want to look at what it contained, not yet anyway, so he stuffed it under his pillow. How could he think clearly what to do when he still felt dazed and stupid with shock? Well, it wasn't every day that your whole world was turned upside down, was it?

He didn't say anything to his landlady or his fellow lodgers about his unexpected inheritance. Unusually for him, he didn't eat much, couldn't seem to swallow food easily. That made his landlady frown at him and ask, 'Are you feeling all right, Adam? You're not sickening for something?'

'I'm fine. It's just that I, um, heard today of a relative dying and it was a bit of a shock.'

'Oh, dear. I'm so sorry. Why didn't you say?'

He shrugged. 'I can't seem to think about it clearly. It . . . wasn't expected. I'll go up to my bedroom and have a quiet think about him, try to come to terms with it, I suppose.'

'Well, there's nothing you can do about death, Adam. We all have to face it one day, for ourselves and for those we love.'

'Yes. I know.' He stood up and went quickly to his room before any of the other lodgers could offer their condolences or try to find out if he'd inherited anything. Eight young men sharing lodgings made it difficult to do anything secretly.

He lit the gas fire, putting another shilling in the meter so that it'd last all evening and made himself comfortable in front of its cosy warmth, reading and re-reading the detailed list of what he'd inherited, utterly amazed to find that there were six small houses as well as the larger one where his father had lived and the one where he had spent most of his life with his mother. That made *eight!* And there was a lot of money in the bank, too, an enormous amount it seemed to him.

As it sank in that he really would be more than comfortably off, he thanked his father mentally and tried to think what to do first about it all. He could normally work out quite easily how to deal with difficult situations, prided himself on coping with whatever life threw at him. But he had never before inherited a fortune, had he?

The lawyer might think it was a modest one but to Adam it sounded like a huge amount of money. And eight houses altogether. *Eight!*

Eventually he started yawning, switched off the gas fire and went to bed. Even though he felt tired, he lay awake for what seemed a long time before he started to feel truly sleepy.

When he woke, it was just getting light and he knew exactly what he had to do first – it was as if the idea had slipped into his mind while he was asleep. He was going to this Eastby End place to have a look at his inheritance without anyone there knowing who he was. That would make it feel real, surely?

He'd look at the house where his father had lived. Would that make the man seem real at last? Who knew? Would that house make a home for him from now on? Could a place feel like a home when you lived there alone? When he thought of his own home of many years, his mother was always there too.

Ironically, he'd have to ask Mr Genner to advance him a little money to pay his expenses for the journey because most of what he'd earned had been going on lodgings and buying parts for the motor car he was building for himself in his spare time, doing this in a shed rented from a neighbour of his landlady.

He suddenly realised that he'd be able to work on the car full-time and without skimping from now on. He'd be able to build his car properly and would enjoy that. They were starting to build cheaper cars for ordinary people in America now, and he supposed that was what most people would want, but he was going to enjoy building his own.

He'd see Mr Genner this morning and then start making proper plans.

He'd have a chat with Tom, too. He was sure his friend would understand that Adam couldn't go on working for him now that he'd been thrown on to another track in life. Surely he'd understand? Adam could think of two other men who'd jump at the chance to take his job, so he'd not be leaving his friend in the lurch.

He went to see Tom first, because they started work early at the garage. The two of them had a long chat, then he packed all his things ready to collect later today and left them in the rented shed with the car.

Next he went to the library to look at a map book and find out exactly where this Ollindale valley was situated.

By then it was time to go and see the kindly lawyer to discuss the visit to Ollindale.

16

When they were about halfway from their farm on their way to pick up Rachel and show her round Eastby End the morning after her arrival, Flora said suddenly, 'Something came to me during the night that might help Rachel and help us to reach more people with the district nursing services. I've been thinking about it ever since I woke up.'

'Go on.'

'If Miss Norris seems suitable, I think we should provide her with an assistant to accompany her when she makes calls, especially when she goes out at night. She won't be as vulnerable then.'

Walter let the pony slow down to a halt and glanced at her in surprise. 'That'll make it more expensive to set things up.'

'Yes, but what she said made me realise there was actually too much work for one person. Eastby End might not cover a large area, but there are a lot of people crammed into those ramshackle buildings and a lot of them don't look well.'

'Too many of them in such a small space by far and too few jobs.'

'Everyone agrees about that, but the council can hardly throw them out of their homes, can it?'

'If only there were somewhere to throw them to!'

'Most of all, though, Walter love, I don't like the thought of our nurse going out alone on night calls in that part of the valley. I'd not like to do that myself. Why didn't I think of that when I was setting things up? I was too eager to start and take advantage of Miss Norris becoming available, I suppose, and of the charity money you have control over.'

She let that sink in for a moment then went on, 'A practical person working with our nurse could help her and the patients in lots of ways. And another woman will make her situation more respectable too.'

Walter nodded his head slowly. 'I never even thought of that aspect. District nursing is such a new thing outside some of the big towns and cities, isn't it? And we definitely rushed into it too quickly.'

'The most important thing to sort out next, to me, is the safety aspect. Do you think having two women will be enough to deter people from attacking Rachel physically if she has to go out at night? Or attacking her morals, knowing what some folk can be like, how suspicious they can be of women who go out to work, especially younger women.'

'Yes, two women working together will make a big difference to safety and look better.'

But he continued to frown, so she asked, 'What else is worrying you about my idea, Walter love?'

'There would be two of them most of the time, but the assistant would have to live close by to be easily available for any night visits and even then, it would mean Rachel needing to go out alone in the dark to fetch her assistant.'

'Well, she wouldn't want to share her flat even if there was another bedroom. You saw how delighted she was to have a place of her own.'

They were both quiet, thinking it through, then Flora said, 'I wonder if Mrs Prior would let us make a simple room to house an assistant in her cellar if we pay extra rent for it? I'd guess she'd be happy to earn more money. Would it be very expensive to enclose an area down there and fit it out with a water supply and gas ring?'

Walter frowned, considering the details needed for living in reasonable comfort. 'No. I don't think it'd cost much to create a cellar room for one person. It already has a door leading outside and a window, on account of it being on a slope with one side above ground and the rear built into the hill. So there will be adequate ventilation without the cost of knocking holes into walls.'

'Didn't Mrs Prior say there was a cold water tap there already as well? We could have another tap and sink connected to it quite easily. What about a gas ring?'

'I don't think that would be hard to install so that she could heat water and cook simple meals. Anything else essential?'

'How about a small gas fire, Walter? She'd need heating of some sort.'

'If we're putting in a gas ring, we can add a small fire at the same time.'

'And she could use the old outside lavatory across the yard.'

'Would doing that upset her?'

Flora gave him a wry smile. 'Believe me, a person who's lived mainly in slums with shared and crowded facilities would find having their own room and conveniences a big step up in the world, even if she had to go outside to use the lav.' She patted his hand. 'I shan't say anything to Miss Norris about an assistant till I see how she goes this morning. If she doesn't get on with the sort of people she'll need to deal with here in Eastby End, I doubt she'll want to stay anyway.'

'But surely someone who's been nursing for several years and has recently completed a special course on district nursing will already be used to dealing with poorer people?' he protested.

'You'd hope so. From what I hear about that course, it teaches them that there's a lot of good old-fashioned scrubbing involved in treating such people in their own homes and getting them up to Nightingale standards of cleanliness. The latter change on its own can actually reduce sickness in general quite markedly.'

'Does it really make that much difference?'

'Oh, yes, Walter. You get a big improvement even without doctors and medicines.'

'Well, we'll soon see how it goes, one way or the other. And if you think she's going to be all right, I'll find the money from that fund to pay for an assistant and creating a cellar room. I don't want anything to stop what we're trying to do in Eastby End. That part of town needs bringing out of the Dark Ages in several ways.'

She nodded decisively. 'We'll start making a difference to Eastby, somehow.'

Rachel woke early on her first morning in the valley and was ready long before Walter and Flora arrived to show her round Eastby End. She felt nervous, worrying alternately about taking on too much if she attempted to do a job like this on her own, and also concerned about her personal safety if the area was too rough after dark.

She'd put on her uniform today, both to give herself courage and to start getting the locals used to the sight of it. She'd adapted it herself from the type of uniform the Queen herself had approved for other groups of nurses. Like many of the poorer women she served, she wore a separate skirt and blouse. The skirt was shorter than those worn by most ladies because that was more practical when you were doing a lot of walking round poorer areas.

She was considering getting a bicycle to ride but how would you keep it safe when you were inside tending to a patient? No, she might just get one for her own use and like other women who rode them, keep her skirts shorter.

Her starched white pinafore covered a dark blue skirt in a hard-wearing heavy cotton material and her top was made of the same blue cotton. As always, she wore the brightly polished brassard with its insignia hanging from a ribbon round her neck and was very proud of it because the professional status it showed had been hard earned.

She wore a cap that was ornate and flattering, and also useful for keeping one's hair out of the way. No one would mistake that sort of cap for part of a servant's uniform, which the nurses had been told during their training was important because they needed what they were doing to be respected.

The cotton material was very sturdy and washed well, so she'd be able to keep it clean. She had to have two or three skirts and tops, because even though she'd wear a smock over her clothes for messy work, the garments underneath it sometimes got soiled, what with showing patients and their families how to scrub a floor and surfaces until they were truly clean, and because of wounds leaking various kinds of body fluids.

In one sense district nursing was based on a battle for cleanliness of both surroundings and patients. This could make a surprising difference to poor people's health and it wasn't too expensive to achieve and keep up once they'd got into the habit. She showed the way by example a lot of the time and the fact that she didn't shirk the most dirty jobs and was willing to help scrub their floors could make a big difference to the respect she was accorded by patients and their families once they got to know her.

She smiled to see Walter and Flora draw up in front of her house. They were so kind and friendly, it made her feel that things would turn out well here.

She was so tired of moving from one place to another, had been feeling desperate for a home of her own for quite a while. But not marriage. She could never risk that. But at least she'd got rid of Pershore now. And she'd do nothing to attract any other men.

When Rachel joined them outside, Flora said, 'The uniform looks very smart, Miss Norris. I'm glad you're wearing it from the start. It'll be good for people to start recognising it.'

'That's what I thought.'

Walter joined in. 'We plan to drive you round Eastby End first to get a feel for the place and you'll see more from up here on the trap than you would on foot. Then we'll leave the pony and trap at some nearby livery stables so that we can walk round the centre with you, ending up at the former shop we've rented for you to work from.'

'I shall be interested to get a feel for the whole area first.'

'Good.' Flora stared up at the cloudy sky. 'I just hope the rain will hold off for the rest of the morning at least.'

It didn't take long for them to get from the flat to the central part of Eastby, which was a good thing to know, because it meant she'd be able to walk to and fro easily to visit her patients. But Rachel's heart sank at what she saw as she stared round from her vantage point.

There was a central space of scruffy ground, not large or cared for in any way that she could see. Near it were a few dwellings, which included a few shabby shops. Two women were standing chatting nearby and had turned to stare at the pony trap and their expressions said they mistrusted the people riding in it.

These ramshackle buildings were surrounded by houses that had been crammed together in terraces, some of them looking ready to fall down had they not been able to lean against one another. Even the better ones were often in need of repairs.

There was a small and very simply built church at one end of the central area and even that looked shabby and neglected.

Walter saw her studying it and said, 'That's an offshoot of the main church in Ollerthwaite, built in better times. It's now as shabby inside as out, I'm afraid. The curate comes to take a service on the first and third Sundays of the month; otherwise a caretaker opens it in the mornings and locks it up at night, letting people shelter there in bad weather.'

As for the people they passed in the streets, most of them looked hungry and even if not actually ill then not truly well either, Rachel thought. The scrawny children in particular tore at her heartstrings and made her wish she were rich enough to feed them all properly. Children often did that to her.

What had she got herself into? How could one person, even a trained district nurse, do much against all this need and hunger?

'The place seems worse than I'd remembered now we're seeing it on foot. I don't often get out here,' Walter said abruptly after they'd walked part of the way round the central area, passing the general store and a small greengrocer with no stock displayed outside the shop and a butcher with very little meat on display in the window. At the end furthest from the church was an empty shop.

'That's the one available for a clinic.'

'Oh. It looks . . . rather run-down.'

He shook his head and turned to the younger woman. 'That window wasn't broken when I came out here to look round. I'll send someone to repair it.'

Never mind the empty shop, Rachel didn't like the looks of the area and couldn't think what to say. She wasn't surprised at Mr Crossley's next words.

'I'll be frank about one thing, Miss Norris. I don't think you should go out to visit patients in Eastby End after dark on your own. Maybe we should just set up a clinic in this shop as planned, which people can come to during the day for help, as we have done in the centre of town for the nurse there.'

Rachel told him the truth, which was one of the reasons she believed in the value of district nursing. 'The trouble is the people who need my help most won't be able to walk to where they can get it, and there can be

emergencies after dark as well as by day and— Oh, no!'
She stopped walking to stare across the street to where an
older woman had suddenly crumpled up and collapsed.

The younger woman who'd been walking with her let
out a wail and tried to pull her companion to her feet but
she was clearly unconscious.

Rachel's instincts took over and without thinking she
ran across the street and crouched down beside the
unconscious woman.

A shabby man who had been watching them from a
group standing on one corner moved slightly to keep his
eye on them.

'Who's that female wearing the fancy uniform?' He
wasn't fond of uniforms, not after his months in jail. 'She
must be a newcomer. She's pretty, isn't she?'

'Yes. Very pretty.'

'Don't you know who she is?'

'Probably the new nurse. I heard them Crossleys were
bringing one to work in Eastby.'

'I'd like to be nursed by her.'

'You'll not get near her, Pete.'

'They can't watch her every hour of the day and night,
can they?' Her connection with the Crossleys only made
her more interesting, as far as Pete was concerned. He
had a score to settle with Mr-Walter-Bloody-Crossley
and he'd do it too, however long it took. And now that
he'd seen her, he fancied having a go at the nurse at some
point, too. He'd missed that sort of hanky-panky in jail.

'It's not worth it,' his companion said. 'They'll guard
her carefully. I'm not getting involved if you're intending
to get up to that sort of thing again.'

He laughed.

But his companion had moved away and was striding off down an alley, so he stopped talking to himself and followed.

The trio had moved away now as well, but he'd find out about her.

And he'd pay Walter Crossley back for helping put him in jail – one way or another.

17

Rachel felt the unconscious woman's pulse, which was a bit fluttery but not too bad. 'Do you know anything that's wrong with her?' she asked the younger woman, who had stood up again now.

'She's not had much to eat, miss, an' she's got a big sore on her leg. We were going to see if there was any food been left out at the church. Sometimes they give it away to people. She's got a voucher for it.'

Rachel studied her patient. This didn't seem like a seizure, but the poor woman was still only semi-conscious and had made no attempt to get up. She looked as if she wasn't eating properly.

'She fainted yesterday as well, but not for this long,' the younger woman said. 'She's my aunty, an' I knew she'd had nothing to eat, so I cut her a slice of our loaf last night an' made her take a bite or two before she went back home. But I bet she gave most of the rest to her grandkids. Their father's run off an' now they're all living in one room, her as well. He said he was fed up of kids skriking, only how can you stop them crying when they're hungry, eh? Well, you can't. An' their mother isn't well, neither.'

Walter had stood listening to this tale of woe and looking round for help to move the woman, because he and Flora were getting too old to do heavy lifting.

'Don't try to lift her yourself, Miss Norris,' he said. 'And Flora, you stand back. That wrist has only just got better so you can't risk damaging it. Let's see if there's someone else around who can help.'

Since there were no men to be seen, he beckoned to a tall woman standing nearby who looked strong. 'A shilling for you if you'll help me carry this poor woman along to the church. Can you manage that, do you think?'

The woman's face brightened. 'I can do it more easily on my own, sir. She's that thin, she probably won't weigh much more than a child.'

She proved how easy it was to pick the woman up and Rachel hurried ahead of them into the church. Only one of the double entrance doors was open but she quickly unbolted the other one and while Walter joined his helper to lift the woman up the uneven steps, she went inside and called out for help.

But there was no response. Walter had been right. There was no one on duty there during the day nor was there anyone inside praying.

The niece of the semi-conscious woman looked round, not hiding her disappointment that no one was offering food to poor people today.

'They've not given out anything to eat all week,' the woman carrying the patient said. 'Someone told me Mrs Dudson is ill and no one else has took over. Where shall I put her, Mr Crossley?'

'You know who I am?'

'Most people in the valley do, sir.'

'Lay her down on that bench at the side.'

The woman did that and looked round. 'The caretaker's opened the doors but I bet he's gone home again till it's time to close it up. It's a godsend sometimes, this place is, when it rains and you have to seek shelter quickly. An' so far no one's damaged anything, thank goodness. Well, even them lads use it sometimes. They know there's nothing here to pinch an' it won't get opened if anything's damaged.'

Rachel checked the patient's pulse again and asked her to open her eyes, but received only an incoherent murmur in response, a flutter of the eyelids and a groan.

'Is there some drinking water here at least?' she asked. 'She looks dehydrated as well as hungry.'

'I know where it is,' Walter said. 'It's a water fountain though, so I'll have to see if I can find something to bring her a drink in.'

The woman who'd carried their patient had been staring at Rachel's uniform. 'Can I ask where you're from, miss? I haven't never seen anyone dressed like that before.'

'I'm the new district nurse for Eastby,' Rachel said. 'And what I'm wearing is a copy of the uniform the Queen herself chose for her special nurses to show the people needing help who we are. And so is this.' She touched the brassard hanging round her neck.

'The Queen chose it? Well, I never!' She was still staring. 'What does a district nurse do that's different from other nurses, if you don't mind me asking?'

'I don't mind at all.' The woman had an intelligent look on her face and Rachel had found that people who asked a lot of sensible questions usually turned out to be the clever ones. 'We run clinics where sick people can get help but we also go to visit some of them in their own homes.'

Walter came back just then, carrying a battered tin beaker without a handle carefully. 'District nurses only visit the ones who can't get to the clinic,' he put in hastily.

Rachel held her patient's head up and managed to persuade her to swallow a few mouthfuls of water. When she laid her down again, she said, 'I think we should try to get her something to eat as well. Could you buy us a loaf, do you think, Mr Crossley?'

Before he could answer, the woman turned to him. 'Beg pardon, sir, but you said you'd give me a shilling an' I'm a bit hungry myself.'

He felt in his pocket and pulled out a shilling coin. 'Sorry. You've certainly earned it. There you are and thank you for your help.'

'Thank you for the chance to earn some money, sir.'

'I'm not quite sure where the baker's shop is. I don't know Eastby End very well. Could you tell me?'

'I can show you where it is. No charge for that. Now that I've got some money, I'll be going there myself to see if I can get some broken bits of loaf for my sister's kids. You get more bread that way.'

'I might need your help again so if you can wait to buy the bread and stay with us for a while longer, I'll give you another shilling.'

The woman nodded eagerly. 'Happy to do that, sir.'

When the two of them came back to the church with the bread they found that the patient had regained consciousness and was sitting up on the bench, leaning back against the wall.

Flora was standing to one side, watching Rachel, whose attention was mainly on her patient.

'I made a preliminary check of her leg,' Rachel said. 'It needs careful attention or it'll go septic. Can we take her into the empty shop we're going to use as a clinic, Mr Crossley? You said you'd left some basic medical supplies there and I need to clean and dress that leg properly.'

'There's not much there. I was expecting to get what's needed when you start and can give me a list.'

'Is there a kettle and any gas to boil it on? It'd be better to use boiled water to clean up that sore properly.'

He looked at her in dismay. 'There isn't a kettle there yet and the gas isn't getting connected till tomorrow, I'm afraid. I'll obtain one for you of course and anything else you think important.' He held out the loaf.

'My hands are probably cleaner than yours, Miss Norris,' Flora said. 'Let me see to giving her some bread.'

She broke off some of the softer bread from inside the loaf and gave it to their patient, who seemed to be lacking several of her teeth and would have found it difficult to bite the crust properly. After managing to chew and swallow a couple of mouthfuls, the woman closed her eyes and leaned back again. She was obviously in no fit state to walk.

'I can carry her again if you like,' their helper offered. 'She doesn't weigh much, poor thing. I can allus go to the baker's afterwards for my own loaf, like you said. '

'This woman is in desperate need of food, but she must eat slowly, only a mouthful or two at a time, then wait to make sure it stays down,' Rachel said. 'We don't want her vomiting anything up.'

Flora turned to give Walter a quick nod to show her approval of how Rachel was dealing with this situation.

He was surprised at how confident the young woman suddenly seemed, and was pleased with how she'd taken charge without needing to be told what to do after she saw the woman collapse.

'Let's take her to the clinic and allow her to rest for a while, Walter.' Flora turned to the woman's companion. 'What's your friend's name?'

'She's my Auntie Wilma. I can't help carry her because of this.' She patted her bulging stomach. 'Not due for another three months, but kicking a lot already.'

Rachel bent over the patient. 'Wilma, we're going to take you somewhere more comfortable to lie down for a while.' She beckoned to their strong helper and whispered, 'Are you sure you can manage on your own?'

'Aye, miss. I'm as strong as most men, allus have been.' She proved it by picking up the woman again and saying, 'Right. I'm ready.'

Walter led the way round the corner to the former shop and unlocked the door. Their helper didn't wait to be told but walked inside and set her burden down on the threadbare old sofa, then stepped to one side and waited.

Flora went over to her and murmured, 'Don't leave yet. Are you looking for steady work?'

'Yes. Isn't everybody round here? There isn't much going though, especially for women.'

'If you wait till we've seen to this poor woman, I may know of a job for you. If I don't, I'll still pay you another shilling for waiting.'

'I'll wait as long as you need.' She smiled. This must be her lucky day to run into these people.

18

The former shop was almost bare except for a short counter of well-scratched wood, a few old pieces of furniture and several oddments of crockery on one of the shelves behind the counter.

Rachel found an old sink in one corner and a few rags stuffed behind the chipped old bowls on the shelf.

'I'll manage with these for the moment.' She used one cleaner-looking rag to wipe a couple of bowls under the cold water tap. Sadly, there was no way to heat the water yet, so that was the best she could do.

'Sorry about the lack of a kettle,' Flora said apologetically. 'We didn't expect to be using this place so soon.'

There was a broom and some other cleaning equipment jumbled together in a corner. These were well worn but still had some use in them, Rachel noted. She understood only too well people's need to keep costs down in these hungry times.

Epidemics seemed to have been coming and going all her adult life, both major and minor local ones. The Queen's Diamond Jubilee last year had cheered people up, but not for long. And even the Queen was getting so old people kept wondering how long she'd last and dreading her leaving them. How strange it'd feel to have a king.

When she'd cleaned and wrapped up the wound as carefully as she could, Rachel stood up and stretched, then saw Flora beckoning to her. She asked Walter to keep an eye on the sick woman and to call her back if Wilma grew restless then moved across to join his wife.

'I have an idea to make the job of district nurse here easier and more efficient for you.' Flora explained that they could hire an assistant and house her in the cellar of the same building as the flat. 'What do you think? That would mean two of you to go out on calls – far safer as well as getting the work done more quickly. And that woman who's helped us today might be suitable.'

Rachel looked at Flora in surprise then studied the woman waiting patiently near the entrance, watching what was going on with a bright, alert look on her face.

'She's certainly strong and seems sensible. It would help greatly to have someone to assist me. I feel guilty saying it but with the best will in the world, it'd be hard for me to do the work efficiently if I were completely on my own here, Mrs Crossley.'

'How about offering her the job, then?'

'I'd like to ask her a few questions first, if you don't mind.'

'Go ahead. It'd be no use hiring someone you don't approve of or like. I'll stand to one side in case I can give you any information about the job but I'll leave it to you otherwise.' Flora moved away a little.

Rachel went across to the woman and introduced herself properly. 'What's your name?'

'Hanny Best, miss.'

'The job Mrs Crossley has been talking about would be working with me. It wouldn't suit everybody, so I need to tell you a little more about it. Have you had much to do with sick people before?'

The woman stared at her, unable to hide her surprise. 'We all have round here, miss. It's not a healthy place to live.'

Rachel patted her arm. 'Do you usually have good health yourself?'

'I do nowadays. I make sure I get food for myself before I give it to anyone else. I make no excuse for putting myself first because there's no one else to look after me if I fall ill. As it is I can sometimes help my family and friends.'

'I agree that's sensible if you're alone in the world. Do you get upset at the sight of blood or injuries?'

Hanny rolled her eyes. 'Of course not. Can I ask what the job of yours pays and what exactly it'd involve? That's important too. I'm sleeping on my sister's floor at the moment so I'll jump at a chance to get a bed of my own, however humble the lodgings.'

'Good.' Rachel turned to Flora. 'Perhaps you'd tell Hanny something about what an assistant might earn, Mrs Crossley?'

So Flora explained about the wages and spoke about the possibility of Hanny having a room of her own in a half-cellar.

'A room of my own!'

Rachel watched Hanny beam at the thought of that. She'd liked the woman's steady, thoughtful expression and her smile was warm, but she was worried about how poorly clothed she was. How would she cope if her garments got badly soiled and had to be changed, as they often did in the work involved in this sort of nursing? They'd been taught to try to bring their patients' surrounding up to nursing standards of cleanliness so there was a lot of scrubbing to do as well as tending to injuries or trying to bring down fevers.

She asked about clothes after Flora had finished telling them about the potential room.

'I only have one other set of clothes, miss, an' they're worse than these. I could maybe get a clean sack or two and make aprons out of them an' I'd buy other things to wear as soon as I'd earned enough money.' She looked from Rachel to Mrs Crossley anxiously.

'I can supply her with some second-hand clothes at no charge,' Flora said quietly. 'They'd still have some wear in them but will be old-fashioned and shabby.'

Hanny waved one hand dismissively. 'I don't care what they look like as long as they cover me decently and keep me warm.' She waited, anxiety still radiating from her.

Rachel could understand how unhappy she would be to lose this chance of employment so didn't keep her waiting. 'Would you like to work with me, then, Hanny? I think you'd do well. Don't you agree, Flora?'

'Yes, I do. Will fifteen shillings a week, together with lodgings that have light and heating provided suit you, Hanny?'

It was more than most women would be able to earn, but the wages people paid women always made Flora angry because these women still had to eat and put a roof over their heads, didn't they? Yet people expected them to manage on half a man's wages, even if they had no man to support them.

'Yes. Oh, yes please. It'd suit me just fine.' Hanny gulped a couple of times then her control slipped and tears welled in her eyes and rolled down her cheeks. 'You won't regret it, miss. I promise you won't. I'll work really hard and I'm sorry to cry on you. It's just . . . such a wonderful chance. An' to think I was feeling down in the dumps only this morning.'

Rachel gave her a quick hug. 'Now, stop crying and let's see if we can make this poor woman more comfortable and feed her another mouthful or two of bread. Do you know where exactly she lives, Hanny?'

'Not exactly but her friend will know. Shall I ask her? She's still waiting outside.'

'Yes. And take her a chunk of bread too.'

Hanny tore more off the loaf, for lack of a knife, and took it outside, coming back with the necessary information. 'I can carry Wilma there. It isn't far from here. Well, nowhere's very far in Eastby, is it? All the houses and people are piled on top of one another like dirty rubbish round here.' She cast a quick, disapproving look round and Rachel had to agree with her description of the area.

'I think Hanny will do well as an assistant,' Walter whispered to his wife in a low voice. 'She's very strong for a woman, isn't she?'

'Yes.' But Flora turned to Rachel first to confirm the position. 'I'm assuming you'll be all right to take the nursing job if you have an assistant?'

'Yes. I'd been wondering whether I could manage everything on my own but I'm sure two of us will be able to cope reasonably well.'

'We hadn't planned the details of your job very well, I'm afraid.'

'No, you hadn't.'

Flora gave a wry smile at this bluntness. 'I don't usually mess things up, but I got a bit distracted by spraining my wrist and district nursing is such a new way of doing things, we're still learning about the practicalities of what's involved.'

Walter joined in. 'Now that we know you're staying, I'll start looking for other ways of improving things for you and your patients, Rachel. There are people in the valley who like to help others now and then. Sometimes they can only manage to do it in small ways, but every little counts, doesn't it?'

'It certainly does. A bit of help at the right time can make the difference between life and death.'

'Right then. We can turn this empty shop into a proper clinic now. People have already offered donations to help set it up.'

Flora gave his arm a nudge. 'Don't forget to include Joss Townley. He told you he wanted to help improve Eastby End, didn't he?'

'I won't forget him.' He turned to explain to Rachel who Townley was. 'He lives just outside Eastby, you see, so he doesn't want a big slum on his doorstep and anyway he seems a decent chap who cares about his fellow human beings.'

'Is he a farmer?'

'No. He owns Townley House. It's not exactly a manor house but it's the biggest house at this side of Ollerthwaite. No one's quite sure what he's going to do with it as it's been standing empty for years. He doesn't seem short of money and he's already said he wants to help improve living conditions and general safety round here.'

'Safety?'

'There are one or two villains around, and some groups of older lads who cause a bit of trouble, but then I don't think there's anywhere that doesn't breed a few rascals.

There isn't enough money in Eastby to attract big-scale villains and crime.'

As Rachel bent over the patient to check something, Flora dug her elbow in her husband's side and whispered, 'Talking of danger is no way to tempt Rachel to settle here.' When Rachel turned back to them she said more cheerfully, 'I'm so glad you're coming to work here, my dear.'

Rachel was wondering what she'd got herself into but it was too late to back out.

19

The sick woman's house was in a shabby terrace of dwellings, each of which was obviously divided into two or more smaller homes. Rubbish was lying around here and there, and Rachel frowned at the sight of the mess.

'Tell them to pile it up outside and I'll get the council to clear it up,' Walter said quietly. 'Some folk can be very lazy but some are simply too weak to carry their rubbish to the nearest street bin. With these houses they tend to have communal bins in one spot.'

Rachel looked round, intending to speak to Wilma's niece, but she wasn't with them any longer. No one had noticed the woman leave them but perhaps she hadn't wanted to be asked to help clean up her family's rooms. Or maybe she'd been ashamed to be associated with such a dirty place.

She followed Hanny and her burden inside a house without waiting to be asked. She needed to check exactly how clean the family's two rooms were, not to mention whether there was someone to look after Wilma.

The rooms were at the back part of the ground floor and were filthy. She exchanged disgusted looks with Hanny then said firmly and loudly to the woman who'd stood up and was looking across at them anxiously, 'Wilma won't get better lying among this filth. We'll have to do something about it. Who are you?'

'I'm her sister. We have to share rooms just now because we can't afford to pay a bigger rent.' The woman looked round in embarrassment. 'I know it's a bit of a mess, but I can't keep up. I do my best, really I do, miss, but I can't do everything on my own.' Her voice wobbled on the last phrase.

Rachel looked at the man who was staying as far away from them as he could in such a small room. 'Who are you?'

When he didn't reply, the woman said, 'He's Nick, my husband, miss.'

'Surely he can answer for himself?'

'I have to go out,' he said suddenly.

Rachel moved to bar the doorway, set her hands on her hips and glared at him. 'Not at the moment, you don't.'

'Don't leave me, Nick,' the woman begged.

He scowled but stayed where he was.

Rachel took over again. 'We'll give you a start today then you must find a way to avoid it getting this bad again. And *you* must help her, if necessary, Nick – unless you *want* your family to keep falling ill. Dirt breeds illness you know.'

He shuffled his feet and muttered, 'The other chaps will laugh at me if I do *housework*.'

'Let them laugh. I'm not ashamed to do it so why should you be? And after all, you helped dirty it. My assistant and I are going to help you clean it up now. You must want to get ill yourself to let it get so dirty.'

'Get ill from being dirty?' He sounded surprised.

'Yes. It's a proven fact. Clean people are healthier.'

He looked at her again, clearly unable to work out what to do about the situation.

'We'll help you to clean up now, only this once though. After that I'll be keeping an eye on you all, calling in regularly to make sure you don't let things go so badly downhill again. Promise me you'll keep it clean.'

He hesitated then nodded, clearly still reluctant. His wife made the same promise, looking much happier about it than he did.

Rachel turned back to Hanny. 'You and I will share the work with them today and make sure it gets a thorough scrubbing but first it needs sweeping out. We can't do that till we get a proper broom.'

Walter had been standing with his wife nearby, concerned that the husband might attack the nurse who was daring to boss him around.

Rachel looked across at him. 'Mr Crossley, if someone can bring us the old brushes and rags from the shop, we'll set to work. Was there a bucket there too? I don't remember. If not, I shall need one, as well a bar of strong carbolic soap and a stiff scrubbing brush.'

He beckoned to his wife. 'I'll fetch the cleaning materials from the clinic and hurry back with them. Flora love, perhaps while I'm doing that you can sort out some clean clothing for Hanny from that second-hand shop of mine near Rachel's flat? You know your way round it. Just take anything you think suitable.'

'Good thinking. If she's scrubbing floors she'll get wet and dirty, so she'll need something to change into straight away afterwards. In fact, she'll need several changes of clothing to cope with this job.'

'Doesn't matter what they look like,' Hanny said quietly.

Once the Crossleys had left, she turned to Rachel. 'Thank you for taking me on, miss. I won't let you down.'

'No, I don't think you will.' Rachel looked at the couple. 'You two can start picking things up while we wait for the cleaning equipment.'

When she turned to Hanny she realised her assistant was looking a bit pale and suddenly remembered her saying she was hungry a short time ago. 'Have a piece of bread while we're waiting for Walter to bring the things we need. I can tell you're hungry.'

'I can wait.'

'No need to. And anyway, you'll work better if you have something in your belly.'

Rachel watched the wife nudge her husband and start picking up litter and piling it to one side. She noted he was still hesitant but then he suddenly let out a loud sigh and started to help pick up the mess from the floor. She was determined that he should join in fully. She wouldn't clean up for someone who refused to share the tasks.

She went to the door to see if there was any sign of Mr Crossley and the equipment. She'd expected to be dealing with poverty and filth but not such desperate hunger or so many horribly gaunt people as she'd seen in this part of town.

Oh, heavens, what had she taken on? This was going to be a huge job, even with an assistant.

Well, she couldn't perform miracles and if they succeeded in improving this part of town even a little, it'd be progress and would save lives, wouldn't it?

Walter received a message from his wife scribbled on a scrap of wrapping paper brought by a scrawny lad. It said that she'd commandeered a cab, and by the time she'd got some clothes sorted out, Walter would no doubt have delivered the scrubbing equipment. She'd catch up with him there and they'd go to Mrs Prior's house to ask her whether they could create a small room in part of the cellar for Hanny. They were both sure the landlady would be happy to earn more money every week.

Walter knocked on Mrs Prior's front door and when she opened it, she looked surprised to see the two of them again.

'May we come in and speak to you, Mrs Prior? We have a suggestion that will help us and bring you in a little more money each week, if you're interested.'

Flora had been right, he thought, noticing the way the other woman's eyes brightened at the word money. As soon as they were inside the hall, he explained that they needed a room for Miss Norris's new assistant.

'Oh dear. I don't have any other flats.'

'No, but you do have a large half-cellar and my husband thinks we could turn the part next to one of the windows into a simple but comfortable room for the assistant.'

He smiled at her. 'She won't need anything fancy, just clean and able to be heated. If you could come down with us I'll explain how we could do it.'

Mrs Prior moved down the stairs slowly and she obviously found the movements painful.

He gestured to the window. 'We could put up an inside wall to make this half of the cellar into a room, with its own sink under the window and a gas ring for her to cook on. She could use your outside lavatory and—'

Flora interrupted. 'And she'd keep that clean for you, which would save you a job, wouldn't it?'

Mrs Prior brightened visibly. 'Yes. Yes, it would. Um, how much would it cost to make the changes? I don't have a lot of spare money, I'm afraid.'

'We'd pay for everything. I know people who would do the necessary work for me very cheaply,' Walter said.

'Oh. And . . . how much rent might she pay?'

'How about five shillings a week?'

He saw her form the words 'five shillings a week' silently and tears well in her eyes, and added gently, 'But we'd be paying that for her as part of her wages. Would that amount be all right for you?'

She clapped one hand to her mouth and gulped. It was a moment before she could speak. 'Oh yes. It'd make such a difference to me, such a *useful* difference. It took nearly all my savings to make the flat, you see, and I've felt very insecure since then waiting for the rent to start coming in. What if I fell ill and had to pay for the doctor, for instance?'

'Well, you won't need to worry now, will you. Just one other detail: Miss Best would want to sleep in the cellar from tonight onwards, even though the work won't be finished for a few days. So we'd start paying the rent at once. Would that be all right too? We can bring in some furniture later today and she'll leave the cellar during the daytime to let the various workmen do the jobs. Only, she doesn't have a room of her own at the moment, poor thing, so you'd be helping her greatly.'

Mrs Prior dabbed at her eyes. 'Of course she can come here.'

He pulled out a ten shilling note and offered it to her. 'Two weeks' rent in advance.'

'Thank you so much. You'll be helping me greatly too, as I'm sure you realise. I can't thank you enough, Mr and Mrs Crossley.'

'We all help one another when we can see a need, don't we?' Flora patted her arm and for a moment Mrs Prior grasped her hand convulsively in a quick squeeze of gratitude.

Walter was studying the cellar. 'We'll be back in an hour or two with a few bits of furniture. They can be piled to one side during the daytime while the men are working. I'll just stay down here for a short time longer and take some rough measurements, if that's all right, then we can let ourselves out.'

'You have a key to the front door already, don't you?'

'Yes.'

'Stay as long as you like, then.' She nodded goodbye and went slowly back up the cellar stairs.

'It's working out well, isn't it?' Walter said quietly to his wife.

'Even better than I'd expected if we're helping that poor woman too.'

'I'm so glad we seized the moment.' He grabbed her round the waist and danced her round the cellar, making her laugh.

She loved these occasional boyish moments. They made her feel young again, too.

Then he plonked a quick kiss on her cheek and started pacing the space out to get a better idea of the size. He studied the position of the tap with its old-fashioned slop-stone, and the gas pipes connecting it to the house, which were nearby on the outside, while she took notes for him.

He plonked another kiss on her cheek when they'd finished. 'We make such a good team when there's a job to be planned or done, don't we?'

She gave him a hug then stepped back. 'Yes. And I enjoy the occasional cuddle but now we have work to do.'

Once the floors of the family's rooms had been swept and were ready for scrubbing, Rachel insisted the eldest daughter and both parents join them in doing the work. The younger one kept watch on the furniture outside till they could bring it in again. She was to shout for help if anyone tried to take it.

After they'd finished, Rachel again warned the whole family that she'd be calling in every few days from now on to make sure they were keeping their home clean. 'And if you're not, I'll stop helping you with your health problems because there will be other people needing my help who'll do the right thing in return.'

They didn't protest at this, just kept nodding and saying, 'Yes, miss. Yes, of course. Yes, we definitely will, miss.'

The father was still looking sulky but at least he had joined in the work.

Rachel removed her filthy, damp smock and bundled it up, but had to keep wearing the rest of her clothes, which were slightly damp. They would, she told her assistant cheerfully when Hanny worried about that, soon dry in the fresh air.

'I hope Flora brings back your new clothes soon, Hanny, because yours are much wetter than mine.'

'I'm used to that.'

'Well, get un-used to it.'

When Flora and Walter returned they looked pleased with themselves and they all got into the cab, sitting with bundles of clothes on their laps.

'Mrs Prior has agreed to let us make a room for Hanny in the outer part of her cellar. Actually, I think she'll be very glad of the extra money,' Flora said.

'What's it like?' Hanny asked eagerly. 'Is the cellar dry? Is it very dark?'

Walter took over. 'It's more like a normal room because the house is built on sloping ground. We just have to wall that part of the main cellar off so that you can be private. And there's even a lav across the yard.'

'How long will it take to make the changes?' Hanny asked, clearly eager to move in.

Walter smiled at her. 'Not long. I know a man who will do the necessary jobs for me quickly, three or four days at most. He's always glad of work and I know I can rely on him to do things properly.'

'What are we going to do about some furnishings for Hanny?' Rachel asked. 'Do you have any cooking equipment and crockery?'

Hanny's face fell. 'I had to give mine to my sister. There's not much but I can't take them away from her and the children.'

'Well, that's another thing we can sort out today,' Walter said. 'I have a collection of second-hand items that I keep for those in need. People know I put such things to good use, so they give their discarded bits and pieces to me. We can take you to my furniture storage shed straight away and find whatever you consider necessary, Hanny, plus cooking equipment.'

A happy sigh was his answer.

As they'd left her patient's family, Rachel had seen Walter slip a florin to the woman's daughter, so knew the family they'd helped would have food for at least one more day.

She didn't know what would happen to them after that. She had to get used to leaving her patients to struggle on. She couldn't deal with every detail of their ongoing lives, only step in when there was a medical problem.

20

Walter let the cab driver take them back to the livery stables after they left Rachel's flat. They needed to use his little cart so that they could fit the items they chose in the back, which was where Hanny would have to sit too. He then took them to what he called his second-hand furniture shop, which was more like a shabby little warehouse than a shop.

Inside he led the way straight through it to a big shed out at the back, which was piled high with all sorts of old, mismatched furniture. He gestured to it. 'This may look scruffy but it has all been repaired and is fit for purpose. Choose what you'll need from it to furnish your room, Hanny, and I'll have it delivered straight away. No cost.'

'Oh! Thank you so much.'

'You'll have to sleep on the new bed in the open cellar for a few nights because the work to make it a private room will be under way. But you'll have the cellar all to yourself after the men have finished work each day.'

She was so overwhelmed by the shock of being told to choose what she wanted that she could only look pleadingly at Rachel for help. 'I don't need much to manage, miss. I'm not extravagant. What do you suggest?'

'There's no charge, remember,' Walter said gently. 'Take what you will *need* and don't skimp. We want you to be comfortable. And you should choose things you like best. You'll be the one living with them, after all.'

Rachel saw that Hanny still didn't dare do anything and turned to him. 'Can you help us decide, Mr Crossley? You'll know how big Hanny's room will be and therefore how much will fit into it.'

'Happy to do that. I have a fair eye for fitting things into spaces, if I do say so myself.'

He helped them choose a narrow bed, two upright chairs to go with a small table, a chest of drawers and he coaxed Hanny into saying which armchair she found the most comfortable. Then he stood back and had a think. 'I reckon that's about all that will fit in without being over-crowded, Hanny.'

Flora took over. 'We have some boxes of mismatched crockery and cooking oddments in the shop to give people setting up homes. They're things that aren't sell-able but are still perfectly OK to use. I'll grab one of those for you, too, as we go back to our cart, Hanny.'

More tears welled in her eyes but she managed to hold these back as she whispered, 'Thank you.'

'Come back into the shop now,' Flora said. 'We can find you a few other clothes and some underwear too. Don't worry. It's been thoroughly washed.' She turned to Rachel. 'Will half a dozen working outfits be enough, do you think?'

'Oh yes, I'm sure they will.'

This caused Hanny another shocked moment where she was unable to fit two words together, so Rachel inter-vened again. 'She'll need mostly dark colours and prefer-ably clothes made of sturdy cotton material for working in and washing regularly. Oh, and a warm cloak, which is easier to put on and off in a hurry than a coat if there's an emergency.'

'Six outfits!' Hanny muttered faintly. 'Six.'

'Yes. We both need to look as smart as possible.'

'Oh, my. I can't . . . it's so hard to . . . to believe this.'

Rachel tried not to smile as she turned back to Flora. 'She'll also need some sort of cap or no, a white headsquare might be better to match her white pinafore. I'll sew on a little red cross near to where the scarf folds across the top of her head, and another cross on the bib of the pinafores. It was always stressed to us during the training that we mustn't look like housemaids or we won't get respected, hence the sort of caps we nurses wear. As a result my cap is far fancier than I'd ever have chosen myself.' She turned back to Hanny. 'As my assistant you need to take care about the same type of thing.'

When they'd finished sorting out the clothes, Walter pulled out his watch and flipped the top open. 'Time we were getting home now, Flora love. Shall I drop you and Hanny off at your flat, Miss Norris?'

'I'd like one more look round the clinic, so that I can think about how best to organise things,' Rachel said. 'Are you all right to walk home afterwards with me, Hanny?'

'Yes. Oh, no. I shall have my other new clothes to carry. I won't want to get them dirty before I start.'

'We can easily drop them off at your flat,' Flora said. 'It's on our way.'

She slipped some coins into Rachel's hand and said cheerfully. 'Why don't you two let us buy you some fish and chips for tea as a celebration of starting work together? I'm told the chippie just along the street from your flat is a good one. And there's a bit of that loaf left for Hanny's breakfast. I'm afraid I've nothing to wrap it up in.'

'Doesn't matter, Mrs Crossley.'

The two women waved goodbye and went inside the clinic, locking the entrance door carefully behind them. 'Let's go and see what's upstairs,' Rachel suggested.

They found only three dusty, unfurnished rooms and some narrow stairs leading to an open attic space, which housed plenty of dust and mouse droppings.

Hanny shuddered. 'We'll need to get several mouse traps! I can't stand having the little devils around, getting into the food.'

'We'll buy a dozen traps and scatter them round upstairs and down.'

'Eh, it's big, isn't it? I've never worked in a place with so many rooms.'

'And I've spent a lot of my time sleeping in dormitories for nurses. I've been longing for my own home, and now I've got a shop to turn into a clinic as well as my own flat. Isn't that marvellous?'

Hanny smiled. 'So we're both getting better accommodation than before.'

'Yes. And tomorrow we'll start sorting out the clinic, giving it a good clean and working out how best to use the space.'

'I'll do the cleaning.'

'I'm not afraid to clean.'

'I've seen that, but I still think that should be my job,' said Hanny.

'All right this time, as I'll need to sort out our medical supplies and arrangements. Thank you.'

Rachel stood looking round and frowning. 'It's still got big shop windows and if people see shelves of items, they might break in and help themselves. I think we should store most of our medical supplies in one of the upstairs rooms and bring them down as needed. I know it'll make extra work but it'll be safer.'

'We should also shut some of them in a big tin box so the mice can't get at them either,' Hanny said.

'So we'll only keep a few basic items in view downstairs.' Rachel stopped and stared towards the rear. 'Is that the door to a cellar?'

'Looks like it.'

'We'd better check it out. We should have done that before.'

It didn't take long. There were a few open shelves and one big cupboard the size of a wardrobe but apart from that, the cellar was empty.

When they went upstairs again, Rachel said, 'I don't know about you but I'm ready for my tea.'

As she moved towards the door, Hanny said, 'Um, can I just call in on my sister and get the rest of my possessions on the way back? I don't want Mavis pawning them, you see. She's hopeless with money. I haven't got much stuff and it's only a bit out of our way. There are a couple of things that used to belong to our mother that I particularly don't want to lose.'

'Of course we can do that.'

Her sister couldn't hide her relief that Hanny had got a job, not only for the money but because a little more space could be made in the cluttered and overcrowded single room they all slept in.

When Hanny slipped her sister one of the shilling pieces she'd earned today to buy some food for the kids, Mavis blinked her eyes furiously and whispered, 'Thanks, love. I've been wondering what to give them for tea.'

As they left her sister's room, Rachel said, 'Come on. Let's get back to the flat now. I'm exhausted.'

'So am I. It's been an amazing day.'

'A good one for both of us, I hope. It should only take us about ten minutes to walk back from here and we'll be able to pick up the fish and chips on our way.'

As they were walking along Hanny muttered, 'I can't thank you enough for giving me this chance, miss.'

'You're welcome. And do call me Rachel when we're on our own.'

'Are you sure? I don't want to sound disrespectful.'

'I'm sure. I call you Hanny, after all.'

'That's really kind and friendly of you . . . Rachel. The Crossleys are kind too. I can't believe how many clothes Mrs Crossley's given me . . . just given. I've never had so many at once in my whole life, or such nice warm ones, either.'

'You'll need the clothes for other reasons than looking nice. You'll be doing plenty of laundering in this job because there's quite a lot of dirty work involved and we pride ourselves on setting an example by being clean. I shall be using the services of the laundry part of the time. It's not expensive if you want to use it, too. Though if there's room for it, I might buy a small mangle to put in the cellar. We'd both find that useful, I'm sure.'

'I'll do all my own washing, if you don't mind. It'll make my money spin out more.'

She'd never had savings before and hoped she could manage to put a few pennies by each week, at least. And she'd slip a little to her sister too, even if it was only six-pence or so. 'I shall be happy to be able to keep my things clean so easily. I haven't often had that luxury before.'

They didn't have to queue for long in the chippie and came out holding warm, newspaper wrapped bundles of food but at the corner Hanny stopped and said, 'I think that chap's following us. I saw his reflection in a couple of shop windows before we arrived at the chippie. He was always the same sort of distance behind us. And now he's there again.'

Rachel swung round to stare and the man scowled at them then crossed the road and disappeared down an alley. 'He might have been following us, but I can't think why.'

'I think he definitely was. Men do that sometimes, espe-cially with pretty women like you if you don't mind me saying so.'

'It's the bane of my life,' Rachel muttered.

Hanny looked surprised at that comment, then said slowly, 'We should each carry a walking stick, just in case we get attacked when we're out at night, one with a weighted handle.'

'Goodness.'

'Better safe than sorry.'

'I suppose so. I've never had to do that before. Where would we get those?'

'I can show you the best ones to buy.'

'Yes, we'll do that. Definitely.'

When they got back to the flat, Mrs Prior came out into the hall to meet her new tenants and then gestured to the stairs, where there was a big bundle of clothes.

'The Crossleys left these for you and your assistant, Miss Norris.'

'Thank you.'

'And then two men brought some furniture and put that downstairs.'

'Already!'

'Mr Crossley always gets good service. I'll let you look at the downstairs area yourselves later, ladies. My knees are a bit stiff on stairs these days and you'll want to eat the fish and chips before they go cold.'

'Yes, we will. Thank you.'

Mrs Prior pushed open the door to her flat, then turned to call, 'I left an oil lamp and some matches down in the cellar for you, Miss Best. There's one gas light on the wall, but you'll need the lamp to go across to the lav at night, which is the door on the left as you look across at the far side of the yard. The other door is the coal house. They said you'd want to sleep down there tonight, but you'll need to be up early, because the men who brought the furniture said they'll be starting work at dawn every day.'

'I'll be up as soon as it gets light, Mrs Prior, and you can be sure I'll leave the place tidy. And if you want me to fill your coal scuttle at any time, just leave it out at the top of the stairs and I'll do it for you.'

Mrs Prior stared in surprise. 'That very kind of you.'

'Well, you've been kind to me.'

'I'd be grateful for help with heavy things, I must admit.'

They went up to the flat and ate their food, which was still fairly warm, then Hanny said she'd go down to what would be her bedroom and sort out her things before having an early night.

'You can come upstairs and have breakfast with me tomorrow once the workmen start,' Rachel added. 'I'm an early riser and I'll make us each a fried egg on toast for breakfast.'

'You don't need to. I've enough bread left to manage.'

'I want to. A lot's happened today, hasn't it?'

Hanny smiled at her. 'Yes, but such good things. I'll say goodnight, then.'

Once she'd crossed the backyard to use the lav, Hanny came back and had a quick all-over wash, before going straight to bed. She moved the bundle of clothes the Crossleys had given her on to the armchair, finding two blankets included with them, a bit worn but still fairly fluffy. Two! How wonderful!

She was utterly exhausted now, not just with hard work but with emotional and physical changes that had left her amazed that such good things could ever happen to someone like her. She smiled in the darkness.

The next thing she knew it was starting to get light and she had to bustle round to get dressed ready to go upstairs for breakfast.

She found the coal scuttle at the top of the stairs and ran back down with it and across the yard to fill it, glad it wasn't raining.

The two workmen had just arrived and one of them looked at her and said, 'Coal? Let me help you.' He insisted on carrying the scuttle upstairs for her, though she could perfectly well have managed it. He left it at the top of the stairs, then she went up to the flat to find the door slightly ajar.

Rachel smiled across at her from the gas fire where she was toasting slices of bread. 'Here. You finish the toast and I'll fry our eggs.'

It was a long time since Hanny had started the day with a good meal like this. There was even jam to put on the last piece of toast.

'Ready for our day's work?' Rachel asked as they set off.

'Ready and looking forward to it, miss. I mean, Rachel.'

21

A few days after he moved into his new home, Joss woke to hear rain drumming on the windowpanes. When a flash of lightning outlined the edges of the curtains and was followed by thunder rumbling in the distance, he got up and padded across to the window to hold back one of the curtains and study the weather prospects.

Outside were dark grey lowering skies heavy with clouds containing, he had no doubt, more rain. Lightning flashed again, reflecting briefly on the silver puddles and runnels of water that dotted the garden.

The rain eased off for a few moments then suddenly beat another tattoo against the windowpanes as if to tell him it wasn't done with his part of the world yet.

He let the curtain fall, sighing. Drat! He'd planned to walk all over his grounds this morning to get a feel for the whole place. If he tried he'd get soaked in minutes, even with an umbrella because the stronger gusts of wind were blowing the rain sideways part of the time. And if he tried to cycle anywhere he'd be soaked within seconds.

Feeling annoyed he went downstairs to have his breakfast, sharing the kitchen table with his staff as usual. Given Sybil's confident way of chatting to him, Megan had soon relaxed with him as well, and he hoped the two maids enjoyed his company as much as he enjoyed theirs. They were old enough to have some wry thoughts about the world they now lived in and the people from round here.

'I can't do much when it's raining like this.' He couldn't hold back another sigh.

'Now's a good time to start going through the piles of stuff in the attic, then,' Sybil said in a brisk tone of voice. 'Make a virtue out of a necessity, Mr Townley. Me and Megan have been too busy cleaning this house and washing down the paintwork room by room to do more than glance at whatever is up there.'

'Didn't you find anything of interest when you swept the attic floors?'

'I was too busy to read all them papers full of words in small print. I piled them in one corner for you to enjoy. I need to buy myself some new reading glasses to read the smaller print. My daughter-in-law had an accident with mine, smashed them to pieces, she did.'

When she scowled as she said that, it seemed to be at some memory her remark had raised and she fell silent for a few moments, staring into space. She didn't frown very often but he guessed the glasses must have been broken on purpose.

He usually only saw Lionel's wife in the distance but she always seemed to be scowling. He realised Sybil was speaking again and turned back to her. 'Sorry. What did you say?'

'I said: there are piles of papers up there. I've no idea what they're about, your family's business, I suppose. As I just told you, I put them all in a corner for your attention when convenient. Well, dealing with your paperwork isn't part of my job, is it?'

'Of course not. I much prefer being out of doors, though not on days like this.'

'No one would want to go out who didn't have to. Today's a good time to make a start up there, then, isn't it?'

'I suppose so. I'd forgotten that I needed to look through them.'

When he didn't say anything more, she added quietly, 'I don't think that rain is going to let up till this afternoon.'

'I should make a start on the papers, then.'

She let out a crack of laughter. 'I've never heard anyone sound as enthusiastic about a job.'

Which won her a reluctant smile.

'My advice is that any time you have an hour or two to spare, you go up and look at some more of them. Do it bit by bit. We get a lot of rainy days here in Lancashire.'

'I've noticed.'

'What's more, you know precious little about that side of your family from what you've told me. Who knows what you'll find out?'

That he knew nothing was thanks to his father insisting his only son work in the factory and stay well away from the Ollerthwaite branch of the family, he thought. But he felt it'd be disloyal to say that, even if it was only to Sybil and Megan, who could be trusted not to blab his secrets to the world, he was quite sure.

'There's another thing, sir, while you're in the attic. There are two or three big boxes full of what look like old clothes up there, some of them children's things. If you don't want them, there are little lads in Eastby with their backsides hanging out of their britches, not to mention lasses growing so quickly both upwards and outwards – ' she gestured towards her own chest – 'that their skirts are too short an' their bodices too tight, so they're embarrassed to go outside to play.'

'You're welcome to go through them and take anything you think will be useful to someone.'

'Really?'

'Yes, of course.'

'I'll do that, then. They'll be a godsend to some folk.'

She fixed her employer with a very firm gaze and added, 'But if you don't fancy dealing with them papers all day, you could plan for a little outing this afternoon. I think the rain will ease off for a while.' She gave him a sideways glance and added, 'We not only need bread for this household, but a couple of loaves for the new nurse at the clinic.'

'What does she want with that much bread if there's only her working there? And why do we have to provide it?'

'She has an assistant now who needs feeding regularly too and they give out the bread from one of the loaves slice by slice to hungry people, especially the children. And we provide it because it's a way of helping some of the folk who're going short.'

'Ah. I see.'

'She's got a good heart, that nurse has. There are a lot of hungry children in Eastby, so you buy her a loaf each day to give away to them.'

'I do?' He grinned at her. 'I must have forgotten that.'

Sybil flushed slightly. 'I can pay for that extra loaf if you don't want to. I don't like to see them children going hungry.'

He stopped teasing her. 'No, I don't like to see that, either. It's good of you to arrange it and I'm happy to pay, as I'm sure you realised. How do you usually get the bread to them?'

'Megan or I pick the loaves up whenever we do the shopping to save her the trouble. If we don't get them to her by mid-afternoon, the baker saves them for her and her assistant picks them up. The clinic they're setting up is in the town centre and quite close by. But someone from here usually has to go into town shopping each day because you have a hearty appetite, my lad.'

She clapped one hand to her mouth and pretended to be worried at what she'd said. 'Er, sorry, I should have said *sir*, not my lad.'

But he could see the laughter in her eyes. 'I don't mind you calling me lad. I suppose I seem like one to you. And you feel more like an aunt than a housekeeper, if you don't mind me saying so.'

'Of course I don't.'

'And I've been meaning to say that I'm very satisfied with your work and Megan's. As for the bread, I'll go and get that later. I haven't met the new nurse yet, haven't even seen her in the distance and I'm feeling nosy. She's settled in well, has she? Won people's trust?'

'She has. And it's not just her who's settled in to do the nursing that people need, her assistant is doing well too. They go out to see people together.' She chuckled suddenly. 'And they're making people clean up their houses. Never thought I'd see the days some of them mopped their floors. But they say she has a way of looking at them that makes them feel they'd better do it.'

'Good for her.'

'But there's still plenty for them two to do in town setting up the clinic and seeing folk there who've had no one to help them for years.'

'What's she like? Is she very fierce?'

'She's nice enough but usually brisk with folk. She's helping sick people, which is what counts with me. She's not here to make friends.'

Sybil shot a quick mischievous glance at Megan when he wasn't looking then said airily, 'You'll see for yourself what she looks like later today if you deliver her bread for me, sir. You'll feel good going out into the fresh air after breathing in all the dust you'll be raising in the attic. Going up now, are you?'

'Yes, ma'am. I know when to do as I'm told. The attic it is.'

Her smile faded and she got a sad expression on her face as she added, 'We can and should joke about things, but there are a lot of needy people in Eastby, sir, and some of them, especially the women and children, actually deserve help. So don't forget that pile of old clothes.'

'Are there some who don't deserve help?'

'Oh, yes. I'd not lift a finger to help that group of young chaps who hang about at street corners and annoy decent people. If *I* were rich, I'd buy food for the women and children, though, I would indeed.'

As he'd suspected when he hired her, Sybil proved regularly that she wasn't afraid to speak her mind. But she usually talked sense, and anyway her frankness amused him. He was learning important things about his new home from her, and he appreciated that too.

She seemed a bit sharper than usual today, however, and he wondered if something had upset her. He'd noticed her son nip across the field that separated the two houses and call in to see her before breakfast. She'd taken Lionel into the scullery to speak privately, then after his visit, she'd been rather tight-lipped. He hadn't looked happy as he left, either.

'Once it stops raining I'll cycle into town, then. The carrier will hold several loaves easily. Tell me again how many to buy, and give me a shopping bag or two not a basket. Bags sit much more easily in those big metal baskets on the trike.'

'Useful gadget that, better than a bicycle because it's a lot easier for an old woman like me to ride, I can tell you. I don't know why they aren't more popular.'

'I don't think they go fast enough for most younger folk and bicycles can slip in and out of the traffic far more easily in the towns. Even the trams don't hold bicycles up for long, but they do hold up tricycles sometimes, the few that there are on urban roads.'

He got the trike ready to escape from the dusty attics once the rain stopped, then went up there to continue going through the papers, still not reading them, only sorting them out into piles of what looked like accounts, miscellaneous letters and a few books with handwritten pages that looked like diaries.

He didn't want to read about the past but to get on with the present and prepare for the future so he set the diaries aside without even glancing at them.

The rain didn't stop or the sun peep out from between clouds till an hour after they'd finished their midday meal. When it looked as if the sun actually meant to hang around for a while, he set off for Eastby. He'd breathed in enough dust for one day, had lost count of the number of times he'd gone to the attic window to stare out at the weather. Too bad if he got wet coming back.

He paused by the side of the road when he saw a rainbow shimmer slowly into place across the sky in the distance. He didn't believe it was a sign of something good coming his way, as credulous people had several times told him on his travels, but it was so beautiful it made him feel happy to gaze at it for a few peaceful moments.

When he got to the baker's, he found that they'd saved Sybil's loaves plus the two extra ones. They also had a couple of big paper bags of broken bread pieces standing at the end of the counter with a sign saying they were for sale cheaply, so he bought them too. He'd ask this nurse to give them to deserving families because he'd like to improve matters for some of the poor in his little corner of the world and this might be a small step towards it.

He hoped the nurse wouldn't be too fierce. They could be very sharp and grumpy he'd found as a lad on the rare occasions he'd needed their services.

Later on he would work out something more useful to help people in the area and get it properly organised. This was still high on his mental list of things to do because the more he lived there, the more he loved his new home. There was something so welcoming about it and the views over the moors were superb. He'd fallen in love with them and had taken a couple of walks up the nearest slopes to places from which he could sit on one of the many drystone walls or an outcropping of rock and study the world around his home.

It was obvious from the central group of buildings which part of Eastby had been the original village. It might even have looked pretty for its first century of existence but it certainly didn't now. There were some better cottages on the outskirts which looked slightly newer, but some of the central ones were in a dreadful state now and looked ready to fall down if you pushed them too hard. In fact, none of that area looked really good these days. Why did the owners not look after them better?

After he left the baker's, he couldn't help noticing that most of the street signs had been ripped off the walls in the central area. This new nurse was apparently making a clinic out of an old abandoned shop on Upper West Street (wherever that was) and was planning to see patients there as well as visiting the ones who couldn't get to the clinic in their own homes.

It took him a while but at last he found what he thought was the right place. He then had the problem of how to keep his trike and contents safe while he took her share of the bread inside to her, because there was a group of older lads standing on a nearby corner watching him intently. He didn't like the looks of them and he hadn't been born yesterday so he wasn't leaving his trike where they could pilfer its load, or even pinch the whole thing.

A young lad came up to him hesitantly. 'Keep an eye on your bicycle for a penny, mister?'

'Will you be able to keep it safe, though? This bread is for the nurse to give to her poorer patients but I don't want to come out and find my own bread gone or even the trike missing. That lot are bigger than you.'

'Me an' my brother will keep it safe, sir. We can yell for you if one of them lot tries to take it away from us. He's got a really loud yell, our Carson has.' He beckoned to an even younger boy who looked curiously at Joss then stationed himself next to the tricycle and tried to make himself look taller and fiercer – but didn't really succeed.

Joss managed not to smile at the younger boy's efforts. 'You're hired. In fact, I'll give you twopence each if you keep it safe.'

'Each? Thanks, mister.'

They beamed at that and the bigger lad stationed himself next to the trike as well.

Joss went to the door of the empty shop and tried to go inside, but found it locked so had to knock on it for attention.

A gaunt young woman wearing what looked like some sort of uniform came out from behind a screen, saw him, studied him for a moment, then called to someone else.

An extremely pretty young woman in an elegant uniform of the sort he'd seen nurses wear in bigger towns came out and walked confidently towards the door.

He couldn't help staring at her. This couldn't be the new district nurse, surely? She was too young . . . and far too pretty.

She unlocked the door and opened it. 'Can I help you, sir?'

'I'm Joss Townley. Sybil Entwistle, my housekeeper, sent me to deliver the bread she gives you. Are you Miss Norris, the new nurse?'

'Yes, I am.'

It was out before he could stop himself. 'Goodness, I thought you'd be much older.'

She looked at him scornfully. 'Like everyone else, I hope to be older one day.'

He held out the paper bag with two loaves in it. 'Sorry. I didn't mean to be rude. She sent these. Apparently you give bread to hungry people most days.'

'Yes, it's very kind of her to provide it.'

He held out the second bag. 'I'd like to provide some too, so I bought some bags of broken crusts from the baker. If I give them to you to hand out, I'm presuming you can use them?'

Her expression softened. 'Oh, yes. I can always use more, unfortunately. Thank you for thinking of us.' She glanced outside. 'You'd have been safer wheeling the tricycle into the shop doorway or even into the shop itself. This door is wider than usual and it'd fit through it easily.'

'The door was locked but I'd not have done that to your clean floor. It's a muddy sort of day.'

'The floor gets mopped every day.'

'I'll bring the tricycle in now, if I may. I'd like to discuss helping you regularly, if you can spare me a few minutes.'

'I can always spare time for discussions like that.'

Good, because he'd like to spend more time with her too. She wasn't just pretty, she looked intelligent and . . . well, rather nice. Extremely nice, in fact.

She gave him a rather suspicious glance then nodded and gestured. 'Bring the tricycle inside, then.'

He went out to the two lads, who were still standing guard, but now a couple of the larger lads had moved to stand directly opposite them on the other side of the street. They were watching the two with the trike as if about to pounce but stepped back a little when he came out.

'Thank you for your help. I'm going to take the trike into the shop now while I talk to the nurse.' He then yelled across to the hovering youths, 'I'll remember your faces and if you lot ever touch my tricycle or what's on it, I'll come after you myself and give you a good thumping before handing you over to the police.' There were times when it was good to be tall and strong, and this was one of them.

They looked startled and edged backwards, so he turned to the young lads. 'Here's your money and thank you for your help. Keep it all.' The minute they had the money they ran off. The ones who'd been hovering nearby ran after them but he doubted they'd catch those two.

A tall lad, who'd been standing slightly to one side on his own, stayed where he was, still watching Joss.

He couldn't resist asking, 'Why didn't you go with your friends?'

'Because they're not my friends. I don't knock around with that sort. I don't want to bash people or steal things. Don't worry, mister. They won't catch Eli and his brother. They're the fastest runners in the village, them two are.'

'What about you? Are you a good runner?'

'I can't run, only walk. See.' He turned and started walking along the pavement, limping awkwardly. He was another ragged lad who looked hungry.

'How did you hurt your foot?'

'Born like this. I've allus limped.'

'Just a minute. Here.' Joss held out another threepenny bit to the lad, who gaped at him but came across quickly to take it from him.

'What's this for, mister?'

'Telling me things and also, because I'm feeling generous.'

'Oh. Well, thank you.' He grinned. 'You can give me money any time you feel generous.'

The nurse had been watching them from the doorway and as Joss wheeled his tricycle inside, she stepped out of the way and murmured, 'I wonder why exactly he's limping. Something must have gone wrong with the birth or perhaps he has one leg shorter than the other. But if that's it, why hasn't he had a special shoe made?'

'His family probably can't afford it.'

'Yes. That's sad. You'd think the local doctor would have found a charity to get him one.'

'I gather she's got too much to do already, but they're going to hire another doctor apparently. If I see the lad again, I'll try to find out what's causing his problem and then see whether Walter can help me to get him a special shoe. If you see him, would you tell him to come and find me?'

She waited till he'd pushed the tricycle inside before closing the door, sliding a bolt next to the handle to lock it straight away.

'Is it so dangerous round here that you have to keep the door locked when you're working?'

'I don't know about dangerous in the sense of us getting injured but Eastby has definitely got more than its share of thieves, a lot of them young. I lost several items on my first day here because I only closed the door and didn't lock it. Hanny thought I had or she'd have done it. I know better now.'

'You need a policeman or someone similar patrolling the village centre if things are that bad, especially if people are coming and going into your clinic.'

'Who's to pay for that? Or find a spare policeman with time to do it?' the gaunt woman standing to one side asked scathingly. 'No one really cares about this part of the valley. Even Mr Crossley can only offer us help occasionally.'

The nurse smiled at her companion then looked out of the shop window. 'Actually, I can't help wondering who all these crumbling buildings belong to and why their owners don't care for them properly.'

'I've been wondering that, too. I own one or two of them, I gather. I've not found out exactly which ones they are yet because I've only just inherited Townley House. I might see if I can find out who the other owners are. Some of them might want to get together to make improvements.'

The gaunt woman rolled her eyes, looking at him scornfully as if she thought he was being naive.

'Don't you agree?' he asked her directly.

'They don't usually buy houses to be kind to people who need homes, but to make as much money as they can from the rents.'

He needed to find out which properties he owned, anyway, and he'd make sure they'd been properly maintained. He couldn't tell other people to pay attention to their properties if his own needed work.

Miss Norris smiled at him, a genuine smile this time. 'Thank you for the extra bread. Not a crumb of it will be wasted, I promise you.'

'I'll bring you some more next time I'm in town.' He looked out of the window and could see the sky had clouded over while he'd been chatting. 'Oh, dear. I think I'd better cycle home again now before it starts raining again. I don't want to get soaked.'

She walked to the door with him, unlocked it and barely waited for him to edge his tricycle through it, before locking it carefully again.

When he turned to glance back, intending to wave goodbye, she had already turned away and was walking towards the rear of the clinic. He'd expected her to wait and wave a final farewell, as people normally did. He was left wondering whether he'd made a good impression on her or not, or she was just very busy.

She'd certainly made a good impression on him, not only because she was so pretty but because she clearly had a passion for her job and equally clearly, was a hard worker and intelligent. You didn't find many women that pretty working for their living. They usually married young.

He wondered why she hadn't got married. Surely she must have had offers. And why was he still thinking about her? She's not your business, he told himself firmly.

He passed a couple of lads pushing one another as if about to start fighting and his thoughts went back to that group of rough lads who'd been watching the clinic. Did they hang around the centre of Eastby all the time? He'd maybe talk to the police sergeant in Ollerthwaite, who seemed to be in charge of law and order in this valley, about how best to stop them frightening people and bullying smaller kids.

He felt it was his duty, as the largest landowner round here, to try to help the folk who lived so close to his family home. From what Crossley had said, the people who lived here were mainly ignored by the rest of the residents of the valley.

And he might try to find out who owned the other houses near the run-down shops near the church. The owners ought to be looking after their investments better than this.

Could he make a difference?

He could try.

22

Mr Genner didn't think it a good idea for Adam to go to Eastby End on his own and incognito, and tried very hard to persuade his client to take someone with him.

'The centre of Eastby End is a very rough area,' he said several times. 'You have no idea how bad. I always avoid going there. I live elsewhere in the valley, near the lake.'

'I'm well able to look after myself,' Adam insisted. 'And have done for twenty-nine years, if you count when I was a baby.' He'd hoped to lighten the mood with that vaguely joking remark, but Mr Genner ignored it completely.

'I'll come and see you when I arrive in Ollindale,' Adam said in the end. 'Or at least, after I've had a look round at my inheritance. You've given me the addresses of the houses I now own, and the address of your legal premises. I have a few things to sort out here then I'll join you.'

'I'd better warn you that the houses you've inherited aren't in good repair. I sent my clerk to check them out before I came to see you and he was shocked, absolutely shocked. I'm afraid your father skimped on that side of things, concentrating mainly on how much money he could make from them.'

Adam didn't like the idea of that. 'Then I'll take careful notes on each one myself and set about having them repaired as necessary. I disapprove of landlords who don't give a fair return to the tenants who pay rent to them each week out of their hard-earned wages. No, I don't approve of it at all.'

'Sadly, I could never persuade your father to do that. He wanted to leave you as much money and property as he could, was absolutely certain that outcome was the best thing he could do for his son in his poor state of health.'

'I see. Well, what's done is done. We'll move on from that approach once I've seen them and made plans to do whatever's needed.'

'If you come to see me as soon as you arrive, I'll get someone to show you round Eastby. There is only one hotel to stay at in Ollerthwaite, by the way. It's run by a Mr and Mrs Shorrocks and it's in the centre of town. It's plain but gives very good value. When do you think you'll be coming? I could book you a room.'

'I'm not sure yet.' He'd pretended he still had to work out his notice at the garage, insisting to the lawyer that it was only fair to do that. But he had no intention of hanging around in Blackpool and Tom had made no attempt to persuade him to stay.

Adam wanted to see Eastby and his inheritance for himself, not to be shown it by someone else. He also wanted to try to find out more about his father, what sort of man he'd been, felt quite desperate to do that now that he'd found out who he was.

He'd always wished he had a father, and had also envied other children their families of brothers and sisters. But if his father had been so hungry for money that he'd skimped on maintaining his houses, Adam didn't like the sound of that, which was a huge disappointment.

People said what you'd never had you didn't miss. But they were wrong. Oh well, he'd have to wait and see what he found in this Ollindale valley before he took any life-changing decisions about what to do now that he had a comfortable amount of money behind him – however it had been earned.

The train journey seemed long and tiresome, and the train stopped at every single village on the mainly single-line track that formed the final stage of the journey. Every single village!

It seemed a tediously long time until they arrived at the final stop, the town of Ollerthwaite, which was, he'd been told, the place from which you got to Eastby. It took Adam a minute or two to realise that he really had arrived, could get off this small chugging train, which had seemed more of an instrument of 'torture by boredom' to him. It hadn't occurred to him to bring a book to read. He'd thought he'd be entertained by the scenery. Only, each one of these small villages seemed just like its neighbours.

He got up and paused for a moment on the top step of his compartment before stepping out because he got a better view from up there. The town looked peaceful and there weren't a lot of people around. It wasn't pretty, but it wasn't ugly either.

Before he got down he glanced at the station clock rather than fiddling around with his waistcoat chain and pulling out his watch. If he found the hotel quickly and left his bag there, he would surely have time to walk up to this Eastby place and get some idea of what it was like before nightfall?

'Do you need a cab, sir?'

He jerked out of his thoughts to see an elderly porter waiting patiently for his response. 'Yes, please. And I need somewhere to spend a night or two, possibly a little longer. Is there a hotel you can recommend?'

The man gave him a wry smile and said the same as Mr Genner, 'There is only one hotel here, sir, but Mr and Mrs Shorrocks provide every comfort and if you order in advance, they can supply evening meals as well as the breakfasts that come with the cost of the room.' He too glanced up at the station clock. 'You'd be wise to book a room and order a meal straight away, if you don't mind me saying so, sir. That'll give Mrs Shorrocks plenty of time to get something nice ready for you.'

'I don't mind at all.' He had a coin ready to tip the man with. 'Can you get me a cab?'

'There is only one, sir, but I can see that it's free.' He waved one hand in the air and a neat little pony clopped forward pulling a vehicle that was a cross between a cart and a trap, but bigger than the latter usually was and with some shelter from the weather.

The driver jumped down, left the pony standing without seeming to need to tether it and came to take Adam's bag and find out where he wanted to go.

In fact the hotel was on a corner of the main street only a few hundred yards up from the station and Adam could easily have strolled there and carried his own bag, which wasn't all that heavy because he didn't own a lot of clothes. He didn't comment on that, however. Everyone had to earn a living as best they could and at least he was now in a position to help others, so he happily added a tip to the fare for this smiling young fellow after the short journey had ended.

Half an hour later, he set off on foot from the hotel, armed with instructions as to how to get to Eastby, and warnings not to stay long enough to be wandering round in the central area on his own after dark. That repeated Mr Genner's warning and made it more credible, which surprised him. He hadn't thought any town in England could be this dangerous and had put the warnings from the lawyer down to him being an older and more cautious man.

He would definitely have to take care how long he stayed there.

As he walked he saw the lake they'd told him about glinting in the distance on the left just outside the town centre and mentally made a vow to walk round it one day soon. But for the moment he was eager to see his inheritance, or at least some of it, so he strode quickly up the gentle slope towards Eastby, following the road the landlord had said was the most direct way to get there.

After a few minutes Adam found one house which was on the list of those he now owned, and stopped to look at it, marvelling that he owned it. Then he began to frown as he studied it more carefully. It was distinctly shabby and the paint on the front door was peeling in parts, definitely needed repainting, which the previous owner, in other words his father, should have seen to before it got this bad.

The windows could have done with a thorough cleaning, but that was usually done by the tenant. That at least could have been attended to at no cost other than a little effort and whoever collected the rent should have told the occupants to see to it.

As he watched, an older woman walked slowly past him and turned into the gate of his house, which had about two yards of neglected garden at the front. She looked worn out by life and her slow, painful movements showed why she hadn't cleaned any windows.

He carried on, surprised at how markedly the whole area had deteriorated by the time he reached the street where Mrs Shorrocks had told him Eastby was considered to begin. He owned a couple of houses near here as well, if he remembered correctly, but he couldn't go hunting for them because the street signs were missing from the walls of the corner houses of most of the various terraces. Faded patches showed where they had once been – but clearly that hadn't been recently.

When he got to what must have once been the centre of the village, his heart sank and he let out an involuntary groan. His houses must be near here, and if they were anything like all the others he could see, they'd be downright dilapidated. They might even be among the group on his right. He hoped not.

This was the last thing he'd expected to find about his inheritance.

23

As Adam started to walk again, he was jerked out of his thoughts by a man stopping in front of him and barring his way with an outstretched hand, not from malice but, judging by the expression on this stranger's face, from sheer shock.

'Who the hell are you?' he demanded.

Adam stared at him in surprise. 'What business is that of yours? Please move out of my way.'

'Not till you've told me who you are. You're the spitting image of my half-brother, could be his twin, only he's dead and he never had any children.' He studied the younger man's face again, shook his head and then added slowly, 'At least . . . none that anyone knew about.'

Adam was startled. Did he resemble this unknown father so closely? The lawyer had also said he was the 'spitting image' of the man but Adam wouldn't have believed it could be such a close resemblance as to stop a passing stranger in his tracks. He hesitated, not knowing what to say or do.

The man glanced round, saw that they were attracting attention and lowered his voice, saying abruptly, 'You can only be Jim's son. You look just like he did when he was younger. I remember it so clearly. Are you going to deny that relationship?'

'No. But you haven't told me your name. Or said what concern this is of yours.'

'I'm Lionel Entwistle, his younger half-brother. Which means that I'm your uncle.' After another frown and glance round he said, 'I think we need to talk. My farm's just up the road, on the other side of Eastby. Only five minutes' walk away. Will you come there with me and discuss this? If we're relatives, we ought to know one another, don't you think?'

Adam hesitated then gave in. He'd come here to look into his family background and hadn't needed to do any searching because it seemed to have immediately found him. 'Yes, of course I'll come with you. I'm Adam Dean, by the way. And for your information, I only found out a few days ago that Jim Entwistle was my father. I've never actually met him.'

That brought another surprised look to Lionel's face, then after another glance round he said, 'Come on. People are staring at us and I'd rather keep our business private, or as private as we can in such a small place. Not to mention that I won't be the only person to notice your resemblance to Jim.'

'Weren't you going somewhere?'

'It can wait. This is far more important.'

They walked briskly along a couple more streets of shabby dwellings, after which the terraces of houses seemed to be in a slightly better condition with each street they came to. And there were street names showing at the corners of houses here. Adam noticed one he'd been looking for. 'Just a minute.' He stopped outside Number 12 and pulled the crumpled piece of paper out of his pocket, giving it a quick glance. 'Isn't this one of your brother's properties?'

'I wouldn't know. You tell me. He and I hadn't talked for years, not since I inherited the farm and he didn't.'

'Well, I may never have met him but he left me some properties in Eastby and I think this is one of them.'

'Properties? He owned more than one house? He must have done better than anyone realised.'

A woman passing by stopped to gape at the pair of them and Lionel tugged Adam's arm. 'The explanation can wait till we have some privacy. You must be here for some reason today. Why did you wait so long to come here if you'd inherited several properties? He's been dead for a few months.'

'The lawyer only just found out where I was living. My mother had always refused to tell me anything about my father so I knew nothing about him.'

'I wonder why Jim didn't get to know you.'

'I have no idea. He wrote me a goodbye letter, one page long, and that was the only contact I've ever had from him.' And that lack made him feel angry every time he thought about it.

'Jim turned into a right old miser as he grew older, only spoke to people he was doing business with or to the old woman who looked after the cottage at the edge of the family farm where he lived. That cottage and a modest sum of money were all he'd inherited from our father.' He shook his head sadly before going on. 'He became a recluse and for the last few years he didn't even go down to the pub to have a drink and chat. He stopped seeing every single one of his former friends. May I ask? Who is your mother?'

'Was. She died over a year before he did, from the influenza.'

'I'm sorry.'

'And just so we get things straight, she might not have been married to him but she was a decent woman and a good mother to me. I still miss her.' Adam waited, quite prepared to walk away from this man, uncle or not, if he said anything bad about his mother. To his surprise, he didn't.

'I didn't know her but you sound to have been lucky in her as a mother. Jim's legal wife was a horrible woman. Our father pushed him into marrying her because she had a big dowry. He was a bully, did the same to me, forced me to marry a woman when I didn't want to. I only did it because he'd promised me the farm, and at least he kept that promise. We had a sister too, but Mavis died young, leaving a small daughter. Her husband was killed the year after in a farm accident. Eh, we've had some bad luck in our family, lost a lot of people too young.'

Lionel stopped, blew his nose, dabbed his eyes and set off walking again. This time Adam didn't need telling to walk along beside him. He rather liked the looks of this man. He couldn't help noticing that they were about the same height, had the same dark, unruly hair, bar a few grey threads at his uncle's temples. And the determined expression on his uncle's face was similar to the one he saw on his own face sometimes in the bathroom mirror.

They passed a piece of land with a low wall round it and Lionel stopped for a moment to wave one hand towards it. 'This land isn't a farm, though it's next to ours. These few acres belong to the Townley family and have done for over a hundred years. They call it their "estate". The wall marks the border of what used to be Eastby village.'

'It'll have nice views.'

'Yes, it does. A youngish fellow has just inherited the land and house. I don't know much about him yet but he's made a good start, as far as I'm concerned. He's recently done me a big favour, so I intend to give him a chance to show what he's worth and wait to pass judgement on him just because his name's Townley.'

Adam spoke without thinking, 'Imagine knowing that much about your family.'

'I can tell you about ours if you're interested, the last two or three generations anyway. As for the Townley family, there's been a feud between them and the Entwistles for a few decades, only as I said, give him his due, this new heir doesn't seem to want to continue at odds with us.'

He started moving again, walked in silence for a few paces then said abruptly, 'My life has been changing in a few ways lately and now that you've turned up, it'll affect the whole family too, I dare say. I never saw such a strong resemblance in my life as there is between you and my half-brother. I near died of shock when I saw you walking towards me in the village.'

Adam gave him a wry smile. 'So much for me coming to have a quiet look round Eastby without telling anyone who I was before I made myself known. This was my first visit. Oh well . . . ' He stopped and held out his hand. 'Let's do this properly. Pleased to meet you, Uncle Lionel.'

The man not only shook Adam's hand but clasped it between both of his for a few seconds with an earnest look. 'I'm pleased to meet you too, Adam lad, truly pleased. Welcome to the family.'

'Thank you.'

They walked on in silence then Lionel slowed down and indicated a farm track on the left. 'We're down here.'

As they turned on to it he said, 'This is more than just my farm, it's the Entwistle family farm. We've lived here for a few generations. That cottage at the far right belonged to your father so I suppose it's yours now. The old lady who acted as his housekeeper is still living there. Edie was loyal to him so I hope you're not going to throw her out. It's her only home nowadays because her husband died and the rest of her family moved away. But she'd not be happy living in Yorkshire with them, I've heard her say Ollindale is her home.'

'No, of course I won't throw her out.'

'Good. The farm isn't a big place, but I care deeply about it. I married my present wife, Thelma, after my first wife died in childbirth. I was trying to give the place an heir and my father approved because she brought me some money as well. I thought we'd manage to rub along together and we'd be all right if there were more bad times.' He sighed and slowed down, adding, 'Only, she hasn't given me the child I was looking for, so what use is it having money? And she's grown more and more bad-tempered, not just with me but in the way she deals with everyone. Eh, marrying for money isn't worth it, lad. When you marry, do it for love or don't do it at all.'

Adam was surprised his uncle would be so frank, but only made a non-committal sound because he didn't know what to say for the best. He'd never rush into marriage, had never met a woman he'd want to spend his life with anyway, been too busy with his job to look for one seriously.

At the door of the farmhouse Lionel stopped and looked a bit embarrassed. 'Please ignore Thelma if she's rude to you. Well, it's not "if", she will be for sure. It's not you.

She's rude to everyone these days. I don't know what's got into her lately. She even chased my young niece away, my dead sister's child. How can a quiet little ten-year-old be causing trouble as Thelma claimed? Good thing Minnie has grandparents on her father's side to take her in but I miss her.'

He opened a gate and gestured to Adam to go through, then closed it carefully. He grabbed the younger man's sleeve to hold him back and said, 'We'll get mugs of tea and take them out into the barn to talk, if that's all right with you? Don't discuss anything important till we're out there.'

'Can I ask why the farm was left to you? Was there a particular reason?'

'Yes. Because I'm a much better farmer than Jim was and my father didn't think he'd have any children, said he was a sickly fellow. Dad knew I cared about the farm.' He looked at his nephew pleadingly. 'Don't let my wife upset you and drive you away.'

'No one can control what other people say and do, can they? I shan't blame you for what your wife says or does.'

'No one can control her in any way these days, that's for sure.' Lionel reached out to open the door, looked back and paused with his hand in mid-air to stare yet again. 'Eh, I can't get over how like Jim you are.'

'Your reaction has given me a big surprise too.'

But he'd longed for a family and now it looked like he'd found one person at least. Surely his relationship with this man would be a good thing? He hoped so because Lionel seemed a nice chap, basically.

24

The door led into a broad hall with high coat hooks on one side and a low metal rack for footwear running along just above the floor beneath them. Lionel wiped his feet on the doormat and opened the inner door to reveal a large farm kitchen. 'I've brought a visitor, Thelma.'

Adam thought it better to hover in the hall side of the doorway till Lionel had explained who he was but he could see and hear what was going on in the kitchen.

An extremely scrawny woman of indeterminate age had been cutting a slice of bread, but dropped the knife and leaned heavily against the table, scowling across the room at her husband and making a gesture as if to push him away.

'Now that your mother's left, I can't cope with visitors, Lionel, as I told you yesterday and again this morning. You can jolly well take that man away again and send him off to visit someone else.'

'I don't think so. This is my nephew. I ran into him in town.'

She'd turned away but spun back to glare at her husband. '*Nephew!* You haven't got a nephew. What lies are you cooking up now?'

'None. It seems I do have a nephew. And there's no doubt he's Jim's lad. See for yourself.' He beckoned to Adam to come fully into the kitchen. She glanced at him and gasped, pressing her right hand against her chest and breathing in ragged gasps.

This time Adam didn't need to ask why she was so shocked so he waited for his uncle to take the lead.

'Adam, this is my wife, your aunt Thelma.'

She stepped back, making another of those pushing away gestures and saying in a harsh voice, 'I don't care whether he's your nephew or the king's uncle, I still can't cope with visitors.'

'I'll do the coping. I'm perfectly capable of making us mugs of tea, after which we'll leave you in peace and take them out to the barn so we can have a little chat and start getting to know one another.'

'No, I said! Send him away from here. I don't want a stranger poking his nose into our affairs.'

To Adam's surprise she tried to get between her husband and the kettle to stop him using it.

Lionel moved her gently out of the way, filling the kettle from a single cold tap then pushing it on to the hot part of the kitchen range.

She continued to screech at her husband to leave her in peace and tried to shove him out of the room.

At that Lionel sat her down forcibly at the table, frowning and studying her face. 'Are you feeling ill again, Thelma? You're bone white and you look absolutely haggard.'

'How do you expect me to look when your mother walks out on us and leaves everything in this big house to me? And then, to cap it all, you bring home a guest.'

'My mother wasn't our slave and if you hadn't treated her so badly, she might not have left. It's a free country, you know, and it was up to her not you whether she stayed or left. We now have to respect her decision and get on with our lives without her.'

He still kept an eye on his wife while he rinsed out the teapot with a little hot water, spooned in some tea leaves and deftly poured the boiling water into it without spilling a drop.

This time she didn't attempt to prevent him but the looks she threw at him would have curdled milk, Adam thought. He leaned against the door frame and waited, feeling extremely uncomfortable but trying not to show it.

When the tea had brewed sufficiently for two mugs of it to be poured through a little hand-held sieve to catch the tea leaves, his uncle asked, 'Sugar and milk?'

'No sugar, thanks. Just milk.'

'Here you are, then.' Lionel held out the full mug and Adam took it, careful not to spill any with his uncle's wife glaring at him from nearby.

'Come this way.' Lionel stopped at the door and looked back at his wife. 'We'll leave you in peace, Thelma. If you're still ill when I come back, though, I'm calling in the doctor.'

'I won't see that Dr Coxton, even if you do. Women aren't proper doctors. They can't be. And don't expect a meal to be waiting for you when you've got rid of *him*, either. You'll have to make do with bread and cheese.'

She got up, stumbling and looking dizzy for a moment or two, then going out of the kitchen by a door on the other side. She banged it shut behind her and stamped the whole way up the stairs to judge from the sounds filtering back.

'This way, lad. We'll still have our chat in the barn, if you don't mind, because it's more private there. She might not want to talk to people but she's a devil for eavesdropping.'

When they got there, Lionel gestured to some bales of hay. 'Take a seat. I'm sorry about your reception. My mother, who must be your great-aunt come to think of it, had stayed on to help us after my father died. She'd been doing most of the housekeeping here but recently found a good job as a housekeeper. I don't blame her at all for leaving because Thelma made her life a misery and didn't show any gratitude for all the hard work she put in.'

'I see. So I have another relative to meet as well as you.'

'Yes. And a far more pleasant one than my wife. Everyone round here likes and respects my mother. I hadn't realised how bad Thelma was at coping with the housework till I had her to myself. It must have been my mother's efficiency that kept things up to scratch. And . . . well, I'm beginning to suspect that Thelma is seriously ill, far worse than she admits and she's . . . to be honest, not thinking straight. I do my best to help her but if you can't get someone to go and see a doctor, it's difficult to help them get better, isn't it?'

Adam felt sorry for him. 'It is. And I hate to add to your troubles.'

'You're not adding to them; you're cheering me up. I'm very glad to meet you, glad you exist to be frank, since I haven't managed to produce an heir. But I shall have to do something about Thelma now. She's becoming very aggressive, throws things at people, dangerous things sometimes like a pan of boiling water I only just managed to dodge the other day.'

He shook his head at that memory then gave Adam another worried glance. 'I think only my mother knew how bad Thelma was and I don't blame her for leaving.

Eh, the whole situation has got me right mithered about what to do for the best, it has that.'

He stared down into his mug for a moment then looked across at Adam. 'Ah well, this is no way to make you feel welcome and you'll like my mother, at least. And don't think I blame her for leaving because I don't. She stuck it out here for longer than anyone else would have done. Mum's too young and full of energy to hover at the fringes of my life and she's found herself a really good job as housekeeper to Mr Townley, him with the estate next to the farm. You're bound to meet her – and him. It's a small place, Eastby.'

He took a long slurp of tea, gave a murmur of pleasure and took another before saying quietly, 'Tell me how you found out about our family and why you came here, what you plan to do next.'

So Adam did his best to explain succinctly a situation that still puzzled him, if truth be told.

'I didn't realise Jim owned all those houses in the village,' Lionel said when he'd finished. 'I thought he only owned the farm cottage our father left him. You'd think I would have known about them, wouldn't you, him being my half-brother? But he and I were never close, and he was always a secretive sod.' Another pause, then, 'I'd have expected him to look after his properties better than that, though. He didn't even mend the roof on the cottage he lived in here. I had to do that last year for shame because it was on the family farm. Whatever was he thinking of?'

'Money.'

'Aye, I suppose so. It does come in useful but it makes a poor master if it's the only thing you live your life for. I saw that in my own father as well. He wasn't a kind man.'

Adam waited, letting his uncle continue to guide the conversation.

'Well, there you are, lad. Every family has problems of some sort and difficult people in it to deal with, don't they?'

'I suppose they do. I think one of my first tasks here is going to be setting the properties I inherited to rights. I can't bear to leave them so shabby, looking as if they're about to fall down. And it's not fair to those living in them and paying rent, either. After I've done that, I don't know whether I'll stay in Ollindale or find somewhere else to live. It never occurred to me that I'd one day have enough money to choose.'

'I'd be the same about repairing the houses but I hope you'll stay here, obviously. You didn't say how you've been earning your living, what sort of work you've been doing?'

'Working in a garage. I enjoy repairing motor cars and bicycles and I'd like to manufacture them to my own design one day. I'd not make all the parts myself, obviously, but you can buy a chassis and a variety of different parts and put them together in your own way.' He stopped for a moment then said, sounding faintly surprised, 'I may be able to do that now. I haven't got used to the idea yet that I have enough money behind me to do what I want.'

'I wonder anyone would want to fiddle around with motor cars. They seem like dirty, smelly things to me.'

'Not if they're looked after properly. They're the coming way of people getting places and will gradually replace horses and perhaps even trams in towns, believe me. They can go much further and faster, and they don't need feeding and mucking out when they're not being used. And why I'm telling you all this when we've only just met, I can't figure out. I don't usually tell strangers the story of my life or what I want to do with it.'

'I may be a stranger, but I think I'm your closest relative now, so I hope I won't *stay* a stranger. And you're one of my closest relatives too, you, my mother and young Minnie, my niece. I'm only sorry that I can't offer to put you up, for obvious reasons.' He stood up abruptly. 'I'd better get back to keep an eye on what she's doing. Please don't leave town, lad. Close relatives should know one another, don't you think?'

'I won't leave without telling you and I'll stay in touch whatever happens and wherever I go.'

'Thank you.' Lionel sighed and looked towards the house. 'I'd better find out how Thelma is really feeling. I'm pretty certain I'll have to get the doctor to come out and see her, or I'd spend longer with you today.'

'Can I do anything to help?'

'I doubt it, but thank you for offering. If Thelma needs to see the doctor then I need to be there to know what Dr Coxton says about her state of health. She's a decent person, our doctor is, woman or not, and I reckon she knows what she's doing as well as any male doctor. And other people say the same.'

'I'd have thought a woman would actually prefer to have a female doctor looking at her.'

'Thelma doesn't seem to like anything or anyone these days.'

'I'd see anyone I had to if I were ill.'

'Me too. I don't know why people make such a fuss about women touching men's bodies. That's what doctors need to do, isn't it? They must think about bodies like we think about our tools when we're doing a job around the farm.'

Lionel began walking towards the door of the barn. 'You should go straight back to the hotel now, lad.'

'I was going to look in at the cottage and meet the woman who's been doing the housekeeping there.'

'You'd better leave that till another time. I'll pop in and tell her you're happy for her to stay there and that'll relieve her worries. You don't want to be anywhere near the centre of Eastby on your own after dark.'

'So everyone tells me.'

'It's good advice. I'll be in touch when I can, within a day or two for sure.'

'I shall look forward to chatting to you again, Uncle Lionel.'

The older man stopped and smiled at him. 'Uncle,' he said. 'How good that sounds.'

Lionel was rather young to be his uncle, Adam thought with a smile.

He'd been warned by several people now about how rough Eastby was at night, so he kept that in mind as he walked briskly back into Ollerthwaite town centre and made his way to the hotel. He had a lot to think about, had encountered one surprise after another today. His aunt was very strange. An aunt by marriage, thank goodness. None of her family in his body. And maybe his uncle was going to need his support in the near future. If Adam had ever seen a woman who was terminally ill, it was Thelma Entwistle. She had what he thought of as 'that death look' on her face. He'd seen it before on his own mother's face.

He was greeted pleasantly by the owners of the hotel, enjoyed a delicious but solitary meal and then had an early night. It had been a busy day so he doubted he'd have any trouble getting to sleep.

He couldn't help wondering as he snuggled down in the comfortable bed whether tomorrow would bring him further shocks. He'd better go and see the lawyer in the morning before he did anything else. Get that out of the way at least.

25

The following morning Lionel found the kitchen unoccupied when he got up, which was unusual, so set the fire to burn up again in the range and went upstairs to check on Thelma. She'd had her own bedroom for a while and it had been a relief to him to be able to sleep in peace on his own, but he still kept an eye on her because something wasn't 'right'. He didn't know what sort of illness to call it, though, and she wouldn't discuss how she felt, let alone see the doctor.

She greeted him with, 'Go away. I feel tired so I'm going to stay in bed today.'

She refused to say anything else and when he pressed for details of how she felt, she simply turned her head away from him and closed her eyes. The trouble was, she looked so pale today as to seem almost transparent and to him she appeared to be getting worse. She'd never kept to her bed all day before, that was sure.

Lionel didn't tell her what he was going to do but sent the farm lad into town to leave a message at Dr Coxton's to call in and see his wife as a matter of urgency. To his surprise the doctor turned up an hour later. As he let her in, he said in a low voice, 'My wife is still in bed, doctor, and she looks dreadful. She doesn't know I've asked you to come and see her.'

'I saw her in town a few weeks ago and thought she was looking unwell but when I went over to speak to her, she walked right past me without even a hello. Tell me what she's been like lately and exactly why you sent for me today before I go up to see her.'

So Lionel explained and answered a couple of questions as best he could, ending, 'I can't let her go on like this, Dr Coxton. She's getting worse all the time, even though she insists she's all right. She's so thin now she tries to hide it by wearing extra layers of clothes, but if she thinks I don't notice that, she's wrong. The truth is, she looks more like a walking skeleton these days.'

'Would you say she was in her right mind?'

He stared in shock at that, then shook his head and admitted it, something he was always reluctant to do. 'No. Sadly, she's become very strange – though she was always a bit different from other people.'

'That's important for how I feel it's right to treat her. Who knows her better than you, after all?'

As they went upstairs Thelma called from inside the room for him to go away and leave her in peace.

Dr Coxton whispered, 'You'd better stay within earshot in case I need help persuading her to let me examine her. Even her voice sounds breathless today, doesn't it?'

The minute the doctor entered the bedroom, Thelma found enough breath to yell, 'Who sent for you? Go away! I'm not seeing anyone. *Go – away!*' She choked on the last words and started coughing, couldn't stop for a few moments.

Lionel followed the doctor in without waiting to be summoned. He hadn't seen his wife wearing only a thin nightgown for a while, and it revealed all too clearly how skeletal she'd become – and it betrayed something else as well, something that made him exchange surprised glances with the doctor.

'Please let me check you, Mrs Entwistle,' Dr Coxton said gently, stretching out one hand.

Thelma batted the hand away. 'No! Leave me alone. I don't want you here.' She had trouble continuing, sounded to be forcing out words. 'I don't want . . . to see *anyone*. And I don't want anyone to see me.'

'The doctor has only come to check how you are so that she can help you,' Lionel said.

'I don't want help! *Go away this minute!*'

The doctor gave him a sad look and said in a low voice, 'There may be nothing we can do, but I do think I should check her more thoroughly, just to be sure. Did you see a large lump to one side of her chest?'

'Yes.'

'I need to look at it properly.'

She stepped forward and beckoned to him to help, so he braced himself to hold his wife still while the doctor checked her body gently, especially the area where a large lump was clearly visible under the skin. This didn't take long and the whole time Thelma struggled and spluttered as she tried to yell at them. He had his work cut out to hold her still.

When the doctor let go and stepped away from the bed, gesturing to him to move back too, Thelma said, 'You're a fool, doctor or not. I know what's wrong. It's a growth. My grandmother died of the same thing. Why can't you leave me to spend my final weeks in peace?'

The doctor didn't attempt to deny that her patient was extremely ill. 'Someone will have to help you as you get weaker, Mrs Entwistle.'

'I'll ask for help if and when I need it.' She gave Lionel a sneering look. 'And don't you be bringing that mother of yours back to my house because I'll stab her with the nearest kitchen knife if she ever sets one foot over this threshold again.'

Both Lionel and Dr Coxton gasped at this, but Thelma rolled over and pulled the covers up again, dragging the top of the sheet up to cover her whole head.

The doctor gestured towards the door with a movement of her head, so Lionel followed her out and back down to the kitchen.

'I didn't even know about that lump, doctor. How could she have hidden it for so long? That must be why she demanded a separate bedroom. She insisted it was my fault, said I was so restless at night I was keeping her awake. I was glad to get away from her by then so I didn't argue.'

'People who're in distress can do the most surprising things at times. Why is she so fierce about not having your mother back to help out? I have a great deal of respect for Mrs Entwistle. Well, everyone round here does. She's kind as well as efficient.'

'Thelma has never got on well with my mother, or even tried to, but strangely, when my mother found herself a job and left, she was furious about Mum leaving.'

'She was perhaps expecting your mother to care for her as she grew weaker.'

'Who'd want to care for someone who was so unpleasant and rude? But surely Mum must have noticed something about her?'

'Your mother may have been trying to respect your wife's wishes to keep her problem secret. Maybe something pushed her over the edge recently and she couldn't stand it here a minute longer. Whatever it was, I don't think you should try to bring her back, not if that recent reaction from your wife is anything to judge by. She really might try to carry out the threat to kill your mother.'

'I have to do something though. I can't run the house as well as the farm.'

'Can you hire someone else from Eastby to help out, perhaps? Someone she will put up with?'

He ran one hand through his hair, struggling to think clearly, he was so upset, then shaking his head. 'I have the money to pay for help but I don't know of anyone suitable who's free to come here. Have you heard of anyone looking for work?'

She stood frowning for a moment then said, 'I think I have, actually. Young Mrs Lucas in Ollerthwaite just lost her husband in that accident with the runaway horse and cart. She's strong and sensible.'

'That driver was shockingly careless. Good thing he's run off and left the area. He'd never have got a job in the valley again.'

'I heard that Mrs Lucas is about to move back in with her parents but perhaps she might welcome the house-keeping job here instead. Once women have had their independence, they don't usually want to go back to being bossed around by their parents. Mrs Lucas hasn't got any children, nor is she expecting, by the way. It certainly won't do any harm to ask her if she's interested in coming to work here.'

'You'd better tell her how difficult Thelma is. We don't want to waste her time.'

'I'll do that.'

'Look, I'm so busy I don't know whether I'm coming or going, as well as having to keep an eye on Thelma. Could you possibly ask Mrs Lucas if she's interested in the job? I know it's a lot to ask of a busy person like you, but . . .' He spread out his arms in a helpless gesture.

She patted his hand. 'Yes, I can do that. I have to go into that part of Ollerthwaite later so it won't be far out of my way. I'm really sorry I can't help your wife. I don't see any purpose in forcing my attentions on her because there's nothing to be done for that sort of growth. However, if she needs relief from pain, as she probably will later, I can prescribe something strong enough to help her through.'

'Thank you. I'll remember that.'

'What about wages? How much are you offering to pay Mrs Lucas?'

'Whatever she thinks suitable. And she'll be in total charge of the house because I reckon Thelma's done very little lately. She looked to me to be struggling to move about yesterday. I've never seen her so weak.'

'She might not have any choice about keeping to her bed. At this stage people with a problem like that can go downhill very quickly.'

He saw the doctor out and then went to sit in the kitchen on his own, elbows on the table, head resting on his hands, trying to come to terms with the situation. Thelma had been very cunning to have hidden her problem from him for so long. Hah! She had always been cunning, manipulating him and getting her own way, abusing his mother's kindness – though he knew now that wasn't from laziness but because she was ill.

So many times he'd wished he hadn't given in to his father's pressure and married her. Ironically his father had died soon after the wedding and it turned out the dowry money had gone to paying off some debts, because the farm hadn't been doing well. No wonder he'd been hard to live with till his younger son agreed to do as he demanded and marry Thelma. Maybe that was why their father had left the farm to him.

But although Lionel had quickly regretted the marriage, even to save his beloved farm, he wouldn't have wished to get out of it by his wife dying so young.

Feeling the need to get some fresh air Lionel went to do some jobs outside. Then he looked across the field and decided to nip over to Townley House to tell his mother what was going on with Thelma before he began work. She would spread the word for him to those it might affect. There wouldn't be many.

He hoped she might have some useful advice for him on how to cope with the situation when things went downhill, as the doctor said they would. He felt to be floundering around at the moment, not knowing what to think or do about the situation.

His mother was a very wise woman in the old-fashioned sense of the word, seemed to know things instinctively without the need for modern science to guide her or articles in magazines and newspapers. There weren't many women like her around these days or at any time, come to that.

He kept remembering how bad Thelma had looked. Eh, no wonder she'd stopped going out and about. People would have noticed how she'd changed. Why would she not let anyone help her, though?

He answered that himself after only a moment's thought. Because she was a fiercely private sort of person, that's why. Even with him. For all they were married and had been trying for a child, he'd never seen her naked and she'd merely put up with the attentions he'd found hard to summon up towards her because she too would have welcomed a child.

He shuddered at the unhappy memories of trying to do that. He was glad now that it hadn't worked. He didn't want to bring children like her into the world.

He found Megan outside at the back of the house pegging out some washing.

When she saw him coming she waved to him with her usual cheerful smile. 'Your mother's in the kitchen. Mr Townley is out and she's on her own, so you can go straight in.'

'Thanks.'

His mother was getting something out of a cupboard. When she heard the door open, she swung round, saying, 'Megan, will you — Oh, it's you, Lionel. We don't usually see you at this time of day.'

He stared at her, not sure how to start.

As she stared back her voice grew gentle. 'Eh, what's wrong, love?'

'You can always tell when I'm having trouble, can't you, Ma?' He told her about Thelma.

She stared for a moment then said, 'I knew something wasn't right with her but I couldn't work out what it was. Then she was so rude to me I couldn't wait to leave when I got the chance. I'll come back and help out now, though.

Well, I will as long as she stays out of my way. I'm sure Mr Townley will understand.'

'Thank you but better not. She'll go mad if she sees you. She gets angry if I even mention your name and she threatened to kill you if you step inside the house again.'

Shock made her stand perfectly still and stare at him. 'She said that?'

'Yes. She's gone insane, I think. Dr Coxton agrees. But Thelma is also very ill and getting rapidly worse, so we'll not need to do anything about locking her away.'

'Insane,' she whispered.

'She's grown a lot worse in the past few days. Anyway, you'd better not even try to visit me, but thanks for offering to help. Dr Coxton says she might let someone else come and work as housekeeper and has suggested Emmy Lucas. The doctor is going to ask her for me. Do you know anything about her?'

'Yes. She's a very capable young woman. Sam Lucas getting killed in that accident at work was a shock to everyone. I don't know whether it's good or bad that they hadn't started a child. They'd only been married a few weeks, but actually, I didn't think they were looking happy when they were together so maybe she's not as upset as some might be about losing him. I never liked him.'

There was a moment's silence, then she went on, 'Anyway, that's irrelevant now he's dead, isn't it? There must be something I can do to help you, though.'

'I'll ask you if something crops up. I came today not only to ask what you think about Emmy, but because I thought you should know about Thelma. Will you tell anyone who might need to know that she's dying from a growth?'

'I can't think of anyone because her parents have moved away to live with her brother. But I will spread the word vaguely that she's ill. Come here, love.' She walked across and pulled him into a long hug, rocking him slightly then pushing him gently to arm's length to caress his face. 'If there's anything I can do, anything at all, you have only to ask me, Lionel love. You know that, don't you?'

'Yes, I do. You've always been there for me.'

She stepped away. 'Cup of tea?'

'Not now, thanks. I'd better get back. I'm hoping Emmy Lucas will come round soon after Dr Coxton speaks to her. In the meantime, you know what it's like on a farm. There's always something to attend to.'

'Yes. I know. Takes a man and wife to run one properly and they're neither of them allowed time off to be ill.'

He couldn't resist asking, 'Did you have any idea at all that Thelma was so bad?'

'I did wonder if something was wrong with her, but only recently. Eh, poor lass. Whether you like her or not, you wouldn't wish that on her so young.' She patted his cheek gently. 'Or on you who will have to watch it happen.'

'I agree. I can't think what to do to help her. I feel absolutely helpless.'

'Some folk, like some animals, prefer to hide away and die on their own. I think your Thelma is one of those. Just stand ready to help her if she asks, lad. No one can do more.'

26

Mrs Lucas turned up at the farm an hour later. Lionel saw a woman coming along the lane towards the farm, looking rosy and energetic, so absolutely normal it lifted his spirits just to see her! Like most younger women she wore her skirts shorter than his wife and mother had, so was able to stride out.

Could this be his possible housekeeper? He did hope so. The way she was smiling made him feel that her presence would brighten his life if she came to work for him, which surprised him. He went out to meet her, not waiting for her to knock at the door.

She spoke first. 'Mr Entwistle?'

'Yes, and you must be Mrs Lucas.'

'I am. Dr Coxton said you needed a housekeeper and I need a job.'

'I do. Did she explain why?'

'Yes. She not only told me about your wife being ill but also how it would be best to deal with her if I came to work here.'

'And that didn't put you off?'

'Not at all. No job is perfect.'

'Let's go inside, then, and you can look round, see if you're willing to take on the care of this house.'

He showed her round the downstairs rooms then took her upstairs, pointing out Thelma's bedroom but not taking her into it. They ended up in the attic where there were two bedrooms as well as a big open area where some rarely used or damaged items were stored.

'One of these bedrooms can be yours if you come here and as they're so small, you're welcome to use the other as a sort of sitting room if it's warm enough and you want to spend your spare time on your own – or you can join me downstairs in the kitchen in the evenings. I'm happy either way.' He risked adding, 'I don't think I'm hard to get on with, unlike my wife.'

'So people tell me.' She didn't wait for him to comment but went to check whether the dormer windows opened and closed properly, which they did.

That seemed promising, but though she'd now seen nearly all of the house, she hadn't yet given any real hint of what she was thinking.

He looked at her anxiously when they were standing in the kitchen again. 'Will you . . . take the job? I think we could get along. I'd try not to be too demanding.'

She gave a decisive nod. 'Yes. I'll be happy to, Mr Entwistle. You've been polite to me the whole time I've been here. I always appreciate being treated civilly.'

Such a comment surprised him. Who hadn't been polite to her? 'How soon can you start?'

'I can go back and get my things straight away. Mum's been helping me to clear out the house where my husband and I have been living. I have to leave it by tomorrow because even if I found a job, I couldn't afford the rent on a woman's wages. Um, you haven't said what wages you're paying?'

'Oh, sorry! I'll pay whatever you think fair. It'll be awkward at times with Thelma being the way she is, so I'm happy for you to decide what you'll feel will be right. Higher wages than usual, I'm sure.'

'That's a very generous way of looking at it but I've never worked as a housekeeper before so I don't really know what to ask for.'

'You might like to discuss it with my mother, then. She'd tell you what's fair. Do you know her?'

'I've met her a few times. She's a kind woman, always helping people. Yes, good idea. I'll ask her.'

'I'll happily pay whatever she thinks right.'

'Thank you. And just so that you know, I'm particularly happy to take the job because I didn't want to go back to live at the farm where my father would have me working hard without wages.'

He walked to the door with her. 'I'm afraid I can't offer to take you back in my cart to collect your things because I feel someone needs to be here to keep an eye on my wife at the moment. She's been acting even more strangely than usual today. If you give me your address and you leave your things ready just inside the front door, I can go and collect them once you're here.'

'No need for that, Mr Entwistle. My brother's already offered to bring me and my possessions here if I got the job. Is it all right if I bring a few more things than Mum says live-in workers usually do? I have some bits and pieces of furniture, you see, and if I leave them at my parents' farm they'll get used and damaged, or even sold. One is a rather pretty workbox I inherited from my god-mother. I'm particularly fond of it.'

'Of course it's all right. There's plenty of room in the attic, as you've seen.'

'And will it be all right if my brother and Mum visit me occasionally? We'll be very quiet.'

'Yes. Just behave as if you're one of the family while you're working here, which you will be, practically speaking. You don't need to ask permission for your relatives to pop in, and I'm not the sort of employer to stand on my dignity either. In fact, I shall feel more comfortable if you call me by my first name from now on: which is Lionel.'

She smiled at him. 'I'm a bit that way too, given the chance. You can call me Emmy. My full name is Emmeline, but that's such a mouthful it never gets used in full.'

'It's a pretty name but I'll call you Emmy if that's what you prefer.'

'I do. Thank you, Lionel.'

'You're welcome, Emmy.'

As he saw her out, he thought what a nice change it had been to chat to a smiling, friendly person. In fact, her presence had done what he'd hoped and brightened his day. He couldn't remember the last time Thelma had actually smiled or spoken pleasantly to anyone.

He suddenly realised there had been no sound from upstairs the whole time Emmy was here, so he could only suppose Thelma really had been asleep – or eavesdropping again. Though she'd not have heard anything wrong being said or done.

He sighed, worried about how she'd behave towards the new housekeeper. He'd do whatever was needed to keep her from causing trouble. She had grown so strange lately he was getting very concerned about her behaviour. She'd started throwing the nearest object at him when something upset her. Surely she wouldn't do that to Emmy?

It had been so difficult here since his mother left. The fact that other people had lives to lead and work they needed to get on with was something Thelma never seemed to allow for. In fact she'd only really been concerned about her own needs all the time he'd been married to her, now he came to think of it. Why hadn't he realised what she was really like during their brief courtship?

She must have held back her temper then. If she'd been anything like this even his father's threats to disinherit him wouldn't have been enough to persuade him to marry her. The dowry she brought had never been the only reason for his decision. He'd wanted so much to start a family.

People should pay less attention to money when looking to find marriage partners and more to what people were like. Bad tempers were hard to live with. He'd never push a child of his to marry a difficult person for the money. Only, he wasn't likely to have children with Thelma so ill, was he?

And if she died – no, *when* she died, because there was little doubt now how ill she was – he doubted he could face trying marriage again. How could you ever be sure you'd be happy with someone?

When Emmy's brother brought her and her possessions to Moor House later that afternoon, Lionel went out to help carry her things in.

He thought he heard a noise upstairs as he was going out of the front door and looked up to see the bedroom curtain in Thelma's room moving about, even though the window wasn't open. He hoped she wasn't going to make one of her fusses about the newcomer. Surely even she would see the need to have the house looked after and meals prepared each day?

He helped carry Emmy's possessions into the house then waved goodbye to her brother. He'd not had much to do with any of the family before, because their farm was on the far side of Eastby, but her brother seemed pleasant enough. She hadn't mentioned her father though, not once, let alone him coming to visit her, only her mother and brother. Did she not get on with him?

When he and Emmy went back inside he suggested they have a cup of tea before doing anything else. 'I bet you've been rushing round packing and clearing up most of the day. And I've been busy too. I usually make myself a pot around now anyway. You can have it in a cup or a mug.'

'I prefer a mug, then you don't have to refill it as often. I don't mind being busy but it has been a bit too hectic today, I will admit. I'll make the tea under your guidance, shall I? I need to get used to where things are kept and how you like it.'

'Yes. Thank you. And you can rearrange the kitchen to your own liking as you settle in. I doubt Thelma will ever use it again.'

'She must be very ill, poor thing.'

'She is. But she's not a poor thing. She's a nasty creature. Don't trust her an inch.'

Emmy looked surprised then nodded. 'All right.' She looked round appraisingly and said quietly, 'Having things organised to suit both of us would be best, don't you think? You must have ways you like to do things.'

'I'm not a fussy person.' He really appreciated this attitude.

While they were waiting for the kettle to boil, there was a thumping sound from upstairs. It was repeated after a short time and he sighed. 'That'll be my wife knocking on the floor for attention. I didn't realise she had anything up there to knock with. I suppose I'd better go and see what she wants but before I do, I need to say that I'm the one in charge here not her now. If she bangs for attention, you don't have to go running up to see what the matter is until it's convenient.'

She nodded so he went on, 'I'm not letting her take absolute charge of your work because she's selfish and unrealistic about other people, expecting them to drop everything and come running the minute she wants something. Though of course if she needs help in any reasonable way, you should do what she asks. But you can't always break off in the middle of a different job, can you? And she'll need meals taking up. I'll do it if I'm at home, otherwise you can take hers up.'

'Dr Coxton said I should start as I meant to continue and make my position very clear.'

'Yes.'

The banging started again.

'I'll just nip up and see what she wants, then come back for my drink of tea.' Feeling reluctant he went up to his wife's bedroom, took a deep breath and opened the door.

Thelma greeted him with, 'I'd prefer you to knock on the door and wait until I tell you to come in.'

He wasn't having that. 'And I would prefer you to remember that this is my family's house, always has been and always will be so I have the right to go where I please when I please. You're not even well enough these days to oversee the housework, so you have no reason to order the new housekeeper about.'

He'd tried to say it gently but it clearly upset her and she let out one of her sudden screeches of rage. 'Don't you dare speak to me like that! I'm still your wife.'

'I shall speak to you how I choose from now on because you're never polite to me.'

She glared at him then asked, 'Who is that woman you've been showing round? I don't recognise her.'

'Mrs Lucas, our new housekeeper.'

She tried to haul herself into a more upright position in the bed but didn't manage to do it so had to sag back down on her pillows. 'Well, if you've chosen her she won't be good at her job, so you can just tell her to go away and I'll find my own housekeeper, thank you very much.'

'And how would you manage to do that? You're in no state to go hunting for one when you struggle even to sit up in bed. You had a good housekeeper but you drove my mother away so when Dr Coxton recommended Mrs Lucas, who has recently been widowed, I asked her to come and see me. She seems pleasant and competent, so I gave her the job. And I told her that I'm her employer, not you. So she is staying here whatever you say or do, *thank you very much.*'

He threw her own phrase back at her as he ended because he'd suddenly noticed his father's walking stick by the side of her bed. It had been in the hall stand earlier today. She hadn't been too feeble to go down and get it while he was working outside, had she? Had that tired her out? Was that why she'd had trouble pulling herself upright?

She followed his gaze. 'I needed some way of summoning help. I had to *crawl* up and down the stairs. I can't go up and down stairs now for every little thing I need so when I need something she'll have to help me.'

'Not when she's in the middle of another job or nothing will ever get done, let alone food being cooked properly.'

He let that sink in, then said firmly, 'I've mentioned your needs to Mrs Lucas, naturally, but I made it plain to her that she isn't *your* servant; she's here as *my* house-keeper. I'll bring her up and introduce her when she and I have finished our discussion about the job.'

'She's only staying if she's a good worker. I'll be watching her carefully.'

He was quite sure Thelma would try to find a way to interrupt Emmy's work and had a sudden idea, so said loudly and clearly, 'If you make it impossible for Mrs Lucas to do her job, I shall have to put you in the asylum, that place out on the moors, because I won't be able to take care of both you and the farm now that you're bedridden.'

She froze and stared at him open-mouthed looking suddenly terrified.

'I mean it, Thelma.' He didn't, couldn't have done that to anyone, because the asylum was notorious for ill-treating those incarcerated there. He hoped he'd hidden his true feelings, though, for Emmy's sake. He had to try to make his wife behave decently.

He waited a moment then pointed his right forefinger at her, jabbing it a few times as he spoke, for emphasis. 'Think about that as an alternative and try to be polite to her.'

He went downstairs before she could speak again and for once she didn't call after him.

Would this threat do the trick? Would she leave Emmy in peace to do the work needed to keep the house running?

He could only hope so.

27

When he got back to the kitchen Lionel shut the door to the hall and stairs quietly, though it was an effort not to slam it to vent his feelings about Thelma. He sank into a chair and asked, 'Is there any tea left in that pot? I need something to get a nasty taste out of my mouth.'

'She's upset you.'

'She often does. I'll calm down in a minute.'

'I'll make a new pot,' Emmy said quietly. 'You don't need to chat to me. You can just sit quietly for a while.'

By the time she set a mug of steaming tea down in front of him, he had more or less recovered. He looked at her very seriously. 'She's utterly beyond reason lately. I'm quite sure she's sick mentally.' He tapped his forehead. 'Well, the doctor has said as much. If you don't want to take the job, I'll understand, I really will, but if you can bear to stay I'd be so grateful. I've just told Thelma that if she drives you away, I'll put her in the asylum.'

She studied him, head on one side. 'I doubt you meant that.'

'No, but I think she believed me, though. But I meant one thing: don't feel you have to go rushing to answer when she calls.'

'I do understand that but I'll do my best to help Mrs Entwistle, as I would any sick creature.'

'Thank you. Why don't we each have another mug of tea then I'll take you up to meet her?'

He reached for the teapot, intending to refill his own mug but it was closer to Emmy's hand and she'd reached out at the same time, so their hands collided. Hers felt so warm and soft against his he wished he could hold it for the sheer comfort. And how stupid was it to think like that? He wasn't a child, was he?

He took his time, sipping the tea slowly because he didn't want to end this pleasant interlude and anyway, they should deal with a few of the practicalities of her job. 'Feel free to look in all the cupboards anywhere in the house, not just in the kitchen. My bedroom's a bit of a mess, as you saw, and I'll need to send a lot of clothes to the laundry this Friday because I forgot last week and Thelma didn't remind me.'

'It's easily done when you're busy. If you're running out of clean clothes, I can wash a few things by hand for you.'

'Thanks but I can manage. The laundry does all the sheets and towels, so you can change the sheets in rotation. They come every week on a Friday afternoon to take away the dirty clothes and bring back the clean ones. You're welcome to add your clothing to them and I'll pay.'

'Thank you.'

'Oh, and Mrs Harton comes in on Tuesdays and Thursdays to do the scrubbing and any other heavy work needed. If there's anything lacking, just say so.'

She looked round the kitchen, smiling. 'Actually, I'm looking forward to sorting everything out. This could be such a nice room. Is it all right if I put some pots of herbs on the windowsill?'

'Of course it is. It'll be good to see some plants brightening up the room again as they did when my mother was living here. Thelma never bothered with them and threw out the few my mother had left behind, pretended that they were dead, but she hadn't even attempted to water them.'

'What a waste! Oh, and I have a busy lizzy plant which would look nice at that side window across there. I've always had one since I was a child.' She took a deep breath as if facing something difficult and added, 'The plant I've got now is still quite small because my husband smashed my big one into the hearth in a fit of temper.'

He stared at her in shock.

'I prefer to start off with the truth between us, Lionel. You've no need to treat me as if I'm in mourning for my husband, because I'm not. Like you, I had problems with my marriage.'

'I'm sorry to hear that, but somehow, you're making me feel better already, as if life can go back to near normal in spite of Thelma.'

When he fell silent and gave her an enquiring look, she decided to tell him more about how things had been for her and then never mention her late husband again if she could help it.

'Things turned sour quite quickly once we were married, because Clarry stopped being kind or even polite, just started ordering me around. He thumped me for the first time a couple of weeks after the wedding. I wouldn't put up with that so I threw the nearest thing at him, which happened to be a jug.'

'I hope it wasn't empty.'

She smiled. 'No, it wasn't. It had some gravy in it. He looked silly with that dripping down his face.'

There was silence for a few moments, but it was a companionable silence, as if the confidences they'd exchanged had drawn them closer together.

Then Lionel caught sight of the clock and sighed. 'I'd better take you upstairs and introduce you properly, then I'll have to get on with my farm work.'

The bedroom smelled sour after the fresh air in the kitchen where the back door was open.

'Thelma, this is Mrs Lucas, who will be looking after the house from now on and cooking our meals.'

She scowled at Emmy. 'I hope you're a hard worker because *he* expects miracles.'

'I'm a very hard worker.' She went to stand by the window. 'You have a nice view from here, Mrs Entwistle. Would you like me to open the window for a few minutes to let some fresh air in?'

'No. I can still get across to it. I'll open it myself if I need to. I'd get blown away today by such a stupid suggestion.'

They left the bedroom quickly and both let out sighs of relief as they went back into the kitchen.

'Thelma made less fuss than I'd expected. I think she must have believed my threat.'

'She wasn't polite though, was she? And she looks very ill. Has she always been so unhappy?'

'Yes.'

'Why did you marry her, then, if you don't mind me asking? At least Clarry pretended to be nice to me for a while.'

'My father pushed me into it by threatening to leave the farm to my half-brother. But she didn't let her temper loose until after we were married so I hadn't realised quite how strange she was.'

'I was a fool not to get to know Clarry better before getting married. Only, my father wasn't good to live with either, and my mother always let him have his own way. I hated watching him boss her around. She's pleasant enough when we're on our own, so is my brother, but when he's there she's on edge all the time and only pays attention to him.'

She shrugged and started collecting the dirty dishes, clearly done with sharing information. 'I'll concentrate on getting this room looking nice first, shall I?'

'That'll be good. I'll get on with the farm work.' He stopped near the door. 'One more thing. We still keep a few chickens for the eggs. Do you want to look after them? If you've enough spare eggs to sell, you can keep the money they bring.'

'I can do that. I like chickens. They're companionable little creatures, given a bit of attention.'

'I'll check their water as I go out. You have enough on your plate here for the moment. Oh, and there's some ham in the larder, and I've been getting bread delivered. We could have ham and eggs for tea .

'Good.'

No sooner had Lionel left the house than there was a thumping from upstairs. Emmy doubted there could be anything urgent because it wasn't long since they'd seen her, so waited a while. She let two more sets of thumps go unanswered before getting so annoyed by it that she went up to see what Mrs Entwistle wanted.

She was definitely taking the advice of the doctor and Lionel and starting off as she meant to continue, acting politely but firmly. She didn't intend that woman to think she'd drop everything and go running upstairs whenever she heard thumping.

She was greeted by, 'I expect you to answer more quickly than this next time I knock for your attention, Lucas.'

'I'll do my best but I won't be able to come straight away if I'm in the middle of doing something that can't be left, like cooking.'

'*What?* Let me make it plain: you will obey my orders and serve me promptly while you're working here.'

Emmy looked at the spiteful face and her dislike of the woman in the bed grew stronger but she kept her voice level. 'Lionel has made it plain that I'm hired mainly as a housekeeper, not as a nurse, though of course I'll do what I can to help you.'

Thelma gaped at her. '*Lionel!* You aren't allowed to call your employer by his first name!'

'He asked me to. And when you address me, I'll be happy to answer to Mrs Lucas or Emmy but not to "Lucas".'

'You'll regret speaking to me like that – and he'll regret hiring you without my approval.'

Emmy didn't attempt to answer, just turned towards the door.

'Where are you going? I haven't dismissed you yet.'

'I'm going back to work, of course. The whole house is in a mess and you haven't asked me to do anything.'

'Bring me up a cup of tea at once, with two spoonfuls of sugar.'

'I'll do that as soon as I have time.'

As Emmy left the room and closed the door, something thumped against the inside of it and she wondered what that horrible woman had thrown. Well, it could lie there.

She hurried downstairs, closing the door to the kitchen behind her and leaning against it for a moment, shuddering in reaction. It had taken all her courage to speak up like that because she liked to get on with people and be polite. The sheer malevolence on that woman's face was horrible to see. Eh, poor Lionel, married to a woman like that!

And poor herself, too, having to run the house with that horrible creature hovering upstairs like a big, black cockroach. But she'd do it because Lionel was a nice chap, polite as you please, and was clearly in desperate need of help. Also, she admitted to herself a few moments later, because she didn't want to go back to live with her father. He had only seen her as a general dogsbody and had never paid her properly. She was going to save her wages carefully while she worked here because she never wanted to feel helpless for lack of money again.

She smiled at a sudden memory of Lionel's smile. Not only had he been polite and friendly towards her, but for some reason she felt quite certain he always would be. It was so different here from living with Clarry. She'd been shocked to the core the first time her husband had slapped her, because even her father hadn't done that to her mother.

She'd made sure his meal was late being served that evening but he'd had a couple of drinks and was a bit more relaxed, so only said, 'Don't be late again with my tea.'

'Don't hit me again then.'

But he'd thumped her, and she wasn't going to let him keep doing that, so she'd thrown the nearest thing at him again, which was her half-drunk mug of tea. Then she'd picked up a chair and fought back when he turned on her with his fists. That had taken him by surprise and she'd managed to give him a big bruise on the forehead to explain to his friends at the pub. She'd received several bruises of her own in return because he was stronger than she was, but that had never stopped her fighting back. Her determination must have got through to him because he'd stopped doing it, but he'd turned very grumpy and awkward to deal with.

But before his wariness had worn off and he'd started hitting her again, he'd been killed in the accident. She'd been glad to be rid of him. After only a couple of months of marriage, glad to be widowed! How terrible was that? She brushed tears away from her eyes and concentrated on the present.

Lionel was kind to the farm animals too, even the lame little cat that she'd seen creeping out of the barn. It was afraid of the whole world, poor thing, but not of him and he'd picked it up to cuddle.

That horrible woman upstairs didn't realise what a treasure she'd married

28

Joss decided to make a start the very next day on finding out who owned which of the small, run-down properties in the central area of Eastby End. He'd begin by trying to get something happening in a small way, maybe with places on the main street itself which would be a very obvious sign of change: the shops and the couple of houses near them.

He went along to the council offices, expecting the information about owners to be there and relatively easy to obtain. It was certainly there, as the official who came to the counter acknowledged, but the man refused point-blank to tell him anything there and then, said he'd have to apply in writing.

After he had spent some time arguing and trying to stay reasonable, Walter Crossley strolled into the building. To Joss's embarrassment this was just at the moment he lost control of his anger at the clerk's arrogant attitude and thumped his fist down on the counter.

Walter immediately changed direction and came across to him. 'May I ask what the problem is?'

As Joss explained, he tried to speak calmly but couldn't manage it and knew his anger was still showing.

'Why can this gentleman not be given that information? It should be simple enough to find and it's always been available to people before,' Walter asked the clerk in his usual quiet way.

'We don't give that sort of information out to anyone who just walks in off the street any longer,' the man said, with a sneering look in Joss's direction.

Walter looked at him in surprise, not only at what he'd said but at how he'd spoken to a ratepayer. The new manager for this section needed to keep a closer eye on his staff's manners and attitude. This chap seemed to think he was superior to their ratepayers, for some weird reason.

'Mr Townley has recently come to live in the valley and owns a large home and a few acres of land just outside Eastby, together with some houses in the town itself. If anyone has the right to be given such information, it's surely someone like him, don't you think?'

The man continued to speak arrogantly, treating them more like a pair of naughty schoolboys than the ratepayers whose money paid his wages.

'Mr Foscoe has given me strict instructions not to give that sort of information to any member of the public from now on.'

'Does that also include me?'

The clerk hesitated then spoke a little more quietly, 'I haven't to give it to anyone who asks for it at the counter.'

'In that case, I'll come *behind* the counter and find out the information for myself and then I'll share it with Mr Townley. As a councillor I definitely have the right to come into the offices.'

Walter took out a notebook and a pencil, handing them to Joss. 'Please write down which streets you need to know about, one on each page, and the house numbers if relevant. I'll get the names and home addresses of each of their owners for you, Townley. I doubt any of them live out in Eastby though.'

Walter didn't wait for that to be done but walked along to one side of the public area and raised the barrier set at the end of the gleaming mahogany counter before walking behind it and waiting near where Joss was standing writing.

The dirty look the clerk gave him made him furious.

When Joss had finished making his list and handed the notebook back to him, Walter went further back into the building past an office where two employees were working and trying to pretend they weren't also watching and listening to what was going on at the front desk.

The counter clerk had now moved across to block off access to the records section. Walter simply walked straight at him, hand outstretched as if about to push him out of the way. That made the fellow skip hurriedly aside.

This was a place to which the general public were not admitted but as a councillor, Walter could go into most parts of the town hall, and there was even a room near here where councillors could sit and discuss matters informally or simply relax between meetings.

When he got to the entrance to the records section, the clerk came forward again and held his arm out to bar the way. 'I *can't* allow you to go in there, sir. The information is confidential. If you need to know something, I have to refer your request to the manager.'

Walter looked at him in astonishment. 'You're definitely allowed to give the information stored there to *me*. As you well know, those of us who are serving our community as councillors regularly need to seek information about the town and its inhabitants because we're partly responsible for its governance. And we need to know these things promptly.'

Still the man shook his head, looking unhappier by the minute but continuing to stand in front of the door. 'It's orders.'

Walter continued to stare at him, seeing the fear in his face now. 'You're Donald Roper, are you not?'

'Yes, sir.' He looked at the older man warily.

'I knew your father. A sad loss to the town for him to die so young. He was one of the most helpful clerks it's ever been my pleasure to work with. He'd be thoroughly ashamed of how you're behaving today.'

Roper looked near to panic now. 'I'm sorry to deny you entry, sir, truly I am. But I have to obey my manager's orders.'

'You're making a mistake then, Roper, because the prime orders you are required to obey are those set out in the rules and regulations of this organisation, and also the requests of myself and any other councillors who serve here. Now, let me go through to the records section at once.'

There was dead silence and then Roper began wringing his hands and jigging to and fro. 'I really do have to check with Mr Foscoe first. My job depends on it.'

Walter raised his voice. 'I think not. In fact, I shall lay a formal complaint against you personally if you continue refusing to move aside and admit me. And if anyone tries to sack you for obeying the rules, I'll lay a complaint against them as well.'

A man came out of the manager's office at the other end of the reception counter. Tall, thin-faced with a sour expression on his face, Foscoe had only recently been appointed and Walter hadn't had any dealings with him yet. However, he'd instinctively disliked the look of him at the interview and had been sorry when the mayor used his deciding vote to settle a disagreement between those interviewing for the post of manager about who to appoint.

Foscoe came towards them, taking his time. 'I heard voices. Ah, Crossley. It's you.'

'*Mr* Crossley to you, if you please!'

A pause then, 'Mr Crossley if you insist.'

'I do.' Walter wasn't an acquaintance let alone a friend of Foscoe and was never likely to be, so wouldn't accept this casual use of his surname.

'May I ask why you are here on the staff side of the counter, sir? Is something wrong?'

'Yes, indeed there is. As a councillor I have every right to enter this part of the town hall, as you should know. And this clerk is denying me access to the records I need to consult today and regularly in future.'

Roper's voice sounded desperate. 'You said not to let anyone into the records section or give out information without consulting you, Mr Foscoe.'

'I did indeed. We no longer allow the public in here, Mr Crossley, or hand out information willy-nilly. Dealing with such requests takes up too much of our clerks' time and who knows what unauthorised people will do with this information?'

'I am not *the public* in that sense and I must reiterate that I have the right to come and go in the town hall as I please, as well as to search for any information I need.'

'The new rule is that you must apply for such information to be furnished by council staff and give us two days' notice to do that.'

Walter stared at him in astonishment. 'Since when?'

'Since I began to rationalise our services to be more efficient, which is one of the main purposes of my job. We can't have our clerks disturbed at any time of day because some outsider chooses to wander in here. They have their own work to get on with.'

'I see. And here was I thinking the counter clerk was hired specifically to assist and serve the public, and more especially the ratepayers and councillors of this town. Before he refused to help me today, this fellow was also refusing to help Mr Townley, a landowner who owns several properties here. I gather that's at your orders as well.'

'Yes, it is. Did you not hear me say so just now? Didn't you understand what I told you?'

Walter was surprised both by this remark and the loud, patronising tone in which he was now being spoken to. He'd met this tone of voice before from arrogant young idiots who seemed to assume that all older folk were slow witted.

'I'm not the one who doesn't understand the situation, so let me inform you of what the rules are, Foscoe, because you don't seem to have bothered to read the book of rules and regulations you were given when you came here.

'And you should know that you do not have the right to change anything in that book without the permission of a two-thirds majority of the town council.'

He waited a moment for that to sink in and when the manager didn't respond, just swelled visibly with anger and glared at him, he continued, 'The legal framework under which we all work has not been changed at all recently, Foscoe. I'd have known if it had because I've attended every single council meeting for the past several years. In fact, I probably know more about the rules and regulations than any man in this town.'

The pregnant silence was broken by Foscoe breathing deeply then saying, 'Let *Mr* Crossley in until we get the rules changed officially, Roper.' He turned to glare across the counter at Joss and add, 'However the general public are still not allowed access to such information.'

'Wrong again.' Walter's usual softly polite tone of voice was now icy and sharp. 'Such information is freely available to all ratepayers as well. Just satisfy my curiosity about one detail, Foscoe. Did you take this decision about changing the rules on your own?'

He flushed slightly. 'I did devise the new rules, but they have the mayor's approval, I can assure you, Mr Crossley.'

This mayor was a weak idiot and wouldn't get voted in again, Walter was sure. '*He* doesn't have the right to change the rules on his own either. Let me repeat how it's done here: a change needs a formal vote of support by a two-thirds majority of the town council, a month after the idea has been first mooted. Please remember that in future.' He turned to Roper. 'Are you going to move out of my way or do I have to call in someone to help me manhandle you.'

The man gaped at him and when Walter took a step forward he moved rapidly sideways.

Walter stopped in the entrance to Records and beckoned to Joss. 'Come round and allow me the pleasure of helping you to find out the information you need, Mr Townley. It'll be quicker with two of us and I know my way around the records section after many years of using them.'

'Very kind of you, Mr Crossley.'

'My pleasure. We should all help one another whenever we can.'

The manager continued to glare at him but Walter ignored him and waited for Joss, who strode rapidly round to the other side of the counter.

It would have been more accurate to say that Roper scuttled out of their way this time than that he simply moved aside. Walter was hard put not to laugh out loud at that as he led the younger man through into the records section.

He beckoned to the lady clerk standing waiting nearby. 'How are you doing, Trudy?'

'Very well, sir.' She added in a whisper, 'And enjoying the show.'

'Good.' He winked at her and turned back to Joss, introducing him to her. 'Now tell us exactly what information you need, Mr Townley, and why so that this lady can help us.'

After standing glaring through the entrance to the records section at them and hovering there for a few moments, Foscoe walked away, presumably to return to his office.

Walter had worked with Trudy many times before and knew how efficient she was, but it still took them over an hour to finish gathering all the pieces of information they needed, and some others she suggested they add to the list in case her manager made it difficult for them to gain access to it again at a later date.

'He won't manage to do that,' Walter said grimly.

'He's already moved some documents into his own storeroom,' she said.

'Has he indeed? Could you tell me which they are?'

'I'm keeping a list. I'll make you a copy of it.'

Joss smiled as he watched. This was a man people helped willingly.

When they'd finished and were walking away from the town hall, they met two other councillors whom Walter knew, so he asked Joss to wait for a moment and stopped Don and Morris to tell them what had just happened.

They both stared at him in surprise. 'No one's told me about any changes,' Don said. 'And I only missed one meeting.'

'Well, I've not missed any meetings and as you say, Walter lad, there haven't been any changes to the rules discussed let alone given the necessary approval. I don't like the sounds of that. Foscoe's a new appointment to the job and was highly recommended by the mayor, but I've since heard that the chap is a nephew of the mayor's wife.'

'Is he indeed?' Walter said thoughtfully. 'Where did you hear that, Morris?'

'My wife overheard the mayor's wife talking to a friend in one of the shops. They didn't see her behind a corner, but sound carries and when she heard what they were talking about she stayed to listen. She didn't want to bump into them and have to chat, anyway. She thinks the mayor's wife is a dreadful snob.'

Don frowned. 'I'm not fond of this mayor. Do you think he's intending to sneak in a few changes which will be to the advantage of his own businesses and family? I was sorry when our former mayor fell ill and that chap had to take over.'

Walter nodded. 'I was too. Such little empires can lead to irregularities of all sorts, not to mention waste of public money.'

'Foscoe seems to be setting up hedges of petty rules to keep us out so that he and the mayor can become what my father used to call the senior rabbits in the warren,' Don said. 'I'm not having that.'

Morris grinned. 'I feel a sudden urge to obtain some information about the street in which I live.'

'Now, there's a coincidence. So do I,' Don said.

Walter chuckled. 'Please do that. I'm quite sure you won't let them forbid you to go into the records section, either. Trudy is still working there, by the way. I'm certain she'll be as helpful to you as she was to me a short time ago. Let me know how things go for you.'

He stopped at the end of the street and turned to Joss. 'I'm sure you'll now have enough information to keep you busy for a while, my dear chap. Let me know if I can help you in any other way. And I'd just like to say that I think this is an excellent idea of yours. It's more than time we did something about Eastby End, but unfortunately there are only twenty-four hours in a day and I simply haven't been able to give it my full attention.'

'I'd be happy to help from now on. This valley has become my home too.'

'Good. You should speak to our police sergeant about the troubles in Eastby. He's a helpful chap. Don't hesitate to ask me about the general situation for the rest of the area, which I know much better than I do Eastby. In fact, I probably know this town better than most people, and I'm certainly one of the longest standing councillors.'

'I'll bear that offer in mind. I certainly enjoyed watching you in action today, all with a faint smile on your face and calm, quiet words that nonetheless struck home and made that uppity new manager obey the rules.'

'It's useful to have grown up in a place and stayed there one's whole life. Foscoe is a newcomer to the town and must be both arrogant and stupid to have got in *my* way without finding out how well I get on with most people. I shall raise the matter of rules and regulations at our next council meeting, for a start. Petty clerks do not control this town and I hope they never will. No one person should control a whole town, not even the mayor.'

29

Joss walked slowly away from Walter, looking forward to studying the lists his new friend had obtained for him. When he passed a stationery shop the window display gave him another idea, so he turned back and went inside.

He bought a few big sheets of drawing paper, some pencils with softer lead in them, which the shopkeeper said would be easier to rub out if – no, *when* he made mistakes – and an artist's rubber. To his delight he also found a volume of recent street maps of Ollerthwaite on a shelf of miscellaneous books.

After paying for these he left behind a beaming proprietor, but he was by far the happier of the two of them because he'd now found out who owned which house and got the tools to make usable records to work from.

He intended to sketch out a map of central Eastby showing where certain run-down properties were situated then choose an area to start working on. He'd contact the owners in that area to see if they were interested in getting together with him to renovate the district in which their properties were located. But whether they all joined him or not, surely some owners would care enough and this could be a good first step towards doing something about Eastby, a run-down area of town that some folk still called 'the village' as if it were a separate place. He was utterly determined to change the atmosphere here and make it safer, yes, and cleaner too. Dirt bred disease.

He wasn't very good at drawing but he should be able to manage a recognisable diagram or two good enough to guide himself and anyone he could persuade to join him in taking the initiative and improving their properties.

On the way back he met Miss Norris returning from a visit to a patient. He stopped to greet her and her assistant, feeling so excited about his project he simply had to tell her what he was about to start doing.

She commented on the big cardboard tube he was carrying and that gave him a start. 'It contains some big sheets of drawing paper.'

'Oh? Are you an artist?'

'Heavens no! I just want to make some big diagrams.' He waggled the carrier bag at her. 'This is full of drawing equipment.'

He didn't wait to be asked but told her exactly what he was going to try to do but ended by admitting wryly that he wasn't the world's best artist. 'However, I think I can manage to do it well enough to show who owns the various houses and help me persuade some of them to join in and improve their properties.'

She stared at him approvingly. 'I think that's a wonderful thing you're trying to do, Mr Townley. If ever a place needed setting to rights, it's the central part of Eastby. It's a disgrace.'

They stared at one another for a moment then she looked away from him and gestured with one hand. 'I can't understand how the town council can have allowed Eastby to get into this state, let alone why they seem to be making no attempt to clean up the area. It's downright dangerous for women to go out at night, which is why I only go out with Hanny after dark.' She smiled at her assistant then asked, 'How are you going to start improving matters, Mr Townley?'

'Well, apart from starting to repair my own properties, I'm thinking of asking Walter Crossley's advice about how else I can tackle things. He seems to have managed to change the situation for the better in other parts of Ollerthwaite.'

She nodded. 'I've heard that too. The town could do with more like him but he's only one man and I've never seen him when he wasn't busy. His wife watches him with a worried expression at times.'

'She usually seems busy too. What good human beings they are!'

Rachel was looking thoughtful. 'I was thinking of complaining to the police sergeant who's in charge of law and order in the valley about the dangers Hanny and I have to face every time we go out at night. We had to threaten to hit a drunken man with our walking sticks the other night to get him to leave us alone.'

'That's dreadful!'

'It's a good thing that we haven't had many calls to go out after dark so far. I'm hoping when more people recognise our uniform they'll treat us with more respect.'

'Is it all right in the daytime? You've been staring round occasionally as if expecting trouble.'

She hesitated. 'I'm maybe a bit too sensitive still because I had a rather horrible man following me around for a time while I was finishing my studies. I don't think he knows where I've come to live now, though.'

'What does he look like? It won't hurt for me to keep my eyes open too.'

'Bald and rather fat around the middle. It's how he stares at women that gives away what he's like.' She shuddered.

'What exactly are you going to do in this clinic?'

'I'm hoping to encourage mothers to bring their young children to me for check-ups as well as if they have specific problems, but without much luck so far. It's good that we've been vaccinating babies against smallpox in this country since 1853, but there's so much more we could do.'

'You should definitely make a formal complaint to Sergeant McGill about night-time safety because it's the job of the police to sort out such problems not just in Ollerthwaite but in Eastby End.'

He looked down at the tube and carrier bag. 'I suppose I'd better get back and make a start. It's been nice chatting to you.'

'Um, I wonder, could you use some help with drawing the maps and diagrams, Mr Townley?' She went slightly pink. 'It's just, well, I'm quite good at drawing and I still amuse myself occasionally by sketching. Not that I have a lot of time to do that since I've come here, but still, what you are going to try to do is so important for my job I almost consider it part of my duties to help you.'

He beamed at her. Not only would he welcome some help with the drawing, but it'd be a chance to get to know her better. Not because she was beautiful, though she was, very beautiful, but because of the kindness in her face and the way she seemed to care about other people. To him those things were very important.

He suddenly realised he was keeping her waiting for an answer. 'I would very much welcome some help, Miss Norris, especially if you have more skill than I do. But you have to promise not to laugh too loudly at my efforts. I'm not good at drawing, never have been.' He watched her relax a little.

'I won't laugh, I promise. I'm sure you'll be doing your best.'

'It still won't be very good. Um, you and Hanny couldn't come round to my house this afternoon, could you? I'm really eager to make a start on this job and we'd be able to spread things out on my dining table and leave them there. I'm sure my housekeeper would agree to stay clear of it. Mrs Entwistle is always very helpful.'

Rachel turned to her companion. 'Would you mind helping with that, Hanny?'

'Not at all.' She nodded her own approval to Joss at what he was planning.

Rachel gave him a rueful smile. 'There's another good reason for bringing Hanny with me. With her and your housekeeper there, it will be clear to any nosy-parkers taking an interest in my doings that this is a perfectly respectable meeting.'

'Are you having trouble with gossips?'

'I always do when I start in a new place, to be frank. You know how spiteful some people can be, especially with um, a younger woman who goes out to work with both men and women. Unfortunately a person in my position always needs to be particularly careful of the proprieties.' She sighed and added, 'I met that nice Mr Dean in the street and stopped to chat about motor cars, and one lady stopped me the next day and told me I shouldn't be flirting with young men.'

'Good heavens.'

He could guess she suffered spiteful gossip more than most younger women did because of envy about her looks. She must be in her late twenties by now, he'd guess, and had a rosy complexion, trim figure and gleaming hair, the sort of hair you'd like to stroke .

He cut his thoughts short and tried to speak crisply, surprised at himself for the way he kept thinking about her and for feeling jealous about Adam spending time chatting to her. He'd admired other women before but never as strongly as this.

'I'd be happy for both of you to help me in any way you can. I'm sure Mrs Entwistle will be happy to counter any gossip your visit may give rise to. My housekeeper is not one to suffer fools gladly or to allow any spitefulness concerning people she respects without speaking out.'

'I know Mrs Entwistle and enjoy her company,' Rachel said. 'We have some interesting chats when she brings the loaves. She's an impressive woman.' She took a step back. 'We mustn't delay you any longer, Mr Townley. You're a busy man and we still have a lot to do to set up the clinic properly. We'll see you this afternoon.'

As she and Hanny walked away she took a deep breath and turned her attention firmly to the clinic. She feared they were going to need a caretaker to keep an eye on it while they were out during the daytime and during the night. She was gradually getting busier.

She found it extremely satisfying to help people and to work with someone like Dr Coxton, who was living proof that women could make good doctors.

They were starting to move away from one another when Joss suddenly saw someone he recognised coming towards them. 'Just a minute, Miss Norris. Don't leave yet! Here comes our police sergeant. I was introduced to him myself a couple of days ago, so I'll introduce you now.'

He beckoned to Hector, who had been walking towards them on the other side of the road as if he was simply out enjoying a stroll until you looked more closely and saw how carefully he was studying his town and its citizens. The sergeant immediately crossed the road to join them. 'Can I help you with something?'

'Hello, Sergeant. May I introduce these two ladies to you? They were just saying they wanted to talk to you about something.'

'I know who you are by sight, Miss Norris and Miss Best, and have heard about the good work you're doing,' Hector said politely. 'How can I help?'

Rachel explained about her job and the problems she was having staying safe.

The sergeant listened intently, frowning as her tale went on. 'I've been up to Eastby End, of course, but I must admit it all looked fairly peaceful if rather run-down when I was there. And even though it was dusk, there were no louts hanging around on street corners.'

'They probably hid when they saw you coming,' Joss said. 'I've seen people hide from you, even in the town itself, but I too have heard that it can be much more dangerous in Eastby after dark.'

'I'll definitely put it higher on my list of places to investigate, then, and deal with any trouble I find. Sadly, however, there is only myself to police the whole valley with the help of one constable.'

Joss looked at him thoughtfully. 'I've been thinking about that, Sergeant, because I live near Eastby and I'm concerned about people's safety there after dark. My housekeeper won't go into the village on her own later in the day. Would you have any problem with me hiring a watchman or two to patrol that area after dark, if I paid their wages? You could perhaps even utilise their services yourself if you needed extra help?'

Hector looked at him in surprise, then grew thoughtful. 'It's a wonderful suggestion. How about coming to see me at the police station so that we can discuss the possibilities in more detail, after which I'd better talk to my superintendent about it? He does like to be kept informed. And we don't want to bore the ladies.'

'The ladies are two of the people who suffer most, because Miss Norris's duties as a district nurse require her to go out and about to help people at all hours of the day or night.'

'Since you haven't been here for long, I didn't realise you went out at night to visit patients, Miss Norris. I don't think that's safe for you to do.'

'We each carry a walking stick with a weighted handle and we wouldn't hesitate to use them to defend ourselves, Sergeant,' Rachel said.

Both men gaped at her.

'Have you had to use them already?' Joss asked.

'Not exactly. But we've had to threaten to use them more than once.'

'Then I'm definitely hiring some watchmen!'

'Perhaps we could come and discuss the general situation with you, Sergeant McGill?' Joss suggested. 'I really do have some money available and would be happy to use it for help in making the area near my new home safer.'

The town hall clock struck the hour just then and the sergeant said, 'I'm afraid I have to be at a meeting shortly but I'd be happy to talk to you about it and hear more details of your encounters. How about you come and see me tomorrow afternoon?'

'I could call for you around half-past one,' Joss said to Rachel, 'and then we can all walk into the town centre together.'

'That would be very pleasant,' she said.

'In the meantime we'll let the sergeant go to his meeting and we'll meet at my house later today.'

When the two women walked out to Mr Townley's house that afternoon, Hanny was at first awed by it. She had never been inside as large a place as this, let alone going there as a guest. She kept quiet at the beginning, watching what the others did and listening to how they talked to one another. But they included her in their conversations and she gradually gained confidence and even made one or two suggestions.

They took over the dining table as he'd suggested, though not till Mrs Entwistle had put a cover over it and found a piece of lino to put the drawing paper on. Then Rachel and Mr Townley settled down at one side to create a map of the street and lists of who lived where, while Hanny sat opposite watching them and doing small jobs like sharpening pencils.

It was mainly Rachel who did the drawing and wrote in the names neatly, while Mr Townley read out details from his scribbled notes. He also did a lot of looking at her, Hanny noticed with some amusement. Even posh people got that look in their eyes when they found someone attractive, it seemed. She'd never met anyone who made her feel like that and wondered if she ever would. Apart from anything else, she was taller than most men and they didn't like that.

When she thought of her own childish handwriting compared to Rachel's, which looked really elegant, she felt downright ashamed. Even Mr Townley said how pretty it looked and admitted that he couldn't compete with his guest in that area any more than he could draw. But his writing still looked neat and he too did what Hanny thought of as 'running writing'.

She had only been to primary school and had left part-time at eleven and full-time at twelve. She hadn't even been able to attend regularly in the last year or two, depending on when her mother needed help with the family's washing or other big jobs like looking after a sick baby. There had nearly always been a baby in the house. Thank goodness her mother had moved away now with her new husband.

The sight of Rachel's writing made her wonder whether she could learn to do what they called 'cursive writing'. It looked a lot nicer than her uneven printing. Working so closely with Rachel was like living part of the time in a different world but Hanny really enjoyed learning so many new things.

When Rachel had finished drawing the street plans and Mr Townley had helped her label them correctly, she began to make copies. Hanny saw Mrs Entwistle struggling to carry in a tray of tea things as well as open the door and rushed to help.

When she'd set them down the housekeeper clapped her hands and told them it was about time they took a break, then lingered to look at the names of the owners on the big sheets of paper spread out across the table. Mr Townley didn't stop her and when she suddenly exclaimed, 'I'd never have thought it of some of those people!' he asked her what she meant.

'I thought they were decent folk who treated their poor neighbours well. That's what they pose as in church, anyway, but then they don't look after the houses they rent out.'

Hanny spoke without thinking and pointed to another name. 'That man's the same.'

Mr Townley scribbled some quick notes. 'I wonder what they'll say when I approach them later about improving their properties. But for the moment I want to make a start with the shops near the church, and perhaps just a few of the nearest houses.'

He stared at the list of owners' names and suddenly realised what had been nudging at his attention. One of them was in the name of Jim Entwistle, but of course he was dead now and his son Adam had inherited them and just turned up in town and been upset by the state of those houses. He'd speak to him first, because Adam had already said he intended to repair the houses that needed it and set them in good order.

The following afternoon, Joss picked up the two ladies and they walked into town to see Sergeant McGill. He received them in the back room of the police station, which also seemed to be serving as his office as well as a meeting place, judging by the desk under the window and the chairs set out neatly.

He listened gravely to their detailed description of what Eastby was like after dark, asking a few questions and then sitting frowning for a few moments before looking at them.

'I'd not be surprised if some of them go out into other areas to break into shops and houses, which is what I shall tell certain people here who are bound to complain about Eastby getting too much attention. I feel I've been remiss in not checking the area more carefully.'

'You can't deal with every possibility with only a single constable to help you,' Joss said. 'And I should think the regional police authorities don't much care what goes on in our valley.'

'I'll bear all that in mind but I think the main thing to start with is to make the streets of Eastby safer at night. I'm very much in favour of your watchmen, Mr Townley.'

He inclined his head to Rachel then turned back to Joss. 'Go ahead and hire a couple of men. I think it'll be very helpful, and I'll write to my inspector to tell him about it. If I get the letter off straight away, it'll arrive by second post tomorrow afternoon.'

'It'll be easier if I can find some men from here in the valley who'd do the job, then they'd have some idea of what they're facing before they even start. I'll look into it straight away.'

Joss escorted the ladies home, again enjoying Rachel's company, then returned home to spend a very thoughtful evening considering the situation and how to make a start.

He'd heard that Adam Dean was planning to move into one of the houses and had hired men to put the place in better order before he did that. He'd be the first owner to contact, maybe even tomorrow while he waited for the sergeant to get back to him.

It'd be good if he and Adam could work together to renovate the properties they owned in the centre of Eastby and set an example. Surely if they made a start others would gradually follow suit?

30

Two days later the lad with the limp woke up in the small cellar room he shared with his mother and heard her wheezing and blowing her nose on one of the rags they used for handkerchiefs. She'd shown signs of starting a cold yesterday, but had said it was nothing, would soon pass.

It sounded to have got much worse during the night, though, and fear shivered through him at the sound. He got up and lit the candle. He'd be utterly on his own in the world if anything happened to her and he'd miss her dreadfully.

'Blow that candle out, love,' she said in a husky voice. 'You're wasting it. And go back to sleep. You've got that little job to do for Mr Godwin tomorrow.'

But he couldn't get to sleep, kept hearing her sneeze and try to smother a cough, then toss and turn for a while, then sneeze again. As soon as it started to grow light, he got up and went across to crouch beside the thin mattress she used as her bed. She was shivering and looked ill, and it took her a minute to focus properly on him.

'It's cold this morning, isn't it? I don't think . . . I'll be well enough . . . to go to work today.'

Even her words were coming in jerky gasps now and when she kept shivering violently, that was it. They had no way of heating this small room and the one window didn't fit well enough to keep the draughts out, even when they stuffed the edges with bits of newspaper. He had to do something, had to try to get help for her.

'I'm going to see if that nurse can come out to you,' he said abruptly.

'Theo, don't. It's just a bad cold. We can't afford it.'

But he murmured, 'Love you, Mum,' and left her, limping through the streets as quickly as he could, hardly seeing anyone else out at this early hour. He knew where the nurse lived, had seen her go in and out of one house with her assistant. The bell labelled 'Nurse' was beside the front door and it looked new and shiny.

When he rang it he heard a faint sound inside the house. Surely she'd come and see his mother, find out if she could help? There had to be something they could do.

To his surprise he didn't have to wait long for someone to answer the door. But it wasn't the nurse; it was Hanny Best, who now worked as her assistant. He and his mother had lived in the same street as Hanny for a couple of years.

She took one look at him and said, 'Tell me what's wrong, Theo. I can see how upset you are.'

'It's Mum. She's the one who's ill.'

'Lally's sick? What's wrong with her?'

'Yesterday she said it was only a bit of a cold but it's got a lot worse during the night. Can the nurse come and see her, please? Will she come even if we can't pay her straight away? Mum was supposed to work today, doing some scrubbing, but she won't be able to, and I had a little job lined up, too.'

Hanny gestured to him to come into the hall. 'Sit on that chair and wait. Do not move around or you'll wake up the lady whose house it is. She lives on the ground floor.'

She ran up the stairs and knocked on a door. It was opened immediately and he heard Hanny explaining about his mother.

'He's a sensible lad and wouldn't make a fuss for nothing. And, Rachel love, he's only got his mother so he's desperate. He's such a loving lad, not one of those rough ones. I've known him and his mother since before I started working with you because I used to live nearby. Lally's a really nice woman. Couldn't you go and see her?'

'You know there's not much we can do about colds.'

'Yes, but if the worst happens he'll feel he did his best. That'll make a big difference to him.'

'All right. We'll go and see her.' She didn't put it into words, because everyone knew, but colds could quickly turn into pneumonia, which was one of the biggest killers of poor people and they couldn't really do much to help unless this lad's mother needed getting to hospital.

The three of them hurried through the streets and when they got to the house, Theo took them round the back and down to a half-cellar. He opened the door and gestured to them to go inside.

It looked at first like the place Hanny called home, but this one was smaller and poorly furnished. It felt not only icy cold but damp inside.

Rachel went across to kneel beside the mattress and check Lally's breathing, then turned to the boy. 'Don't you have any way of heating this room?'

Theo shook his head. 'No.'

'You mother needs to be kept warm if she's to get better. Do you have any family you can stay with for a while, somewhere warmer?'

'No one. There's only us two now.'

Rachel glanced at Hanny and said in a low voice, 'She can't stay here. And the hospital won't take her in unless she's dying. I tried to get someone in last week and they told me they only have room for the worst cases.'

She saw the terror on the boy's face as he heard what she said and knew she couldn't leave him alone here to watch his mother die, just couldn't do it. Some people touched your heart more than others and for some reason, he was one of them. And the love between him and his mother made her long for something she didn't dare name even to herself.

'It'll help your mother if we can find a way to keep her warm.' There might be a slim chance of helping the poor woman recover, after all, because this woman had a strong motive for holding on to life: her son. That was important.

She looked down. Not many lads his age would hold his mother's hand so openly. Sometimes the sight of love like that touched Rachel, reminding her that she'd borne a child, making her wonder if she'd have made a good mother. Making her angry at herself too. Stop thinking of that, she always told herself. It was over and done with long ago. But she couldn't always do that.

She looked across at Hanny. 'We'll take her to the clinic. We can put her in one of the bedrooms and light a fire there.'

'Bless you,' Hanny said quietly. 'You and I can carry her. It's not far from here.'

'I can help you,' Theo said.

Hanny shook her head. 'You need to stay here and do something else first.' She turned to Rachel. 'If it's known they've had to move out for a while, their possessions will get stolen.'

She didn't have to say that the cellar contained the only things they owned because it was all too obvious how poor they were.

Rachel hesitated only for a few seconds, then turned to Theo. 'You can stay at the clinic with your mother, but first you need to get someone to help you take everything you own there. You can offer them this to help you.' She fumbled in her pocket and held out two sixpences to him.

The relief on his face made her feel good. How could you not want to help a lad with such a bright eager face, who looked at his mother in such a loving way?

'Thank you, miss. I have a friend who lives in the next street. I can run and fetch him.' He walked across to one corner and pulled some sacking aside to reveal a ramshackle old pram, a big old-fashioned one. 'You don't have to carry Mum. You can take her in this. We use it when we move. It rattles about a lot but it still goes. Mum lets people pay her to borrow it. Only – ' He hesitated then added, 'the landlord will put someone else in to live here if we take our things away and can't pay the rent, then where can we go if, I mean *after*, she gets better?'

'We'll help you find somewhere to live afterwards,' Rachel promised rashly. 'The main thing is to make sure your mother doesn't get worse and for that we need to help her get warm as soon as possible. You know where the clinic is, don't you?'

'Yes. I'll come and fetch the pram back to take our things later.'

Hanny laid one hand on his shoulder. 'I'll bring the pram back to you once we've got your mother to the clinic, Theo. It's not far away.'

'Is Mum going to die?' he asked in a croaky whisper, staring at her so anxiously he didn't look like a child but more like a worried old man.

She couldn't lie to him 'You can never be sure either way. But she still has a chance and we'll do our best to help her, I promise you.'

'Thank you. I'll go and fetch my friend and he'll help me push the pram to the clinic when it's loaded with our things.' He didn't say it but she knew he'd want his friend with him to help protect the pram's contents as well as push.

'We'll not leave here till you get back.'

He set off, running awkwardly.

When he got back they left with the sick woman huddled in the rackety old pram. It was hard to keep it going straight, even with two of them, but easier than trying to carry her to the clinic.

'Let me help you.' Mr Townley suddenly appeared and moved Rachel gently aside, then took hold of the handle next to Hanny.

It was a lot easier to push with his strength added.

'Thank you.' Rachel moved to walk beside the pram, keeping an eye on the sick woman.

'Where are you taking her, Miss Norris?' he asked.

'To the clinic. She'd die if we left her in the damp cellar they were living in. There was no way of even heating it and yet they were being charged rent and threatened with being thrown out if they fell behind with it.'

More people preying on the poor, he thought angrily.

'What are you doing out at this early hour, Mr Townley?'

'I'm still getting to know Eastby. I wanted to check what it was like in the early morning. It seems fairly quiet at the moment.'

'One of the few times it is quiet. Some folk will be sleeping off their night's thieving,' Hanny said bitterly.

'I intend to stop most of the local thieving with my nightwatchmen.'

'That should help, even if it doesn't stop it all. The sooner they start work the better.'

They reached the clinic just then so Rachel hurried ahead to unlock the door.

He helped push the pram inside and said, 'I can carry her if you'll show me where to go?'

As Rachel locked the front door again, Hanny said, 'You go up with him and settle Lally, Rachel love. I'll fetch up the makings for a fire.' She bustled off towards the kitchen area at the back.

'Can you manage to carry her upstairs on your own or shall I help?' Rachel asked.

He picked Lally up and hefted her into a carrying position, then nodded as if satisfied. 'I can manage. She doesn't weigh much, does she? Lead on.'

And how kind it was of him to help them like this, Rachel thought as she watched him. What a lovely man he was!

She moved up the stairs ahead of him and opened a door at the back of the landing. 'We'll put her in this bedroom.' She turned down the rather ragged bedcovers on one of the beds and he set the sick woman down carefully.

'We were given this pair of old single beds and they even had usable mattresses on them, very old and saggy ones but fairly clean. And Mr Crossley had some old bedding in his stores. The word seems to be spreading about the clinic and a few other people have promised us more odds and ends of furniture. We won't turn anything down because even if we can't use it, I've no doubt some of our poorer patients' families will welcome it.'

'Where's Lally's son?'

'Theo stayed behind to guard their possessions, which will get stolen if people find out they're leaving. He'll be staying here with his mother for a while.'

'Those two are very close. It warms your heart to see them, doesn't it?'

She gave him a sad look and added, 'They own so little he can store everything in one corner of our basement without it being at all in the way. It's clean and not damp, unlike the place they were living in. How anyone could charge money for a room like that beggars belief.'

'And yet desperate people pay rent for such places.'

He stood beside the door, watching Rachel settle the sick woman in the bed and tuck her up under a faded old quilt.

As she stepped back he asked, 'Do you need anything else? Don't hesitate to ask me if you do.'

'Not at the moment. Thank you so much for your help. When Hanny's brought up the kindling and wood, I'll light the fire and she can take you down and unlock the door to let you out.'

He frowned. 'That's another thing that I don't like to see. You shouldn't have to keep the door so carefully locked when the clinic is occupied.'

'Tell that to those folk who go round stealing things,' Rachel said bitterly.

'I shall, one way or another.'

When Hanny came up, Lally was getting a bit restless, so he said, 'I can wait a little longer to leave. You see to her, Rachel, and let Hanny start the fire. It's more important to warm this room for that poor woman than to send me on my way at this exact minute.'

After she'd got the kindling burning Hanny left the fire for Rachel to tend and as she and Joss went downstairs, he said, 'I'd take the pram back to Theo for you, but I don't know where they're living. I'll come with you, though, to help keep you safe.'

After she'd locked the door again he took over pushing the empty pram and asked, 'Your patient's son is the lad with the limp, isn't he? I've seen him around but he doesn't seem to be involved in causing mischief.'

'He isn't. He's too busy trying to earn money and help his mother in any way he can. He and Lally are very close.'

'Where's the father?'

'Vanished even before Theo was born, apparently, but she had her parents alive to help her then.'

'Do you think Lally will recover?

'I hope so. She has a better chance of it now at least. There wasn't even a fireplace in the cellar of theirs. It was better than sleeping rough, but only just.'

He shook his head in disgust. 'People like that shouldn't be allowed to rent out hovels. Some towns insist on inspections for rental places because cramming people in has led to minor epidemics of flu and other illnesses, and also places catching fire. We have to change things. We just have to.'

A few paces further on he said, 'Let me know if you need anything extra for Lally or for the clinic. I have some money to spare for good causes.'

'Thank you. I will. And we need to turn off the street here and go round the back to get in.'

She gave the pram to Theo then Mr Townley insisted on escorting her back to the clinic even though it was getting light by then.

She stood in the doorway and watched him stride away along the street. What a nice man he was. If she were Rachel she'd be encouraging his attentions. There was no mistaking the attraction between them. Hanny doubted anything would come of it, though. Rachel had said more than once that she'd never marry. Who knew why she was so adamant?

Mr Townley was a bit optimistic if he thought he could change Eastby End on his own and make it a safer place to live.

When she went upstairs at the clinic the fire was burning up nicely and Rachel was standing in front of it warming her hands. She pointed to the bed and put one finger on her lips so Hanny didn't try to talk but took a quick look at Lally. Was it her imagination or did she look a bit easier for being kept warm? Eh, she hoped so.

A short time later she heard someone knock on the front door and ran downstairs again to let Theo and the other lad inside with the pram full of Lally and Theo's possessions. There were pitifully few things.

She realised the lad was looking at her anxiously and knew what he was afraid of asking.

'Your mother is comfier now and stands a better chance. She's in a proper bed and there's one for you next to hers. And we've lit a fire in that bedroom. You two put that stuff in the basement, that door there, then I'll let your friend out and you can go up to your mother. I'll be staying here so I can help her if needed.'

Hanny supervised them unloading the pram, saw Theo give the other lad sixpence and look at her guiltily. She winked at him, knowing he was trying to save some of the shilling Rachel had given him for his mother's needs. The other lad would no doubt be happy with sixpence anyway. If you didn't have any money, every extra farthing was welcome.

Eh, they looked hungry, the poor things. 'How about a quick jam buttie, you two?'

They both brightened and nodded, so she cut slices of bread and put both butter and jam on them. It wouldn't hurt for it to be known that Theo's friends might get food slipped to them occasionally here.

She nodded in satisfaction when she heard the other lad say before he left, 'Let me know if you need any other help, Theo.'

'Thanks but I won't always have money to spare.'

The lad shrugged. 'We help one another when we can, don't we?'

After showing him out Hanny took Theo upstairs. He went to stand beside the bed and as if she felt his presence, Lally opened her eyes, blinked to bring him into focus and immediately smiled at the sight of her son. She held out one hand to clasp his, but when she tried to speak it made her cough.

Rachel moved closer to the bed. 'Don't try to talk, Lally. Theo can see for himself that you're doing a bit better already because you've got some colour in your cheeks now. What you need is to sleep and drink lots of fluid, so have a drink every time you wake up.'

Lally managed a smile then her eyes went back to her son, who was still holding her hand.

'No need to worry about Theo,' Rachel said quietly. 'We'll keep him safe here and Hanny's given him something to eat. He'll be sleeping on that bed next to yours so you'll see him there whenever you wake up.'

Lally mouthed the words, 'Thank you.' After that she closed her eyes and snuggled down.

Rachel moved towards the door and gestured to Theo to follow her.

'Is Mum going to die?' he whispered when they had joined Hanny on the landing. 'She looks bad and that coughing sounded terrible.'

'She won't die if we can help it,' Hanny said firmly. 'Now, let's find you something else to eat, then you can get some sleep too. I bet you didn't get much during the night.'

'No, I didn't.'

'I've got a thank-you letter to write to a donor,' Rachel said. 'I might as well get an early start on the paperwork. Can you make me a sandwich and a cup of tea as well, Hanny?'

She opened a tin of ham for a treat and made them all sandwiches. Theo ate his in big happy gulps. After that Hanny reminded him to use the lav before he went upstairs again and told him to wash his hands and face properly after he'd finished there.

'You sound just like my mum,' he said, trying to wipe tears from his eyes without her seeing.

The next time she peeped into the back bedroom, mother and son were both sound asleep. And when she went downstairs, even Rachel was sitting on the big sofa next to the fire in the main room dozing peacefully.

Hanny sat down nearby, ate her own sandwich quickly, then followed their example. She felt some hope that Lally would get better, but only time would tell for certain. They'd done all they could for now and were all more than due a rest.

It felt so good to help people. This was the best job she'd ever had.

31

Lally didn't get any worse the following day but she didn't seem to get much better either. Theo spent time sitting beside her bed, except when there were any little jobs he could do to help around the place, such as bringing in buckets of coal and tending the fires.

In the middle of the following night he jerked suddenly awake because he thought he'd heard his mother say something. He looked across to her bed and could see that she was sound asleep. What had he heard then?

When the noise sounded again he realised it was coming from downstairs. He knew Hanny had taken one of the other upstairs rooms to sleep in, so tiptoed out to peep through her door and check whether she'd got up.

There was enough moonlight shining round the edges of the ragged curtains at the window to see her lying under the bedclothes, as still as his mother had been, so the noise hadn't been made by her either.

Had he been mistaken and the noise was coming from outside? He stood motionless on the landing, listening carefully, and heard it again, but was still unable to work out what it was.

Noises didn't usually keep happening unless someone was making them, though, and he knew he'd not be able to get back to sleep till he found out what it was and made sure nothing was wrong. He went quietly downstairs to have a look round – just in case there was a problem.

The noise sounded again as he got to the bottom of the stairs and it sounded louder down here. It was coming from the kitchen at the rear of the house. He didn't try to light a lamp but continued in that direction, trying not to make a noise.

Was someone trying to break into the clinic? If so, that was a mean thing to do when this was a place set up to help people who were ill! And there was definitely no money lying around so what were they looking for?

He stayed in the shadows next to the kitchen doorway and was horrified to see the dark figure of a man outside the window next to the back door. He couldn't see the man's face because the would-be burglar was bent over, fiddling with the lock on the door! The fellow didn't notice him, thank goodness.

Theo didn't think he should risk confronting the intruder on his own so ran upstairs and woke Hanny, telling her in a low voice what he'd seen.

'I'll go down with you and have a look. Move quietly!' She jumped out of bed, dragging on a dressing gown but not bothering about shoes. She led the way down, stopping at the bottom of the stairs to grab one of the battered old walking sticks the clinic had been given to lend to injured people, wishing she hadn't left her weighted stick at home. Theo followed her example and took one for himself.

Hanny again led the way. She was taller than him and in the semi-darkness could be mistaken for a man. His heart was thumping with fear of what might happen but he wasn't going to let her tackle an intruder on her own.

They both stopped at the kitchen doorway just as the person gave the back door a big shake, as if angry with it, but failed to get the lock to give way. He then picked up a piece of metal that looked as if it had once been part of some railings and smashed the glass of the window. Fragments flew in all directions and he put his hand through the hole to try to open the door from the inside.

Hanny rushed forward, brandishing her stick and surprised the man, who pulled his arm back from the hole and trying to unlock the door from the inside. As he did that he gashed his arm on a piece of broken glass and yelped in pain, jerking away and banging his head against the side of the window, knocking off his improvised mask.

Even in the dimness Theo could see blood start pouring from the cut on his hand, which must be a bad one. He could now see the man's face quite clearly too, see it and recognise it.

As the fellow ran off across the little yard and out into the lane that lay along the back of that group of houses, Hanny put an arm round the boy's shoulder. 'Don't try to go after him. We'd never catch up with him. I saw who he was, though. Did you?'

Theo nodded. 'Yes. Pete Donahue.'

'Can't mistake him, with that big, crooked nose. He's only just come out of jail after serving six months for theft, and he's at it again already. He must be utterly stupid. What does he think we keep here? Bags of gold?'

'Shall I fetch the police?'

She shook her head. 'There's no one on duty at night and even if we did wake the sergeant, he wouldn't be able to look round properly outside till it's light. But you can go for him then.'

'I'll stay down here and keep watch on this window to be sure he doesn't try to come back in, shall I?'

'Good lad. I'll nip upstairs and get dressed. Yell, if you need help.' She let out an annoyed growl of noise as she started walking away. 'We'll have to get someone in to repair this pane of glass, too. What a waste of the clinic's money.'

There was a sound from upstairs. 'I'd better go and check your mother before I do anything else, Theo. Donahue's shouting must have disturbed her.'

He wanted to go with her and see for himself that his mother was all right but he knew he owed it to these kind people to stay on watch. 'Give her my love if she's awake.'

'If she is, I'll come and change places with you for a few moments as soon as I'm dressed and let you have a quick word with her.'

But Lally had already fallen asleep again by the time Hanny bent over her. Thank goodness for the moonlight. It showed her to be sleeping more peacefully and breathing more easily.

When she went back down she'd tell Theo his mother seemed to be holding her own but had gone back to sleep. She wouldn't say Lally seemed better because she didn't want to raise his hopes till it was utterly certain his mother was recovering. At this stage an illness like that could be chancy, and there was always the fear of it turning into pneumonia. There was so little anyone could do against that, it was one of people's worst fears.

When she came down, fully dressed now, she joined him in the kitchen and he looked at her anxiously.

'Your mother's fast asleep so we'll leave her in peace.'

He jigged about from one foot to the other and she smiled. 'Oh, go on. Nip up and stand in the doorway. Do not disturb her.'

He was gone before she'd finished speaking and came back down shortly afterwards smiling slightly. 'She looks peaceful.'

'Yes. A good sound sleep can work wonders. How about I make us both a mug of cocoa? We've earned it, don't you think? You did really well tonight, saved us from having things stolen. We'll report Pete Donahue to the police as soon as they open up for the day.'

Once it started to grow light she prepared to send Theo off to tell the police sergeant what had happened. Surely with the cut on the wrist and two people seeing Donahue's face there would be no trouble convicting him?

After seeing the sergeant Theo was to go round to the handyman's home and ask him to come and fix their smashed window. She let him run upstairs and see his mother before he left, and he came back looking even happier.

'She looks so cosy, snuggled up in bed, and she's not gasping for breath.'

Hanny smiled as she watched him leave. It was so nice to see how devoted that lad was to his mother.

To her surprise, Rachel arrived at the clinic soon after that, which was far earlier than usual and she'd walked there on her own.

Hanny greeted her with, 'You shouldn't have risked coming here alone.'

'I waited till I could see other people in the streets. I wanted to check on Lally.'

She too thought their patient was looking better and she was fully conscious now as well. She drank a full cup of water that Hanny held for her, another good sign, then the two women went back downstairs, promising to bring her up a mug of tea.

'Well, I'm glad you're early because we've had an eventful night.' Hanny led the way into the kitchen and didn't need to point to the window, because there was cold air coming in through it and she hadn't been able to sweep up all the pieces of glass.

'We had a would-be burglar, but luckily Theo heard him and came to investigate. He and I drove him off this time, but it's left me feeling worried about leaving the clinic unoccupied at night.'

Rachel nodded. 'I am too.'

When they took up a cup of tea and some bread and butter for their patient, Hanny told her how Theo had saved them from being broken into, and Lally said proudly that he was a good lad.

Hanny saw Rachel look at her as if she was envious. She'd seen that look before on the faces of women longing for a child and on Rachel's face once or twice lately. Such a pity she had never married. She'd have made a lovely mother.

Theo came back soon afterwards and said the sergeant would be there shortly but the handyman had sent a message that he wouldn't come till he'd finished his breakfast because the sergeant would want to see the damage before they disturbed things by measuring up for a new windowpane and clearing the shards of glass out of the wooden frame.

In the meantime Hanny let Theo go upstairs to see his mother.

Lally held her hand out to him. 'Theo, love, I'm so proud of you, helping to stop a burglar.'

He beamed at that but was more interested in asking, 'How do you feel now? You sound a lot better.'

'I am feeling better,' she said in a husky whisper.

But though that was good, he couldn't help worrying now about where they'd live after they left here. If it was somewhere damp and uncomfortable, which was all they were likely to afford, she might fall ill again.

Rachel followed him up and stayed near the door of the bedroom, watching mother and son hold each other's hands with such looks of affection on their faces that it sent a pang of envy through her. Moments like this could make her wonder what had happened to her own daughter, and wish she had someone who loved her so deeply, someone she could love in return.

She was glad when she heard the sergeant arrive and she could concentrate on helping him. You couldn't change the past, just had to carry on with the next part of your life. At least her baby had gone to a good family. And the man who'd been pursuing her before she came here didn't seem to have followed. That was good.

Downstairs she found the sergeant studying the broken window, with Hanny watching him and looking angry. 'You're certain it was Donahue, Miss Best?'

'I'd stake my life on it. Theo is just as certain.'

'That nasty oik didn't wait long to start thieving again, did he?'

'No. He was pinching things from other kids even when he was a little lad.'

'Will you be prepared to stand up before the magistrate and swear that it was him? You wouldn't be afraid of him coming after you one day if you did that?'

'Just let him try to come after me. Anyway, he cut the side of his right wrist on the glass really badly, so that'll help prove what we say. You can see the blood on the windowsill and frame.'

He studied them then went outside to study the footprints equally carefully. 'The left boot has a broken corner at the heel. That could be another bit of proof.' He nodded in satisfaction. 'There shouldn't be much difficulty getting him convicted and he'll spend a lot longer in jail this time. I'll see if I can find him straight away.'

When he'd gone, both women let out sighs of relief at the same time then smiled at one another.

'Let's hope the rest of the day is more peaceful,' Rachel said. 'We've still got a lot to do here. Mr Crossley is sending me some more bits and pieces of furniture from his second-hand stores today.

The sergeant went to Donahue's last known address accompanied by his constable. They found the fellow's wife there, but no sign of her husband.

'Where's your husband?' the sergeant asked, hoping that oik hadn't managed to leave town.

She wouldn't meet his eyes as she said, 'He's gone off to Manchester. He went yesterday because he'd heard about a job there. He's going to send for me an' our son when he's found us somewhere to live.'

He knew she was lying because she'd never been able to lie easily. When he looked at her more closely, he saw a bruise on her cheek and she looked as if she'd been crying. He also knew Donahue wouldn't have been able to leave Eastby in the middle of the night because there were no trains running then. That fellow had failed in what he'd set out to do last night so he'd probably not have enough money to pay for escaping by train.

'Are you sure about that, Mrs Donahue?' he asked in his sternest voice.

'That's what he told me, sergeant.'

But he saw she was trembling and pity filled him so he pretended to accept what she'd said.

Hector searched the pitiful pair of rooms where Mrs Donahue lived with her husband and young child. There might be no sign of Donahue, but there were some men's clothes still there. He didn't comment on them but surely Donahue wouldn't have left without taking his spare clothes?

He'd probably gone into hiding now, but he'd need to get hold of some money to pay for his travel out of the valley, so they'd have to keep watch for him.

That same morning, Joss asked his housekeeper if she knew a couple of strong men who'd like a job keeping watch for a few weeks.

Sybil stared at him, rather surprised at this. 'I could find you a dozen men in Eastby who'd do anything to earn some steady money. What exactly do you need watching and when?'

'I want some strong chaps to patrol the centre of Eastby during the evenings and nights, random patrols so that people never know where to expect them next. If they catch anyone misbehaving or trying to break in somewhere they'll be expected to catch them and hand them over to the police.'

'Good heavens! Does the sergeant know about this?'

'Of course he does. They'd be working partly with him and partly with me. Keeping watch is one of the tactics I hope will start making that part of Eastby safer after dark. Those unmarried young fellows are running wild, especially since they split into two groups and started fighting to be top dogs.'

'They need jobs to take up all that energy. But this keeping watch does sound like a good idea. How much would you be paying the watchmen?'

He gave her one of his rueful smiles. 'I was hoping you'd suggest a reasonable wage.'

'Hmm.' She stared into space for a few moments, then named an amount and when he nodded, she said, 'Keith Fulton's a good chap and maybe his brother Norman could help too.'

'Why do you say "maybe" for this Norman fellow?'

'Because he'd only be able to work with his brother, not on his own. He's very strong but he's a bit simple-minded. He's a gentle soul but he can't bear to see violence and if other people start causing trouble when he's around, he sometimes tries to intervene. He's known for stopping bigger kids in the street if he sees them bullying smaller kids.'

Joss frowned at her. 'It sounds a bit of a risk having him keeping watch. He might hurt someone if he sees anything violent or get hurt himself.'

'I doubt it. He's strong enough to stop a fight without much risk to himself, and quickly too. I've seen him do it quite often. You could pay him less because he'd need to work under his brother's supervision. The family would be happy if he got half what you'll be paying the others.'

She waited and when he still frowned, said, 'Why not give him a try?'

'You're sure he wouldn't *cause* trouble by misunderstanding a situation?'

At her nod, he said, 'Hmm. I could certainly afford it and we'd get an extra watchman. Yes, let's try it.'

She looked at him, head on one side, and asked, 'Are you going to tell people in Eastby about the patrols?'

'I'm not sure. It's another thing I'll ask the sergeant about and I'd appreciate your opinion on that, too.'

'I'd not tell them anything in advance, just let it come as a shock to some of those louts when they get caught and hauled off to the police station. And if the one and only cell gets full, we can always shut them in the crypt underneath the little church in Eastby. There's a room at one side with a good strong door on it.'

'You're a fount of good ideas, Sybil.'

'I appreciate you listening to me. Some men think women don't know anything except how to cook and look after kids.'

'Well, they're wrong. And I feel particularly lucky to have a woman as intelligent as you for my housekeeper.'

He left her looking pink and flushed at the compliment and trying to hide her pleasure at that.

Joss cycled into Ollerthwaite to visit the police station again. He loved being so close to the moors and had found some paths up there from the edge of his land. It could be such a pretty village and the people who called it home deserved to live their lives safely. He got more and more determined to make Eastby safer every time he saw how pretty it could be here.

They might even be able to attract hikers one day. There was money to be made in that from refreshments and cheap rooms for the night.

The only thing he hadn't managed to make a proper start on was to persuade Rachel to spend more time with him and he was determined to find a way so that they could see if they really were suited. He knew she liked him, you could tell, somehow, and sometimes she forgot to keep her distance for a while when they got chatting. He so enjoyed her company at those times.

He'd keep his eye open for opportunities to chat to her and spend time with her. He could be very determined when he wanted something this much.

Sergeant McGill wrote to his inspector, catching the early post, and he turned up unexpectedly a couple of days later to talk about Joss's offer. He came in a motor car he had bought for his personal use, driven by a chauffeur.

Lucky him, having a rich wife to pay for such luxuries and a job that gave him good reason to use his car whenever he needed to see someone at the edge of his area.

The sergeant dutifully admired the vehicle. 'It must be very convenient, sir.'

The inspector patted the side of the bonnet and beamed at him. 'It is. Now that the stupid law restricting speed to four miles an hour in the country has been repealed and the speed limit raised to a decent fourteen miles an hour, we shall start to make real progress with making cars in this country.'

'Yes, indeed.' The sergeant tried to look interested though he'd heard all this before, and more than once too.

'One day the police will all use motor cars to get around in, just you wait and see. More people are buying cars already in America and in some European countries, not just the rich. They're trying to make cars that are cheaper here too, but we're lagging behind those countries still. We won't always, though.'

Hector couldn't see motor cars being widely used in Britain for a long time yet, if ever, partly because of the expense but also because of their unreliability. People laughed at the way they broke down so often. But he knew better than to contradict the inspector who was known to have a bee in his bonnet about his ideas of progress.

'In the meantime I wouldn't mind bicycles for me and my constable,' Hector dared to say. 'Lots of people have them nowadays, women as well as men, and criminals can use them to get away from policemen who can't keep up with them on foot.'

The inspector frowned and then nodded slowly. 'I've been thinking about bicycles as an interim measure, actually. We might run to buying them for you and your constable. I'll see what I can do.'

Hector couldn't believe his ears. Someone higher must have been talking to the inspector. 'They'd be a big help, sir, and the sooner the better. You've hit the nail on the head about what a help they'd be. There's a lot of ground to cover here in the valley and no public transport system at all, apart from the railway terminal.'

'Exactly. I'll see what I can do. Now, to get back to your philanthropic gentleman. Are you sure there's not some hidden motive behind his offer? There aren't many people who'd do what he's suggesting. It'll cost a lot and how will he reap a profit from it?'

'I'm quite sure there's no hidden motive except to make where he lives a better place. He doesn't seem short of money so I doubt he's after a financial benefit. And the more I see of Mr Townley, the more I like him, and so do some of the people whose opinions I respect, like Walter Crossley.'

'Ah well, if that chap Crossley approves of him you can be sure Townley is a decent chap. Tell him to go ahead and make some arrangements but you keep an eye on what these watchmen actually do. I think we'd better let the public know the patrols are going to start, though. Some folk don't like any changes and seize any chance to complain.'

Hector didn't agree but he knew when to back off. He did manage to get his inspector to agree to compromise by making an announcement that some new police-approved nightwatchmen would be starting work soon in the valley, but not saying exactly when or where they'd be starting.

Hector watched the inspector drive away then went to discuss the details of the scheme with Joss. He also went to study the crypt of the church and found the side room very suitable if they caught a few villains, though he'd need to have a better lock put on the door to make it truly secure.

He hoped that when the patrols got going and people saw work being done on the room in the crypt, folk would start to realise the authorities were serious about improving law and order in Eastby.

Then he sighed. Did those groups of young men care about the future? He doubted it. They wanted things to happen now and it'd take a few incidents and some of them being carted off to jail to make them see that folk had had enough of their thieving and fighting.

He made sure no one could find out the details of when and where exactly these patrols were going to operate, or even who was going to be doing the job. But sadly there were even a few people who worried publicly about these watchmen causing more trouble with the younger locals than they prevented.

Well, let them worry, the sergeant thought grimly. Things were going to change, whatever it took.

Walter Crossley watched all this from a distance and chatted to those involved in actually making arrangements. A couple of times he even came up with minor suggestions for how things might be more efficiently organised. But on the whole he left it to others to take charge of setting all this up.

It particularly pleased him to see Joss Townley at the centre of it all. Last year Walter had been worrying about what would happen as he grew even older and eventually needed to step back from playing an active role in local life. He'd been lucky to stay fit and healthy till over seventy but you never knew what was waiting for you round the corner at this age. With Joss taking a hand, he felt more hopeful about the future.

His wife had been telling him he couldn't do everything and shouldn't even try. He had to admit, though only to himself, that he did get tired more easily these days, but he could still help people in small ways and watch the next generation start taking hold, couldn't he?

He discussed the situation with other people on the town council and most agreed with him that the future was looking better in Eastby which, for the first time in years, was receiving some of the attention it needed to keep its residents safe.

And he accepted, though reluctantly when it came to motor cars, that they all needed to keep up with some of the modern developments that were improving people's daily lives.

He didn't like cars and never would, because his son and grandson had been killed in an accident involving one. He considered them best left as toys for richer people to play with. However, telephones did appear to be a useful and safe invention and he wanted to persuade the authorities to set up a better telephone exchange here in Ollindale, or whatever it was you did to keep up with the world.

It was only about ten years since Mr Bell had demonstrated the telephone to the Queen, and she had approved of it. And if they were good enough for Her Majesty, they were good enough for him, by George.

Sadly Her Majesty appeared to be getting rather frail but he hoped she would live past a hundred. She had been there for most of his life and it would be hard to say 'His Majesty' when the worst happened.

Developments with telephones had been rapid and safe, and Walter loved to read about them in the newspapers. Nowadays any respectable person could buy a licence from their local Post Office to possess and operate a telephone, and once they had one of the gadgets, people could even make long-distance phone calls between cities as far apart as London and Bristol.

The thought of that amazed him, and it was what he called real progress.

32

When Joss met Adam strolling round the centre of
Eastby he was struck again by how closely he resem-
bled Lionel. He seized the opportunity to chat to him about
the houses they both owned near the group of run-down
shops as well as the shops themselves. He found the man
he was already starting to consider a friend very receptive
to the idea of a group of house owners improving that part
of town and setting an example to other landlords.

'I'm thrilled to have inherited so much from my father,
naturally, but I'm also upset that he didn't maintain the
houses properly,' Adam admitted at one point in their
conversation.

'Have you started work on improvements to any of
them?'

'Yes. But only the one I intend to occupy myself, which
isn't in the centre of Eastby but not far from it. I don't
want to live out at the cottage on the farm, even though
I'd have the pleasure of you as a neighbour, and I don't
want to be in the village centre either. I need a workshop,
you see, or somewhere to erect one, because I intend to
start up a business dealing with motor cars.'

Joss looked at him in surprise.

He chuckled. 'First of all I'm going to build one for
myself using a pre-made chassis but also, I hope, I'll start
to repair them for others.'

'Do you think there will be enough work for you to make a living? I don't think there's anyone in the valley who actually owns a car yet, though some have been talking about buying one for a while so we're on the verge of starting to see them around. People do use them to visit friends here, though.'

'It'll happen quickly once enough people see the benefits.'

'You should chat to Riley Callan about it. He's a plumber who's intending to get into making and repairing cars one day. People smile when they hear him talk about wanting to do that, but the police inspector comes to visit our sergeant in a motor car and that has set quite a few people off talking more positively about the idea lately.'

'Perhaps if they knew there was a good mechanic available they'd actually risk buying a car.' Adam grinned. 'And in the meantime, having that inheritance and no one dependent on me means I don't need to scrape for every penny but can please myself what I do with my life and put together my own car.'

His smile faded. 'Unfortunately, I do feel guilty about the state of the houses I inherited so I will have to deal with that problem if I'm to live at peace with my conscience. I like your idea about several of us setting a good example by doing some much-needed repairs on our houses.'

After a short discussion they decided that Joss would contact the owners of the other shops and houses in the group in the centre of Eastby and Adam would keep an eye open for suitable craftsmen to do the actual work, preferably people who lived nearby.

So Joss started asking around. He felt angry to be met with refusals to join in from several gentlemen whose properties needed the most attention. He was told quite sharply by one that it didn't do to coddle the lower classes and no good would come of this. That arrogant, old-fashioned attitude annoyed him hugely, but fortunately he did find three other shop and house owners who were willing to join him and Adam in such a venture.

His biggest surprise was to find that one owner was an older lady, a former teacher who had terrified two generations of local children into behaving perfectly in her classes and learning whatever she presented to them. He hadn't even realised a woman owned that house because the information from the town hall just gave initials and surnames. It wasn't the worst one by any means though it did need some attention.

He hadn't expected her to join in their venture and yet she proved to be one of the most enthusiastic members of the group. He acknowledged to himself then that he had been displaying a rather old-fashioned attitude to women.

Miss Scholes questioned him at length and eventually pronounced it to be an excellent civic initiative. She added that since she had recently retired from teaching to live with her sister, she'd welcome some new interests and would be happy to help him organise things.

He walked away full of respect for her, which only grew as he got to know her. It was she who arranged a time for them all to meet, booking the church hall so they could discuss the situation 'properly'. And she went on to say, 'I shall take notes at this meeting so that people don't forget what has been agreed, and I shall be able to help Mr Dean and yourself with any other paperwork needed.'

In fact, things were off to a good start and Joss was pleased with what he'd done so far.

The only area of interest to him in which he was not making nearly as much progress as he'd have liked was in getting Rachel to spend more time with him. And yet, she occasionally lingered to chat to him for much longer than was necessary, ranging over a variety of topics and shared interests as well as the original topic of conversation. It was these encounters that made him certain he wasn't fooling himself in thinking she liked him and found his company congenial. You could tell that sort of attraction somehow.

Why would she not take the next step? He'd racked his brain trying to work that out.

She reminded him of a horse he'd encountered on his travels that had been ill-treated. He'd helped the owner soothe it and get it to trust human beings again but it had taken a while and he'd delayed his departure to help see the job through.

It suddenly occurred to him that something bad could have happened to Rachel in the past that had put her off marriage. She didn't seem to have any family, never talked about relatives or her childhood years. What had happened to her when she was younger? He grew increasingly certain there had been something.

One day they started talking about the improvements to houses that were needed, and she pointed a few more things out from a woman's viewpoint. Half an hour passed discussing them before they realised it.

Another day they were walking back into town with Hanny trailing behind when he commented on a family walking down the road ahead of them, children and parents laughing together, and the two parents swinging a small lad up in the air every now and then.

He spoke without thinking. 'I hope to have a family like that one day.'

He saw Rachel stiffen visibly and just couldn't bear it any longer, asking involuntarily, 'What am I doing wrong? Why will you not even consider going for a walk with me when we get on so well? And what did I say just now to make you end our discussion so abruptly?'

She looked at him and said quietly, 'I don't intend to marry and stop being a nurse, so I was wrong to give you the wrong ideas about our – our friendship.'

'Modern women don't always stop work after they marry these days, if that's what upsets you,' he dared say. 'Flora Crossley, whose maiden name was Vardy, is a nurse and she hasn't stopped work.'

Rachel's voice grew sharper. 'She was too old to have children when she married him. It's younger women who get criticised if they continue working after they marry.'

In for a penny, in for a pound, he thought. 'I'd never ask any wife of mine to stop doing something she cared about as much as you obviously care about nursing. I can afford to hire a nanny and I already have an excellent housekeeper. What I don't have is a beloved companion and children of my own. And I long for them, Rachel. What's more, I've seen you look at families in the street and it seems to me that you do too.'

He stopped walking, staring at her, hoping she'd be as honest with him as he had just been with her.

When she didn't speak he prompted gently, 'What happened to you, Rachel? I don't think you dislike me, but something must have made you determined never to marry.' He hadn't expected the expression of agony this brought to her face. He knew then that whatever had happened must have been far worse than he'd guessed.

Someone walked past just then, staring at them, and she glanced round looking uncomfortable and upset. 'We can't talk about such things in a public place.'

'Then where can we talk about them, Rachel? I've been honest with you. I think I deserve the truth in return. Most women would consider it a compliment to be asked to go steady with someone who cares about them as much as I've started to care about you.'

'It is a compliment, an honour even.' Tears welled in her eyes and she said in a low voice, 'Let me . . . I can't . . . give me some time to consider what I ought to say to you.'

'And then?'

'Then I'll tell you why I can't marry anyone.'

Before he could say anything else, she fell back to walk next to Hanny and they reached the clinic soon afterwards.

Someone was waiting for her outside it, a careworn woman with a lad who had a badly cut arm, judging by the blood on the cloth wrapped round it. Rachel muttered goodbye and hurried to unlock the door and take the injured lad inside.

Joss looked sideways at Hanny, wondering what she thought of the situation. She must have heard some of what they'd said, not to mention seeing how upset Rachel was.

She hesitated and said, 'I'm sorry, Mr Townley. I couldn't help overhearing and it'd have looked strange if I'd walked away from the two of you.' She stared down, biting the corner of her mouth, clearly wanting to say something else, so he waited. When she looked up she said, 'Rachel does like you in the way you like her, I'm sure of that. But she's convinced herself that she can't get married for some reason. I don't know why but it's obviously to do with something that upsets her greatly. She was in tears today trying to answer you and I've never seen her like that before.'

'Would *you* get married if you met someone you could care for or are people involved in nursing all against marriage?'

'I hope to marry one day. I like children. But I don't want to do that yet. Only, Rachel is several years older than me and the way she looks at children sometimes makes me think she'd love to be a mother.' She hesitated and added, 'Give her time. Treat her gently and be patient.' Then she hurried inside the clinic.

He walked slowly away, lost in thought, going over in his mind what had happened, wondering if he had made things worse today or simply brought matters to a head, to a confrontation that had been inevitable.

But Hanny's encouragement had made him feel a little more hopeful. Surely if he and Rachel could talk privately, spend time together, she would see that they could build a happy marriage?

He'd never met a woman he found so attractive or wanted so badly to share the rest of his life with. And this had happened so quickly. He desperately wanted to help her step out from whatever shadow was clouding her life. Seeing her look so unhappy upset him.

33

Emmy Lucas spent the first week at the farm working hard to give the whole house a thorough cleaning. However, she kept a wary eye on the woman upstairs, who was eating very little and seeming to get thinner by the day.

Every time Thelma looked at Emmy she radiated barely suppressed hatred of the new housekeeper. Why? What on earth had Emmy ever done to her?

As the days passed things got worse, not better. Thelma began to say things, expressing her disgust at Emmy's presence and tossing the nastiest accusations and insults at her, though never when Lionel was around to hear them.

Well, she mistook her target, Emmy thought. She had grown up with a father who never said anything good about anyone, even his own children, and she had learned from an early age to ignore insults and scorn. She cared less about how this woman felt than she had about her father's attitude, far less. It was irritating rather than painful.

Then Thelma began to spill her food and drink on purpose. She smeared it on the tray at first then after a day or two began leaving a mess on the bedcovers. Each day there was more mess and in a more prominent position.

Emmy didn't hurry to clear it up after the first time, leaving it there to annoy the invalid. But eventually it had to be cleared up and Thelma half lay in the chair next to the bed with a sneering half smile on her face watching her do that.

Then one day, not realising that her husband was still in the house, Thelma threw her plate of food at the nearest wall. When he heard the crash of something breaking Lionel came running upstairs.

He stopped in the doorway unseen by the two women just as Thelma shouted, 'Clear that up at once, you slut.'

'Why did you do that?' Emmy asked.

'It was too vile to eat.'

'I've a good mind to leave it there to rot.'

'Don't you dare answer me back, you—' She saw her husband and broke off abruptly.

He studied the mess at one side of the room and then glared at his wife. 'So you did that on purpose, did you?'

'It was inedible. She can't cook. I wonder you put up with her nasty messes.'

He looked scornfully at his wife. 'I really enjoy Emmy's cooking. And you're the one who will have to put up with the mess you've just made here because I'm not clearing it up till tomorrow. And what's more I'm not letting Emmy clear up this or any further deliberate messes you make ever again. I mean that. See how you enjoy having it there. You'll have to be careful how you lie in bed, won't you? There's some food on the covers as well as on the floor.'

Then he took Emmy's arm and led her gently but firmly out of the bedroom. On the landing he set his hands on her shoulders, looked her in the eyes and said very firmly, 'Leave it!'

Thelma yelled insults after them and threw a fit of hysterics, but though Lionel stayed outside the door in case she tried to harm herself, he wouldn't let Emmy go back inside to clear up and he didn't do so himself, either.

He kept his word, not clearing up till the next afternoon and doing the job himself, saying as he left the bedroom. 'I meant what I said yesterday: I'll not let Emmy clear up after you and if you do anything like this again, I'll leave you to enjoy your mess for three days, perhaps even longer.'

There wasn't another incident for several days, then Thelma had a fit of shrieking hysterics at what Emmy took up for her midday meal and threw the whole tray and its contents on to the floor. Then she got out of bed and thumped the pieces of crockery with an old shoe to make sure they were all broken.

She must have planned to do this, Emmy thought as she walked out of the bedroom. She left the mess lying there as Lionel had ordered, feeling sickened by the situation.

Thelma was getting worse. What would she do next?

If she hadn't been working for someone as nice as Lionel, Emmy would have left. She stood motionless, staring out of the kitchen window and thinking about what he had to put up with, poor man. Marriage could be like being held fast by a heavy chain sometimes.

What slowly sank in was how much she was starting to care for him. How had she let that happen? And yet, how could she have stopped it happening? He was always so pleasant with her, smiling whenever she walked into a room to join him. And the time they spent together in the evenings was perfect, even though there was nothing spectacular about it. They chatted about their day's work, about how well the chickens were laying, how the crops were growing. Or they sat quietly reading the newspapers and commenting on the wider world when they found articles of interest.

Yesterday he'd bought Emmy a woman's magazine in the town because he thought she might enjoy some lighter reading. That had been so kind. How could she not care for him?

And how could she not know that he cared for her too, even though neither of them had ever put their feelings into words?

Oh, heavens, she hoped no one else in town else had noticed.

When Lionel came in from working on the kitchen garden, which she guessed was a job chosen to keep him close to the house, she was still standing by the window staring out, thinking about Thelma now and wondering if there was any way to deal with this latest set of bad behaviour to make things easier for him.

'What has she done now?' he asked at once.

'How did you know she'd done something?'

'You're looking upset. And her tray isn't in its usual place.' He gestured towards a shelf.

'She's thrown the tray on the floor and probably broken all the crockery on it. It's made a far worse mess than ever before.'

'What brought that on?'

'I can't work that out, Lionel. All I did was take up her meal and leave her to it.'

'Perhaps I really should put her in the asylum. I've been reluctant to do it, but she's making things more and more difficult.'

'We're coping.'

'Yes, but for how long can we manage? I saw Dr Coxton in town and she asked how Thelma was. When I told her my wife seemed to be getting worse, she looked worried. I asked if she'd known Thelma's behaviour would deteriorate so quickly and she reminded me that she'd warned me about that last time she came to see her.'

Emmy looked at him in sympathy. He'd put up with so much from his wife.

'Next time I see the doctor I'd better ask her if we need to put Thelma away. I don't want to but we don't want to risk her hurting anyone else, especially you.'

'I don't like the thought of putting anyone in that place on the moors, even her, if half the rumours about it are true,' Emmy said.

'No. I don't, either.'

'We're coping.'

'You at least shouldn't have to cope with such behaviour.'

He sighed and moved towards the door to the stairs. 'I'd better go up and clear the mess. I'll bring the remains down and I'll see to her tonight. You're not to go up to her to help her get ready for bed. I'll do anything that's necessary and if she makes another mess, she can sleep in the dirty sheets for a week because we're running out of clean ones, and so I'll tell her.'

He went upstairs and there were shrieks and yells from Thelma but only one or two low rumbles of sound from him.

He came down with the tray. There was a jumble of food and broken crockery on it, hardly any piece left intact. Automatically Emmy started to sort it out.

'Leave that. I'll do it later. I think I'd better get her some clean clothes first and a facecloth to wash herself with. I've never seen her in such a mess.'

While he went back upstairs to his wife, Emmy began to clear up the things from the tray because he had enough to do without this. She could only throw away the broken crockery, but she sorted out the cutlery and put it in the sink, ready to wash. As she stared down at it she froze, checking the mess out again.

No. The knife was definitely missing!

There was another shriek from upstairs and she heard Thelma's words clearly.

'That bitch is after you, you fool. But she's not having you, Lionel. Never ever. I'm going to make sure of that.'

Another rumble of sound from Lionel then Thelma shrieked, 'No, no, no! I won't stop. She's *not* having you. I'm your wife.'

For some reason fear shot through Emmy, partly at what Thelma was saying and partly at the way she was shrieking these words.

She had never heard anyone make sounds so utterly inhuman and something terrified her suddenly, and made her hurry up the stairs not realising till she got to the top that she was still holding the kitchen towel.

She didn't want to leave him alone with his wife. She felt afraid Thelma might hurt him.

She got to the bedroom door in time to see Lionel bend to pick up something from the floor, having trouble picking up what looked like pieces of food.

Thelma was standing at the end of the bed whose sheets had been pulled off.

Everything seemed to happen slowly as Thelma raised her right hand and the blade of the knife she was holding glinted in the sunbeams shining through the window.

Lionel didn't seem at all aware of the danger behind him, but Emmy could tell that the woman was getting ready to use the knife.

Thelma didn't even notice her standing in the doorway. She didn't seem aware of anything except her husband and the knife, staring from him to it and smiling as she started to raise the hand holding it.

Emmy jerked into action, yelling as she leaped forward and grabbed Thelma's hand. She pulled it away from Lionel's back only with a struggle. She tried to use the towel to protect herself as she grabbed it, desperate to get it away from the woman she was now sure had run completely mad. But tonight Thelma seemed stronger than ever before and though Emmy was bigger than her, she couldn't get the knife away.

Thelma let out another of those inhuman shrieks and struggled even more wildly.

Lionel had turned round and seen what was happening. He also reached out towards the arm holding up the knife. But Thelma somehow seemed to be finding the strength to keep hold of it and she managed to jab it forward.

When Emmy felt a burning sensation in her outstretched arm, she didn't at first realise she'd been injured, not till she heard him shout, 'Move back quickly, Emmy! Move back!'

She felt him push her away and lost her balance, tumbling to the floor away from Thelma and the knife.

Things seemed to be happening more quickly now.

Lionel reached out for his wife and managed to thump her arm so sharply that the knife clattered to the floor then he reached out to grab her.

Thelma screamed and threw herself backwards through the doorway in what looked like a desperate attempt to get away from him.

As he stumbled on the jumble of bedcovers and missed getting hold of her flailing arm, Thelma jerked backwards into the end of the bannisters so violently that she lost her balance and was thrown away from them into the stairwell.

She tumbled helplessly backwards, screaming shrilly.

He tried but couldn't get to her quickly enough to stop her tumbling down the stairs. Then he lost his balance and only just managed to grab the end of the bannisters and save himself from following her down.

He and Emmy could only stare in horror as Thelma bumped helplessly down the stairs, tossed about like a rag doll and ending up in a twisted heap at the bottom.

She lay there, not moving, her head at an unnatural angle.

Emmy sobbed aloud as she realised what had happened.

The other woman's eyes remained wide and staring, her features still fixed in a wild grimace. She had not made the slightest attempt to move and it was clear that she never would again.

'Are you all right?' Lionel shot an anguished look at Emmy, then exclaimed, 'No, you're not.' He saw the blood dripping from the wound on her arm before she did and before she could move, he put an arm round her shoulders and pulled her further back.

'Look away, my darling. She's beyond our help now. It's you who need attention. You're bleeding. Let me get a clean towel.'

She looked down in bewilderment, hadn't realised she had such a big gash along her arm.

It was much more important to her that he'd called her darling.

He opened the door of the linen cupboard and pulled a clean towel out, wrapping it round her arm. Then he picked her up and carried her slowly down the stairs, edging with difficulty past the dead woman at the bottom and going into the kitchen, where he laid Emmy down gently on the old sofa in the corner.

'See to your wife.'

'No one can help Thelma now. I need to stop this bleeding.'

'You can't just leave her lying there.'

'I think I have to so that the sergeant can see how it happened. The doctor will bear witness that Thelma wasn't in her right mind.'

When he'd finished wrapping the towel tightly round her arm, he asked, 'Will you be all right if I run across to Mr Townley's house and fetch my mother to help you? She's good with injuries and a tower of strength in an emergency. Joss will go for the doctor and the sergeant, I'm sure.'

Emmy didn't want him to leave her, wanted to huddle against him, wanted it desperately, and she absolutely hated the thought of being left alone in the house with the dead woman. But somehow she pulled herself together and said, 'Yes, of course. You do what you have to. I'll be fine.'

And just like that he was gone.

She couldn't see Thelma's body from where she was lying, thank goodness, but she still couldn't seem to pull her thoughts together. So she stayed huddled in the corner of the sofa, kept the towel wrapped round her arm, which was throbbing with pain now, and listened for him coming back.

It seemed a very long time before she heard people running across the farm yard and Lionel burst into the house, followed by his mother.

'Are you all right?'

Only then did Emmy let herself go, not quite fainting but feeling as if she were hovering a long way above the terrible scene nearby.

Then his arms were there, and she clung to him.

After one quick look at the foot of the stairs, Sybil joined them and her soft voice began to slip a cloak of comfort and love around them both.

'That poor woman is at peace now and you two can get on with your lives.'

Lionel said, 'Emmy saved my life. That's how she got hurt.'

Sybil leaned forward to hug Emmy. 'Then I can never thank you enough.'

'I tried to save Thelma,' Lionel said. 'I really did try.'

'Of course you did. No one will ever doubt that. Now let me pour the boiled water from the kettle into a bowl, and you can boil some more for me, Lionel. I have to attend to your arm, Emmy, and clean it up. Though you'll need the doctor to stitch it up properly for you.'

While he filled the kettle again and set it on to boil, Sybil washed the wound then beckoned to him. 'You hold her till they come, Lionel. You both need the comfort of that.'

The motherly tone and the series of instructions and gentle comments helped them both to pull themselves together and by the time the sergeant arrived they had moved apart and were ready to face the world again.

Hector went to stare at Thelma's body then spoke gently to them, asking a few questions. But he didn't try to move the dead woman until the doctor had arrived.

Dr Coxton also studied the scene and said quietly, 'I'm not surprised by this, Sergeant. She was getting worse each time I visited her. I've told Lionel several times that he should put his wife in the asylum but he wouldn't. I knew she was losing what little was left of her reason, but I didn't expect her to try to murder him and Emmy. She must have gone downhill very rapidly.'

'You'll speak to the coroner about that, explain what she was like at the end?' the sergeant asked.

'Yes, of course.' She looked back towards the body and shook her head sadly.

'I think we can move her now and send for the undertaker from Ollerthwaite,' he said quietly. 'You're as sure as I am now that this wasn't Mr Entwistle's fault?'

'It's obvious, especially with the wound on Mrs Lucas's arm.'

No one said much after that as they waited for the undertaker.

And though they might not be able to touch one another now, Emmy and Lionel were still able to sit near one another and draw comfort from that as they waited.

It wasn't till the afternoon was nearly over and everyone except Sybil had left the farm that peace seemed to start settling around them again.

Sybil waited till the three of them were alone to say, 'You should get someone to live here with you until you can decently get married, son, or it won't look good.'

Lionel looked at her in shock. 'Is it so obvious how I feel about Emmy?'

'Yes. And I approve. But you still need some sort of chaperone figure here for a while. I'll stay tonight and I'd suggest old Mrs Gibbins be invited to move in for a few weeks, say a couple of months. She's a nice, quiet old woman and won't drive you mad nattering and asking questions.'

He smiled at her. 'Good idea and thank you for your help.'

She moved to give Emmy a hug. 'Welcome to the family, dear.'

Soon afterwards Mrs Gibbins came to stay. It was she who suggested to Sybil that Lionel and Emmy would make a lovely couple and then boasted to her friends a few weeks later that it had been her idea to bring them together.

Sybil didn't contradict her, just smiled and nodded.

Mrs Gibbins had set the seal on the respectability of their engagement and coming marriage. Their deep love for one another would ensure they were happy together.

34

The attempted murder had caught people in the whole valley by surprise, shocking them so much at the thought of a woman running mad and trying to kill her husband that little else was talked about for a long time. In Eastby it was even more prominent in people's minds because they felt they had been so close to it.

The sergeant was kept busy dealing with the formalities following an unexpected death and answering questions from worried residents and it was several days before he was able to give the necessity to capture Pete Donahue his full attention again. After all, an attempted burglary wasn't nearly as important as calming people down and making them feel that they were safe in their own homes after a murder had only just been prevented.

Donahue was even able to meet his friends in the back room of the sleazy little pub where the cheapest beer in the valley was sold. He'd had time to think while hiding in an old hut at the edge of the moors, supplied with food by his wife, when she could.

He came up with a plan to earn the money to fund him leaving Eastby for good and starting up a new life elsewhere. He told everyone he knew that he needed money to take his wife and child away from here and give them all a new start in life, but in actual fact, once he'd got hold of some money he intended to run away and leave them behind. She was a weak, stupid creature and got pregnant far too easily. If he hadn't given her a good punching last time she started a child, he'd be lumbered with two of the little sods now, not just the one, and he'd never get a peaceful night's sleep again, let alone have money to buy himself a beer when he wanted one.

He told a couple of his friends about his plan and they thought it a good idea, but he was well aware that they'd mainly agreed to help him because of the share of the money that he'd told them he'd make sure they got, not out of mere friendship.

He also knew that being in prison for several months had taught him a lot about getting what you wanted out of the world. He knew more than these former friends now, that's for certain, as well as more about defending himself. He'd seen that some of them were rather nervous of the differences in him these days, especially after he'd beaten up a chap who'd tried to take over his plan and use it for his own purposes.

He knew his relatives had discussed handing him in to the sergeant, before he got them into trouble, but he made it plain to them that he'd make them regret it if they tried, even if he had to wait years to do so.

Once he'd got the support of a few useful people he set about arranging a meeting between two of the best fighters in Eastby, one from each of the rival groups in the village, telling potential spectators that he'd be selling special tickets to watch it, with a prize draw of money for the number on the ticket stub pulled out of a hat afterwards.

He offered to pay the two fighters good money for taking part but didn't intend to pay that or the prize money if he could help it.

He was sure the police would come and break the fight up and he intended to use the resultant chaos to get away with all the takings, which he'd put in a money belt. This time he'd have his spare clothes and a few other bits and pieces packed and ready to grab from a hiding place at the edge of Eastby as he left.

He knew various ways across the moors from his boyhood wanderings and he'd wait a day or two up there then find a way down to a railway station further along the line and simply catch a train to the nearest main line station.

He was going to head for London. He'd never been there but it sounded like a good place to disappear into. He knew a couple of fellows who lived there from his time in jail. They'd seen how strong he was, in spite of not being a big man and promised him plenty of work if he joined them there.

With money in his pocket he'd be set for a comfortable future elsewhere.

The coming fight was known about in Eastby, because you couldn't keep such a thing secret if you wanted to attract the local idiots to pay to see it. But Donahue made sure that several different rumours were circulated about when exactly it would occur.

Men wanting to watch were sold numbered tickets and watched as the stub was put into a pouch held by a respected old fellow in the village, who would draw out the prizewinning ticket. They'd only find out the actual time and place for the fight a couple of hours beforehand. They wouldn't be able to attend unless they had a ticket or paid at the entrance.

As for the patrol by the new watchmen, which was known about and approved of by most people, the day it was planned to start hadn't yet been revealed. The two watchmen slipped into the police station the night before their first patrol was to take place, so that they could discuss the details with the sergeant and Joss about where exactly they would each go on their patrol.

'And if you can find out on your travels when and where exactly that damned fight is going to take place, I'd be much obliged,' the sergeant said sourly. 'I don't trust that Donahue to keep it all peaceful.'

It wasn't till after this meeting that Keith Fulton went home and told his mother about his new job. He'd hinted that they'd soon be making a start but asked her not to talk about it to any of her friends. She was delighted for him and even more delighted that Norman would have a chance to earn some steady money for a while. He might have a child's mind but he had a big strong man's body and ate so heartily she found it hard to keep him satisfied.

It wasn't until the next day at teatime that Keith explained to his brother that they were going to keep watch on Eastby town centre by walking round it after dark that night and every evening from now on, and would get paid for this.

To his surprise, Norman nodded vigorously. 'Need to stop the fight tonight, though. People are paying to watch them do it. Fighting is bad, very bad.'

'*What?* How do you know about it?'

'I heard Eddie telling someone and I hid like you told me so they wouldn't see me listening and bash me.'

'Good lad.' Keith was glad his patient repeating of hints at how to behave was working. His brother was such a lovely, gentle fellow.

But Norman hadn't finished and tugged his sleeve to get his attention. 'I don't like fighting, Keith. I don't like people getting hurt. We have to stop them doing it tonight.'

'Are you absolutely sure it's tonight?'

Norman nodded vigorously. 'Yes. I said. Tonight.'

Their mother shook her head. 'They're getting worse, that group of rough heads are. No one will be safe at this rate. They need a job that tires them out. That'd keep them out of mischief. Only who'd give them jobs? No one who has any sense, that's for sure.'

Keith was worried now, because Norman was so sure it was tonight. He decided he'd better tell Mr Townley what Norman had overheard and leave it to him to get word to the sergeant. He could cycle to the police station in town far more quickly than Keith could walk. He'd better tell Mr Townley as quickly as possible, before he and his brother set off on patrol in case the sergeant decided to change where they were to go tonight. He glanced at the clock. He had time to do that before they set off but he'd have to hurry.

He turned to his mother. 'I'll go and see Mr Townley, Mam. Can you make sure our Norman stays at home till I get back. We don't want him giving anything away.'

She nodded. 'I'll do that. You get off, love.'

When he heard that the worst group of louts in Eastby was intending to hold their big fight that very night, Joss sighed. His new patrols would be mocked if they didn't do something to stop it, so he'd have to change the arrangements as well as informing the police.

'I'll cycle into Ollerthwaite and let the sergeant know. You go and keep watch behind the church, Keith, so we can call you in to assist the sergeant if need be.'

By half-past six the sergeant and constable had been warned and had followed Joss back to Eastby secretly on borrowed bicycles. They were going to wait behind the run-down shops in the centre of the village till the rival groups had gathered for the fight, then pounce on them.

'I'm not letting them get started if I can help it,' the sergeant said. 'You can't trust that lot to behave themselves if they get overexcited. And if they think they've kept it secret from me about where it's going to take place, I'll have even more difficulty stopping them causing trouble.' He breathed deeply. 'Thanks, lad. I needed confirmation of exactly when and where. That bare patch of ground behind the church always seemed like the most likely place, unless they decided to go up on the moors.'

Mr Fulton wished his sons well on their first evening and told his wife those damned louts had gone too far this time and he hoped they all got arrested. Then he sat down with his evening paper and refused to speculate about what might happen.

At half-past six Joss and the sergeant went into hiding behind some fancy headstones in the graveyard next to the patch of bare ground where the fight was to take place. People didn't often go there because relatives of the dead tended to make a fuss and cause trouble.

Men were already gathering and they watched Donahue and a friend finish hammering in some stakes in a rough circle and tie ropes to the tops of them.

Some of the wilder young men from the village and nearby smallholdings and farms had already started to trickle in but for once they were mostly quiet, having been warned not to attract attention to what was about to happen by making a noise.

'It's like an avalanche getting ready to roll down the hill,' Joss whispered to the sergeant as the minutes passed and more people joined the gathering.

'Look at them, shoving one another about and arguing in whispers. They're getting restless and there are still ten minutes to go, even if it starts on time, which I doubt it will with Donahue organising it.'

'I agree. Given the slightest provocation there could be more than two so-called fighters getting active here.'

Joss was worried about his watchmen's personal safety. 'I certainly didn't expect those men to have to deal with something like this on their first day of work. I'm worried about Norman.'

'His brother always looks after him. Eh, look at that Pete Donahue ordering people about and collecting money. He looks very pleased with himself but those having to pay don't like it.' The sergeant grinned. 'Well, I'm going to make them even more unhappy when I stop the fight and confiscate the takings.'

He turned to Joss. 'I shall have to go after one of the fighters first of all because they'll be the centre of attention. I have to make sure of stopping them fighting. I'm worried Donahue might sneak away, so could you go and grab hold of him for me, Joss? He's a scrawny little oik, so I doubt a big chap like you will have much trouble keeping him under restraint.'

Joss hadn't intended to get personally involved in the fighting, had always loathed violence but sometimes you just had to do something about a bad situation. Besides, what credibility would he have in the community if he didn't back up his promise to help make Eastby safer. 'Yes, I'll do that.'

'It'll make my day to put Donahue behind bars for a long time. He's been beating that poor little wife of his again, the sod. If Thelma Entwistle hadn't caused all that trouble and got killed, I'd have locked him away days ago because he was bound over to keep the peace when they let him out of jail early.'

He scowled at the crowd of men gathered in a rough circle, pushing to and fro as they argued about who was likely to win. 'I'm glad those two groups of younger chaps are on opposite sides of the circle and I hope they stay there. We can do without a battle in the audience as well.'

It had been arranged that the fight would start immediately after the church clock had chimed seven. By five minutes to seven the crowd was distinctly restless and a couple of arguments between members of rival groups had had to be stopped by the men organising the fight.

By the time the minute hand drew close to the top of the clock, the spectators had formed a ring round the two fighters, shouting encouragement or insults, depending on which fighter they were supporting and Donahue had given up collecting money and was planning how to get away quickly.

The two young fighters were wearing ragged shorts and vests, and strutted forward as the clock finger crawled towards the top.

The crowd began to count off the last few seconds loudly, impatient for the fight to start.

As the clock began to chime, the two fighters moved towards one another, raising their clenched fists, violence radiating from them. The crowd had fallen silent now.

Then the sergeant came out of hiding and strode forward, pushing his way through the group of spectators and towering over most of them. Before anyone had realised what he intended, he grabbed the nearest of the two fighters by the arm and twisted it behind his back, yelling in a voice famous for its loudness, 'Stop this fight at once! And stay where you are.'

There were cries and yells, and men instantly began to do the opposite, those at the rear of the audience running away in every direction and some who were hemmed in trying desperately to shove others out of their way so that they could do the same.

The constable had tackled the other fighter as he'd been told and when he too tried to run away, he hooked the man's legs from under him and grabbed an arm, twisting it into a painful position few would even try to escape from.

Donahue was quick off the mark and turned to escape, but ran into Joss.

'It'd make my day to have to thump you, Donahue,' Joss shouted.

He had to prove that, however, because Donahue was desperate not to get sent back to prison and struggled wildly, unfortunately managing to keep the bigger man from grabbing his arm.

'I give in!' he yelled after Joss punched him in the face and stood still, arms slightly raised as if surrendering.

Joss relaxed a little. Which was a big mistake, because Donahue whacked him on the nose and forehead with two quick blows, in a manoeuvre he'd been taught in prison, then kneed him hard in the groin.

As Joss folded up helplessly because of the pain, Donahue set off running, dodging in and out of the rapidly thinning crowd. He might have got away if Norman Fulton hadn't been hovering at that side and seen him hurt Mr Townley.

'Not hurt people!' he yelled and grabbed Donahue by the hair, shoving him to the ground and sitting on him.

As Donahue struggled to get up, the sergeant left his own troublemaker, now handcuffed, in his constable's care and pulled out his second pair of handcuffs. He snapped these into place on Donahue, then asked Norman to stay with him. 'Don't let him get away. Sit on him again if he tries.'

'Not let him get away,' Norman repeated obediently. 'Sit on him.'

Donahue didn't give him reason to do that, he was still hurting where he'd been sat on already.

By that time Joss had struggled into a sitting position on the ground, but was fighting dizziness after the vicious blows to his face and was still in great pain that only a man would understand.

Most of the audience had got away, but the sergeant was more interested in helping Joss than fiddling around with a few more bystanders. When he helped him up, Joss was too dizzy to stand on his own, so the sergeant took him across to the nearest gravestone. 'Come and sit here, lad,' he said. 'We'll get you some help once I've arrested this sod formally. After that your watchmen can help my deputy get him to the station.

He turned to Donahue. 'You'll serve longer than six months this time, I'm sure.'

'The fight didn't even start! We didn't do anything wrong.'

'I don't think the magistrate will agree with you. You had no licence to hold a fight. And while I think about it, I'll look after your takings for you. With a bit of luck there will be enough to pay the fines.'

The sergeant grinned even more broadly as he unbuck-led the money belt and handed it to one of the watchmen.

'Let's see your left wrist now, Donahue. Dear me, that's a bad cut and it's not been done tonight because it's started healing. Just the sort of cut you'd get from broken glass in the window of a house you were breaking into.'

Donahue glared at him but didn't say anything else.

The sergeant turned back to Joss. 'You're going to have a lovely black eye, lad. And you're still dizzy, aren't you?'

'Mmm.'

'Well the clinic is just round the corner and if that new nurse is there I'll get her to keep an eye on you for a while. I don't like you being that dizzy.'

'No, don't. I'll just go home to bed. She'll think me a fool.'

'Nonsense. She'll think you a hero, which you are, help-ing capture that violent chap.'

Joss would have shaken his head, but he still felt too dizzy to risk doing that.

The sergeant beckoned to two men, complete strangers to him, and they helped him to his feet and walked with him round the corner.

It took such a big effort to move forward he stopped protesting and left the sergeant and his helpers sorting out the aftermath of the fight.

What on earth would Rachel think of him?

35

Rachel was sleeping at the clinic. She said it was because she didn't want to leave all the work of looking after Lally and Theo to Hanny, but she admitted to herself that she'd been feeling a bit left out. It was also because being there distracted her somewhat from her personal worries.

She owed Joss a response, she really did. He had honoured her with his affection and hinted at wanting something more permanent.

The trouble was, she had been utterly certain for many years that she'd never marry. She'd fooled herself about not finding any man appealing enough.

Joss was. And yet even after she met him, she'd continued to tell herself it was merely 'friendship' and shared interests. That was a nice part of their relationship but he had become much more than that, so very much more, she now realised. She had even dreamed about him holding her in his arms last night, and it had felt so right. But it had been followed by another dream, or rather nightmare, that was a jumbled mass of worries about what might happen if she dared tell him the truth about her earlier life.

How scornfully would he look at her if she told him about the baby she'd borne? She didn't think she could bear that.

She had tried to keep that part of her life completely hidden, tried not to dwell on it, only she hadn't been able to help wondering at times what had happened to the child.

But the midwife who'd helped her had said she'd regret it deeply if she never held her child and had put the baby gently in her arms as she was clearing up after the birth.

Rachel had never been able to forget the sight of that little face, its soft breaths, and how tiny it had seemed, too tiny to be sent out to face the world away from its mother.

Only how could a penniless lass who was still not really a woman have looked after it? She couldn't have done and people would have taken it from her one way or another. At times she still felt guilty, though, and sad. How could you not?

She tossed and turned in the narrow bed at the clinic, unable to settle. Then she gave in and got up because she was desperately thirsty and needed a drink of water. She tried not to make any noise, didn't even attempt to light a lamp let alone turn on one of the brighter gas lights. She didn't want brightness anyway; she wanted oblivion from her own thoughts.

When she heard voices outside, she assumed it was someone passing in the street, as occasionally happened, and nearly jumped out of her skin when someone knocked on the front door of the clinic.

As she tied her dressing gown more tightly around her and hurried towards the front door, she heard Hanny get up and paused to call up the stairs, 'I'm down here already. I'll answer that.' People only usually knocked on the door at this time of night when there was a serious emergency.

She peered through the window beside the front door to check that this wasn't a trick and saw in the light of the street lamp two men supporting another who was sagging as if hurt.

It wasn't till she unlocked the door that she realised who the injured man was: Joss Townley. 'Come in. I'll light a lamp.'

'I'll do that,' Hanny called from across the room. 'You see to the patient.'

She gestured to the old sofa. 'He can lie down there.'

'Rather sit up,' he mumbled.

She helped sit him in a corner of the sofa, asking, 'What happened?'

They told her about the fight and a man called Donahue attacking Joss and she examined the bruising where he'd been punched.

'I'm all right,' he insisted.

He didn't look too bad, but his voice was still blurry as if he were having difficulty forming the words.

'I'm just a bit dizzy.'

'If you're dizzy you need to stay here and let me keep an eye on you, Joss.'

She looked at the men. 'Just tell me how it happened then I can check his injuries and if they're not too bad, you can leave him with me.'

One of the men told her about the fighting, ending, 'We'd better get back now in case the sergeant needs our help.'

The other added, 'I bet the sergeant is going to make a big fuss about this and see if he can get the magistrate to caution them all. We knew a lot of them by sight so we can tell him their names. If they think it'll mean arrest if they step out of line again, they might behave a bit better for a while.'

She sat down on the sofa next to Joss and felt his pulse, then examined his eyes. 'I don't think you're concussed or there's anything else seriously wrong, but you do need to rest for a while and give your body time to recover.'

One of his companions chuckled and said, 'He's going to have a nice black eye there, isn't he?'

Joss sighed and leaned back, staring at her now with a rueful smile.

And she found herself smiling back involuntarily.

Hanny passed her a pillow and she put it at the end of the sofa and patted it. 'Lie down. Give yourself time to recover.'

He did that with a sigh and she helped him get comfortable, still sitting on the edge of the sofa. Someone must have whacked him hard to make his eye bruise and swell up like that.

'Sorry to be a trouble,' he muttered.

'It's what we're here for.'

'It's not serious, then?' one of the men asked.

'No, I don't think so.'

'Then we'd better get back and see if the sergeant needs more help.'

Hanny saw them out, locked the door again and looked across at her. 'Do you want me to do anything?'

'No. I think it's just time to recover that he needs.'

'Then I'll go back to bed. And Rachel – talk to him, give him a chance.'

She gaped in shock at this and couldn't think what to say as she watched Hanny run lightly up the stairs, then looked back at Joss.

He took hold of her hand and she looked down at him, took a deep breath and said, 'If you feel you're better enough to listen, I'll tell you about . . . what happened to me when I was going on fourteen.'

'Something bad. It won't change how I feel about you, though.'

'You don't know that.'

'I do. I've fallen in love with you, with who you are now, not what you were like before whatever it was happened.'

The silence went on for a long time as she summoned up all her courage. When she started speaking the words came in little spurts as she fumbled for the best way to tell him.

He kept hold of her hand the whole time and it was a comfort that he didn't let go, a big comfort. At one stage, he lifted her hand to his lips and kissed it gently, then said, 'Go on. I'm still here.'

When she'd finished she didn't know where to look, could only wait for him to say he was sorry but he couldn't marry her after that.

His voice sounded stronger now. 'You've carried that inside you all these years with no one to help you, haven't you?'

She could only shrug.

He took her by surprise, sitting up and pulling her into his arms. 'What happened was terrible, but it's what made you into the woman you are now, the one who's helped so many people, the one I love and admire. Will you marry me, Rachel?'

She looked at him in shock. It was the last thing she'd expected to hear.

'I mean it. And you won't have to give up being a nurse either. In fact, I'll help set things up so that we can help as many others as possible to become nurses. I'm not short of money.'

He had pulled her close to kiss her before she realised what he was doing. And she had started returning his kiss before she could stop herself from responding.

He smiled at her, his face still close to hers. 'You still haven't said you love me.'

'I love you more than I would ever have believed possible, Joss.'

'Good. We'll get married as soon as we can, but not till this goes away.' He chuckled suddenly and pointed across the room at their reflections in a mirror. 'If you can love me when I look as bad as this, it must be true love.'

'It is.' But she felt overwhelmed and suddenly buried her face in his shoulder and wept.

He let her cry for a while, then kissed her tears and wiped them away, saying quietly, 'That's enough. You've washed it all away. From now on we'll plan for happiness, for ourselves and for others.'

Epilogue

Rachel had tried to arrange for a quiet wedding, but though it wasn't a fancy affair, it was attended by everyone she knew, including some former patients.

She had thought she'd be nervous but when she woke up she was filled with a surge of joy and lay for a while revelling in it. And to make her day, it was sunny, a bright day to match her feelings.

She'd had a bath the night before and hadn't cared that she'd had to use the bathroom downstairs.

She didn't feel like eating much but Hanny had given her a small apple pie and that made her breakfast seem special as well as different.

Of course she didn't stay on her own for long. She'd only just started to get dressed when Hanny knocked on the door.

When she opened it, her friend said, 'I brought these for you.'

'But we said no flowers.'

'*You* said no flowers. I've got a corsage for myself too. I've never had one before. And I'm sure Joss will be wearing a buttonhole. Where's your hat?'

Rachel smiled and could feel herself flushing. 'I nipped out yesterday afternoon and bought that hat we saw in town. I know it's vain but I wanted to look my best for him.' She went into her bedroom and brought it out.

'Perfect!' Hanny said. 'Much nicer than your old one.'

The next surprise was when the Crossleys drove up just before they were about to set off in a trap decorated with ribbons, spring flowers and foliage.

'That's perfect!' Hanny said. 'Come on. You deserve to ride to church in style.

Rachel went down and found a few of the neighbours gathered in the street to wish her well, too.

'You look truly beautiful, dear,' Mrs Crossley said.

And for the first time in many years Rachel was glad of her appearance. She wanted to look the very best she could for the very best man she'd ever met.

Walter drove slowly across town to the church, and many of the people they passed waved and called out to wish her well.

At the church a man stepped forward to hold the pony and cart and Walter helped the three women, who were all dressed in their best, carefully down.

The other two women went into the church, leaving Rachel standing with Walter.

He echoed his wife's words. 'You make a beautiful bride, my dear. And I'm sure you two will be happy together. Ready?'

At her nod, he held out one arm and she took it.

Inside she stopped and gasped. They'd invited a few people but the church was full and everyone had turned to smile at her.

There was a movement at the front of the church and Joss came forward to stand there, looking down the aisle at her. She forgot about the other people then, the crowds and the fuss, seeing only him.

'Shall we start moving?' Walter asked.

'Yes, please.' She felt as if she floated down the aisle to take her place next to the man she loved with all her heart and soul.

She supposed she said the right words but didn't notice anything except the way Joss smiled and the love in his eyes.

When they walked back down the aisle again, people cheered and shouted, and the organist filled the church with joyful music.

They walked round to the church hall, which was now full of tables and chairs.

'How did all this happen without me knowing?' she whispered to Joss.

'I didn't know either, because you were so insistent on no fuss and keeping it simple that I did as you asked. But I'll have to delay kissing you again for a while now and pretend I'm hungry.'

She had to pretend she was hungry too.

It seemed a long time till they could get away, and this time Walter's trap was being driven by someone else who didn't bother them with conversation.

At the house he stopped and Joss said quickly, 'I'll help my wife get down. Thank you for bringing us here.'

'My pleasure. You won't remember, missus, but you helped my son into the world.'

They waved him goodbye, then as they turned to go inside, Joss surprised her by picking her up in his arms and carrying her over the threshold.

'Welcome home.'

In the house they both sighed then he pulled her into his arms and kissed her in a way that made her wish he need never stop.

'This is what it feels like when you love someone as much as I love you,' he said quietly. 'I won't hurt you, my love.'

'I know.'

They walked up the stairs together and into the bedroom, shutting the door on the world, and on the bad memories that had upset her whole life.

She proved her trust by kissing him before he could kiss her again, then starting to unbutton her pretty new lace blouse.

As she stepped out of her clothes she stepped into a tender new world that made it feel as if the sun would shine for ever.

'That was love,' he said softly afterwards and she had to pull his head towards her again and kiss him gently on the lips.

CONTACT ANNA

Anna is always delighted to hear from readers and can be contacted via the Internet.

Anna has her own web page, with details of her books, some behind-the-scenes information that is available nowhere else and the first chapters of her books to try out, as well as a picture gallery.

Anna can be contacted by email at
anna@annajacobs.com

You can also find Anna on Facebook at
www.facebook.com/AnnaJacobsBooks

If you'd like to receive an email newsletter about Anna and her books every month or two, you are cordially invited to join her announcements list. Just email her and ask to be added to the list, or follow the link from her web page.

www.annajacobs.com